JOSEPH CONNOLLY

THIS IS 64

riverrun

First published in Great Britain in 2017 by riverrun
This paperback edition published in 2018 by

riverrun

riverrun
an imprint of
Quercus Editions Ltd
Carmelite House
50 Victoria Embankment
London EC4Y 0DZ

An Hachette UK company

A CIP catalogue record for this book is available
from the British Library

PB ISBN 978 1 84866 635 1
EBOOK ISBN 978 1 84866 634 4

10 9 8 7 6 5 4 3 2 1

Typeset by CC Book Production

Printed and bound in Great Britain by Clays Ltd, St Ives plc

To David Harper

Bliss was it in that dawn to be alive,
But to be young was very heaven!

William Wordsworth

When I'm sixty-four.

Lennon–McCartney

A MEMOIR. YOU MIGHT CALL IT THAT. REALLY JUST A JUMBLE OF RANDOM AND TATTERED, MORE OR LESS IDLE AND INCONSEQUENTIAL LITTLE SCRAPS OF RECOLLECTION FROM THE JOYOUS AND LONG AGO PAST. NOW THAT TODAY IS MY BIRTHDAY. AND I'M OLD.

Julie Christie. In an E-Type Jaguar. Red – it had to be red, the E-Type. And she, she would be all in white. Minidress, A-line – Biba, conceivably. Those long and shiny white boots by Courrèges. PVC, were they . . .? Amazing what lodges, the things you remember – words like Courrèges. So that was my absolute, my ultimate fantasy. That's what I always wanted. Well – that certainly was always a primary, a motivating desire, anyway. Driving force. Because in truth, I wanted everything. Who didn't? But there were so many people, all around me, who actually seemed to have it. They truly did seem to have everything: the cars, the clothes – the money, the glamour and all the dolly birds. Ah yes – the dolly birds. They didn't at all mind it, being called that – loved it, actually. Badge of honour. Feather in your cap, being a bird. A mark, the tacit recognition of being slim and long-blonde-haired and fashionable and desirable – so why ever would they object to that? The best of them had pale pink lipstick, and sootily shadowed eyes. Nowadays, well – you daren't open your mouth: women, I don't know – they're just on to you, all over you, whatever you say.

And it's not that they were all that much older than I was, this glittering coterie of blessed and so groovy people who truly seemed to have it all. I'm not talking about red-faced fat cats with chauffeurs, cigars and mistresses – I'm talking about the young ones. Not Cliff Richard's young ones, though – time, it had already moved on. Because it's 64 I'm remembering, 1964. And I was nineteen years old. Kid, really. But young was the thing, well naturally – young was truly the only thing to be. We felt sorry for old people, middle-aged people – even people who can only have been in their thirties. And hated them too a bit, I think. Just for being there – just for not being young and cool and slim and desirable: they messed up the look. It's hard to describe . . . and certainly it's hard, beyond hard, to summon up the bubble of the sheer high feeling, the kick inside . . . but just to be young in London in 1964 was simply so very viscerally thrilling: the gorgeous smugness and the rippling joy, it made your heart sing out as it thrummed within you.

Golden age . . .? Well yeh, I suppose – and particularly if you were one of the anointed, one of those who had everything. I didn't. I was never one of them. It's not that I had nothing – I was by no means a hopeless case, I think that's got to be more or less made clear. I was reasonably good-looking, or so I was told (and not just by my mother, but mainly, admittedly) – so hardly one of the beautiful people, but still. Thick and longish hair, skinny legs, not stupid – everything you need. I had a job, not much of a one. I had a room – I wasn't still living with my parents, and that was a mercy, I can tell you. You'd understand if you'd ever met my parents. Well, Mum – she wasn't too bad, I suppose. She did her best. No idea what she was feeling, most of the time: about anything she might have been going through. But Dad, oh my God. My children today – I say children: all grown-up, of course – they're constantly telling me how out of touch I am, how increasingly intolerant, how I don't understand even the very simplest element of technology (not true, any of that, but let it lie). My father, though – oh Jesus. Once, he put his foot through the television because the Rolling Stones were on: I'm telling you – it was as bad as that. He gaped with fury at the fizzy grey close-up of Mick Jagger's lips, and his own were practically foaming. My mother, she was just looking down at the floor – she did that quite a lot. The noise of the exploding television, the scattered drizzle of dangerous shards, the buzzing and the smell of burning, all of it had been so absolutely startling that still I was just staring – open-mouthed, I should think, though none of this had actually frightened me. He did this sort of thing, my father – an otherwise highly introverted and mean man who hated 'breaking a note' – and this thing with the television, this was merely the most extreme example. He regretted it immediately, you could tell – Radio Rentals: he didn't even own the bloody thing – but still, though . . . that was the moment when the blend of contempt and indifference that up till then was all I ever remember feeling for the man, deepened, and then hardened into an abiding hatred.

I didn't go to university. A couple of my friends did, not that many actually, because whatever it was they wanted to go into – can't remember, something dull: law, accountancy, whatever – it was expected and required. But nobody really felt they had to do it, not in those days: it was hardly the norm. Loads did for the sake of the grant, of course, and because the thought of actually working was just too bloody frightening, or else (in the light of the times) terminally depressing and very unswinging. But I must admit I considered it, I did consider it. I could have breezed into a redbrick, but anywhere decent,

Oxford or Cambridge, would have been out of the question because one of the first things I had ditched was Latin, so I never got the O level, and that, back then, was non-negotiable. Can't remember quite why I was so very down on Latin – simply didn't get on with it. Like Milton, in English. Loved Chaucer – thought he was enormous fun – but Milton, oh dear me no. But in the end I just couldn't face the thought of another pile of set books to plough through, the prospect of more exams. Now, of course, everyone ends up with a perfectly useless degree in, I don't know – social studies, or some damn nonsense, from the University of Bogtown, and still they can't get even the lousiest job, is what you're reading in the papers. Whereas I, well – I walked right in. Didn't take any time off after I left school – gap years, they hadn't even been invented. So I just went straight into it, and suddenly I was earning a bit of money. It wasn't a trendy job, though – I worked for the wholesale side of W. H. Smith's: baling up bundles of newsprint, basically . . . writing out labels. So although it was great for nicking the odd free copy of *Fabulous* and *Rave* and the *Melody Maker* (which I far preferred to the *New Musical Express* because, I don't know . . . it didn't take itself quite so seriously) and of course *Beatles Monthly*, loved that . . . still the job was hardly what they now call 'cutting-edge'. We didn't say that then, cutting-edge. What did we say . . .? Don't know. Cool, I suppose. One of the only words of that sort that seems to have survived. All the others – fab, gear, groovy, can't remember but there were more – you have to mime ironic inverted commas if ever you use them, or people will look at you. Hip . . . hip is another one: hip, that seems to have come back into use just lately, but it doesn't really mean any more, so far as I can make out, quite what it used to. Was an old jazz term, of course – before my time – but then it was all sort of, I don't know . . . Hippy Hippy Shake, all that sort of thing. The song. Swinging Blue Jeans, pretty sure. Young men these days who seem to be described as hip, though . . . they don't seem to have a lot of hair. Thin on top – or else they are very foolishly and deliberately razoring it to the bone. My God . . . when I was young, if you didn't have hair, and plenty of it, you were dead in the water, really: no bird was going to look at you. I seem to have kept most of mine, anyway. White, of course – well, greyish mostly . . . but still it's pretty thick, and I suppose I wear it longer than I ought to. Still it's over my collar, covering the tops of my ears. A lot of men of my generation seem to be the same – similarly blessed, as it were – and the pop groups of the time as well: into their seventies, some of them – still packing out the world's auditoria with the only music that ever really mattered a damn, and still their hair is swinging around them.

But the point I'm making – getting back to what I was doing, and everything – is that I wasn't working for EMI in Abbey Road or even in Lord John or Take Six in Carnaby Street or in some nightclub or other like the Scotch of St James's, or somewhere like that. Which I never went to, of course – but I read about it. All the pop and film stars went there, and I yearned to; didn't even know where it was.

And the room, the bedsit I had, it couldn't really ever be described as a 'pad'. Not one of those glossy and miraculous penthouses – the palaces you see in all the films about the Sixties that somehow, although on paper perfectly accurate in the detail, still always somehow seem to get it so ridiculously wrong. So no – it wasn't all acres of white leather sofas and coloured Perspex mobiles and G-Plan swivel chairs and a conversation pit and swirly orange wallpaper and a sunken bath and Julie Christie in those white Courrèges boots rolling about invitingly on a circular bed (and in that particular fantasy, that is all she was wearing, Julie: just the boots). It wasn't in the King's Road, is what I'm saying. It was in Kilburn, my room. I did what I could with it: various posters – Ursula Andress coming out of the sea in *Dr No*, Bond's DB5 as well as an E-Type and a Mini Cooper and also that Lautrec thing for the Moulin Rouge and some other rather sinuous numbers by Beardsley and Mucha, although they might have come later – they were maybe a couple of years on, along with my Union Jack rubbish bin and that rather fusty old military jacket with only the one epaulette that I got for next to nothing in a market. Knocked up very rudimentary shelves with planks and bricks, like we all did. Loads of Penguins and Pans. One of the only good things about getting older was being able to afford hardbacks, which I always did prefer: no time at all for all this Kindle rubbish – you want to touch a book, you want to smell it. And orange light bulbs from Woolworth's, they went quite a long way in setting the atmosphere if you were having a bird round, or something. I'd buy some dreadful wine – all wine was dreadful in those days, or at least the stuff I ever came into contact with (even at a wedding, the champagne was vile) – and a Vesta chicken chow mein which I'd do in the Baby Belling. I actually felt really rather sophisticated, if you can believe it. Like John Steed, or someone – whose clothes made me practically faint; mine were largely from C&A: you play the cards you're dealt, right? I recall with particular affection a pair of bright blue elephant cord hipsters with enormous belt loops – not from C&A, those . . . some much smaller place in Oxford Street, as I recall, with a name that was something on the lines of Mr Man or Guy or something – and my extreme frustration at being unable to afford the bloody belt to go with them. Oh yes and Wall's ice cream, we always finished off with that, after the Vesta mess – which was never right because that little fridge I had was just a joke. Even a tin of mandarin oranges, sometimes.

But the really great thing was that it was *mine*, that room, you see. I'd never before had a room that was mine and mine alone. Right up until I finally escaped the parental cavern, I was bunking up with my brother, Tom. He hated it too, of course – probably even more acutely than I did, being that much older than me. The whole place always smelled of Brylcreem, because dear old Tom, he was forever trying to get his hair to look like Elvis's, because he was of that generation, that's what he was into – but it always flopped down again over his brow, and it just drove him wild, when it did that. It was a tiny and pretty awful room, actually – stacked with lumber, not all of it ours – though never so profoundly worrying as my parents' room at the end of the corridor: that was a stifling nightmare. I never went in there if I could possibly avoid it (why would I?) but it seemed to be made up of little more than candlewick and wallpaper and filmy curtains that kept out no sunlight and never quite met in the middle, with a smell of something musty as well as the sweet and acrid tang of Old Holborn. My mother, she hated him smoking in bed, the pig, but of course he never gave a flying fuck about anything she thought or wanted, nor anyone else. Already it was at the stage where I could barely stand being in the same room as him . . . but the thought of my poor little mother having actually to share that bed . . . and it was hardly bigger than a single: they would have lain there, like a couple of rank sardines. More than that I cannot think. There was a greenish quilt that had been charred during the war, I was always told, and my mother, she called it the counterpane. What really drove me crazy about the useless little space I was sharing with Tom though was that we had this perfectly fine bay-windowed front room – the best in the house, though admittedly that was hardly saying a great deal – and this was not just unused but actually locked. My mother went in there once a week on a Tuesday to Hoover the square of carpet, Mansion Wax the surrounding parquet, dust the clock which my father always said he was going to repair, ha bloody ha, and the pair of dark and maybe oak candlesticks on the beige and mottled tile fireplace that had never seen a fire . . . polish the silver-plated and ugly cylindrical biscuit barrel which we all knew had come to us from Auntie Joan, without ever having the remotest idea as to who in blue blazes Auntie Joan might actually have been. There was a three-piece suite with plastic covers so that it wouldn't mark – though still I don't think anyone had ever been allowed to sit on it. In the back room, which all of us infested nightly, because the rest of the house was generally freezing (the room with the lousy little Radio Rentals telly that didn't even get ITV and you constantly had to fool around with the bloody useless aerial – all this before my most excellent father elected to kick the whole damn shooting match to absolute buggery), there was a sofa so very collapsed that it had long ago been shored up beneath with a length of plywood, which needless to say improved its comfort not a jot. Also in the front room was this lovely little cocktail cabinet, though – 1930s, I should think – and when you opened it, the top rose up and there was a chromium rack of swizzle sticks with differently coloured ends. The interior was pale figured veneer and pinkish mirror. The thought of there being a cocktail cabinet in our house, of course, was just so far beyond hilarious: a cocktail was about as likely as a mink coat for my mother. Or going to a restaurant. India Pale Ale and Haig were the nearest my father ever got: Harvey's Bristol Cream for Christmas, and De Kuyper cherry brandy. The same sticky bottles for years and years and years, kept in the bottom of the sideboard alongside my mother's wicker and gingham-lined sewing basket and the gardening shoes. I said to my father one time: look – we never use that front room, we never even open the door, it's such a stupid waste. Why can't I have it? Why do Tom and I have to be crammed into the box room when there's all this space going begging . . .? He looked at me as if I were criminally deranged. The subject never came up again, and we all continued to never enter that room – except for my mother, on a Tuesday, to clean its perfect cleanness. I never did know what happened to that cocktail cabinet, though – the only decent piece of furniture we ever owned. Maybe that too had come to us from Auntie Joan, who was to say? Very fashionable these days, that sort of thing: worth a fortune, I shouldn't wonder. Anyway: long gone now.

So the tatty little room in Kilburn was something of a step up – that's the way I saw it, anyway. Didn't have a car, obviously – let alone a bloody E-Type. And as to Julie Christie, well . . . but I did know a good few girls, quite briefly (it's how they seemed to like it). I had by then what I suppose you'd call a sort of a proper girlfriend, Dorothy. She was okay. I maybe quite unfairly remember her as being just a little bit boring – but I don't suppose that I was much of a riot either, in those days: I hardly bring the house down now. She was amenable enough though, Dorothy. Quite eager and willing, if you know what I'm saying. Pill – that did help things along. Her hair wasn't very long but it was pale-ish without being blonde and she kept on tugging at it, I'm remembering now, and moaning about what she called her dreadful split ends. Like I cared. Thighs a bit chunky for the skirts she wore – but I didn't blame her for that: girls, they had to wear them, miniskirts: they just had to. Never seemed to have much to say for herself – I thought at first that she was maybe not really that bright, little Dorothy, slow to catch on . . . but it wasn't that, it wasn't that at all – just terribly young and slightly shy, that's all. And then, though, she became just a little bit too clingy. You know how they can get: she was trying to make me like all the largely spastic things that she was so devotedly into. Funny how one so easily falls back into the language of the time. Haven't used that word for decades. (Try it today, and they'd string you up, shouldn't wonder. Do you know: if some very able and high-profile person were just to let it slip out, the word spastic, he would be pilloried by the voluble po-faced self-righteous mob, and probably jobless by teatime.) I shouldn't have stayed with her as long as I did, little Dorothy, but you sort of fall into a pattern, don't you really? It just becomes easy.

I wanted to be a pop star. Who didn't? Dreamed of my debut single shooting up the charts, and me in an Italian mohair suit rather self-consciously miming to it on *Top of the Pops*: that was new in 1964 – we were all so ridiculously excited when it first came on. And most of the groups – they were pretty much all our age, you see, so anything was possible. I wanted to be interviewed by Cathy McGowan on *Ready, Steady, Go!* Not Keith Fordyce, though: what was that fat and square old man doing on the programme anyway? Dorothy and I, we could never understand it. She had a thing about Mike somebody, the singer in The Dave Clark Five: we weren't even slightly similar – I bore no resemblance at all to the singer in The Dave Clark Five, so it irked me, that. Can you believe it? Just so amazing even to recall such a thing. But look – I was nineteen, wasn't I? That's all. Kid, really. I watched all of those pop programmes. Who didn't? There weren't that many, actually – and radio, that was even worse. If it hadn't been for Alan Freeman's *Pick of the Pops* and *Savile's Travels* on a Sunday, we would have been done for. Everyone went on about Radio Luxembourg, but it was hopeless, really – on my little transistor it was, anyway: more crackle than anything, no matter how much you were twiddling the dial. I eagerly fantasised about my first number one, which would be voted a hit on *Juke Box Jury* and given 'foive' by that funny little girl on *Thank Your Lucky Stars*. Janet, was she . . .? Janice . . .? Something. Extraordinary, though . . . all this ages-ago nonsense, and yet it seems as fresh – fresher, actually – than yesterday. I've become that cliché of an oldie, I suppose: can't recollect where I was last Friday, and yet I can taste and inhale the dizzying aroma of such long distant youth. All that stuff about if you remember the Sixties, you just weren't there – that what they say? Well maybe for the druggies – but that was never really my 'bag', as we used to call it. Otherwise it's nonsense, isn't it? The purest nonsense. Because me, well . . . I can hardly remember anything else.

And never mind The Dave Clark bloody Five – mindless stomping anyway – it was The Beatles, well of course it was. Oh my Lord – The Beatles, I just idolised them, really. Right from the word go. Who didn't? From the very first time I heard 'Please Please Me', that was it: bang! I missed out on 'Love Me Do', the first single. Passed me by, somehow. But that very first time I heard 'Please Please Me' in a booth in Smith's, I was gone. Bought it – 6s 8d, quite a lot of money in those days, and particularly if you were earning only six pounds fifteen a week, as I was. It's funny how you never ever forget these figures: it's like your first phone number. Mine was Primrose 5056 – that was later, though: that wasn't in Kilburn. Had to use the box on the corner next to the pub, when I was still in Kilburn – or go downstairs and beg to use the one that the drunken Irish people had. My mobile number now, though – can't remember that: I have to have it written down, or I couldn't give it to anyone. Not that I do, very often – don't want to be pestered. Two pounds eight-and-six went on rent, but the bus to work, that cost next to nothing in those days: not like now. Same with stamps – can't bloody believe it: nearly fifteen shillings to post a letter . . .? Anna, my youngest, she tells me not to think like that because not only does it age me, but it's stupid, and she's probably right. But I got the LP *With The Beatles* that Christmas, thirty-two bob – major outlay, best money I ever spent. Played it to death – loved it, just loved it so much. I've got the original sleeve framed now, the mono one, moody black-and-white photo, you know it, and still I play the CD. Love it, just love it so much. Well all of their albums, of course – but at the time I'm harking back to, that was it, that was the one. Apart from the *Please Please Me* LP, of course, which I didn't have. That was the one that Larkin, that poet Larkin went on about, wasn't it? Their first LP. In 1963, when he says sex was invented, or something like that. People go on about Larkin, but I can't see it. Same few quotes, and not much in any of them, so far as I'm concerned. Anyway – wasn't true for me. That year, 63, I was still at school. 64 – that was the time: 64, that's when it all started happening for me: that was the year when the Sixties just erupted.

I had a portable record player that weighed a bloody ton. They put a handle on anything in those days and called it portable. Wasn't a Dansette – couldn't afford a Dansette. Pye, I think it was. Yes – pretty sure it was a Pye. My mate Sammy – rich parents – he had a Grundig, and a matching tape recorder. He also had a Rickenbacker electric guitar exactly like John Lennon's – couldn't play a note: I doubt if he knew how to plug it in. So: did I want to be a Beatle? Well yeh – who didn't? Wanted the jacket, the collarless jacket. Wanted the boots – Anello & Davide is what I had read they were. Whoever Anello and bloody Davide were – sounded like a circus act. Had the black knitted tie, though – that's the nearest I got to their look. Tab-collar shirt came later – it was the colour of a lemon and I wore it for three days straight, washed it in the sink in my curtained-off kitchenette, dried it in front of the popping and stinky gas fire, and put it on again. Wanted a pink one as well, but I couldn't afford it. Not a phrase you ever hear, nowadays. Can't afford it . . .? Don't make me laugh. Young people, they get whatever they want the second they want it with money they haven't yet earned: normal now. And not just the young either – I know people of my own age who are in so way over their heads, splashing the cash like it's water: don't know how they sleep at night. Credit. It used to be called debt – a thing to be feared and ashamed of, and now it's almost a bloody status symbol, the more they allow you to owe them. Just one of the very many things that have gone so very badly wrong with this bloody country. You want more . . .? I could be here all night. Immigration . . .? Don't get me started. Anyway, what was I . . .? Oh yes: Beatles. Had a go at the hairstyle – complete joke. Did it myself with the only pair of scissors I owned, which were useless anyway – arching my eyebrows in Beatle-like surprise in front of this mottled little mirror . . . and when I had done my terrible worst and relaxed my face back down into normal, the jagged and raggedy result of all this well-intentioned hacking was halfway up my forehead and not right at all. I looked retarded: bloody awful mess – my very own lunatic fringe. One thing, though – up till then, I'd really hated my name. I always thought it was a drag, my name: sounded so square, so completely Victorian. But because of the Fab Four, suddenly it was wonderful to be called George: it was utterly cool. It was really only that that made me always say that George was my favourite Beatle (because you had to have one: it was a rule. Just as you could only like The Beatles or the Rolling Stones: that was another rule). So I made out that it was subtle and mysterious to have George as my favourite Beatle – the quiet one, the interesting one, the deep one: the dark horse, as he came to be known. He was probably none of those things – but who can ever know? It was John I liked really – who didn't? I wanted to be him, John Lennon. It's Paul I'm a huge fan of now, but back then it was John: loved him. Yeh I did. I couldn't believe it, when he was killed. I remember some old bloke at the time – probably younger than I am now, though – and he said out loud and with enormous relish: 'One down – three to go!' I was sick, Just sick. And George, my namesake . . . when George went, I actually did even cry a bit. Amazed myself. But it was maybe for me – those tears, they were maybe for me. Because Beatles . . . dying. So wrong. They were youth – they were my boyhood. So Beatles dying . . . it wasn't meant to be. Like getting old. When I was a kid, I thought there were four genders: boys, girls, old people and nuns. So . . . getting old: it wasn't meant to be. Because how can you just change gender . . .?

I didn't keep a diary – I wish I had. I was given the odd one for Christmas, but I never really used to write much in them. There was never anything to write. Just if I'd bought a Penguin or a new LP or something. Or if it rained. That was the sort of thing I noted down. Though I did turn out to be something of a thoroughly unsystematic hoarder. Never really cared to throw things away. I came across quite recently a dented old Roses tin that was full of all sorts of bits of junk – and how did I think to take that with me through, oh . . . must be six or seven changes of address? Ticket stubs – Odeon mostly, all from 1964 – book matches, tin badges . . . Uncle Holly from Selfridges Santa grotto, a Robertson's Golly, the Ban the Bomb thing, one saying 'I'm a Beatles Fan!' Also folded up in there was a poem, or the beginning of one, anyway. I used to want to be a writer as well as a pop star. Bestselling novelist. Yeh – why not? I was young, remember? So anything was possible – that's the way I think I was thinking. Astonishing, really. I mean, I did have a taste for reading – Waugh, Greene, Amis, Sartre, Orwell . . . went through a phase of Agatha Christie. I used to hide the Mickey Spillanes – though in truth he was probably my favourite. These days, I don't read a bloody thing, not sure why: too damned idle. But I never had any real desire or talent for committing my own thoughts to paper – though now I do find I am rather more inclined in that direction: I jot things down like this. I think all I really wanted was to see my name and photograph on a book cover, together with a brilliant quote from the *Sunday Times*. To see someone reading my book (Penguin, for preference) on the Tube or on a bus – that would have been an unimaginable blast. A uniform collected edition in my bookcase. It would have impressed the birds: can't imagine I was thinking any further than that. Anyway, this poem – I have it just here. Now where are my . . .? Oh – I've got them on. That happens quite a bit. Right, then – this poem:

Morning has broken.
Look – it's all over the floor.
It happened before I had woken.
It just bloody well kicked in the door.

Is that good? Witty? Puerile? Christ knows. Rhymes, anyway – something, these days. Quite subversive, did I imagine it was? Maybe it was part of a lyric, I really couldn't tell you – I have not the slightest memory of even having written it. I would say someone else had done it and given it to me, but that is definitely my handwriting: I was experimenting with turquoise Quink at the time. Still had my Parker from school: never really into Bics. I probably wanted to be a songwriter as well. I shouldn't be at all surprised. Watch out Lennon–McCartney . . .! Because look – I wanted everything, you see: all of it. Who didn't?

As I say, I'd left school just the year before. Minor public school, is what they used to call the sort of rather obscure establishment I went to. Maybe still do. It still is chugging along – saw a mention of it in the paper not that long ago, though of course I have had no further contact with the place. Never really understood all that – the old boy thing. Your parents happened to send you to the same school as someone else. So what? Hardly the basis for a lifelong bond, I shouldn't have said. I neither loved nor hated it – apart from my time as a fag, I absolutely detested that. Brats, we used to call them. And the food was perfectly unspeakable: I was permanently starving – lived on Mars bars, smoky bacon crisps and Lyons Swiss rolls, if ever I could afford them. A tin of Pork Luncheon Meat was an unimaginable treat. Otherwise it was just Lea & Perrins' sandwiches. My father expected thirty shillings to last me the term. Yes – and he later cut it down to a pound: Christ Almighty. Headmaster – nasty man – when I was leaving he called me in and he said to me, 'Reilly . . . Reilly . . . Reilly.' On a descending and histrionic note of cumulative disappointment. 'Oh George Reilly. You – you had the potential. You know that, boy? You were really *going* somewhere . . .! And then, and then Reilly . . . well then you just *didn't*.' No well – he maybe had something there. I mean to say – I'm pretty smart, I think. Always quite good at the things I'm good at. But laziness, you see – that's what always has done for me. If someone at an early age had dumped upon me a million pounds and said to me okay then, George: live off that for the rest of your life and don't ever do a damn single thing, I would have said okay, right mate – terrific, you're on: no problems there. And not a lot has changed. I never really went anywhere, I suppose. Became a printer – went into printing: classy letterheads, engraved invitations, memorial and wedding stuff – all that sort of thing. Upper end, is what they say now. Word got round in the better circles that we were easily as good as Smythson, but nowhere near the price. So all fairly lucrative, if rather pedestrian. Got a house . . . then I got a better house. Got a wife, Enid . . . had two children, David and Anna. I was the reverse of what they refer to these days as a hands-on father: my hands were always far too busy with rather more interesting things. Thought of divorce, didn't go through with it. Stopped seeing the woman who was the trigger to the nearly-divorce, and not long after I started it all up again. Then she went to Australia, some reason, leaving me clueless and stunned, knowing nothing at all. Oddly, though – and certainly in 1964 when I was nineteen years old – I was convinced I knew the lot: that no one could teach me a single damn thing because me, well . . . I knew the lot. Looking back,

I think I must actually have been about forty before I came to know anything at all. Now, though . . . now I'm of the age to know that the only thing I know is that I don't know a damned bloody thing about anything at all. Yes . . . but where is wisdom when most you need it? Because I tell you, matey – in common with advice, it's no fucking use to me now.

And the journey, the journey through life, as it's sometimes rather fatuously termed . . . well I can't even decide if I enjoyed it. When I was young I did, when I was nineteen I did . . . but that was no journey. There was a plateau in heaven, where I would happily lodge for ever, unseeing and unchanging, savouring the prospect, secure in the certainty of eternal, sweet, untasted days. Apart from, of course, that one great shadow, the defining moment with Dorothy. Which I purposely and for years blanked right out of my consciousness, but now I find myself thinking about it more and more and more, every single day. Anyway. But that journey, if that's what we are to call it . . . well, it's not exactly over, is it? It's not yet done. I haven't yet docked, as it were – still I am sailing, if in an increasingly rickety vessel. But rather than progress much further, I find I'd quite prefer to relive, to live over, the very best bits of the past. Not as an ancient ruminant, with nothing more to live for – I don't mean that, I don't at all mean that. Not like that song, that Paul Simon song – is it 'Bookends' . . .? I think it might be. 'Preserve your memories – they're all that's left you'. Poignant, and rather deeply sad – but that's not me. I'm not there yet. I know that still I am unfulfilled: there are yet things to be done, though Christ alone knows what on earth they might be. Because – and it has to be admitted . . . I am old. Am I old . . .? Or merely elderly? Christ, these days centenarians are said to have died of elderliness. People hate the word old – they shy away from it. It frightens them to death. But no: I'm old – just got to be faced. Jesus – I was born just a couple of weeks after VE Day. Another world. And Tom, my brother – he's five years older. War baby. There was a sister too – Lucy. I wasn't much more than a baby myself when she died – but everyone was most awfully upset about it, that much I do remember.

Old age, though . . . it was never meant to come. And particularly not now, when I'm hardly feeling up to it. It's odd . . . it's really so extraordinarily *odd*. I mean – I know I'm old, I know it, I do know it – I'm not completely stupid. It's just that I can't think, you see, that it's actually meant to *be*. I look in the mirror (not often – I don't seek it out) and what I expect to see there is that fresh-faced and eager young man with longish thick hair who still, I know, is lurking within me. Because I still *feel* quite . . . well, not young – young, I suppose, would be going it a bit . . . but not really quite *old*, if you know what I mean. Generally, I feel really pretty good – and giving up smoking quite a few years back, wasn't easy, but that helped me on, I'm sure of it. Don't start every morning hacking up my guts and fumbling about for the packet of Rothmans. Of course, if I overdo the booze I can feel like absolute shit – stomach, mainly: acid reflux, they call it . . . and not so much a resounding headache as a sort of booming light-headedness that can verge on a kind of quite euphoric giddiness, sometimes rather worryingly. And it hangs around for a couple of days, if you can believe it: could shrug it off in a morning, once. And when I say 'overdo the booze', all I'm talking about is a bottle of wine, for Christ's sake. Jesus: in the old days, that wouldn't even have qualified as a warm-up. But I can't put my mind to a single damn thing, not when I'm feeling like that: even doing an email . . . it just seems quite beyond me. Still I force myself to undergo the humiliation of an annual check-up through BUPA. 'How are we doing?' the doctor always asks me. I tell him that that's what we're here to find out. So far there's been nothing too alarming. I mean – all the usual bits of decay and withering you just have to expect at my age, I suppose, but no dark rumble of an evil and cackling saboteur within. Unlike quite a few of my friends and acquaintances: sudden diagnoses, and then they're either ruined by 'treatments', or else dropping like flies. So I suppose that when I can't actually see before me the evidence of what the passing of time has done to my face, the malevolent etching, I blithely assume that it's simply not yet there, and continue to behave accordingly. I smile at a lovely young girl in the street, and she'll always smile back. Yes, but you just have to ask yourself: is she seeing the blood and danger of the man beneath, and responding as a woman would . . .? Or is she only aware of the white-haired and innocuously soft pink-cheeked old fellow on the surface, grinning like a grandad . . . and all she's thinking is that he's *sweet* . . .?

You see . . . it's difficult: I was irresistibly attracted to beautiful young girls when I was so very young myself – and in common, I think, with many men of my age, my tastes remain true: I see no reason to re-evaluate my position. Men, they will always want this . . . and the girls, well – it's absolutely up to them, isn't it? It always is, it always was, and it always will be: the nature of the beast. As to whether they respond or not, I mean. And very largely it will be not, of course – we all know that – unless you are rich or famous, and preferably both. Women, though – the feminists – they should stop attacking men for what simply comes naturally to them, and start attacking the girls for eagerly pandering to the whim of an idle ancient in blatant exchange for money and status. When they are not out to actively entrap one. If the girls didn't do it, you see, then the fat and bald old rich men would all be lonely, and the feminists cock-a-hoop. And while they are at it, women should also stop affecting to be affronted when a man reacts to the sexual allure which they work so very hard to manufacture and project: because it's silly, isn't it? How much worse to be ignored: because women – they hate that, they really hate that: they hate that more than anything. Used not to be this way – wasn't at all like that, not then: girls were sexy, and they knew it – well of course they knew it, they always do. From puberty onwards, I should think. If not before: the consummate power over a doting father, a lascivious uncle. And you could tell a girl she was gorgeous: you could actually utter the words into her bright and happy face. Touch her lightly, stroke her hair, openly admire her fabulous figure . . . and she wouldn't be calling the bloody police and spending the rest of her days in counselling to counteract the shattering profundity of her lifelong trauma. So there: I remain true to what I always felt, to what I always wanted. Julie Christie, in a nutshell. Julie Christie, yeah – and not in a nutshell actually, but in a red E-Type Jaguar. And no – not as she is now, in a bloody silver Yaris. So you see it's just . . . everything else that has changed. Not me, though: no, not me.

And now . . . well now, I'm afraid, it's 2009 – which doesn't even strike me as a *date*, it looks so bloody futuristic and alien . . . but I've thought that since the millennium. While today . . . well today it's my birthday, so I'll stop all of this now. Family's coming round. Couldn't tell you why – it's not that we're close. Enid's doing. She means well. She always did. Just never seems to come out quite right, anything she ever puts her mind to. Well – not her fault. Another one who hated her name, as a matter of fact: she always wanted to be called Marianne.

Right. Okay. So what have I actually established . . .? That I wanted to be young for ever. Who didn't? And how did all that work out for me, then? Well as you see: not too well – not too well at all. But now that I've started to think about it all, I'm not at all sure that I really feel ready to stop. Rather want to wallow in it all for quite a bit longer, is the way I'm feeling at the moment. Another sign, isn't it? Of being old? But first, though . . . just let me haul myself back into the unforgiving present. Yes. So that I can just get another birthday out of the way: yet another one, just one more, yes indeed. I'll do that then, shall I? I think so. Got to be faced, I suppose. Family's coming round. Couldn't tell you why. It's not that we're close. Do my best to affect a near delirious glee at whatever ghastly variant of a V-neck or hip flask or shoe-shine kit they have grudgingly clubbed together for this time. Christ, it's all such a business. Gets worse every year – and maybe worst of all, this time. Because today . . . well today . . . although I find it quite impossible to believe . . . I'm actually 64.

Yes. I know. But look: it's only a number . . . That's what they say, isn't it? They're always saying that.

CHAPTER ONE

A RATHER STRANGE BOY

'She loves you.'

'Yeah, Sammy – I know. She says it to me all the time. Never stops. Drives me bloody crazy.'

George reached across his old school tuck box that he used as a sort of a makeshift coffee table, and shuffled a cigarette out of Sammy's flipped-open packet of Benson & Hedges. Nicer than his own No. 6 – and certainly better than Embassy, which he used to get only because of the coupons, and after an eon of stuffing them into a drawer, Dorothy had discovered from the catalogue that he didn't have even enough for the lowliest gifts of all – a garden trowel, the After Eight trolley or a roll of raffia placemats. So he junked them.

'Yeah I know but you've really got to try to be a bit, well . . . sort of *nice* to her, Georgie. It's not a bad thing, what she feels about you. Lots of guys, it's what they want. It's all they're after. Fed up with just, you know – some drunken poke after the pub. It's good, having a bird like that. I wouldn't mind it, I'm telling you. Bloody hell – she's a hell of a lot better than the last lot you had. Yeh and particularly that Ellie. Jesus. Right nutcase she was . . .'

'Yeah I know. Ellie, oh Jesus. She was trouble. Yeah you're

right – glad to be shot of that one. Good in other ways, though. But Dorothy, I don't know . . . it's the way she always looks at me when she says it. You know . . .? When she says she loves me. Big sort of expectant eyes. Don't know what she's expecting . . .'

'Well you do know, Georgie – of course you know. She wants you to say it back. Only natural. Birds, they like to feel secure. Can we turn the music down a bit . . .?'

'What's wrong? It's The Beatles . . . you love The Beatles . . .'

'I know I love The Beatles. Just a bit loud, that's all. When we're talking.'

'Yeah . . .? Okay, then. That better . . .? Side's nearly over anyway . . .'

'That's fine. Yeah. So what was I saying? Oh yeah – birds, you see Georgie . . . they need to feel secure. It's what they like. They're funny like that. But yeh, of course they do. They need to feel they're not just another bird. They like to feel more, I don't know . . . valued. Loved, if you like. Birds, they're into all sorts of way-out stuff like that. And she's all right, Dorothy. Don't know what your problem is. I mean – you do *like* her, don't you?'

'Well of course I *like* her. I like her – of course I do. Wouldn't be with her if I didn't *like* her, would I? I think she said she was going to make some coffee actually, Sammy – do you fancy that? Haven't got anything, you know – better, I'm afraid . . . Want one of your own fags?'

'Yeah – coffee's fine. I will have a fag, actually. But, what . . . you just don't love her. That what you're saying?'

'I don't know. I really actually don't know, to be honest with you, Sammy. But what I keep thinking is . . . if I did, if I did love her, then I would, wouldn't I? Know, I mean.'

'Suppose . . . Anyway – all I'm saying is, she's a bit of all right, Dorothy.'

'Hands off.'

'Don't be stupid. Got more than enough to handle at the moment, haven't I?'

'What with groovy Emma . . .'

'What with groovy Emma . . . among other things. But look, Georgie – all I'm saying is, just be careful, that's all.'

'What sense? What do you mean . . .?'

'Well – you don't want to lose her, do you? You don't want to put her off. Because even birds like Dorothy – they do get fed up, you know. Don't hang around for ever.'

'Dorothy would. She would. She'd hang around for ever. But you're right – I know you're right, Sammy. I am pretty lucky. She is okay. Bit chunky . . .'

'Yeah well: nothing's perfect.'

'Julie Christie is.'

'Yeah now that's exactly what I mean, Georgie – that's what I'm talking about: you just can't keep going on like that. It's stupid. It's like saying if you can't get an E-Type, you're never going to drive. It's just stupid. Isn't it? If you were given a Morris Minor, you'd take it. Wouldn't you? Jump at it. Look – I know you like Julie Christie . . .'

'Love her . . .'

'Yeah right: love her. But we all do, don't we? Anyone who's ever seen her at the cinema. You'd have to be blind or dead not to. Yeah but so what? I mean – I feel the same way about Marianne Faithfull, but I don't go on and on about it.'

'Yeah yeah – I know. We're never going to meet Julie Christie and Marianne Faithfull. I know, I know . . .'

'Right. Shame, but there it is. And in the meanwhile, Dorothy . . . well . . .'

'Yeah. She's here. She's now. She's real. Available . . . always available. Sweet and dependable and decidedly chunky . . . It's weird, though: she still goes on about the Bomb, you know. How it could wipe us all out. But that's all over now, isn't it? Never even aware of it in the first place, if I'm honest. Kennedy that was, wasn't it? Don't know much about it. And now she's talking about not eating meat any more – that's the latest bloody thing. And she wants me to do it too – that's the real pain of her. Taken to ironing her hair, if you can believe it. I said to her: listen, Dorothy – look at yourself, can't you? Your hair, it's just not long enough, is it? And what about those split ends you're always banging on about? They'll frazzle. Didn't listen. Only managed to burn her bloody ear . . . and then she goes and does the jeans thing . . .'

'Yeh yeh. You told me about the jeans thing.'

'Yeah . . .? I did? What – the whole of the sitting in the bath thing . . .?'

'Yeh. You told me.'

'I wouldn't mind but the bloody jeans, they fitted fine in the first place. I mean, Christ – it's not like she's a beanpole, is it?'

'Jesus. Give her a break, Georgie, can't you . . .? You just go on and on . . .'

'Bloody bum was blue for a week. And what – I was expected just to put up with that and say nothing at all about it, was I . . .? Bloody great big blue bum . . .'

'Oh Christ's sake, Georgie – you just can't see it, can you? You're missing the whole bloody point. Why can't you just look at the other thing: the big thing?'

'Which is . . .?'

'God almighty – exactly where we came in, mate: you listening, or what? She's really into you, man . . .! She *loves* you . . .'

'Oh God. Oh God oh God oh God . . . I don't know, Sammy – I

just don't know. I just don't want to be dealing with all of this. Drives me bloody crazy . . . all right if I have another fag . . .?'

And Dorothy, who had been standing just outside the open door for quite some time now, silently turned and took the three mugs of coffee down the four steps and back into the kitchenette. Two of them she straight away upended into the sink, while all she was thinking was I am not going to cry – I can't cry again because I'm doing it all the time these days and it's just so stupid and everyone says it never gets you anywhere, crying, and they're right, of course they're right: just a waste of time, that's all. And George, when he sees I've been crying, when my eyes are all puffy – because that concealer I got from Boots, it doesn't work, it doesn't conceal anything, and it wasn't cheap, you know – well he really doesn't like it: goes mad, sometimes. I've just gone and tasted this other coffee now, and I really don't care for it: just as nasty as last time I made it. Nescafé I used not to mind too much if it had plenty of milk and sugar in it, but George, he prefers Maxwell House so it's Maxwell House he always used to get, but now he's discovered some other sort in Tesco that he says is great because it's miles cheaper and tastes just as good, but I think it's completely horrid. I'd much prefer a cup of tea: it's tea I like, really – but George, he says tea is boring and suburban and for old people in a home which I think is such a stupid thing to say, really . . . but I don't tell George that. I wouldn't actually say it to him. He thinks loads of things are suburban – and he really does sneer when he says it. I asked him once what he meant, what he was particularly meaning when he said it – because look, this room of his, it's in Kilburn, okay . . . which isn't exactly Piccadilly Circus, is it? He said that suburban is a state of mind, and you know it when you smell it – but if I wanted to be literal about it, if I was after an actual location, well then somewhere like Edgware. Where I live with my mum.

He can be very, I don't know . . . I'm not really that good, when it comes to words . . . but he's awfully . . . direct, I suppose you could say. Abrupt – that's better. When we first met – and I'll never forget it, well obviously I won't, it was in that bierkeller just off Oxford Street and I was there just after work with Yvonne, who I've known since school, and Sally, who I'd just met quite recently in my temping agency, and she seemed very nice. Yvonne is always up with all the latest trends – you should see those green suede boots of hers! Got them in Dolcis, but heaven knows how she managed to afford them – and she had read about it, this place, this bierkeller, in *Honey*, I think she said, or maybe she just knew someone who'd been . . . but she kept on telling me we just had to go there because it sounded really so fab and groovy: a really happening place. Everything with her has to be fab and groovy, or else she says it's just boring and a drag – bit how George thinks, actually. And I said to her yes but listen, Yvonne: I don't actually like it, beer, and she said it's German, it's Löwenbräu, it's not like English beer, it's all bright yellow and frothy and it tastes like cream soda. Well it doesn't obviously, as I soon found out – it tastes like beer, and I hate it. But anyway – George, he just happened to be there that day, you see, with Sammy (of course with Sammy – he's always with Sammy, far more than he's ever with me), and there were one or two other boys with him as well, forgotten their names, and he came right up to me and he said . . . oh, I'll always remember what he said to me because I was so amazed that a boy was talking to me at all – and then a bit confused and I bet I went bright red and I was kind of excited all at the same time and later that evening

I wrote it all down in my five-year diary with the lock on the front of it which I still do use actually, but my mother, she keeps on finding it wherever I hide it and I just know that she must have a key from something that opens it because she always knows exactly what I'm thinking, what I'm reading, what my favourite record is, where I've been, who I've been with. Drives me a bit crazy, to be honest, still having to live at home – and it's so much worse now, since my dad died: she just won't leave me alone. I want to come and live here with George – I know I could make it so much cosier for the two of us (get rid of all those pictures of cars and women for a start) . . . but George, he just won't ask me, and if I asked him, he'd only go mad. And with just the bits of secretarial work which is all I seem to be able to get at the moment, I can't really afford a place of my own, and God knows what my mum would do if I just suddenly left her: there's no telling, really – not with the way she is now. Maybe sharing, I could – I could maybe afford a sort of a flat-share . . . but it's not really what I want: I only want to be living with George. He's the one I want to be with. Always have done, really – pretty much from that very first moment I set eyes on him. Like I say, he came right up to me. Just suddenly, I saw him standing there.

'You're looking good.'

That's what he said. They were the first words he ever spoke to me.

'Yeah . . .?'

And that's the first word he ever heard from me: 'Yeah'. Oh God . . .

'Yeah. Look good. Saw you from over there, and I thought oh yeah: she's looking good. I'm George.'

'George. Oh wow.'

'You like it down here?'

'Yeah. No – not really.'

'Right. And you are . . .?'

'I am what . . .?'

'No – your name. I meant your name.'

'Oh yeah right – of course. My name. Stupid. No – that's not my name . . .! I'm Dorothy. I'm Dorothy. Like in the Wizard, you know . . .?'

'Like in the what?'

'Doesn't matter. Wizard of . . . no – doesn't matter.'

'Wizard? What you talking about?'

'Nothing. No – nothing. I'm called Dorothy. That's my name.'

'Got it. Right. So you're not a wizard.'

'No, I – no. Not.'

'Well listen, Dorothy: I don't want to buy you a drink.'

'You don't? Well I've got a drink.'

'Well I'm glad. I'm glad, you see – because I don't want to buy you a drink.'

'No. You said.'

'Yeah. And dinner. I don't want to buy you that either.'

'Oh. Right.'

'Not even sure I want to get to know you any better.'

'Are you always like this?'

'Like what?'

'Like this.'

'Don't know. Expect so. What I am.'

'Right.'

'You don't like it? You don't like me?'

'I don't know you.'

'No well. I'm leaving now. Getting out of here. Stuffy. Fed up with it.'

'You're . . . really quite rude, you know. Aren't you? Wouldn't you say?'

'Am I? Never really thought about it. Don't think I mean to be . . .'

'And what about your friends?'

'Sod them. You coming?'

'What . . .?'

'With me. You want to come with me?'

'Well I . . . I can't really. I'm here with friends . . .'

'Sod them. Coming?'

'Well . . . I don't know. Well yeah okay. Okay, then. Yeah. I've just got to go and . . .'

'Yeah well you go and do that, Dorothy. And I'll see you at the door. Okay?'

'Fine. Yeah. Okay, then.'

Even now, after all these months have passed, I can barely believe it – that all that actually happened. And the fact that I even sort of stood up to him, didn't I? Called him rude, and everything. Couldn't ever do that now. Couldn't think of it. It's just not in me. And George, he really wouldn't like it if I did. He completely wouldn't stand for it, actually. He'd tell me I knew nothing – tell me I was stupid. I don't really mind it when he's . . . is it masterful, they call it? When a man is, you know – being all sort of manly. But I don't much like it when he's shouting at me. I hate people shouting: I had enough of all that from my father to last me a lifetime. I've asked him since, George, how I had sort of come over . . . what his first impression of me was like, all that he was thinking . . . but he's never answered me, though. Said he couldn't remember. Said it didn't matter. Said what's gone is gone. Yvonne and Sally, they hadn't at all minded when I had more or less walked out on them. Looking back (because I don't really see them any more – well, Yvonne a bit, but George isn't keen on it: not just Yvonne – anyone, really), I think they had both assumed that that's the whole reason we had gone to this underground pub in the first place: not the beastly German beer, but simply to get picked up. It hadn't even occurred to me.

I was in a total whirl as I walked up the stairs. I kept on asking myself what on earth I imagined I was *doing* . . .?! Because this, this sort of thing, it really wasn't me: I was so completely surprising myself. Before George, I've only ever had one boyfriend, if you could even call him that. Peter, he'd take me to the pictures. He bought me Paynes Poppets (sometimes Sun-Maid chocolate raisins, which I actually much prefer) and he kissed me in the dark. Was forever trying to grapple with my bra, which I didn't like at all. He took my hand and he put it on . . . you know: himself. And I took it away again. This went on for quite a while. Some weeks later – we were in the Odeon and watching *From Russia with Love* – I finally went through with it just to stop him becoming even more bad-tempered. It did quiet him down, I have to admit, and that was a lesson of sorts, I suppose. Afterwards, while I was getting the latest *Photoplay*, he offered me a hot dog in the foyer.

The point is, though . . . I'd gone out with Peter just simply because he'd asked me to: I knew that girls went out with boys: it's what we're meant to do. And because of films like *Summer Holiday* (and I'm still a Cliff fan, whatever people say – it doesn't all have to be about the beat groups, although I do very much like The Dave Clark Five, and especially Mike Smith, the lovely singer) . . . but yes, because of these films, I did, I suppose, quite want it, to go on a date, to be part of a duo . . . but really, it was all a bit like the words in pop songs – it's what they're all about, but I never really thought that any of it could ever apply to me: they were just the words in pop songs, weren't they? Yvonne, she says I'm very naïve. She says I'm backward for my age, which is eighteen, nearly eighteen-and-a-half, now. I don't know if she's right – I suppose she is, in a way. I was never really in step with all the other girls at school – though I do wish now that I'd stayed on to do my A levels, like my mother told me to – and so did Miss Grincham, she was really very keen. But my so-called friends – Yvonne, Sally, Linda and Marion – they all said it was a complete waste of time because this is the nineteen sixties, but I knew it wouldn't be a waste of time – I knew it would be a good thing to do (history and maths, rather oddly – they were my best things, the subjects that I always nearly came top in, and Miss Grincham, she was completely convinced I could get a place in a decent university) . . . but I let them win me over, I don't know why I did. So I left and did a Pitman's course instead: how I came to be a temp. So I'm not nearly so 'modern', or whatever you want to call it, as Yvonne is, that's for sure – not nearly so daring. So when I met George – when I so completely amazed myself by agreeing to leave this horrible cellar with a rather strange boy after just that short and pretty stupid conversation . . . I really did feel sort of, I don't know . . . alive, in a way that I never had before. Sparkling, really. Had no idea what was going to happen. And I was really excited about that. I was tingling, and my eyes – they felt all kind of bulgy and really so huge. I don't know . . . I think that the only way I can really put it is to say that I was feeling . . . glad all over . . .!

He was waiting just outside the door, George – leaning against the wall and smoking a cigarette, as per usual. The sudden whoosh of fresh air, it was a shock but very welcome

– I do remember thinking that – but we're now going back to February, you see, so it was really quite chilly, and I wished I'd brought a scarf: I nearly did, it was in the hall, the striped one that used to be my dad's . . . but then, I don't know . . . last minute, I just didn't. I've told him so many times since, George, that he's smoking too much – I was always telling him, but he only used to grin and look at me with just one of his eyes open and staring really daftly the way he always does, and then he'd just say, 'What's too much?' There's no point in me doing it any more – don't know why I did. He says stuff like 'Life is for living' and 'I'm young – what do I care?' He says that a lot, that he's young and he doesn't care, and I hate it when he does because it's like he's tempting . . . whatever that word is. And then he says that I'm young too and I should remember that because I won't be young for ever and I ought to start 'living a little'. It's all pretty meaningless, all of this: it all sounds so terribly, I don't know . . . second-hand, really. But the way he says it, the way he always tries to put it across, it's like he really does seem to believe that he's all sort of proclaiming, oh God – the profoundest things imaginable . . .! But really it's all just like a series of mottoes, or something. He's a clever boy, George – he's awfully bright, really much cleverer than I am (as he keeps on telling me) . . . but still, he does come out with some pretty stupid things, sometimes. I don't say anything, now – not any more. No point. Just let him get on with it. I think actually that these days I don't even listen to half of it – and the other half, well . . . I've heard it all before. *Providence* – that's it: that's the word I was meaning. Yeh: tempting providence – yeh yeh, that's it.

'You took your time.'

'I had to say goodbye to my friends. I told you.'

'Want a fag, do you . . .?'

'No thanks. No thank you. I don't, actually.'

'What – ever?'

'No – I don't at all. Well – I had a Consulate once. Yvonne said – Yvonne, that's one of my friends, one of the ones who I was with downstairs, yes . . .? She said they're really nice and minty, these Consulates – not like ordinary cigarettes – but I really didn't like it at all and I just had to put it out. Felt a bit guilty, actually, because then she went and told me that they're terribly expensive. I had no idea or I wouldn't have taken one in the first place. I probably didn't do it right – I don't know. But I'm really not keen. Actually seems a bit stupid to me, smoking . . .'

'I'll teach you.'

'No – no thank you. I'd rather not.'

'Okay. Well let's push off then, shall we?'

'Where? Where are we going? Only I can't be too late . . .'

'Where do you live?'

'Oh – miles away. Million miles away from here. And you? Do you live round here? It's getting quite cold . . .'

'Why? Are you inviting yourself over? You think it's cold . . .? I don't feel cold.'

'No! I didn't mean that. I didn't mean that at all! I was just . . . you asked me where I lived, that's all. And so I asked you. Only trying to be polite. Don't much care about where you live actually. And yeh I do think it's cold – I think it's freezing. Are we just going to stand out here all evening? Because if we are, I think I might go back downstairs and be with my friends . . .'

'No – you don't want to do that. And anyway – we're off. We're going to Kilburn.'

'So what's in Killbun? Why do you want to go to Killbun?'

'You'll like it. Come on.'

And I so wished I'd been wearing something else. Over the weeks and months, I've thought about that evening really quite a lot, obviously – well you don't want ever to forget it, do you? The day you met the man you love. And still I'm just *so* embarrassed by, oh God – well nearly all of it, really. That I'd never heard of Kilburn, for a start – that I had no idea how the word was even spelt. That I must have sounded so . . . what is it? I don't know how I sounded. Fussy. No – prissy: prissy, that's it. It was just all so *embarrassing*. But I was nervous, you see. Really scared, actually (still excited, though – my stomach was going up and down, and I kept on swallowing, and my eyes still felt so massive) because I'd never done this, never done anything like this in the whole of my life: first I'm hating beer in a bierkeller and turning down a Consulate from Yvonne (I'm always telling her no, but she will keep on offering me them), then I'm turning down a whatever it was George was smoking outside . . . still Embassy, I think, in those days. And I was wearing a nigger brown corduroy shift under my coat that was really dull and much too long because it was one of the ones I hadn't yet got around to shortening and I'd only put it on because I didn't think I'd be taking my coat off at all, but if now we were going to go somewhere, somewhere in Killbun, well then I probably would be, wouldn't I? And then George, he'd see this really boring thing I was wearing underneath and he'd think, Oh God, she really is boring this girl – or 'dullsville', is what he probably would have said – and everything she says and everything she wears, it's just so b-word *boring* . . .! Because his clothes, the gear he had on that evening, it was really nice, really smart – that's what I remember thinking at the time. It was only that yellow tab-collar shirt and the elephant cords that these days I'm frankly sick of the sight of, but I did think he looked nice that night. The brown jacket with patch pockets which was okay – and then, when I met him outside at the door, this really grotty sort of raincoat with a belt which was the sort of thing you have to wear at school. I later found out that it was the actual one that he did wear at school, and he hated it as much as I did. He's chucked it now, that's long gone, and he got this double-breasted black plastic thing, PVC thing, instead: I think it looks a bit cheap and actually rather effeminate but he clearly thinks it's just so completely cool, so I've never said anything about it. His hair was just over the tops of his ears, which I went for – because I never liked a boy's hair to be really long like the Rolling Stones or something, and that's what I still think now: it just looks dirty, that, or else it looks a bit like a girl. Mike Smith's is just right. But really it was his hands, George's hands, that I noticed most – very slim and pale, with long, thin fingers: I thought that with hands like that, he's just bound to be really sensitive and caring. That's what I thought.

I hadn't even washed my hair that day and I'd quickly gone to the Ladies in the bierkeller after I'd said goodbye to Yvonne and Sally and I nearly did cry when I saw that it had all been flattened, my hair, by this huge floppy hat I'd been wearing which I'd got in the British Home Stores in the January sales and I'd been really pleased with it because the sort of apple-green colour almost exactly matched the slingbacks I got for Christmas from my mum after an awful lot of pleading, and it was only thirteen and eleven – the hat, I mean. Sally had said that she really liked it, but I don't know if she meant it or not. I wish I had really long blonde hair like Yvonne's: mine just doesn't seem to grow, not properly – and even when it does it's just so frizzy and covered in split ends and I didn't then dare iron it like I read you could in *Honey* (which now I do, but it's just so scary because I've got no one to help me with it and George, he just laughs and twice I've burned my ear, now). So in the Ladies I just tried to fluff it up a bit with my hands, which didn't do anything, and then I put on a bit more lipstick – Rimmel, new colour, sort of frosty, it's really good, but that didn't seem to make a lot of difference either, and so George – he's just going to hate me, isn't he? Yes but on the other hand . . . he did ask me, didn't he? To come with him. Plenty of other girls down there, but it was me he asked, wasn't it? So there must have been something. I must have seemed attractive in some way to him, mustn't I? No . . .? Yes . . .? So this is how I was, you see . . . this is how I was thinking: this is the state I was in. Oh look . . . I just drove myself crazy, going over and over and over it. And I can still get like that sometimes – if George ever shouts at me, say . . . or if we're in the pictures or a pub or somewhere and he says that he likes what some girl's wearing because he doesn't mean he likes what she's wearing, does he? We know what boys mean: it's what they always mean. But . . . I think on the whole I'm better than I was. Hope so, anyway.

I can't honestly imagine what we were talking about in the Tube: I was just too knotted up to say anything much – and I kept on looking at my watch. This was a different line from the one to Edgware, so all I remember thinking was that I had to make sure that I knew exactly where I should be changing on the way back so that I'd be certain to get home and that I'd left myself plenty of time or else my mum, if I was in even a minute after ten, she was just going to go mad. Like she always does. But it's her I thought of – she was the first thing that popped into my mind when we came out of the Tube. I thought, oh God – if she could just see me here now, she'd have a fit. And I also was thinking, if I'm honest, that I would actually not at all mind being at home in Edgware, right at this moment, nice and cosy in my room, or else even back in the bierkeller with Yvonne and Sally – because my first impression of this place, it wasn't a good one. There were these men, old mostly, at the entrance to the Tube station, all red-faced and hanging on to one another and staggering about and laughing and gurgling and the smell was just terrible. Irish, George told me: they were always there – a permanent fixture, a local sight. They drink meths, petrol, surgical spirit – anything they can lay their hands on: they wouldn't, George said, know a chateau-bottled vintage if you hit them round the head with it: they'd sell their souls for a bottle of Jameson, I think is what he said. There's a lot of Irish round here, he told me, but don't worry because they're not all as bad as that. Well now that I've been coming here really quite a lot, I can tell you that the place is just full of Irish, nearly nothing else, and most of them, as far as I can see, are just as bad as that. Even the women are pretty terrible. Always swearing and a lot of them seem to be missing half their teeth – don't ever know what they're shouting about (shouting, that's their normal way of speaking) because the accent, as well as disgusting, is just completely incomprehensible. I don't know how they can do it. None of them seems to have a job, or anything. The men are meant to be navvies, but you never see them doing any navvying – and yet they're always drinking. They hold up a bottle of something wrapped in brown paper, and they just upend it down their throat. Then they laugh and scratch their bristly faces and one will stop the other from falling right over. Once, that awful one they all call

Saint Patrick, he made a lunge at me, and I practically died: he stank so badly, and I just ran away as fast as I possibly could. Coloured people too – there are quite a few of those, but they seem quieter, probably quite nice people, but they do rather scare me – just to look at them, and the way they sort of move. George says I'm small-minded and stupid to think all this, but that's what he says about practically all my opinions. Which is why I don't say anything any more – why I never tell him what I think. But I don't know . . . maybe he's right. I don't know . . .

It's not far from the Tube, George's place – his room, bedsit, whatever you want to call it: it's actually not very much – it's really quite small. There's a sort of café – all day they serve breakfast, and even into the night. You can never see in because the windows are always completely steamed up. There's chipped white lettering on the glass that says TEAS, but the actual place doesn't seem to have a name, or anything. George says they do a really good fry-up, is what he calls it, and unbelievably cheap, but I've never wanted to go in. And to the side of this there's a door that's got barely any paint left on it – around the handle it's nearly raw, and also down at the bottom: there's a bit of different-coloured plywood where it looks like it's been kicked in repeatedly. There's all sorts of mismatched bells up the side with scrawled-on bits of paper stuck next to them and one with just a wire hanging out which George said to be careful not to touch or I'd get a shock. It's still just like that now, of course it is. Well – in the months I've been coming here since, nothing about the place has changed at all, and I don't suppose it ever will: the hallway is still that awful brown lino and the wallpaper all rubbed away where people are forever squeezing past one another, or else it's just peeling. There are pieces of a bicycle that no one seems to own that you have to step over every single time you come in or out, but they're never ever going to be moved, I just know it. And on two brackets there's that enormous gas meter which you can easily bash your head on, if you're not very careful. And a really dim light – you press a switch and it comes on (if you're lucky – often people steal the bulbs) but you've got to be really quick getting up the two flights of stairs to George's room, or else it just clicks off again and you're stuck in total darkness outside Sean and Mary's place – more Irish – which always smells so . . . oh, it just makes me gag. George says it's because they fry things on a Bunsen Burner and they've got a baby but they don't ever see to the nappies. I just can't bear to think of it.

Of course, he didn't tell me any of this at the time – I've picked it all up since, bit by horrible bit. If he'd told me at the time – or if I'd been just even slightly more aware – I'd have run a mile, I should think. I didn't like it at all, this house – still don't, not really. How could you? I've asked him, George, why he has to live somewhere quite so awful, and he just says well why do you think? It's cheap. And at first, quite early on, I tried to suggest that there had to be somewhere in London that was just as cheap, or not much more expensive anyway, that wasn't just quite so ghastly. He told me I didn't know what I was talking about. So now I just keep my mouth shut . . . but of course I continue to come back here. It's just that this is where George is, you see . . . and so therefore it follows quite naturally that this is where I want to be. At the time, though . . . that first evening, when he first showed me into this room of his (I say showed me in – he just held back on the landing and just more or less pointed, really), suddenly I was smacked by the thought, the what is it . . .? Realisation . . . the realisation, yes, that here, this room was the last place on earth I actually wanted to be. Not particularly because of the look of it, or anything – I hadn't even begun to take that in – it's just that it had come to me all in a rush exactly what it was I had done here. I was in some rather beastly part of London I had never before been to, in a room two floors above a stinking greasy spoon, and I hadn't observed the house number, nor even the name of the street. Not a single living soul had any idea where I was, and that included me. What's more – and this was really the thing, well of course it was – I was there, all alone with a boy who I'd only just met about, what . . . half an hour ago, maybe? And all I knew about this total stranger was that his name was George, and that his hands were very slim and pale, with long, thin fingers. I don't know . . . I'm still not sure if it was fear that was making me sweat and just shiver a bit, my heart really thumping . . . or just this sort of crazy excitement, and maybe even the beginnings of love.

'Coffee? Do you want . . .?'

'Mm . . .?'

'Want a cup of coffee? Sit, if you like. Over there, if you want . . .'

'Have you got anything else? Not great on coffee . . .'

'Johnny next door, he's probably got some lager, or something . . .'

'Oh no – I meant . . . it doesn't really matter, actually.'

'I maybe got Sunfresh . . .'

'No honestly – nothing. I'm fine. I'm completely fine. So . . . this is where you . . . you didn't actually tell me that we were going to go to where you, um . . .'

'I thought you knew. I said Kilburn.'

'Yes, but . . .'

'Didn't I? Say it. I said it, Kilburn. That that's where we were going . . .'

'Yes but I didn't know that that's where you . . . oh look – it doesn't matter. Honestly. It's fine. Here, shall I sit . . .? Did you say? Or . . .'

'You can go if you like.'

'No no. It's fine. I'm fine. Honestly.'

'Don't have to stay, or anything. Not forcing you . . .'

'I said I'm okay, didn't I?'

'Keep looking at your watch, that's all . . .'

'Yes well I've got to know . . . you know . . . when to go.'

'Only just come.'

'Yes I know but . . . look – maybe I will just have a quick coffee then, if you're going to make it. Yes? You having a coffee?'

'No. I don't want one.'

'No. Well I don't either. Not really.'

'Fag . . .?'

'No thank you. I told you I . . .'

'Oh yeh. Just remembered. Just when I offered you one, I remembered you don't, do you?'

'I don't, no. But you go ahead.'

'Going to.'

'Right. It's, uh . . . nice here . . . Been here long? Have you been living here a long time, or . . .?'

Lies, lies . . . so many lies . . .! That I was fine. That everything was completely okay. And then the biggest lie of all: that it was, oh dear me . . . 'nice here'. Because this room – my God in heaven . . .! That's what I thought then, and it's what I still think now. Where I was sitting, the thing he had told me to sit on was so very low and uncomfortable – just some sort of a crate, it felt like, with a Union Jack draped over it. And that's exactly what it was, I found out later: R. White's lemonade. In front of that was another box with brass handles and a lock – what I now know to be his old tuck box from school, and still we use it as a table because there isn't really anything else, apart from the cronky old ironing board which never got used, until I came along. The tuck box, it's covered in rings from a million mugs of coffee, and I tell him probably about once every month that I could easily go to Woolworth's and get half a yard of Con-Tact, which is what they call Fablon and it's quite a lot cheaper, and cover it all up really nicely, but all he does is just look at me. Maybe I should just go ahead and do it and not say anything about it, but I'm not really sure I've got the courage – and if I got, I don't know, imitation teak or something, he'd only go and say it was suburban. On the wall and right opposite where I was sitting there was this absolutely enormous poster of a girl in a bikini – I thought it was maybe from some film or other, it did look quite familiar, but I wasn't completely sure because I'm not too great on films. I know what it is now, of course – the James Bond film, the first one, what was it called . . .? But still I don't much want to keep on having to stare at a girl in a bikini, actually, and so that is one thing I am totally determined is going to come down, whether George likes it or not. I'll have to get him to agree to it when he's in a good mood, though . . . when he seems pleased with me, or not too displeased, anyway – and I'll also have to find something to replace it, of course. He says he likes Dalí, who I quite like too, miracle of miracles – but the only print I've ever seen, that one with the melting clock, it's in Athena and it's awfully expensive, I think, for what's really only a big piece of paper, after all. I was hoping they'd have it in their sale, but they didn't. They only had Hieronymus Bosch, which frankly is just about the last thing we need.

Then there are cars, pictures of cars, which all look the same to me. What else? A gas fire with two broken elements, which is maybe why it smells. It's actually good that the weather's a bit warmer now, so we don't have to have it on. The Baby Belling, of course, without which George'd starve, or else live on jam sandwiches, which he says he adores (and particularly loganberry ones) but I know it's just because they're quick and cheap and easy (same reason he goes for sausage rolls and Hovis with Dairylea). A cracked pub ashtray crammed with cigarette butts that says Watneys Red Barrel on all four sides of it. A small divan in the corner, not brilliantly clean sheets, and rather rumpled – which, on that very first visit, I tried so hard not to look at. Not much more: a couple of ordinary wooden chairs that George says if we painted purple would look 'really cool and happening', is what he actually said, but first he's got to check with the landlord. Record player, not many records, pretty much all Beatles – which is fine because I actually love The Beatles, who doesn't, but it would be quite nice to have something else occasionally, if only for a change. I once brought round my 'Glad All Over' single which was number one not that long ago and I play it all the time at home but he actually refused to put it on because he said he hates The Dave Clark Five (I sometimes wish I'd never even mentioned that I liked Mike Smith: if it was a Beatle, particularly George Harrison, he'd be completely fine with it. Funny, really). The only encouraging thing, quite frankly, was a pretty impressive collection of books, Penguins mostly, on these sort of makeshift shelves just over by the fireplace. Honestly, though – to say that this room needed a woman's touch would be the understatement of the . . . God, you know, if I'm being completely honest, what it really needed (I remember thinking this at the time) was a total clear-out, complete redecoration – even fumigation, because of the stale cigarette smell – and starting all over again. And there was a beastly draught from the very grubby window – one reason, that first evening, why I didn't take my coat off: he hadn't put on the gas fire, or anything. That, and the horrible nigger brown corduroy shift I had on underneath, and also . . . other things. Still is draughty, that window, despite my having jammed an old pair of tights into the worst of the gaps – but at least I've got a curtain over it now. I got a remnant from John Lewis – blue and green gingham, quite gay – and my mum showed me how to hem it on her machine. I was on at George to get some of that curtain wire with hooks and eyes so I could fix it and he said he would, promised me he would, but he never did, of course, so I just put it up with drawing pins in the end.

'Shall I put on a record? Beatles, yeah . . .?'

'Love The Beatles, yes. Only . . . I can't stay too long. Getting a bit late, isn't it? Maybe we could just, um – you know: talk a bit . . .'

'Okay. What do you want to talk about?'

'Well . . . what do you do, George? I don't know the first thing about you.'

'I'm press. Distribution. Wholesale side.'

'Gosh – really? That sounds awfully exciting . . .'

'It's okay, yeah. Quite like it. Responsibilities, of course . . .'

'I'm just a secretary, I'm afraid. Temp.'

'Is that all right?'

'Yes. It's all right. It's not exactly what I want to be, but . . .'

'So what do you want to be, then? Pop star? You want to be Marianne Faithfull or Cilla or someone?'

'No. No, not really. I don't actually know. What I want to be.

I don't think I've really thought about it very much. Probably why I'm just a temp . . .'

'Do you like *Steptoe*?'

'I'm sorry . . .?'

'*Steptoe & Son*. Do you like it? I like it. You know – on TV.'

'Oh. Yes. I've heard of it, I think. I've never seen it, though. It's good, is it? At home we don't really, um . . .'

'And where's home?'

'I'm still living with my mum, actually. Edgware.'

'Poor you.'

'Oh God I really used to love that record . . . oh no – it was "Poor Me", wasn't it . . .?'

'What . . .?'

'Nothing. No, it's not too bad, actually. Not really. She's all right.'

'Edgware. End of the line.'

'What do you mean . . .?'

'Edgware. It's the end of the Northern Line.'

'Oh I see. Yes.'

'I've never been there.'

'No, well – you wouldn't really, unless you, um . . . it's not very exciting.'

'Morden.'

'Sorry . . .?'

'I've been to Morden. That's the end of some other line. Not sure which.'

'Uh-huh. Okay . . .'

'But I've never been to Edgware. That's all I'm saying.'

'Right . . .'

'Morden's not very exciting either.'

'Isn't it?'

'Don't really remember it, actually. Do you want a Kit-Kat?'

'A . . .? Oh – no thanks, no thank you. Not really hungry.'

'I'm starving.'

'Oh well . . . you have one, then . . .'

'Not sure I've actually got any . . .'

'Right. Okay, then . . .'

'What did you think of the Clay fight?'

'The what . . .?'

'Cassius Clay. Liston. You must have seen it.'

'Oh God no. Boxing . . .? Oh God no. Listen, George – I know you're being polite and making conversation and all that sort of thing . . . which I'm not actually very good at, as you've probably discovered by now . . . but look, what I mean to say is, it's been really nice and everything, but because I really do have to go very soon . . . got to get back, you see? So because I really can't stay for very much longer . . . I was just sort of wondering, George . . .'

And what I was wondering was whether he had any intention of kissing me. Which I was reasonably sure I wanted to happen. I was confused, actually . . . because this isn't how I thought boys behaved, once they had got you alone. I mean – all I had to go on was Peter in the cinema, so I suppose I'd expected him to be suddenly all over me, George . . . I suppose what I thought was that I'd be fighting him off, from the moment I stepped into the room. Well, I say fight him off . . . I was very attracted to him, there's no denying that – why otherwise had I agreed to go with him in the first place? Because there was something about him, George – I had felt it immediately. He was different – different from Peter, anyway, who actually had been really pretty horrible, now I come to think of it. And I knew that I did want to touch his hair, George's hair, just where it came over the tops of his ears . . . and inhale his skin – his neck, you know? Does that sound funny? Because that's always so terribly intimate, I think. When you see it in films. But if he had other ideas – if he thought I was just some sort of an easy pick-up in a pub who was going to go all the way with him, or something, like all these dolly birds in Chelsea and places that you keep on seeing in the *News of the World* . . . well then I'd decided to just scream the place down and then make a run for it. What I really hadn't been expecting, though – the thing that had really surprised me was all these actually pretty stupid questions about TV programmes and Kit-Kats and then blooming boxing, of all things. Yes . . . and he'd asked them all in this same sort of completely flat and expressionless voice that made it pretty clear, I thought, that he didn't remotely give two hoots about the answers – what I actually had to say on the matter. So why was he doing that, then? Was he nervous? He didn't seem to be nervous. Shy, then. But he didn't really seem to be that, either. So probably it's just me . . . has to be, really.

'What? Wondering what?'

'Well . . . you do . . . like me, don't you George . . .?'

'Yeah. I like you. You seem . . . yeah. I like you.'

'Well look . . . I've got to go soon . . .'

'Yeah. You keep saying.'

'Yes. So . . . oh God, you're really making this a bit hard for me actually, George. I don't want to seem as if I'm . . . but look: don't you want to . . .?'

'What? Don't I want to what?'

'Kiss me . . .?'

He stared at me. He just stared at me. I felt . . . oh heavens, I don't know what I felt. Embarrassed mainly, I suppose. Stupid and clumsy and horribly forward. I thought I could scream. I thought I should run. And then he said:

'Yes.'

He stepped towards me, then – I was standing quite close to him by this time – and he just did it. So softly, on the mouth. Just like the touch of a feather, and yet so fantastically warm. I didn't even mind the dull and foggy taste of cigarettes. He didn't try to jam his tongue halfway down my throat like Peter always did. And we just stayed like that for what seemed like hours and days, it seemed like a dreamy eternity . . . and I was touching his hair, just where it went over the tops of his ears . . . and when the kiss had finally ended, I rested my head on his shoulder, and then I could inhale his skin to the side of his neck . . . and oh, it just smelled so divine . . .

He walked me to the Tube station, which was quite a relief. It was really quite late now – by my standards, anyway – completely dark, and the Irish, their noise and all their awful lunacy, it was even worse than it was before. He explained to me, George, all about where I had to change trains, and I gave him the home telephone number – I'd torn a page out of my diary, and I also wrote down the times when it would be best for him to ring. When I'd be back from work, obviously, but also when I thought my mum was a little less likely to be snooping about – when *Coronation Street* was on, say, or else some play on the radio – because it's in the hall, our phone, and you can hear everything all over the house. On the walk to the Tube, I thought that now we had kissed, he might have something romantic to say to me . . . but he didn't. In just that same flat voice as before, he asked me what I'd do if I found a hundred pounds on the pavement. I said I'd hand it in – why, what would he do? He said he'd go round the world, and when the money ran out he'd work as a grease monkey and also jerking sodas. I had not the slightest idea what either of these things meant – what on earth he was talking about. Then he asked me if I knew that Kathy Kirby earned forty thousand pounds a year . . . and I said I doubted whether that was possible, because I didn't think even the Queen could earn that much. He said it was true. I didn't care. I'd never heard of Kathy Kirby – completely unaware of who she was. Didn't care who she was, or how much she earned. I was much too busy . . . falling in love.

On the journey home – which was actually quite quick, much faster than I thought it would be – I was lost in a world that was new to me. I hugged the memory of a rather strange boy . . . I hugged it really close and tight – its colour and its fragrance – and then I went over every single second, repeatedly. Only when I got home – Mum was in the hall, of course, looking at her watch, though we both knew it wasn't nearly ten o'clock yet . . . but yes, it was only when I got home that it occurred to me that he hadn't once, George, throughout the evening, called me by my name: he hadn't once said to me: Dorothy. It was only weeks later when I had suddenly thought to mention it that he admitted that he'd actually forgotten it, my name – forgotten what I was called, and somehow, he just didn't like to ask.

And all that . . . it was more than three, nearly four months ago, now. Sometimes feels like years, the time I've been with George . . . and yet now that I'm thinking of it, going over all of it again, it could be just yesterday, that meeting down in the bierkeller, that first kiss in the room. He's calling for me now. Twice he's done it, while I've just been standing here in the kitchenette, staring ahead of me, and trying not to think. 'Where's that coffee, then . . .?!' That's what he's been shouting at me. Well I'll tell you, George, shall I? It's down the sink. I chucked it down the sink. Because I was going to bring it, I had it made and I was all ready to give it to you, but then I just happened to be outside the door while you were talking to Sammy – talking to Sammy with much more softness, more closeness and far more intimacy than I ever hear when you're talking to me. I don't even remember the last time you did talk to me, actually. And what you were saying – well, you were basically saying that I, your girlfriend – I, your girlfriend, who loves you . . . who really does love you, George – and don't I tell you? Aren't I saying it to you all the time? – is nothing more than a dependable just about okay old boot. Who isn't Julie Christie. And I can't be, can I? How can I ever be? I'm just about a million miles from being even slightly like Julie Christie. It's not my fault. It just isn't my fault. Is it? And as well as that . . . I'm chunky. Apparently. Which may or may not be true, it's not really for me to say. Am I chunky . . .? I don't know. I suppose I must be, if that's what he thinks I am. I really don't know. How can I? But it hurt – it hurt me anyway. All of what he said, it hurt me – I flinched when I heard it, and still I'm burning with what actually feels like a kind of shame. You hurt me, George – you don't know it, but I doubt if you'd care even if you did. You hurt me badly, George, yes you did, yes you did. And that, I suppose . . . that must be the reason why now I just can't stop crying. But I have to . . . I have to just stop, and pull myself together. Because I really don't want him to see me like this . . .

CHAPTER TWO

VAINGLORIOUS TO A FAULT

'Happy birthday, Dad . . .!'

'Thank you, Anna, my dear. How sweet you are. But birthdays, you know . . . they're not for old men. Not for oldies like me. Children – they're for children, birthdays.'

'Oh you always say that. You've been saying all that for just *years*, Dad! I told you – didn't I tell you? You've got to think *young* . . . It's only a number, isn't it? Sixty-four – it's only a number. You could be handy, mending a fuse . . .! Think young, Dad. Just keep thinking *young* . . .'

I eye her with genuine fondness. I nod. Fielding the inevitable allusion to the Beatles song – and of course as soon as I walked into the room she had played the entire track on this miracle phone she was waving around, and quite heartily joining in the chorus: 'when I'm sixty-*four* . . .'. Yes well. And I nod too, and smile, supposedly at her wisdom. Think young, she says . . . and I am thinking, Ah Anna, my dear little girl – how easy, how very easy for you to say that. Because you *are* young, aren't you? Still so young and lovely . . . though I suppose by now you must actually be . . . well I don't know, if I'm honest. Not exactly. How awful. Is that awful? I mean I do know roughly, of course – I more or less know how old you are, my dear, of course I do: you must be what now, Anna? Thirty? Bit more, maybe? Oh yes – it will be more, it will be a bit more than that actually, because we did something, didn't we? For your thirtieth? Restaurant, or something? And now I remember that little Troy, you had little Troy when you were just twenty-nine, that I do remember, and he must be two or maybe even three by now, mustn't he? Not too good at judging the age of children. There he is over on the sofa, little Troy (damned stupid name: said it at the time, made my views felt, I think – now I just shut up about it) – seems quite utterly absorbed, little chap, by whatever it is he is playing with. Electronic, of course. Well I've repeatedly made plain my views about that as well, but you just get the rolling of the eyes from his mother. 'It's the way it is now, Dad,' she patiently explains – barely repressing the sigh of exasperation as she attempts once more to din the alphabet and fundamental numeracy into the obdurate head of the demented and defiantly troglodyte Methuselah who is standing before her . . . mm, probably rather confused, all that, but the thrust and meaning are perfectly plain, surely? 'You've just got to understand that,' is what she's always saying to me. 'Even you – you'd be lost now without email and Google and everything, wouldn't you?' Well no, dear Anna – hardly lost. I would miss the quick convenience, I suppose. I would miss the even quicker pornography. But I would hardly be desolate. 'You see, Dad – all the kids at his school have got it now. They've got just everything. What Troy has is actually pretty basic – but it would be cruel to deprive him.' Whereupon I do it again, all that is expected of me. I nod. Nod and smile, supposedly at her wisdom. And what I am thinking is, Oh dear Christ in heaven, Anna – what can you or he ever comprehend about *deprivation* . . .? And have you stopped, if only just for a second or so, to question why this actually has to be . . .? He would be equally content, more so probably, with bricks, or something – you know, Lego and so forth – or cars or soldiers. I know I was. Do they still make them, soldiers . . .? I doubt it: incitement to murder, or something. Institutionalised violence. But what I am meaning is, the joy of things that don't have to *work* – things where, well . . . the child can make it work. That was what playtime meant. Imagination – do they still do imagination, children? It all went on in your head. And in my case, very much still does, of course. Oh well.

'So you do like it, Dad, yes . . .? Sure? Because you can change it, if you don't like it. I've got the receipt, and everything. David says you won't wear it – that's what you said, isn't it, David? Oh God – he's on his . . . he's making a call, as usual. You talk about me and Troy, Dad – it's David you ought to be on at: he's never off that thing. Anyway – I think it will really suit you. I should think you've got plenty of shirts that go. You like it, don't you Mum . . .?'

Enid . . . she glances across at me before she answers. She will be evasive. She will say . . . what will she say? She will say, 'It's really not up to me to like it or not like it, is it Anna? It's your father – he's the one who'll be wearing it.' Something of that order – that's what she'll be saying. She doesn't know if it will suit me. She doesn't care if it will suit me. It's a tie. Just another tie. Navy, with diagonal stripes. If I had to guess, I would have said that I already possess a dozen at least that are more or less identical. It's a funny thing, though . . . about your wife: that's what has taken me, now: that's the way I'm thinking at the moment. I am watching her, Enid, while I am going over all this in my head – she being perfectly unaware, of course, as now she is fooling with cake. She looks like your wife: same face, give or take, same little mannerisms, for good or ill. She sounds exactly like that person you married all those eons ago . . . and yet one day you wake up to suddenly realise (and this happened to me, oh . . . quite a good long while ago) that you're actually living with somebody else entirely. Or . . . can it be this? Rather more unsettling, but can it be this? Can it be that she is, in fact, your wife, precisely the same woman as she always was, but it is you. Yes – you. You, and your perceptions, you and your urgent memories, your increasingly rickety imaginings . . . that it is not they but you that now are changed beyond all recognition . . .?

'It's not really up to me, is it, Anna? Either way. It's your father – he's the one who's got to wear it.'

'Well he doesn't *have* to wear it . . .'

'No – I didn't mean that, Anna . . .'

'You don't have to, Dad. If you really don't like it, I don't want you feeling you've got to wear it. That would be stupid. I can take it back. I've got the receipt, and everything . . .'

'I will wear it, Anna, I like it very much. It's most unusual, and very well chosen. I might have known that you were the brains behind it, as soon I unwrapped it. Very nice. Very good. Thank you, Anna. Thank you . . . all.'

Yes. That should do it. Enid, she's still slicing away there: portioning out the cake. Don't actually like it, cake – particularly the sort with icing on it; I do keep saying, but more and more now, nobody ever seems to hear me. David . . .? Nothing could distract him from yattering away on his bloody mobile phone – but yes, we all know that. Troy is in a trance as he jabs at buttons. But Anna – she's beaming, anyway. And that was the only point. I am looking at David now, though . . . and always when he speaks . . . I have observed this before about this son of mine, of course, but whenever he is speaking into that bloody little phone of his, David . . . he always will turn away. It is as if he imagines that the sight of the back of his head will somehow render his constant and rabbiting nonsense completely inaudible to ordinary human beings. His turning away – this terse aversion of a shoulder – it is his makeshift disguise: a rudely drawn-across screen, a symbolic divisor between his glorious self and the assembled motley of fools. Making it perfectly clear to how many unseen witnesses – stressing, as if any such stress were required, the very evident truth of the matter, do you see . . .? That while such lamentable futility as his parents, his sister, his little nephew Troy – while these doolally morons continue to fritter their time in airy-headed idleness, and amid the trappings of so worthless a thing as someone else's birthday, he is wholly, and in a thoroughly adult manner, rapt and concerned with the real big thing: life, of course, with which he is grappling manfully. Here is a true toiler at the coalface, glossy with grime and persistent effort. Or maybe a master of the universe, cleaving to the cutting edge. Ha. If only he were either thing. Because no – that is not our David. Not our David at all. Oh, he might well grapple, but always seemingly with a tireless and determinedly aggressive octopus. And David . . . he has not the holds, the strength, nor even the gusto, and so always he is thrown. Or else pinned down. He never will win, it is not in his destiny – even a round, never mind the bout. Not enough energy, too little brain.

He frowns when he speaks – as he growls abrupt instructions into his phone, rammed tight against his ear. That low forehead of his, it is corrugated intensely – I suppose to underline to a thoroughly uncaring and elsewhere world (did he but know it, could he but see it) that here is a matter of supreme importance . . . or even that he is talking sense, or something. But he will only and once again be harassing that poor little idiot Lilian, who still is meek and defeated in the relentless face of all his slack-mouthed bullying. She has worked with him for years on his latest preposterous venture, which still is clinging with extraordinary tenacity to the ground from which it should have been launched, oh God – how long ago? – to spectacular fanfare and applause . . . for was it not, as he repeatedly harangued us, everything our planet had been waiting for . . .? Lilian I myself have encountered only once or twice, on occasions when she had been commanded to bring to him immediately an urgent piece of paper, which always I imagined to be blank. She has a good face, Lilian, I do remember that – wide, expressive eyes and a decent jawline, for a woman. Her body is sadly deficient. But promotion for Lilian to his equal and helpmeet will not ever figure in this boyo's scheme of things. He must be superior to someone, David – or feel himself to be, anyway: he needs it, you can tell. And Lilian . . . well she, I am afraid, is all there is left. Because the rest of us – oh yes, and even his mother – I think we made it perfectly clear to him rather long ago that we were simply having none of it, this spurious superiority he oozily exudes. And so who else, I ask you – who other than Lilian is there who would tolerate even so much as the very idea . . .? Poor little thing. Though I'm not actually sure whether I even have any sympathy for her, if I'm honest – I think, on balance, I probably don't. People have to fight – people just have to stand up for themselves. Show a bit of backbone. Otherwise other people, well . . . they'll just walk right over them. Seen it a thousand times. It's just the way certain people are, I'm afraid. Modern world: what are you going to do?

There was one girl in David's life – woman, I suppose she was, really. Well more than one, of course, over the years . . . but not that many. A father, well – naturally you're not ever going to know in detail what a son of yours is up to (and nor, if you're wise, should you want such a thing – even if you care, which I don't very much). But still I can say that I was never too aware of very much action on David's part – not in that direction, anyway. That's not to say . . . I mean, I never harboured . . . how shall I put it . . .? Fears. You know – that he might be a poof, or something. Because that would just have killed me, to be honest: I make no bones about it. Don't know how a parent can stand that, frankly. I mean . . . not so bad with a girl, of course. That you could pretty much deal with because clearly it's not quite so unnatural. Quite sweet, in one way. But your son, a man . . . well that . . . that's just plain disgusting, to my mind. And I'm not alone in thinking that. Oh I know that in these enlightened days no one is meant to *say* it, that everything's meant to be *fine*: Christ, so far as I can see, it's more or less mandatory now, bloody queers. But it's *not* fine, is it? No it's not – and someone has to say it, or we'll all go mad. So anyway: no – I have to admit I had no worries on that score . . . but good God, though – I should imagine I had more girls, far more girls, by the time I was twenty than David has had in his entire life on earth. Yes well – that was the Sixties, wasn't it? The golden time. Oh Christ, you know – I do so wish I could go back there. Be me again. Yeh well. Anyway. Now . . . I've gone and lost the, um . . . What was I actually, er . . .? Oh yes: David. Well he, now – he can't be much shy of thirty-five, can he? Thirty-five, Christ. When I was thirty-five, I already had a wife, a house, a good little business – not that little, actually – two children. While David, well look at him: all he's got is a couple of rooms in Chalk Farm, and according to Enid he can barely afford that . . . and a nasty little 'office' above a furniture discount store, or is it a cheap carpet shop, in Kilburn. Not too far, actually – just round the corner really from that very first bedsit of mine, all those years ago: ah, glory days . . .! Never see them again, God damn it. Yes . . . and he also has, David, a debt that would dizzy you – because everyone's in debt, these days: everything is built upon a myth. And all this because of his Great Big Idea – which, it is glaringly apparent to everyone but himself, is now no more nor less than the Great Big White Elephant, let us face it please, no matter how difficult . . . but look: what more can I say to the man . . .? Hey? Because I've tried, of course I've tried – to make him see sense. Look David, I've said to him – the time has come, yes? You've invested quite enough now, don't you think? More – far more than enough, wouldn't you say? Too much. Time and money. Cut your losses, why don't you? It's the only sensible thing to do. You had a crack, you gave it a good go, you put all that effort into it . . . but you have to know, David, when to walk away. When just to call it a day. Can't be going on for ever, can you? Throwing good money after bad. Listen to me, David: pack all this in and get a regular job – that's what to do. Makes sense, doesn't it? Yes? Let someone else do all the worrying, and you just draw a nice monthly salary. Doesn't that sound good? Use your contacts. You do *have* contacts, don't you . . .?

Well of course he never listened. But maybe (I've thought about this) he yearns to do exactly as I say – quite possibly he is absolutely desperate to be rid of the entire fiasco . . . yes, I think so: but look at it: how could he be seen to behave in precisely the way his father had advised . . .? For how ever would he live that down? You see? Stubborn as a pig, overbearing, and vainglorious to a fault – I just can't think why he always has to be like that. But it's this woman I'm thinking about now, ex-girlfriend – the only one who ever came even remotely close to actually getting engaged to him, or so Enid was always telling me. I rather liked her: certainly wouldn't have overlooked a woman like that, not back in the day I wouldn't. What – me? I don't think so. I'll get her name in just a minute. It'll come to me. Ridiculous, actually, I can't remember, because she was round here quite a lot. Often I'd come in and she'd be here. I suppose because it's nicer, isn't it? Than a couple of rooms in Chalk Farm. Pretty little laugh. Fabulous legs. What the devil was her bloody name, now . . .? Well I'll get it – I'll get it eventually. Anyway – name doesn't matter. Point is, point I'm making is that I could see that she was definitely a cut above, this one – and I don't mean just above the occasional drib or drab of forgettable females that had drifted in and out before her, but way above David himself: that's what I'm meaning. Another league. She was a solicitor, fully qualified – some practice in the West End, near Grosvenor Square, as I recall. It wasn't Annabel, was it . . .? What she was called? It wasn't, no – but it was something very like that, something pretty close: I'll get it in a minute. And I remember thinking, yes – oh yes, she could be just what he needs, she could be the saving of him: a stimulus, a mind to keep up with, quite a looker, and a damned good little earner into the bargain, which can never be a bad thing. I wouldn't know about that, of course – not from personal experience. Enid, she never had a job. Women, they didn't in those days. Just as well, really – God knows what she would have done. Anyway, this girl . . . Angela, could it have been? Amanda . . .? Pretty sure it started with an A . . . anyway: great puzzle was – to me, at any rate – what in Christ's name she was hanging around David for. I mean – no great catch, I think we can all agree. But there she most certainly was, anyway. And then one day, right out of the blue . . . she wasn't. Gone. Flown. Saw sense, I imagine: who could blame her? We never did get to the bottom of it – all the ins and outs. I suppose you never do, not really, not where other people's relationships are concerned – or even your own, come to that. Enid, she talked to him, asked him questions, did all that, but apparently he was saying very little about it. Was he hurt . . .? Don't know. Hard to say. He wasn't happy, certainly – though hardly destroyed . . . as he would have been, wouldn't he? If here had been some great and crimson passion? Yes . . . but then it is David we're talking about, isn't it? Which you rather do have to bear in mind.

And so this is now what he has become: a pretend businessman with a failed idea, barking at little Lilian down his mobile phone. Well – there it is. And we don't really talk any more – not just about all this, but about anything, really. I mean – there's no rift, no breakdown, no great animus: no lines have been drawn, is what I am saying. But no, we don't really talk . . . because actually, when it comes down to it . . . what is there to say? *Barbara* . . .! Oh Christ yes, of course. It was Barbara, that's what she was called: the one that got away. Amazing I couldn't remember that. She was round here quite a lot. Nice girl, nice person. Very clever woman. Pretty little laugh. Fabulous legs. Barbara . . . yes of course. Don't know if there's a new one – couldn't tell you whether he's seeing someone currently or not. Enid, she normally seems generally aware of anything that's going on in these sorts of directions, but she hasn't said anything. Not to me, anyway – but that's no measure of very much. So I think I'll ask him.

Not that I could give two devil damns either way – why should I care about a thing like that? But I'll ask him, I'll ask him anyway – simply because he's annoying me. Yes: he's bloody well annoying me now. I mean – making a call, yes okay, I don't mind it occasionally – modern world, you have to accept it – but it's been all the bloody time now . . . and so that's just about enough, I think. Look: I don't attach any importance at all to the fact that it's my birthday, but this is supposed to be a family gathering, Christ's sake, and in my honour. Honour . . .? Did I say honour . . .? Well that's a fat laugh for a start: don't get that, don't get any of that, not in this house, not any more. But still: hell with it. I'm going to talk, I'm going to ask him. I've just got to break this.

'So, David. Seeing a young woman currently, are we?'

'Okay. Yes. Okay. I've said I will, but . . .'

'David? Hear me? Talking to you. Met someone new, have you . . .?'

'Sorry – hang on, can you? There's someone here. Yes. I know. Uh – on the phone, Dad . . .'

'Yes, David. I observe that. We're all aware – all of us are very aware, I think, that you're on the phone. You've been on the phone, you see, since the moment you stepped through the door.'

'Oh leave him, George . . .'

'I have left him. I've left him, Enid. We all have. But it's time now, don't you think? For David to join the party. Have a piece of cake. Look, David – cake, you see?'

'I won't be a minute. I've just got to . . .'

'Which your mother has been up all night baking. Probably.'

'Yeh okay. Just a sec, all right . . .?'

'Actually I got it in Waitrose . . .'

'Did you, Enid? Hear that, David? Your mother, she got it in Waitrose.'

'They're better in Waitrose. Better than I could manage . . .'

'Oh Mum – you're great at baking!'

'Well that's kind of you, Anna. But I'm not. Not really.'

'Are you hearing all of this, David? We're talking about cake. Anna says your mother is great at baking, but your mother demurs. She remains a very staunch advocate of the Waitrose version. You're missing all of this. So hang up now, yes? Give little Lilian a break. Give us all a break, actually. Break, yes? And then cake.'

'Right. Okay. Yeh. Look – I'll have to ring you back.'

'Oh *no*, David . . .! Show the child some *mercy* . . .!'

'Yup. Call you back. Soon as I can.'

'Do you want cake, Dad? Only I know you're not too fond . . .'

'A little. I'll have a little bit, Anna. See if Waitrose is all it's cracked up to be. Ah – David! You're with us once again. My, how you've grown. Shot up. Hardly recognised you.'

'Yes all right, Dad. But business, you know? It doesn't run itself.'

'Indeed not. As actually I, a man who has been in it, business, for more than forty years will readily testify. *Actually*, David. But it's supposed to be a party, you see?'

'Dad's quite right. You're always on that phone of yours, David. It's Dad's birthday! And it's rude – I'm always telling you. Troy . . .! Troy – put that down! *Now*, Troy . . .! Yes. That's right. Put it down. Good. Good boy, Troy . . .'

'Would he like a bit of chocolate, do you think, Anna . . .?'

'You've already given him piles, Mum! That's why he's getting hyper.'

'So, David – let me get in quickly, shall I? Before your next call. I was simply wondering . . .'

'Do you want tea? Shall I make us some more tea?'

'No, I don't think so, Enid. Maybe we should open the champagne . . .'

'Oh yes – lovely. I'll get it Dad, shall I?'

'Thank you, Anna. And David can open it, maybe. Don't be thrown, will you David, by all the wire around the cork.'

'Funny, Dad. You're a very funny man.'

'Well no, not really. Just a little bit snide, I'd call it. But what I want to know, David – I'm sure we're all agog – is whether some fresh new flower of English womanhood has recently been, um . . . plucked, as it were . . .'

'Why are you suddenly so interested in my personal life? You don't care. You've never cared about anything I do. No – don't interrupt, Mum . . .'

'Well I can't let you say things like that about your father, David! He does care – of course he cares. Don't you, George?'

'With a raging passion, my dear. So tell us, David. Clue us in . . .'

'Well . . . if you really want to know . . . there's nobody special. At the moment.'

'I see. Run out of specials, had they . . .?'

'You see! You see, Mum? This is what he's like.'

'Thought of trying Waitrose? I hear they're most awfully good . . .'

'Why do you do this, Dad? All this stuff. This is what you do. This is what you do all the bloody time. You don't want to talk. You don't give a shit about what I'm doing. All you wanted – you just wanted to get me off the phone! Never mind that it might be important . . .'

'Quite true. Oh look – champagne! Bound to put us all into the party spirit. Don't you think?'

'Are you going to do it, David? Or shall I?'

'Oh give it to me, Anna – you'll only mess it up.'

'Yeh right. Because a woman is incapable of opening a bloody bottle . . .'

'Okay, then – you open it. I don't care who opens it. I've got to go soon anyway.'

'Pressing business, is it? Something else of huge importance . . .?'

'Well yes it is, Dad. As a matter of fact. We're not *all* retired, you know.'

'I'm not retired. Am I David? I still am chairman of the company, as well you know.'

'Well when was the last time you went in, then?'

'I don't have to go in. Not any more. I have people. Reliable people.'

'Your father has earned a bit of rest – don't you think so, David?'

'Fine. Okay, Mum. He's a success. He's a great success. Here we bloody go again. It's always . . . it always comes down to this, doesn't it? Dad's made millions with his bloody company and his son can't even get a business off the ground because he's just a pathetic fuckwit . . .!'

'*David* . . .!'

'Sorry, Mum. Sorry. But it's just . . . oh Christ. Look – I've got to go.'

'Oh *no*, David . . . look – Anna's just poured you some champagne.'

'Got to go, Mum. Sorry.'

'What – no cake?'

'Don't provoke him, George . . .'

'Provoke him? Just offering him a bit of cake, that's all. High-powered businessmen – they can't run on empty, you know. Need sustenance. So have your cake, David – you can eat it on the hoof. Then you can call in on some woman who is apparently not special, and . . . I don't know – spend the rest of the night on the phone. What . . .? What are you laughing about, Anna . . .?'

'You are very *naughty*, Dad. You're really very *naughty*.'

'Okay, Dad? At least one of your children isn't a total disappointment to you. I'm the hopeless son, and she's the dazzling daughter. You should be happy with that.'

'Oh can't we just *stop* all this . . .?! It's supposed to be your father's *birthday* . . .'

'I'm sorry, Mum. But it's not me. It's him. You just don't see it any more. Been with him too long.'

'Oh stop it, David! You're upsetting Mum now, along with everyone else. Look at your little nephew! Look at Troy. Just look at him! He's just staring at us all. Poor little man – he doesn't understand what's going on!'

'Not the only one . . .'

'Enough now, Dad. Just say goodbye to David, all right?'

'Goodbye, David. Don't be a stranger.'

'And you, David: you say goodbye too. And wish him a happy birthday.'

'Christ . . .'

'It's all right – you don't have to, dear boy. I shall take it as read. Now, then – let's try a little bit of this cake, shall we? Champagne is good, I must say. Love it, Bollinger. Very much hitting the spot . . .'

So . . . it rather would appear that I have been wrong, very wrong, in my earlier and rather throwaway reading of the relationship I have with David. A rift does exist: it seems as though there has been a breakdown and is great animus. Evidently, lines have been drawn. And if this truly is the case, as it surely does inescapably appear, well then it will be me, of course . . . of course it will be me who has drawn them, dark and deep. Because in truth, the boy is beginning to drive me to distraction. It's true that I hardly see him these days . . . but whenever I do, I can't help thinking . . . well, it is constantly borne in upon me, and increasingly forcibly, that he isn't . . . he isn't . . . well he just isn't what a young man ought to be, is what I can't help thinking. I mean to say – where is the blood? And where the thunder? There isn't any. Is there? No volcanic belly, and a complete lack of guts. Simply his anaemic and effetely whimpered protestations, with no suspicion of an underlying fury. Dear God: how can this be a son of mine? Anna, now – she, I have to say, she's much more the thing. There's a bit of fire to her, there's no denying that: stands up for herself, says what she thinks. Goes on about that bloody little child of hers a bit too much, yes of course she does, but show me the mother who doesn't. No matter how fine the woman, a part of her brain will be ritually rendered into mush the moment she comes to give birth. This is known. They always say they'll carry on as usual, be just the woman they always were, but it's never the case. I mean – it's a good thing: in many ways, it's a good thing, that . . . because otherwise, where is the parental obligation? You see? The complete dedication. A lot of it is to do with the nine months of sheer hell they have to go through prior to it all, of course – to say nothing of the total and unimaginable horror of actually giving birth. Christ, I couldn't have gone through that – no way on God's earth could I ever have even begun to go through all of that. Most men feel the same – and if they don't, there's something rather wrong, I'd say. But it forms the bond, you see – gestation, the physical pain . . . it's nature's way, of course it is: all part of the master plan. Why a father, for all his sense of duty and no doubt sincere devotion, can never feel the same way as a mother does. Of course he can't. And there is nothing wrong with this, and nor is it a mystery. All this 'new man' bloody nonsense – wholly artificial and absolute guff. Empathy . . .? Balls. Feeling your feminine side? Total crap. If you want to feel the feminine side you'll stroke the electric warmth of a real female flank, and be done with it. None of this is news or deep thinking: plain to anyone with half a brain. But getting back to what I was talking about – Anna, since becoming a mother, she has retained more than enough of herself to still be completely recognisable: she hasn't, like rather too many of her friends, it seems to me, suddenly been transformed into an utterly useless human being. And the other thing is . . . she seems to like me. She really does seem to genuinely like me. Which I need. Because I don't get it from anywhere else. Enid . . .? No. Oh no. All the signs of affection that she now quite automatically will display, that's no more than, what . . .? Just a sort of a bovine loyalty. Decent in its way, but nothing to do with anything, really. She doesn't like me. Not deep down. And sometimes – when her rather sweet and inherent honesty is shining like the sun, or else whenever her guard is down . . . well at those times, not even on the surface.

It was better, in a way, when she was drinking. I almost could convince myself in those days that a sort of affection, an admittedly only mildly lubricious camaraderie might conceivably, somehow, in some strange manner, be coexisting between the two of us. Her lolling mouth, as it slid into nearly a collaborative leer . . . it could even be lascivious invitation. She became, then, naturally very tactile. The nape of my neck in particular came in for a great deal of probing and attention – her fingernails were still so long and polished in those days: she hadn't yet started biting them, as she took to constantly doing during the endless haul back to a sort of normality . . . so there was a sort of electric titillation that I can't say I didn't enjoy. Initially, indeed, I found it all rather arousing – why I maybe said nothing for a good long while: I liked it, when she was a drinker. It was better for me. But the days when both of us could pretend that here were simply two adult people enjoying a glass of wine or two, laughing and horsing around . . . yes well, those were the very early stages, of course, when still I could pretend to be complicit – to be an equal and eager part of the thing. Then, before dinner . . . during dinner, after dinner . . . she would be topping up her glass very much more often than I could keep up with. She would hold up an empty bottle in mock surprise – make a sort of a joke of it: where did all that go, then? I think this one must have sprung a leak . . . all that sort of nonsense. Frequently then she would open a third, sometimes even a fourth bottle of Beaujolais – her preferred tipple because, she said, it was so light and fruity it wasn't really like drinking at all . . . opening another, yet one more, because she felt she wanted just the one extra small glass, and then saying it was silly, wasn't it, to leave the little that was left . . .? Gulpingly finishing it off, so it wouldn't go to waste. Then she would go up to bed . . . but I knew that there was vodka in the bathroom. In an Evian bottle. More in the kitchen, similarly disguised. Sometimes, when I got in, she'd brightly offer me a welcoming gin and tonic – the big ice cubes she will have clunked into a heavy tumbler, the Bombay Sapphire already chilled . . . but it was so clear from the juniper at the edge of that just peremptory kiss that for her, the cocktail hour was already long established.

The decline after that was shockingly rapid. Put me off drinking altogether, just the sight of her – not to say the state of the house, the lack of simple food. Communication was jarring, then pointless, before it descended into sheer impossibility. I very much resented all that because I've always enjoyed my wine, and a Bordeaux especially. I'd eat out in restaurants more and more – fearful, though, of what I might return to. Enid, she couldn't see it. When I sought to caution her, when I advocated even a degree of moderation – and I did take care never to be hectoring – she said I was a bore: behaving like a stuffy old man . . . that I ought to, God help me, 'loosen up'. She, when she got like this, would be so very shimmeringly loosened as to seem poised upon the heady verge of a practically liquid swoon . . . or else her ungainly body would be slumped into an angular heap of its component parts. And all this, you know, it wasn't really all that long ago. What are we talking about . . .? Three years? Less, probably – probably quite a bit less. A couple of years – could be no more than just, I don't know – eighteen months, maybe: it's hard to work it out. Eventually – oh God, at last – she did very slowly come to see sense: was eventually persuaded that she needed treatment – or if not yet that, then at least to admit to herself that the drinking now was dangerously out of control. It was Anna, of course, who eventually talked her round – got her to see someone. David, who already had taken to visiting us hardly at all – I doubt he'd seen it: doubt he was even aware. Hard, at first – she found it so terribly hard, poor Enid . . . but Christ, give that woman her due: she bloody well stuck to it. Didn't cut down – she knew full well that she couldn't cut down – so she just stopped it completely. One evening, when Anna brought her home from some or other specialist – because the first one she'd been to, he was no good at all, far too aggressive is what Enid had said, but then Anna, she'd found a woman from somewhere, much more sympathetic, apparently . . . yes and so when she got home that evening, she smiled at me resignedly (never forget it, that expression she had on her face – as if she was bashfully owning to having been foolish, while imploring me – imploring her – to please be kind and forgive) . . . well she had a bottle of her Beaujolais, quickly followed by another . . . then she took a long time to sip, not swig, a very large cognac in silence next to the fire. Went to bed, got up in the morning, said she felt like hell, and that was that: never drank again. Well you've got to, haven't you? Admire that? I was in awe, I can tell you. Still used to snoop about, of course, looking for stashes of bottles in all her favourite hiding places . . . but no: absolutely nothing. I am blessed, I suppose, in not being cursed with an addictive personality – I take my pleasures as I may. But had I been condemned to spend my life at the mercy of compulsion, serious addiction . . . well, I'd be dead by now, no two ways about it: I could never have fought against all that. And Enid . . . she never wanted to talk about it. No post-mortem, no discussion. Christ knows what she was going through. And at first, I wouldn't, of course – drink anything at all. Went through a phase of having none in the house. But soon – quite amazingly soon, actually – she said she didn't honestly care either way: that it no longer bothered her. She even had the strength of will – this is amazing, it's quite amazing this, actually – but she even had the strength of will to make light of it, joke about her extraordinary predicament. We fell into an easy banter: she'd yawn very elaborately and she'd say to me, 'How long is it, George, before I can have my next drink . . .?' and I'd make a huge show of looking at my watch and I'd say, 'Ooh well let me see now . . . it's just coming up to two o'clock . . . so why don't we say . . . never?' And she'd be nodding away, and there was such a cheeky complicit grin plastered across her little face, dear Enid – still gaunt, because oh, her cheeks, they'd more or less shrunk and collapsed . . . but now, so very much fuller than when she'd been drinking heavily, and not a bad colour to her these days either – and then she'd clap her hands once and announce with theatrical solemnity, 'Well that sounds good to me!' How many times did we do the routine? That same old bit of nonsense, word for word. It must have helped her – I think it must have, because she wouldn't have gone through it, would she, if it hadn't been helping her in some way? So now – like on this stupid birthday so-called gathering that still I am enduring – Anna and I can enjoy a glass of Bollinger, while Enid . . . she seems quite happy with her tea. I do look over with anxiety from time to time, I still do that . . . because I could not bear the thought, actually, that she is suffering simply to please us, to ease our passage . . . but no, I never detect a flicker of agony, a stifled sigh of desperation. And from the mildness of her platitudes, well . . . you never will know what Enid might be thinking, but I do so very much hope that she isn't in pain. And whatever discontent it was that drove her to so awful a state . . . is it now annihilated? Or merely dormant? Has she conquered, or is she just cruelly jailed within a purgatory of daily toleration? Either way, all I can do is hope that she isn't in pain. Because even though I know, that I am very well aware that Enid, she doesn't at all like me any more . . . I like her, you see. I like her rather a lot. Because how can you not? Like someone, if once you so much loved them.

'Think I'll have to be off soon, Dad. Troy, he's getting a bit . . .'

'Seems all right to me . . .'

'Yeh – he is now, but I know how he gets. All these sweets and things he's had . . . if I don't get him down soon, there'll be not a minute of peace for me tonight, I'm telling you that. And there's work in the morning. All your fault, Mum . . .!'

'Oh – he's such a lovely little boy. I love to spoil him – how can you not? Aren't you, Troy? Aren't you? Such a lovely little boy? Yes you are. Yes you *are* . . .'

'Have you enjoyed your birthday, Dad . . .? Probably not.'

'It's been lovely, Anna. Of course it has. So grateful to you. And the tie – thank you so much for the tie. Sweet of you to go to so much trouble. When will we see you again, my dear?'

'All a bit difficult at the moment, Dad. Work and everything . . . and oh God, that tie! Don't go on about it! Honestly – you don't have to wear it if you really hate it. I'm, um . . . I'm sorry about David . . .'

'Yes, I am too. But there it is.'

'You can always drop Troy off here for the afternoon, you know. If you're busy.'

'I know that, Mum. I know. And I might this week, actually – Maria's not been well. She might be okay now, but she had something . . . I don't know . . . something with her stomach . . .'

'Must cost you a fortune, all this child-minding. Just drop him off here – I'm always telling you.'

'I know, Mum. Thanks. I really do appreciate it.'

'Your mother loves having him. Family, isn't it?'

'Yes Dad. I know. We're all very lucky.'

'Yes well – you'd be a damn sight luckier if you didn't have to go off to work all day, wouldn't you? But then that's what comes of marrying a man who buggers off – walks out on his bloody wife and son . . .'

'Oh Christ Dad, no – not again. Not now. Please don't do all that now . . .'

'Yes well . . . If I ever set eyes on that bastard again . . .'

'Okay. That's it. We're off. I can't go another ten rounds of this. Come on, Troy – going home now, yes? Mum – do you know where his jacket went . . .?'

'Look, Anna – all I'm saying is . . .'

'Yeh. I know. I know, Dad. I know you mean well, I know you want to help, but . . .'

'Well of course I do. You know I'll always help you, Anna. You don't even have to do that bloody job. I'll pay – I'll pay for everything. How many times have I said that?'

'Loads. You're always saying that. I know. I know. But it's my mess, isn't it? It's my problem, yes? And so it's me who's got to deal with it.'

Yes it is. Have to cope – just got to. Somehow. Because Dad – well he wouldn't: he wouldn't just park all his responsibilities on to someone else's shoulders. Would he? And if I did – if I did ever take him up on his offer . . . and he's always saying it: to just sit back, be a mother to Troy and let him take care of all the bills and everything . . . well then, although I know he'd be perfectly happy to do it, I know he's not just saying it . . . but still, I don't think afterwards he'd . . . well, what I mean is, what I'd really be scared about is that he wouldn't look at me, he wouldn't ever see me in the same way again. Difficult to explain. Because he loves me, my dad, I've always known that, always known that I'm special to him – but I think . . . I think this is true . . . I think that he rather sort of admires me as well, you see, and I wouldn't ever want that to change. Because it's important. It's really important that Dad . . . respects me, if you like. Thinks of me as a strong and capable woman. Which, of course, I'm not. No I'm not – not really. I try – I really do try, and sometimes I think I'm on top of it all, pretty much dealing . . . but oh Christ, it's hard – it's really hard, you know? Yes, and getting harder – it's getting harder all the time. And Dad, well – he doesn't know the half of it. Jesus, if I told him everything that's been going on in my life just lately, if I really filled him in on the extent of the mess I'm in . . . oh God, he'd just go mad, he'd simply go completely crazy – and then before he bailed me out he'd start *accusing* me, which I know I absolutely couldn't stand. No, I just couldn't bear that: the look of anger on his face . . . yes and worse than that, his incapacity to disguise a profound disappointment. In me. That would just be too awful. But look . . . not all of it's my fault. I mean – I know that sometimes I do stupid things, make some bloody awful decisions . . . but it's luck as well. I just don't, lately, seem to be getting an awful lot of luck.

I wish I could just be a kid again, really – because when I was younger, when I was a child, a teenager, I truly did think that my life was blessed. Tell you why: because it was – can't believe how fantastically good. God, you know – back then, I was just so amazingly lucky that I had no idea how amazingly lucky I was, if you see what I'm saying: I loved it, my life, I really did enjoy it – but still I just accepted everything, all of it, as being completely normal: it's what children do. Nothing to compare it with, is there? Because my friends at school, they all seemed to have everything they wanted – clothes, holidays, whatever it was they were into. I mean – I don't think I was actually spoiled in the way that some people since have told me they thought I just must have been: I wasn't given loads of money, or anything . . . but it is true that if ever there was something I had convinced myself I would simply die if I didn't get . . . well, then I just had to go to my daddy. So I loved my parents, and they loved me back. Loved where I lived, my room and everything. Oh – my room! It was heaven. Dad let me have anything I wanted, but it was he who sort of designed it – he's really very good at stuff like that. There was this really thick and shaggy orange carpeting and a fold-up bed that became part of the wardrobes and there were fitted cupboards around the bay window with specially made cushions on the top: my very own bathroom – just everything. It's all still exactly the same – nothing's been done to it since I left. I used to go in there a lot and look at all my old books and posters and toys and things, but I don't like to do that any more. It's maybe since Troy was born . . . I don't know, really . . . but these days, it just makes me feel a bit funny. And Mum and Dad's house, oh it's just so gorgeous. Quiet street with all these really tall trees, beautiful architecture . . . can't remember exactly – early eighteenth-century I'm pretty sure Dad says it is . . . anyway, it's just wonderful. Great garden – super big lawn I used to adore running around on during all those truly idyllic childhood summers. People always go on about how wonderful the summers were when they were children, I know they do – but mine, they really were like that: quite marvellous. A lot of the rooms are filled with things that Dad has collected over the years: good stuff, I now realise – he clearly has an eye. At the time I suppose I dismissed it all, really – it was just Dad's junk. But there's some excellent English Georgian furniture and pictures and some great mid-century modern, which I really do love. He's also got a Beatles collection, if you can believe it – all original memorabilia from mainly 1964, I'm pretty sure. Because The Beatles, oh my God – they're just like gods to him: seemingly the best thing that ever happened when he was young, and pretty much ever since. He plays their records all the time – still the old vinyl LPs, only sometimes a CD – and when I was very young, I remember, I used to say I hated them, I don't know why I did. Say that, I mean – because I didn't actually hate them at all: loved it, loved the sound, always did. Maybe why I was never into the music of the Eighties like all of my friends were – people like, I don't know . . . Blondie, was that Eighties? I don't even know. Wham!, Madonna, I really haven't a clue because at our house, the Sixties ruled! Not just The Beatles, but other really good stuff as well – Stones, Kinks, The Who, loads of them. But this particular collection he's got, it's mostly really weird things like Beatles nylon stockings in the original packets, pretty tacky jewellery, little figures of the Fab Four, toy guitars, watches, pens, purses, jigsaws – oh God, just loads of it. A tin of Beatles talcum powder, for God's sake . . .! And this mad-looking Beatle wig – no, honestly! And when I was a kid I used to beg him to let me try it on, but he always said I couldn't because it was still in its unopened packaging. Crazy, really – but Dad, he takes it all really quite seriously: it's fun, he says, it's just a bit of fun . . . but I do think he sees these things as being truly authentic antiques – which they are now, I suppose – and collectively maybe even forming something of sociological significance for the future. I don't know – it's hard to know what Dad is thinking. And it's all in lovely condition – he's got a bit of a thing about condition – and although I suppose it must all have been just cheap stuff for the fans at the time, the fact that he's got it all in glass-fronted display cases probably means he's spent quite a lot on it. It gives him pleasure, though – that I do know. Whenever he's playing with it all, or carefully placing some new acquisition, he's always got this sort of fond and faraway expression on his face – a sort of barely-there and hovering smile. The whole house is much too big for just the two of them now, of course, yes I suppose it is – has been really for ages, since David and I moved out . . . but oh God I'd die if they ever moved. Because coming back here, well . . . it's the nearest I can get to a time when everything in my life was simply, oh . . . just perfect, really. People might laugh at that, but it was – to me it was. Living here, having no responsibilities or worries in the world and being cared for, loved and so well looked after by my dad, it was . . . just perfect.

I even loved going to school – but then it was a pretty terrific school. Made some quite good friends – Sue and Molly I was particularly close to, haven't seen or heard of either of them since, of course . . . I was never really one for keeping up with people: could never see the point. And I did quite well there, really – A levels and so on – but nothing very brilliant. Dad used to drive me every morning before he went to work in this dark green Jaguar we had at the time. I used to inhale his newly applied cologne – loved to watch his manly and capable hand as he reached to the side to change gear: the thicket of darkish hairs below a perfect shirt cuff that sometimes used to catch in the bracelet of his Cartier watch: I'd stroke him, sometimes, and he'd turn to smile at me. Such a handsome man – quite thrillingly so, actually – I always thought he was, anyway. He still is. Well – he's only sixty-four, so why on earth shouldn't he be? He didn't lose his hair, that's the key to it, I suppose. Receding, of course, and gorgeously silver: looks much better than Mum, I have to say – but then, he takes a lot more care. And about that Jaguar, I remember he always used to say to me – God, how many times did he say this, dear old Dad! – that although he didn't altogether identify with the image of Jaguar, he was damned if he'd have a Mercedes or a BMW because they were bloody *German* and he still remembered rationing and we weren't quite Rolls-Royce people, though he hadn't entirely ruled out a Bentley for some time in the future. Which he did actually get, eventually – he still drives it now, his pride and joy. Always keeps it in the garage, and he won't ever let anyone else touch it – he polishes it and everything himself: it's immaculate, like everything Dad owns. It's not one of the new ones though, the Bentley – it's vintage, from the Sixties, which is no surprise: most things Dad loves are. God, though – you should hear what he says about the modern Rolls-Royces these days . . .! Company's owned by *Germans*, great big ugly boats that are driven by foreigners and twats. He's so totally un-PC: just as well it's only me he says these things to (hope it is, anyway).

So look – I was very happy, that's the point . . . and Dad, he told me I always would be. I believed him. I always believed him. If ever I wanted to know something, I wouldn't go to a teacher or look it up in the library . . . I just went and asked my dad. Mum . . . it was very different with Mum. She just looked after the home – it's what women did in those days . . . round here it was, anyway. Wasn't a very good cook, bit better these days, not much . . . Dad and me, we used to smile when she came up with some other new horror – it was really so very naughty of us, but I don't think she ever noticed, or anything. I know she did her very best, but Mum . . . well . . . what can I say? She was just *there*, really. It was Dad who somehow made everything real. Not sure what David thought. He was three years older, and that meant a lot at the time. It's odd . . . he was a constant presence throughout my life until he went off to uni, but he never really, I don't know . . . registered, somehow.

Saw him every day, of course . . . so we did talk, but not about anything much. Nothing that sticks in my memory, anyway. Liked different music, different films, different TV programmes. He didn't laugh much, that I do remember: David, he wasn't ever really in on any joke. We never rowed, though. With David and me . . . it was all really, I don't know . . . pretty much what you might call *non*. Still is.

Then it was my turn to go to university. I was aiming at Cambridge to read history, but that had always been – and even my tutor agreed about this – something of a long shot. So it came down to Exeter in the end, which was reckoned at the time to be decent, though always in a middle-ranking sort of a way. It was really a funny time, though. So odd. Dad, of course – he didn't really want me to go at all. He never said so, early on – he was always encouraging, but he was never at all keen on the idea. I could tell, even before he told me. You could see it in his face: it was so very difficult for him not to look thrilled when Cambridge said no. Nor can it have been easy to appear to be quite so ecstatic when Exeter eventually came through – but he did, and when I got my acceptance, he even gave me a little party, which I thought was really so terribly sweet of him. I understood what he felt, though – what he was going through, of course I did: I completely got it, because I was feeling very much the same myself – which, I don't know . . . he maybe knew. I had only really applied for university in the first place because all the other girls were doing it, and obviously it was something the school expected of you as a matter of course . . . but it was never something I had sat down and consciously thought about: it all seemed so remote. I've never been good about dealing with futures; lately, Jesus, it's all I can do to handle today. But the point is I didn't particularly want to go to Cambridge, nor anywhere else, come to that. I mean . . . I suppose I liked the *idea* of being a Cambridge undergraduate – swanning about the place in a subfusc gown and being taken on a punt by a handsome young man (the actual business of studying did not feature in the vision) – but what I really liked most was just to be at home. You see? Why would I want to leave home? And reading history – did I want to read history? No, not really – not remotely, in fact: I much preferred reading P. D. James, if anything. At home. So yes – when Cambridge said that they were somehow going to struggle to continue running their university without the benefit of my fabulous presence, I did feel a little pang of rejection, sure I did – particularly when I picked up the phone and it was Molly screaming excitedly about how they'd welcomed her with open bloody arms – but overall, I was just flooded with relief: lit up by it, if I'm honest. And it was the same with Exeter, the emotions I went through, but the other way round, if you see what I mean: pleased to be accepted, to have their offer . . . but then immediately after, my stomach just hit the floor as I realised that soon I would have to face the rather awful reality of actually *going* there . . .

Mum, then – she threw herself body and soul into the whole ghastly business of buying all the mountains of stuff she was for some reason convinced that I'd need: she was adding to the list all the time. I think it must have made her feel a part of it all – not something she was used to, I imagine. Not sure if she ever saw how reluctant I was . . . how I would gently set aside all the catalogues she'd sent for, tell her I'd look at them later . . . always found an excuse not to accompany her on yet another day-long trip to the shops. And Dad . . . well Dad, he just seemed to be observing it all from a deliberately silent distance – but eventually he did come clean, and not that long afterwards. He didn't want to talk about what he felt, he said, but simply all that he'd been thinking. Yes well that's what he said: in fact, when he did start talking it was all about exactly what he was feeling – and I knew, because I was feeling it as well. It was late one evening, I'll never forget – a little less than just a week before my inaugural term was due to begin. Mum, she was in bed: I'd got the feeling he'd been waiting for that. He'd opened one of his older clarets – which I do sort of like, but I'm sure I don't get anything like as much out of them as he very evidently seems to: he inhales, he swirls – he *chews*, for God's sake: me, I just swallow it (and sometimes, just because it visibly exasperates him – I know it's silly, but it is quite fun). Anyway – he was stroking my hair, which was still really long at the time: he loved my hair – he was always saying so, and reaching out to touch it. When I later had it cut short – some or other stupid fashion – I nearly burst out crying: not for the loss of my hair, but simply at the sight of this totally forlorn expression that was just all over my daddy's face: he looked so completely defeated – as if someone had just gone and died, or something. Anyway – on that evening with the claret, he'd said he wanted to talk to me about not what he felt, but all that he'd been thinking, and I said fine. Because I was always completely fine with talking to my dad, no matter what it was he ever might have to say to me.

'So, my sweet . . . all ready, are you? For your awfully big adventure . . .?'

'Think so. Well – not really. Ready as I ever will be, I expect.'

'You don't sound, if I may say so, very, um . . . enthusiastic. Or is that just me?'

'No, I'm – yeh, I'm pretty ready. Pretty keen. It's just – you know: all a bit much to take in. It's a lot to suddenly have to think about. That's all.'

'Yes of course I do see that. Ha – your mother, she seems to imagine that you are emigrating to Australia and never coming back. I think we'll have to get you a warehouse in Exeter to store all the things she's been buying for you. Have you seen it all . . .?'

'Oh God I know . . .! I keep telling her, Dad – I won't need a fraction of all that stuff, but she keeps on buying more . . .! I just can't believe it . . .'

'Well. Makes her feel useful. Expect that's what it is.'

'Yes. That's what I thought. I don't mind, really. It's quite sweet of her . . .'

'Course it is. All good intentions. So, then . . . history . . .'

'Mm? Oh yeh – history.'

'Don't gulp the wine, Anna. Just let it insinuate itself across your tongue . . .'

'Insinuate itself, yeh right, Dad. I'll remember that in the student bar. It's pretty yummy, actually. Can we have the music down a bit . . .?'

'It's not "yummy": it's sublime. You think the music's too loud? It's *Revolver* – you love *Revolver*.'

'Yeh I know I do – just a bit loud, that's all. If we're talking . . .'

'Fine. There. Better . . .? It's a Pauillac. Last of the Sixties I've got.'

'Thought you had loads of wine . . .'

'Oh well I do. But this is just a particularly, um . . .'

'So why open it tonight if it's so . . .?'

'Well why not? My only daughter. Off to university. But "history", though . . . I never really had you down as that much of a historian . . .'

'No well I'm not. Not really. It was just, I don't know . . . a subject. I would've preferred English but apparently everyone a bit arty wants to read English so they said to put down something else. Give me a better chance. I don't know . . . didn't seem to matter . . .'

'But you are, um . . . looking forward to it all, are you? Yes? Excited?'

'Well. You know. Sort of. Not really.'

'It's not too late Anna, you know. To change your mind. About the whole thing. Not written in stone, is it . . .?'

'What . . . you mean – not go?'

'Well – why not? Don't have to. Do you?'

'Well what else would I do?'

'Oh my goodness . . .! Anything you like! I mean . . . how about . . . nothing? For a year or two, anyway. Bit of travel. See the world. If you want. Or just stay here, as you have been. And then, well – there's always the business. Isn't there? You'd be invaluable. Always told you that. How many times have I told you that? I've known it since you were tiny: just the right sort – just exactly what I'm needing, you are, Anna. Someone I can completely trust. Someone who can take on the day-to-day running. Can't tell you how much that would help me. Starting salary, well . . . you'd be more than fine, I can assure you of that. Nothing to worry about at all. Living here, just as you've always done . . . or maybe you'd like to become an independent young madam . . .? Come and go as you please? Well in that case . . . nice little flat somewhere . . . I could sort that out, of course I could. No trouble at all. It would be a pleasure, actually, if that's what you'd like . . .'

'You don't want me to go, do you?'

'Well . . . it's not about me, is it? What I want. It's your life, after all – your future, isn't it Anna?'

'But you don't, do you?'

'Well . . . if you're actually asking me . . . I don't want to . . . lose you. Well of course I don't. I mean – I don't at all like the thought of . . . being without you. You – not here in the house, and so on . . .'

'No. Well. I don't either. Like the thought of it. Love it here . . .'

'Well exactly! That's just what I mean. And then, of course, there is another aspect to all of this, you see. One that you may not yet have had the time to consider – or possibly it simply hasn't even occurred to you. Well you can't think of everything, can you? Lot on your mind. But there is this question of, well . . . safety. I mean – I know you're all grown up and everything, capable young woman perfectly able to take care of herself, yes of course I do know all of that. But . . . it's only true up to a point, if you see what I'm saying to you, Anna. Because the thing is, you . . . well, you've never had to, have you? Take care of yourself. That's always been my job, hasn't it? So you don't really know quite how things might go. You see? I'm not in any way trying to alarm you, Anna – I do hope you see that. Quite the reverse – I simply want to be sure that you are easy in your mind. And nor am I trying to influence you in one direction or the other . . . but look: I know it seems quite obvious, but you do have to bear in mind that you will, of course . . . meet people. Won't you? A whole lot of new people. It's the nature of the thing. And naturally most of them will be completely lovely, of course they will – just young students in common with yourself. But they won't *all* be, is what I'm saying, I suppose. And I worry about you, Anna my dearest. Of course I do. I couldn't bear the thought, you see . . . of you being in any sort of . . . well: I hesitate to use the word *danger* . . . but even . . . discomfort. That would make me very unhappy indeed – and you, you wouldn't care for it either, well of course you wouldn't, would you? No. Exactly. So all I'm saying is, maybe you might want to take just a little bit of time to think about all of that. Go over it in your mind. Possibly, I don't know . . . even to reconsider the entire business. I mean – why take the risk? You don't have to, do you? You can simply carry on as you always have. Why not? I mean – look at me: I never went to university, did I? Can't really see that it *damaged* me in any way. So think about it, yes? That's all I'm asking. And then who knows? What you might decide. Either way, you know I'll support you. Don't you, Anna? I'm sure you do know that.'

I remember just sitting there. I was aware of 'Good Day Sunshine', faintly beautiful in the background, and I was in a beautiful drawing room in our beautiful house, and sipping this beautiful wine with my beautiful dad. Who again – yet once more – was wanting to wave his magic wand. He had perceived in me my extreme reluctance to go through with this awful thing I'd somehow got myself into – offered me anything I wanted: promised to make anything beastly, all my anxiety, simply melt away. I have never been so gorgeously seduced, so thrillingly tempted in the whole of my life – and I was all for Oscar Wilde's thinking on the matter of temptation: simply give in to it. What was it he wrote . . .? That he could resist just anything but. Yes well – that's me: that's me to a T. And so do you know what I said to my dad that evening . . .? I said this:

'Yeh, Dad – thank you so, so much. Thank you for caring about me. Thank you for everything you've just said – it really means, oh – just the world to me. I love you, Daddy – you do know that? I really do love you so much . . .'

He smiled – seemed touched. Drank wine – not with any show, but rather the way I do. And then immediately he looked so very terribly sad.

'You're going, aren't you . . .?'

'Yeh, Dad. Yeh I am.'

Mm. And so I did. I still now do try to work out my reasoning here – because I well remember so wanting to have nothing at all to do with it, and Dad's quite wonderful and totally unexpected intervention, this utterly alluring cameo of how my life could go instead – it practically made me keel over with longing. But no – I went through with it. We had to hire a minivan to transport all the gear that Mum had amassed for me: didn't even take most of the stuff out of its wrappings – sold nearly all of it incredibly cheaply during the first two weeks I was up – practically gave it away, no one could believe their luck. Immediately and happily squandered the loot in the student bar, in time-honoured tradition. Which made me briefly popular – I was just chucking it about. There were boys – not just in the bar, but seemingly, oh God . . . simply everywhere: they were always hanging around me. My experience up till then had been practically zero, so I was flattered and terrified all at the same time – which probably led me to being rather more flirty than I actually intended. Shyness can do that. Well – who cares? If any of them got the wrong idea – or any idea at all, actually – I'd just immediately slap them down: tell them to get lost. Some took it better than others.

It didn't take long to discover that I hated history, hated Exeter, hated even being there. Took up very briefly some sort of yoga nonsense – less nuts than most of the stuff that was on offer there, I can tell you – and also with Sven, because he was tall and blond and less aggressively pushy than nearly all of the other boys who still just kept on buzzing around me . . . yes and easily the best-looking: he had the most amazing eyes, like cold blue crystal. Nothing came of that – oh, except the abortion, of course. I know – do you think I don't know? Complete bloody fool, and even now I don't like to think of it: so scary, as well as sad. And of course I dropped out – there was no way on earth I could have stayed there for the full three years. But how to break it to my dad . . .? The decision to leave, that was easy – well obviously easy because I shouldn't have been there in the first place . . . yeh, but the thing was: how was I going to break it to my dad . . .? I mean, I knew he'd be pleased, I knew he'd be happy to have me back – it wasn't his disappointment I was shying away from: I just didn't want him to think I was incapable, that was it really. That I couldn't handle the very first challenge that life had put in my way . . . that, yes, but nor was I looking forward to his face, smarmed with smugness and I Told You So written right across his forehead in red neon lettering. What I eventually told him was that I'd been offered this most amazingly fabulous job in London, and that it was just so fantastic as to be impossible to turn down. He was thrilled, and entirely credulous: it was just the sort of thing that ought to happen to his daughter – he didn't find it surprising in the least. So back in London, I had to pretty quickly find a job – any job really, and then just large it up: somehow pretend that it really was amazingly fabulous. Some clothes shop, it turned out to be. Then after that fell through – God, I was just so bored there – I got a dogsbody job in a sort of a publisher, and made that out to be quite impossibly glamorous: invented lunches with famous authors, and all we were printing was mail order catalogues. Could just about afford the bedsit I was in – it was such a beastly little wreck on the ground floor of a tenement in Willesden, and backing on to what the estate agent had called a garden, but was really just a bit of dirt where they kept all the bins. And mice were all over the place: I hoped they were mice – didn't look too closely. Because still, although I yearned for home, I was stubbornly resisting being supported by Dad. I mean, he gave me wonderful presents and the odd few hundred quid from time to time, but still I could maintain to myself that at least I was self-sufficient. But it's so silly, he used to say: your room at home is waiting for you: we've got all this space, and you love the old homestead, don't you . . .? The garden . . .? So what do you want to be squirrelling yourself away in this bloody hole in Willesden for . . .? To which I had no answer: I thought it was as stupid as he did, and Christ knows how depressing . . . but I just felt deep inside me that I had to cling on to it, my little Willesden hovel. And I sort of knew why.

Had a few boyfriends because it's what people did. They bored me as much as the job in the clothes shop. And sex, frankly . . . after all that business at Exeter, well – it was a duty more than anything, that's honestly how I saw it – and one to be shirked if ever at all I could manage to, because it actually quite frightened me: I just couldn't bear the possibility of any more consequences. So none of these non-relationships was remotely long-lasting, which suited me just fine. And if that didn't please some idiot I was seeing, well then he could just fuck off. Which of course they all did, after not too long. I knew I would have a proper relationship one day, though – get married, and everything – but no hurry: it was just a question of meeting the right man, that was all. And when I did, there'd be a thunderclap and the midnight skies would be lit by stars: the imagery was a shambles, actually, because in this bedazzled vision of mine the sun was beaming down too. And then, not too long ago, four years, bit less, it really did happen – or that's how it felt at the time, anyway. When I ran into Max at that crappy party. One that now I so wish I hadn't gone to . . . because I wasn't meaning to, I wasn't even invited . . . it just turned out that way. But if I hadn't gone . . . if I hadn't met Max . . . well then I wouldn't have my little Troy, would I? And I'd die – I'd die, if I couldn't be with Troy: he's my angel. He's my life. Apart from Dad.

I can't get into it. Because when I think back now over all of it, I just feel so . . . oh Christ: I just can't get into it. Max, he told me he was in diamonds. What does that mean, I asked him. He said what do you mean, what does it mean . . .? I told you: I'm in diamonds. I married him – oh Jesus, not because of the *diamonds*: are you kidding? He just seemed . . . nice. Okay look – I was really powerfully attracted to him, there's no point denying it. He had . . . presence, I suppose you'd call it. He had a strong air of capability about him. He was a man in charge, you know . . .? And the sex, I have to say – that, for the very first time, was exactly all you've ever heard it can and should be. Dad, he hated him on sight.

He had a lovely flat, Max, just off Baker Street. Where Troy and I still are living, actually – though Christ knows for how much longer. There was always money lying around – loads of it. Always had whatever I wanted. Diamonds, he said, it's a cash business. I didn't ask: he wouldn't have told me anything. And Max, by now – he'd taken to calling me Sugartits, even when we were out. I couldn't speak. Not that we did go out together very much . . . and after Troy, not at all – literally, not ever. He was out, though – Max, he was never at home. Not even at night. I didn't mind – I didn't care a bit: pleased to be shot of him by that time. Dad, of course – he'd warned me not to marry him, told me a thousand times . . . and I think if it hadn't been for that, I would have left Max by this time. And then one day – look, I'm leaving out plenty, of course I am, because I can't: I just can't get into it . . . but one day, well – Max was gone. Just like that. Because he was out so much, it took me a day or two to even realise. There was no note, no explanation. His bank account – or, at least, the only one I knew about – that was emptied, cleared out: yeh and so was mine. Suddenly, there was no more money spread about the flat in rubber-banded lumps. And so that was that, really. Dad, well – he was just incandescent, as well you might imagine. Said he'd get him: said he'd kill him. So now I continue in yet another, the latest in a line of useless little jobs that have pretty much made up the milestones along the pointlessly meandering route of my actually pretty useless existence, a job that I tell Dad pays a fortune. It doesn't pay a fortune – it's actually quite ridiculous, so tiny, what they pay me. I'm behind with Troy's nursery fees, because I long ago refused to let Dad see to that . . . and I am so behind in the rent on the flat (because Max, he didn't own it or anything: I had assumed he did, but he didn't). Oh Christ . . . I am *so* behind in the rent . . . and already I've received a solicitor's letter: two, actually – but I haven't opened the second one. I recognised the logo on the envelope and just quickly crammed it into a drawer. There are things going wrong in the flat, and I can't tell the landlord because I owe him so much bloody money: a leak in the kitchen, a fuse in the hall . . . the cooker has started to smell very strangely: think it could be gas, not entirely sure. Can't afford to get anyone in. I just cower. My home, it's ganging up on me: I'm getting quite afraid of it.

But it's more than that, it's worse than that – it's actually quite a lot worse than that. Because I've had these calls, these phone calls – Christ knows how they got hold of my mobile number. Asking me where the diamonds are. Who is this, I kept on saying. No response: just tell us where the diamonds are, and everything will be fine. For you. For your boy. Just like in a bloody awful scary movie . . .! Well I don't *know*, do I? Where the bloody diamonds are, whatever diamonds they're talking about. With Max, I suppose – I never had any diamonds . . . except for my engagement ring. Which he took with him. And then the other evening – night before last, I'd just that moment managed to get Troy down finally, because Jesus, it had been one hell of an evening – the doorbell went. I squinted through the spyhole thing. Two men. Never seen them before. I just stood there more or less petrified on the other side of the door, trying not to breathe. They rang again – the shrillness, it ran right through me: made me shudder. And then they went away. But they'll be back of course: well of course they bloody will. It woke up Troy. He was screaming.

Dad, he always used to tell me that in life you should never take your eyes off the broader picture – take good care of that, and never pay attention to the little things. Because if you dwell, he said, they magnify before your eyes: it's the little things that can get you down. Yeh well . . . what I've never said to him is yeh okay Dad, whatever you say – but it's the big things too: the big things, they can get you down as well.

CHAPTER THREE

BITS AND PIECES

It was my idea, this picnic we're having. Well of course it was – stupid thing to say, really. You can't actually imagine it being George's idea, can you? That would be just such a laugh, quite frankly, because he never really wants to do anything. Not what I'd call anything, anyway. Quite happy just hanging about with Sammy, talking pretty much rubbish and playing his Beatles LPs. And seeing me, I suppose, if and when it suits him – which is only when he goes to the phone box and rings me, or else if I happen to be here already and suddenly he gets that look in his eye, you know what I mean. All other times, I'm just in the way, I can feel it, I can tell – he takes no trouble to hide it. What else does George like to do . . .? Well he's forever looking in the windows of shops like Take Six at clothes he's always moaning about never being able to afford.

'Yes well we're all in the same boat, George. It's not just you, is it? I mean – I'd be going to Bazaar all the time, if only I had the money – I'd just get everything, all of Mary Quant's stuff because I think she's just brilliant, actually. I would – I'd get one of everything in all the different colours. Yes . . . but on what I get for temping, well . . .'

'But it's different for you. Isn't it, Dorothy? Like you say

– you're just a temp. Don't ever know how many hours you're going to get, do you? But me – I'm regular. Proper job. I go to that bloody Smith's depot every bloody morning at half past bloody eight, and I'm never out much before six – sometimes nearly seven, lately. Yeh and I get overtime for that – so how come I . . .? That's what I just can't . . . I just can't understand it because these shops, okay? Take Six, Lord John, Guy, John Stephen . . . all of these shops, all of these really gear clothes . . . well they're meant for *me*. Aren't they? They're meant to be bought by people just like me. Young and trendy. Who've got a job. So why can't I ever bloody well afford them? Why do I have to go to bloody C&A, or else keep on wearing the same old stuff that I'm always wearing?'

'Well . . . I don't know actually, George.'

'You don't? You don't? Well I'll bloody well tell you then, Dorothy. It's this place, isn't it? This room you're standing in. Rent. Ever heard of rent, have you? Electricity meter. Food in the kitchen. That's where it goes. All right for you, isn't it? Hey? Living all nice and cosy with Mummy in Harrow, and then coming over here whenever you damn well feel like it. Oh yeah. It's all right for you . . .'

'Edgware.'

'What? What did you say?'

'Doesn't matter. I just said Edgware. It's Edgware I live in, not Harrow. That's all.'

'Well it doesn't bloody *matter*, does it? Where it is you and Mummy bloody *live*. The point is you don't have any expenses. Do you? Everything you earn is your own – so I don't understand why you say you can never afford Bazaar, or whatever it's called. Or that other place you're always on about. You could afford to buy the whole bloody *shop* . . .'

'Oh don't be *ridiculous,* George . . .! Bazaar is expensive. Everyone knows that.'

'What . . .?'

'Nothing. Nothing, George. Just forget I said anything, okay?'

'What did you call me . . .?'

'Nothing. I didn't call you anything. Look – let's just drop it. Forget the whole thing, all right?'

'No. No it's not all right actually, Dorothy. Not going to drop it. Because I know what you said. *Ridiculous . . .*? You think I'm *ridiculous* now, do you?'

'No. No, of course I don't. It's just that sometimes . . .'

'Sometimes? Sometimes what?'

'Oh. Nothing. Nothing. Look – I've got a really great surprise planned for you. For us. Yes? A treat. Something I've been, you know – thinking about for ages. Arranging. Just for you. For the two of us. You'll love it. Honestly, George – you're just going to love it.'

It's amazing, you know – but his expression, it completely changed. Just like that – in just that split second after I said it. Why I did say it, of course: I've noticed that in him before. He goes from all angry and actually pretty dangerous-looking to suddenly all kind of . . . well – not happy, exactly, but . . . I don't know . . . pleased, anyway. A bit pleased. And his hands, they're not all bunched up any more. His eyes are open and bright – not all screwed sort of tight and threatening, like they can sometimes get.

'Yeh? A surprise? Fab. What sort of surprise? What is it?'

'Well you'll just have to wait and see, won't you? Wouldn't be a surprise, would it? If I went and told you.'

'Tell me. Tell me what it is.'

'No, George. I won't. You'll see. It's Saturday tomorrow.

That's when it will happen. That's when we're going to do it.'

'Do what? What? When what will happen?'

'It'll be fabulous. Promise. But it's no good you going on, George – you've just got to wait because I'm not going to tell you.'

No. And the reason I wasn't going to tell him is because I was now a bit panicking – more than a bit panicking actually, really rather frantic – because I hadn't got the slightest *clue*, had I? What this blessed surprise was supposed to be . . .! I'd just said it. Out of the blue. To stop him going on. To stop him going on at me. Yes well now I had to start thinking really quickly – because it's Saturday tomorrow. And that, oh God, is when it's going to happen, according to me. Whatever it is. And I was also thinking it's mean, it's really mean of him to have said what he did: thoughtless, rude, selfish and just completely wrong – so absolutely typical of George, then – because yes, all right, he pays the weekly rent on this crummy little room, but he doesn't know (because I've never told him, because he wouldn't care) that every Saturday morning I have to hand over to my mum half of anything I take home for what she calls 'bed and board', I can hardly believe it. The more I earn, the more she takes: I have to open the brown envelope in front of her on the dining-room table, and then she goes and checks the payslip, like I'm out to swindle her, or something. I can't really stop her – I've tried to tell her that the cost of this so-called 'bed and board' can't just keep altering like that . . . but I don't really say anything now because it's simply not worth it, and if I do she just goes all funny like she does, and that . . . well that's just worse than anything. And even then it's not the end of it – I have to get her little presents on top of all this rent she charges me – half-a-pound of Dairy Box or a bag of monkey nuts or some of those sherbet dips, all of which she loves to gorge on, in secret. Disgusting, really. And if I don't, she says I'm a bad child. She says I don't love her. She says she's glad my father isn't alive to see it – and so am I, but I'm pretty sure for very different reasons. George, he doesn't know anything about any of this – and as for his 'electricity', well: I'm just always putting shillings in the meter because he just automatically says he hasn't got any: I've taken to bringing them specially – and for the gas as well, or else we'd be shivering and sitting in the dark. And there's been loads of times when I've also brought round things like Scotch eggs and crisps and Swiss rolls and baking potatoes and stuff like that because there's just never anything here except tins of Skol and cigarettes and that horrible coffee that he says is so terribly good – so that's why I can't afford to get anything new for me, let alone go to Bazaar . . . but don't ask me why George can't afford all this trendy Carnaby Street gear he's always going on about, because he earns much more than I do and his money definitely doesn't go into the way he lives, that's for sure – and he certainly never spends anything on me, I can tell you that. Once . . . once, he gave me flowers. Dahlias. I think they must have been going very cheap, or else he just got them for nothing from some rotten little corner shop at the end of the day, because most of them were half dead and the stems when I put them in water had that sort of rather sickly and sewery smell, you know?

So anyway, I was really worried now about this stupid promise I'd made to him . . . and then I suddenly got this idea for a picnic. It's the middle of May, and the weather's been really very nice, just lately. So: a picnic on Hampstead Heath – that would be good, wouldn't it? He'd like it, wouldn't he? We've never done anything like that before. Well, that's tomorrow: it's tomorrow because I stupidly went and said it was. I'll have to be up really early and sort everything out. I can go to the market in Camden Town and get all I need: just hope I can afford it. Write a list. And maybe even a couple of quite special things if they're not too expensive from this little Italian sort of delicatessen, do they call them, in the very same street, Inverness Street I think, that I thought had only just opened up, but one of the Irish women from downstairs was telling me it's been there for ever – though God knows how she knew that, actually, because they all seem to live on just chips and alcohol. And my mum – she's got a hamper somewhere, I'm pretty sure. I'm positive I remember seeing a wicker hamper knocking about somewhere when I was a child – not that we ever used it, or anything. Heaven knows where it can be, though. Loft, maybe. But even if I can't find it, there'll be a Thermos and plates and cutlery and all the rest of it. I wonder what he'd like to drink . . .? Lager, I suppose – but it won't be cold. Well: I'll have to think about it all. Write a list. Because there's no backing out now: I've promised him a really nice surprise, and if he doesn't get it, he'll probably kill me.

Okay: all that's for the morning – but right now we already ought to be on our way up to Sammy's parents' place in Hampstead to watch *Ready, Steady, Go!*, like we always do on Fridays. I don't want to be late . . . what can George be doing? He takes so much longer than I do to get ready . . . because it's easily the best programme of the week, and I really really love it. Sammy, you know, he's a pretty good example – well, the only one I know, actually – of how if you're still living at home it can be really great: everything he's got, the set-up there, it's a million miles from me and Mum in Edgware, I can tell you that. My room at home, oh . . . I just can't put it into words. Same awful flowery wallpaper that has been there since before I was born, I should think – and I'm not even allowed to pin up pictures. I did once – cut up two whole issues of *Fabulous* and had Cliff and The Shadows, Cilla, Dusty – The Beatles, of course, because you can't not, really . . . but mainly The Dave Clark Five, and one really lovely one of Mike Smith all on his own, and smiling really beautifully. My mum, she went completely mad. Screaming that I'd ruined the walls. Kept on yelling at me to take them all down – and it was no good me saying but look, Mum – the holes are there now, aren't they? The drawing pins, they're already in the wall, so if I take down the pictures, all you'll see is the holes. No – didn't listen. Went on and on until I just couldn't stand it any more. So I had to take them down – and you didn't see the holes, actually, because all the big flowers completely blotted them out: you couldn't even tell where the pictures had been. It's just that she doesn't ever want me to have what I want, what I like – I know that's true, because it always has been, really.

But Sammy's room, oh . . . George is just so envious – he doesn't try to hide it, he keeps on saying it – and I can sort of see why: who wouldn't want what Sammy has got? His parents' house is beautiful – they must be awfully rich but I don't know what his father does, or anything – and it's in this really quiet and leafy street overlooking the Heath. It's really big as well, and I think that's a lot of how it works so well for Sammy – he's got his own sort of flat! Well, not exactly – but he does have a whole bathroom all to himself, which I still can't quite believe, and it's all in black and yellow chequered tiling and there's this Spanish woman called I think he said Consuela who comes in every day and cleans it for him, and then she makes his bed and does all his laundry! No honestly – I am not joking. And he can spend loads of time here because he doesn't have to work, or anything: he's on some sort of a course, George was telling me – and sounding pretty miserable about it. His parents are paying, of course – it's not university exactly, so far as I can gather . . . but something to do with higher education anyway, so rather posh, I imagine. No idea what subject or what he wants to become, or anything: never asked him. But this room of his is just so amazing, though – it's got fitted wardrobes and a bay window seat with cupboards underneath and these really lovely cushions on top that have been made specially to fit, you can tell. And sitting on the cushions he's got this sweet and rather bashed-up little teddy bear which is probably the one he had as a child, I should think, and these tremendous Gonks, which I absolutely love and I've wanted to buy one since they first came out but the larger types are thirty-nine-and eleven which is just completely crazy, quite frankly, because they're only stuffed sort of felt – but they really are nice. He's got Gone Gonk, of course – the orange and black one, and he's got Fred Gonk as well, in his braces and little tweed cap. You can get smaller ones, but even those are nearly nine shillings each, so a bit of a luxury, really, and one that I obviously can't afford (along with nearly everything else) – but I saw in *Honey* that Simplicity have done a pattern now, so I wonder if I could maybe make one . . .? I'm not really very good at sewing, but I wouldn't mind giving it a try.

And what else is in Sammy's room . . .? There's striped wallpaper and pictures of veteran cars and he's got a fantastic drum kit that's exactly the same as Ringo's, George says, and it's even got the name on the big drum – not The Beatles' name, I don't mean, but that sort of swirly I suppose it's the maker's name above it, can't remember what it is: George could tell you. And an electric guitar in bright shiny red – more like The Shadows' sort of guitar than the beat groups, but really pretty . . . and I still like The Shadows anyway, but George doesn't: he says Cliff and The Shadows are dead, but seeing as Cliff's latest single 'Constantly', which I do quite like, but it's not nearly as good as his earlier records like 'Living Doll', which I really love, or 'Summer Holiday' . . . but seeing as this new one is at the moment about number twelve or fifteen or something in the charts, that's obviously nonsense, they're not dead at all – but I'm not going to say that to George for obvious reasons. Don't want to start all that up.

I don't think he actually plays anything, Sammy – he's never said so, and certainly when we go round there he never picks up an instrument (because he's got loads: Spanish guitar, saxophone, some other brass thing – loads of them). There are orange lampshades and his bed folds upwards, hard to explain, into this sort of cupboard that links up with the wardrobes so that it doesn't look like a bedroom at all, more like a really cool lounge in *The Avengers*, or something – but this is the really amazing thing: he's got his own TV set! In his room! So he can just watch anything, any time he likes. Now that is pretty groovy, you have to admit – and his record player too, that's very cool-looking, and there's a radio in it as well. His LP collection – oh heavens! It's like being in HMV in Oxford Street! It really is all just so fabulously fantastic . . . so you can see how George is always feeling about this. He doesn't resent Sammy having it all, I don't think, because he really does like Sammy a lot – I think he likes Sammy more than anyone on earth – and he loves going round there, and everything . . . but the trouble is, when we come back afterwards, George and me, to his room in Kilburn, well then . . . then he can be nastier than ever.

We got there just in time. Sammy answered the door – wearing the most amazing lemon-coloured V-neck over a Fred Perry – really soft and fluffy so I think it just has to be cashmere – and the three of us bolted up the two flights of stairs to his room and he was waving around his arms and shouting out frantically, Quick quick quick it's just begun . . .! And just as we walked into the room we heard the Manfreds singing the intro song, '5-4-3-2-1' – which I always think is just so exciting, and on the screen it says 'The Weekend Starts Here', and that really does make me feel really nice and warm inside. Sammy's mum – or maybe it's Consuela, if that's her name, yes it must be Consuela who does it because I've never actually met Sammy's mum but I doubt that she serves people . . . anyway, one of them always leaves us a plate of chocolate biscuits which George hogs more than his fair share of because he loves them so much, as if that's an excuse – and tins of Coca-Cola that are always really cold and not how you get them in places like tea shops. My mum won't let me have what she calls 'carbonated drinks' at home. She won't let me have anything unless she's having it too, so you can imagine what that's like: boiled cod and boiled potatoes and boiled greens, rhubarb and custard, plain digestive biscuits, Typhoo tea . . . it's like the Second World War never ended, in our house. It's like there's still rationing: it's amazing she's still not buying us powdered eggs and whale meat: I bet she would, if she could find them. There's something wrong with her, I've known that for ages . . . but I don't know what I can do about it. But whatever her affliction is, whatever makes her act like this all the time, it's just a shame that it has to affect so badly the whole of my life.

The songs on the programme weren't as good as they usually are – with a couple of exceptions, one of them being The Hollies, who are always great. We all thought The Searchers would be on because 'Don't Throw Your Love Away' is at number one, but they weren't. There was Eden Kane, an odd-looking person who I'd never heard of, and Susan Maughan, who Sammy and George were saying was a real and swinging 'dolly bird', but I actually think she looked quite common: far too much eye make-up . . . which, I don't know . . . is maybe the point, is it? I'm not really sure sometimes what boys really respond to: I'm probably doing everything wrong. I did like when she did 'Bobby's Girl' though, but that was ages ago, years. This new one isn't up to much, I wouldn't say. And then there was this really disgusting new group called The Pretty Things – and yes I know they must have chosen the name to make old people angry, or maybe, I don't know, just to make all of us laugh or something, because obviously they're not pretty at all, quite the reverse . . . but goodness, though – the length of their hair! I've never seen anything like it – well, not on a boy, anyway. It was easily longer than mine – and actually in better condition, which doesn't really help. It made The Beatles and The Dave Clark Five look as if they've all got army-regulation short-back-and-sides. But *talking* of The Dave Clark Five – they were on! Yes! With their new record 'Can't You See that She's Mine', which is just out and I'll probably get it next week if I've got any money left over after this blessed picnic thing – but I don't think it's as good as 'Bits and Pieces', which I really did love – still do. I've played it to pieces: bits and pieces.

The point about them being on, though, was that I had to be really careful about how I was behaving, which I always really hate. Because whenever I watch *Top of the Pops* or *Ready,*

Steady, Go! I really want to get into the spirit of the whole thing of enjoying myself because they're just so great, those programmes, and they're only half-an-hour long and they're over so terribly quickly and it's only once a week and I had just got over moping about the sight of Cathy McGowan's perfect, oh just so perfect, long straight hair and fringe – and suddenly, there they were: The Dave Clark Five . . .! And George, I knew, was looking at me. Sidelong, like he does. Not looking right at me – just enough to see the side of my face and how I'm reacting. Because no matter what I say to him about how very silly he's being (though I have to be careful about that too – how I, you know . . . sort of put it) still he just can't stand the fact that I really do think that Mike Smith is just utterly fantastic: more than any Beatle or anyone else on the whole of the pop scene. I've never said that to George, of course – I've just said I like him, quite like him, but still he can go completely crazy. So throughout the whole song I just had to sit there and nod in time to the beat with my eyes not wavering for even so much as a second, and my hands folded neatly in my lap. And I wanted, I so wanted – I was really yearning to be leaping up and down and dancing about all over the room and swaying my hips and fanning out my hair in my fingers and maybe even going right up to the screen and waiting for the camera to hurry up and do a close-up of my gorgeous Mike when his hair is going from side to side and you can see that he's stamping his Cuban-heeled boot, so I could actually lean right in and just *kiss* him . . .! But I didn't do any of that. Just sat there. And afterwards, I ate a chocolate biscuit, one of only two that George hadn't guzzled, the pig, and tried not to show how much I was still just all fizzing inside.

The following day was sunny, thank goodness, and even

warm enough for me not to have to bother with a jacket or my mac or anything because they said in the forecast that it wasn't going to rain, so I just was wearing a cardigan – which isn't as horrible as that word always seems to sound (God, I always think of my father's awful beige one that he put on every single evening when he was listening to what he called the wireless – the news mostly, or else checking his pools coupon: it had a cable-knit design with brown leather football buttons and was always reeking of stale tobacco). I haven't worn it before, this cardigan, I've been saving it – I got it in the market for only nineteen-and-eleven but it's nearly exactly like the one I really yearned for that I saw in *Honey* which they've just got in at Biba for nearly three pounds ten, with these tiny little buttons all down the front and on the cuffs and just a bit of padding on the shoulders. I had really wanted the pale blue, but they'd run out of that one in my size, so this is a sort of a mauvy colour which actually looks really nice with the plain white shirt that I'm wearing underneath. Or I think so, anyway: George, he's yet to even notice. And because I'm quite small, I can still get these smart little shirts from the school outfitting department at John Lewis – really good-quality cotton, and they're amazing value. I also bought from there the last time I went a mint-green gingham frock – summer uniform for some private school in Kensington, apparently – but when I put it on, George said I looked 'pathetic'. That's what he said – the word he used. And so I know I wouldn't ever wear it again, but still I didn't like to take it back to John Lewis because I had worn it that once, so it wasn't quite new any more, and anyway I'd lost the receipt. Today, I would've gone for jeans to wear on the Heath, but I knew he wouldn't like that, so I'm wearing that soft and floaty pink and white floral skirt that I've had for ages, and although

I don't like my skirts to be long, obviously – I've shortened them all myself on Mum's sewing machine (I say 'all' – I've only got three) – still though this one is a fair bit shorter than I would actually have gone for, but on this particular occasion I'd lugged the machine round to George's place because Mum was being really difficult that evening and George, he had come in when I was in the middle of doing it and he told me take it up more, so I did: he says he likes them like that. Even if when he imagines I'm not listening he goes and says to Sammy that he thinks my legs are, oh God – chunky. They're not, are they . . .? Oh dear. I really don't know why I trouble with him, sometimes. The whole thing . . . it's all such a lot to think about, all the time. Always got to be on my guard. So much work. Why do I do it, that's what I sometimes ask myself. Well because I love him – why else would I do it? Yes but why do I love him? Why do I?

This spot I'd decided on is really lovely – and I said we ought to get there early because it's Saturday and I didn't want it to be packed with people. I've got to know the Heath quite well really, in the short time I've been coming here. I walk here on my own quite a bit – either when work's been awful, or because the agency hasn't given me any work to do at all, or else if Mum or George are being . . . oh, when I simply can't bear either of them for just a minute longer. I always feel perfectly safe – it's all so beautiful, like the Garden of Eden, and so you simply can't believe that anything bad could ever happen there . . . but yes I do know from the local paper that it sadly isn't true. But the Heath . . . no one who doesn't know it will ever believe this, but it really is just like the countryside – really so amazing. Reminds me of when I read Thomas Hardy at school. Tess – and I sort of know how she was feeling, sometimes. Do other girls think that? Don't know. Don't really know any other girls, any more: not since George. When I was little, my dad would take my mum and me on a picnic to Rickmansworth, not often – don't know quite where it is, Rickmansworth – in this big old Austin A40 in a sort of a greenish-blue colour that he had at the time: smelled of petrol, and it was always breaking down. I don't really remember much about those picnics except for egg and cress sandwiches and tepid tea and my father losing his temper almost as soon as we got there and Mum and me just sitting miserably on this old tartan rug with burn holes from his roll-up cigarettes and longing for him to tell us that it was time to go home.

But Hampstead Heath, oh . . . it's so much lovelier than that. George and I, we had taken the little overground train from West Hampstead and got off at South End Green, which is right on the edge of the Heath, and the place I had in mind is only a really short walk from there, but of course he was already moaning, George – of course he was. The thing I had to do now was just sort of contain it, if you know what I'm meaning: make him happy if I could, obviously – but if I couldn't get him in the mood to go quite that far, then at least I had to make sure that he didn't actually explode, or something. You know: really get sort of furious. And yes I did, actually – think back to my dad in Rickmansworth: how could you not, under the circumstances?

'It's heavy, this bag. Weighs a bloody ton. How far is it?'

'I said I'll carry it, George. Not far – I told you. It shouldn't be that heavy – the plates are only paper.'

'Yeh maybe – but the Thermos isn't and the bottles or cans or whatever they are and whatever else you've stuck in here – they're not made of paper, are they?'

Well you see what I mean. I've put so much effort into making this a really proper spread, a really nice day out for the two of us – heavens, I was up not much after dawn, because first I had to wash my hair, obviously. It's gone a bit funny though, a little bit frizzy – just didn't have the time to iron it. This new shampoo Drene that I got the other day in Boots, though, it's so much better than Vosene, which I always used to use, and it smells much nicer too: I saw it advertised in *Honey*, and the girl's hair in the picture looked just wonderful – all straight and long and blonde, not a bit like mine at all, with all the split ends. Then I went out and got cucumber and radishes from the market because they're easy to eat and are all nice and fresh and crunchy. Nearly got celery, but I'm not sure either of us really likes it, and I thought anyway it might have wilted. I've made ham sandwiches – taken the fat away from the edges and trimmed the crusts the way he likes it – and there's a piece of cheddar with apples. And I did go to that little Italian shop – terribly daring! The most wonderful smell when you walk through the door: all fresh pasta – and I had no idea there were so many different shapes and sizes because I only really know about spaghetti, and sometimes I've had that ravioli that comes in tins. They also had these huge and really odd-looking cheeses which don't seem a bit like Cheddar and I'm not sure I'd really go for . . . but I was very brave and I did get some salami! I didn't know it was called that, but the very nice old Italian lady there, she told me. Big sad eyes, and I noticed that her fingers were really so elegant and dainty as she was working this enormous slicing machine that they've got in there. It's sort of like circles of quite fatty-looking ham, this salami, not very pretty – but it smells really wonderful. I was actually thinking of giving up eating meat, not too long ago . . . but I just like it too much. She asked me, the lady, if I'd maybe care for some olives – but I've never had an olive so I said I didn't think so. She offered me one to taste – they had barrels of all different sorts . . . but I thought, no. So that's all the food, anyway: no egg, and definitely no cress. There's also that beastly coffee in the Thermos, two tins of Harp lager because the corner off-licence didn't have any of his usual Skol, so he'll probably go mad about that as well. I've got a small bottle of orange for myself. And then in the newsagent when I was getting the latest *Honey*, I really pushed the boat out and got a carton of Clarnico Mint Chocs: half-a-crown – but I just saw them there and I know that George really loves them because that's what he always buys in the Odeon whenever we go there, which is less and less, just lately. Can't remember the last film we saw – together, I mean, because I know he goes with Sammy, sometimes. I hope they won't melt, the Mint Chocs. Anyway, it's just about cleaned me out, buying all this stuff – almost completely broke, so I jolly well hope that the agency comes up with something for next week, or else Mum will have to make do with half of nothing. It all just barely fitted into this big sort of bucket bag that was hanging on the back of the cupboard door – because I couldn't find that hamper that I'm sure I remembered, couldn't find it anywhere. And also in the bag is Mum's sort of wine-coloured Roberts radio with the handle, which I'm pretty sure has been in the sitting room since before I was born – and I'm hoping she won't miss it until I get home, or else there will be more of all her utter nutsiness that I'll have to cope with. *The Archers* and *Mrs Dale's Diary* – that's what she mainly likes, addicted to them, so far as I can see. But those programmes – are they on every day, or just once a week . . .? No idea – but if either of them's today,

I've completely had it: she'll just go crazy, won't ever let me hear the end of it. Oh well – deal with all that when the time comes, I suppose. It's just that I thought some music might be nice – and it's really a very good radio, actually, with a proper aerial and everything, so we might be able to get Luxembourg without it being all tinny and crackly like it is on my transistor. So yes, just thinking about it . . . I suppose the bag that George is still lugging across the Heath with this awful scowl on his face, and deliberately lagging as far as he can behind me . . . I suppose it would be quite heavy, really.

'How much further . . .? It's killing me, this. A treat, you said. You said it was going to be a *treat* . . .'

'Just over the next sort of hill. You see that big oak tree dead ahead of us? It's just past that. You'll love it, George – honestly you will. Worth the walk, I promise you.'

And I really did think he would, actually – love it. How could anyone not? Anyone with a heart and soul. I only actually had come across this place a week or so ago, and I was pretty sure that George would never have been here. There's a sort of a vale, a glade maybe, with this tall and so terribly romantic old bridge, almost like a Roman viaduct or something, and it's perfectly reflected in the still green water of a pond beneath it. There are even lily pads – and lots of fresh grass to sit on, and the shade of trees, one or two of them willows. Just heaven. We didn't have it completely to ourselves – too much to hope for, I suppose – but there weren't really too many people, and still plenty of nice spots we could go for. George, he just looked around him – the sun, it was glinting brightly off the water, so he was squinting just a bit – and he nodded. Put down the bag in the very place I would have chosen. He liked it, I just knew he did.

'All right, George? You like it? It's beautiful, isn't it?'

He was spreading out the towel – yes, because that's another thing I'd crammed into the bag at the very last moment: a rather garish big beach towel . . . not at all ideal, but all I could seem to find.

'It's all right,' he said slowly. 'Yes. It's pretty good.'

I nearly keeled over with pleasure – and relief too, of course. He loved it. He absolutely loved it. Good. Oh goody-goody . . .! This was going to be great, I just knew it.

'What've we got to drink in here? I'm parched.'

'There's lager, two tins – but it won't be cold, I'm afraid. Here. There's coffee as well, if you want it.'

'Two tins . . .?'

'Oh don't worry – they're both for you. I'm just having orange. Can I sit on the towel as well, George? Can you budge up a bit? I don't want the grass to mark my skirt. Do you like it, by the way? What I'm wearing? This cardigan, it's new. Wore it specially.'

'This isn't Skol . . .'

'I know. But I'm sure it'll be good. You've had it before, haven't you? Harp?'

'Oh yes. It's all right. Nothing wrong with Harp. Just prefer Skol, that's all. Haven't seen that radio before – where did you get it?'

'It's my mum's. It's ancient, actually, but it's terribly good. Let me see what I can get on it. It's always tuned in to either the Light Programme or the Third, so just let me fiddle with it for a bit. So what do you think then, George? About my cardigan?'

'Are these sandwiches . . .?'

'Well what else do you think they can be . . .?'

'What . . .?'

'Nothing. Nothing, George. It's just that they're bread, aren't they? With ham in between. I just don't see what else you think they can be if not, you know . . . sandwiches . . .'

'No need to be sarcastic.'

'I wasn't.'

'There's no need to be bloody sarcastic . . .'

'I wasn't being.'

'Yeh well you were, actually.'

'Oh listen . . .! It's Luxembourg. I've got Luxembourg . . .'

'That's really clear. Can never get it that clear on my radio.'

'I know. I told you it's good. Four Pennies, isn't it? This one?'

'Yeh. Hate this one.'

'It's nearly finished, I think. Here, George – try this. It's new. It's called salami.'

'Salami . . .? Yes . . . I think I've heard of that. Foreign, obviously. But that's all right – a lot of foreign things are really good.'

'Italian. Try it. It might go well with a radish . . .'

'Mm. I like it. Bit greasy . . . but I like it. Oh *Christ* . . .!'

'Oh God, it's going everywhere . . .! Do the other side of the tin, George – pierce the other side quickly, and it'll stop fizzing out. Yes. That's it. Don't worry – most of it went on the towel. Oh listen! It's Millie! "My Boy Lollipop" . . . love this.'

'Some of it's gone on my cords . . .'

'I don't think it'll stain. I haven't brought any water, I'm afraid. You could get some from the pond, but I should think it's pretty dirty, actually. Probably make it worse. I've got a handkerchief, if you want it . . .'

'It's all right. It'll be all right – didn't really spill too much. It's actually quite hot, isn't it? When the sun's on you. The sun'll dry them out. They'll be fine. Any more of that salami . . .?'

'Oh piles. I'm really glad you like it – I didn't know if you would. I only got it this morning from that little shop, the Italian shop where the market is. Do you know it? Been there for ever, according to one of the Irish women downstairs, can't remember what she's called. Some funny name she's got. That one with the red face, you know? She never washes her hair – disgusting. Actually, that shop's really close to the stall where I got this cardigan. Do you like it, George?'

'Like what . . .?'

'Cardigan. I said. My cardigan. This. Do you like it? I haven't worn it before.'

'It's fine. You said you brought two tins, yeh . . .?'

Yes well: that's George, isn't it? I'm afraid. He wasn't quite so inattentive last evening though, was he? Not so careless then – not after we left Sammy's. I said I was going to get the Tube straight back to Edgware – not just because I know exactly just how George can be, sometimes, back in his room in Kilburn after evenings round at Sammy's place (although that was a part of it, I have to admit) – but it was mainly because we'd actually stayed there longer than usual. George had been making an awful row on the drum kit and Sammy had given him a lager and we were all still arguing about the different acts we'd just seen on *Ready, Steady, Go!* Well, I say arguing – it was just George really saying again and again in a really loud voice that The Beatles are better, miles better, than The Hollies, and simply a million times better than The b-word Dave Clark Five . . . again and again and again. Sammy was just laughing, and I made a point of saying nothing. As usual. Anyway, it was nearly a quarter to nine when we eventually left Sammy's – and of course I had to be in by ten, as ever.

'Well just come in for a minute. That's all. I like to . . . be with you.'

'Yes but Kilburn – it's in the opposite direction, isn't it George? I can go direct if I get the Tube from Hampstead . . .'

'It's Friday. There's no work tomorrow. It's early. And you're looking lovely tonight, you know. I meant to say earlier. I mean – you always do, you always do, of course . . . but tonight, well . . . like I just said: particularly so. Yeah? That dress and everything you're wearing – lovely. Really lovely. Looking great.'

'Yes well that's nice, that's really nice of you to say so, George . . . but I've got your *surprise* to arrange in the morning, remember? And it's not a question of early or late, is it? You know I've got to be in by ten . . .'

'Why? What will she do if you're not? Kill you? Stupid old bat . . .'

'She's not. She's not that. It's just that she's . . . oh look: you don't have to live with the consequences, do you, George? It's just not worth it, if I'm late. All I have to go through. How many times have I told you? And we're seeing each other tomorrow, aren't we? And honestly – I've got just loads to see to when I get up. I've really got to go, okay . . .?'

And no I wasn't flattered, actually. I know George. This was nothing to do with him not able to bear being parted from me for an instant. It wasn't *romantic*. I knew what he wanted, of course I did. And it would be 'just a minute' as well, he wasn't wrong about that – and afterwards, he couldn't give two hoots if I stayed, went back to Edgware or just lay dead in the street. Because he would be asleep, and I would have ceased to exist. Yes. I know George. That much about him, anyway. So I had to make a decision, knowing that he was never going to make it easy for me. Because he's just so absolutely selfish – it's like he's wearing blinkers, or something. All he sees is whatever it is he wants at the time, dead ahead of him and sort of, I don't know . . . shimmering irresistibly in the distance, or something. Everything else to either side is not only completely invisible, but it just doesn't matter, not even a tiny bit. And it's all so unfair: whatever I decide, whatever I do, I am always going to be in trouble with either George or my mother . . . and you see, I don't really know anybody else. It's ridiculous, really – but there is no one else, is there? In the whole of the world, who affects me . . . and I am always forced into the position of having to please or displease them – yes but neither ever stops to think for a moment what it is that might please *me*. Do they? And that's just not fair. Is it?

'I'm going, George. I'm sorry. I just have to. But look – I'll come round really early tomorrow morning, okay? So make sure you're up. And we'll go off together. Yes? All right? George . . .? Oh heavens, George – it's no good just walking away from me, is it . . .? Come back. Come back and talk to me, for heaven's sake . . .! George . . .? George . . .! Oh God. Oh God . . . don't just *leave* me . . .!'

Yes. But he did – he left me standing there in the street, just outside Sammy's house – and it's right by the Heath there, and really dark and silent. I didn't enjoy the quite long walk up to Hampstead Village and the Tube, all on my own – all the shadows were making me jump. And while I was sitting in the train, I wondered whether if tomorrow morning he'd even answer the door when I rang the bell. Or answer it, and then just slam it in my face – because he's done that to me before as well. But then I decided that he would, of course – he would let me in, of course he would, because there was this stupid *surprise* coming, wasn't there? A surprise, yes – a treat, yet another treat for George, which naturally he just knows he deserves so terribly much. And when eventually I got in, my mother looked at me accusingly and asked me where I'd been. And I told her: out. And then she called me a young madam, and asked me what sort of a time I called this. And I just looked at her, feeling more than I could say about – oh, just everything, really, and I said to her I call this seven minutes to ten: that's what the time is – look at the clock. So it isn't after ten, is it? Is it? And she said no . . . but it very *nearly* is. Isn't it?

And now it's the picnic: George's latest treat. Idyllic setting, perfect weather . . . but for some reason or another, I am back now to being invisible again. Me, my clothes – all just invisible. And he wants his second tin of Harp, which he's just about prepared to put up with, despite it not being Skol. Maybe this one he'll manage not to spray all over those beastly trousers of his, which he keeps on wearing. Like the shirt he's got on – the same one as yesterday, just picked it up off the floor, I expect. He's always going on and on about clothes, George, but he never looks anything much, not in my eyes. I actually wish he would go to Lord John and Take Six and whatever else he said in Carnaby Street and just *buy* them – because of course he can afford it, I don't know what he's talking about – what else does he spend his money on? Not salami, I don't think. Oh dear . . . it's all just so much work. Why do I do it, that's what I sometimes ask myself. Well because I love him – why else would I do it? Yes but why do I love him? Why *do* I . . .?

And this morning, it was just as if nothing had happened. I didn't say a word about how upset I'd been – but buying all these groceries and things, I had felt something of a fool, if I'm honest . . . and particularly when I went and shelled out a whole half-crown for those blessed Mint Chocs. Why did I do that . . .? It's not like I'm flush, or anything: must have been crazy. And then when he came to the door, I saw at once that he hadn't taken the tiniest bit of trouble over his appearance. With me, he doesn't any more. I think he just thinks: well what's the point? It's only Dorothy. Those clothes he wants, it's all about trying to impress Sammy, as far as I can make out. Make him feel more equal, or something, is all I can think. But it's nothing at all to do with me, that I do know. Anyway . . . we're here now, and it's really lovely, despite how George is being. Do you know what I wish . . .? I wish I could build a pretty little cottage right here on this exact spot on the Heath with a garage just next to it where I could have my own little car, a bit like Noddy's, which I always thought was just so sweet. And live here for ever. Maybe with George. Who is lying on his back now, fully stretched out, with his hands making this kind of cradle behind the back of his head – but still he's managing to hold a cigarette between his fingers. I maybe ought to have brought him a cushion. And . . . I'm quite relieved, actually . . . and a little bit surprised. Because I thought, after last night, that he'd be fumbling away at me by now – which I hate, I absolutely hate it if we're out, and people can see. But I did think he'd be touching me, and everything – because practically all of my legs are on show as I'm just sitting here in this really short skirt and they're all warm and glowing because the sun, it's right on them . . . and I do know that in boys it all gets pent up inside them . . . it sort of grows and grows, that's what Yvonne was always telling me, until they can get really quite urgent about it – and, in George's case, often rather angry. But no – he's not a bit like that, this morning. Which is a little bit strange, actually. Look at him: he's just lying there.

'Here, George – look over here. Look at me. George. I'm going to take your picture.'

'Where did you get that old thing . . .?'

'Box Brownie. Had it ages – got it for my Confirmation.'

'Your what . . .?'

'Doesn't matter. It's old. Had it for ever – but it's really good, actually. Here – look at me, can you, George? Sit up just a bit. Oh God . . . the sun is right in the lens. Can't see what I'm taking . . .'

'Leave it. Just leave it. Don't like having my picture taken. Never liked it.'

'Oh you always come out so well in pictures, George – I don't know what you're talking about. Come on – say cheese! There. That's it. I think you might have moved, though. Just as I took it. I hope it's not blurry . . . Do you want to take one of me, George? It's a shame we can't get one of us together. Do you, George?'

'Do I what?'

'Want to take one? A picture. Of me.'

'Not especially. Just sit down, can't you? Always jumping about . . .'

'Oh. Okay then. Oh look – I've just remembered. There's some Mint Chocs, George. Got them this morning. You like those, don't you?'

'I do. Very much. Maybe later. Quite full at the moment. Shame you didn't buy more lager. But we can go and get a drink somewhere, maybe.'

'Get a drink . . .? What do you mean "get a drink" ? We've got a drink – you've just had a drink. We're sitting in the most beautiful place in the whole wide world and the sun's out and we're together and we've got absolutely everything here because I thought about it, and I bought it and I brought it and it's all just, oh God . . . *perfect* . . .! So what do you mean, "get a drink" . . .?'

'Yes – all right . . .! Jesus – bloody women. You can't say the slightest thing. I don't mean straight away. Later. Bit later. Maybe. If we want. Don't have to. Just thought it might be nice, that's all. Something to do. God . . . this record's awful. Don't you think? Who on earth buys The Bachelors? On and on, moaning away . . . I just thought it might be something to do, that's all.'

'They're very popular. Not a favourite of mine, though. Do you want me to turn it off, then? All I'm saying is, I'm perfectly happy just sitting where we are . . .'

'No, it's okay. They'll play something good in a minute. I wish I could get a reception like this on Luxembourg at home. And yeh – okay: we'll stay for a bit. That's fine.'

'Good. Because it's lovely here. George. Listen – let me ask you something: what do you . . .? I mean – do you ever think about the future? You know – what you'll become, and everything . . .? What will . . . happen . . .?'

'Not really. Well – a bit, I suppose. What I'll become is older – we all will. That's what's going to happen. But I won't be stupid like old people are today. That's for sure. They've just got everything wrong and they just can't see it because they're all just so bloody *stupid* . . .'

'What do you mean "old" . . .? You mean when you're a grandfather, or something?'

'Oh *Christ* no . . .! Grandfather? Me? Ho bloody ho. Who would want to be that? Who wants bloody children – let alone *grand*children. I'll never get that old anyway. No – I just mean people of about thirty, or something. Such a *drag* . . . and just so bloody *stupid*. They all think they know the lot – you just have to look at their faces. And the suits they go to work in and the bloody Ford Anglia. But they don't. They don't know bloody anything. Oh – this one's good . . .! Peter and Gordon. Written by Lennon and McCartney, you know – why it's so good: they're just brilliant. One of them, Gordon I think, he's Jane Asher's sister. Did you know that? Paul's really lucky to have a bird like Jane Asher – but then he would, wouldn't he? Have a bird like that. He's a Beatle. Get any bird he wants . . .'

'Brother.'

'What? What did you say?'

'It's Peter, not Gordon, and he's Jane Asher's brother. You said sister.'

'I said *what* . . .? Of course I didn't say "sister" . . .! I said brother. He's her brother of course he's her bloody brother. Why would I say "sister"? He's a bloke, isn't he, Peter? So how could he be her sister?'

'Well I know, George. I'm just saying what you said, that's all.'

'Oh don't be so bloody *stupid*, Dorothy . . . of course I didn't say that. You don't know what you're talking about. Look . . . let's go, shall we? Let's just clear up all this stuff and get out of here. Fed up, now. Going. You coming? Yes no? And I'm out of fags . . .'

I'm just looking at him in total disbelief. He's already standing up, brushing off his trousers whatever he imagined to be clinging there: they look perfectly all right to me. And when he'd said, George, 'Let's clear up all this stuff', clearly what he actually meant was that I should clear up all this stuff – this 'stuff' being all the lovely food and everything which I've only just recently bought for this great big stupid surprise, the ungrateful beast – while he just stands around and watches me do it. And if I don't get it done pretty quickly, he'll walk off – he'll just wander away across the Heath, I just know he will. It's not fair – it's not fair what he's doing, and it's not right, it's not right at all. But he's never really fair, not to me. A lot of what he does is wrong – but oh God, he'd just be so amazed if you told him. If I said it, if I started to reel off all the things that are wrong with him, do you know what he'd do? He'd stare at me – he'd just stare at me in that really cold and nasty way he's got and then he'd say that I'm not right in the head, or something. That's just the sort of thing he'd say – and he might even twirl around his finger close to his ear so that anyone who happened to be looking could see that he thinks that I'm truly a loony – and anyway only some stupid *girl*, so what can you expect? Because he's above it, criticism. If you accuse him of doing something wrong – anything, anything at all – well then no I'm sorry but it's *you* that's wrong, actually. You see? Because George, he can't be – just can't be: simple as that. He can never be wrong about anything. I don't know why I put up with it. I really, really don't.

'Come on. Hurry up. We'll get there before the crowds.'

'Well you might want to help a bit then, George. If you want to go so terribly urgently, why don't you help me put everything away?'

'Well . . . you've nearly finished now. More or less done it.'

'And where . . .? Get where before the crowds? Where are we going?'

'Oh . . . I don't know. Nice day . . . I thought – Spaniards, maybe.'

'The Spaniards Inn?'

'No, Dorothy – no. I was meaning that we'd walk down to Dover and get the ferry across to France and then maybe, what . . .? Hitch-hike to Barcelona so that we can have a couple of drinks there. What do you reckon? Or Madrid, if you think you'd like that better.'

'Yes all right, George. Made your point.'

'Well *honestly*, Dorothy . . .! Of *course* the Spaniards Inn – what's wrong with you?'

'But why do you want to go there, George? Why? It's a picnic. We were supposed to be having a picnic. Why do you want to go to a pub?'

'I just thought it would be *nice*, that's all. Christ, you know – you really do take the fun out of things. You always have to go *in* to everything. On and on. It's the weekend – the sun is shining, and I'm just suggesting we go to one of the best pubs in London for a drink, that's all. It's not *terrible*, is it? Jesus – the way you just go on and on . . .'

'Here. I've packed it all up. Mint Chocs have melted. Are you carrying it?'

'It'll be lighter now. You can carry it. Not far. I hate carrying things. You should have brought more lager, really. Those little cans, you know . . . go absolutely nowhere. Hot day, isn't it . . .?'

I don't like this. I don't like this one little bit. I am trying, with my face, to make him see, George, that I'm really not pleased. I am holding out the bag to him, knowing he'll just ignore it, and I can feel that my lips are pressed tight, really close together, and I was going to stare at him now, really hard and meaningfully so that he could see all that I'm going through right at this moment . . . I was going to make a point of picking up all of these filthy fag-ends that he's ground into the grass in this perfectly wonderful place . . . but do you know what? He's gone. He's just wandered off. Hands in his pockets, just strolling away through the longer grass that leads back up to the path. Can't believe it. I just can't believe it – except that I *can*, of course, I can well believe it, of course I can, because this is George. Isn't it? So fed up. I feel like just throwing everything into the pond, and him with it. I feel like turning round and catching the Tube and going all the way home. Give Mum back her radio, sit in the garden back at Edgware and just, I don't know . . . read, or something. But I'm not going to do any of those things, am I? I'm not, no. Of course I'm not. Wish I could, though – be like that, sometimes. Just not the sort of thing I do. So I'm carrying the bag now. Still quite heavy. And following him. Quite soon I'm shouting across that he's going the wrong way, and of course he's just shaking his head and bawling back to me that he isn't. Calls over then that I don't know what I'm talking about. But I do – I know the Heath much better than he does: he barely ever comes. So I just veer away in the right direction, if it's the Spaniards we're making for, if it's the Spaniards he really wants to go to. And if he carries on the way he's going, he'll end up in Highgate.

I'm walking on, and I look over my shoulder and he's just standing there now, quite a way away, not knowing quite what to do. He can see that I'm right, now . . . he's understood it finally, but he'd probably rather die on the spot than admit it: I know him – he'll be spittingly angry by now. So I carry on walking, glancing back from time to time, wondering what he's going to decide. He slowly starts coming towards me, so I just hang around for a moment or so, and then he gets closer and still he's just wagging his head from side to side and he's saying oh yes, we can go this way if I really want to, but his way, the way he was headed, it's rather nicer and so very much quicker, but yes, okay, if I really do want to go this way, he doesn't mind, he doesn't mind at all. He's simply happy, you see, to indulge the whim of a stupid little girl – that's what he's basically saying: a stupid little girl who might just stamp her foot and become ill-tempered if she doesn't get her way. And he's not ashamed, you know, of this sort of attitude – because that's exactly the sort of thing he'd say, the sort of thing he'd come out with, if there was anyone around to hear it. He's always like this: he knows it's a lie, he knows full well that he was headed in completely the wrong direction, but he'd say the absolute opposite with all the conviction in the world – he'd be trying to get across, with his eyes so completely wide open, the way he does it when he's desperate for people to go along with him – to believe just how terribly wise and saintly and clever he is. It's a joke, really. A complete and utter joke. Yes but I'm always the butt of it. That's the trouble.

I actually love the Spaniards Inn – but I suppose everybody does because how could you not? I've only been here once or twice before – it was George who first took me, of course, because he said they had draught Bass and he was going through a phase of liking draught Bass at the time – and I loved it, just loved the place, from the moment I walked through the door. It's funny, because although I just adore all the trendy new clothes and music and furniture and Pop Art and stuff, I don't much like modern buildings – all the big concrete things, and skyscrapers like in New York which they're building just loads of now. George does, he likes them – or he says he does, anyway. He doesn't go for old at all, George – and particularly old people, hates them. Yes, but then he's not really awfully keen on people generally, is he? Not so's you'd notice. But anyway – the Spaniards, yes? It's all low ceilings and ancient black beams and loads of interesting alcoves and little cubbyholes off the main bit – amazing, all these sort of ins and outs. Even the outside of it, it just looks so romantic – like Shakespeare's birthplace, or something. Shakespeare didn't come here, I don't suppose – had enough of that sort of thing up in Stratford, I expect – but Dickens, he certainly did. I think it's actually mentioned in *Pickwick*, someone was telling me. Or was it *Great Expectations* . . .? Can't remember – but it doesn't matter because it was one of them, anyway, I'm pretty sure of that. And the highwayman Dick Turpin, he used to water his horse here, Black Bess. I know because after the first time I came I went to the library and looked it all up. I was really quite excited and told George all about it – he didn't know anything at all until I told him, but he didn't really care: just talked about how good the draught Bass was. Now it's just Skol he's always going on about: as if any of it mattered – it's only *beer*, isn't it? Why do boys go on and on about all these boring things? Well at least he's not into football – that I really do not think I could bear. Yes and it's not just the Spaniards . . . the whole of Hampstead, the whole of this area around the Heath, it's all just fabulous, I think – so beautiful, and so long and romantic a history. I wish I lived there instead of Edgware. I wish George's room was in Hampstead Village, maybe Church Row, or lower down in Keats Grove, possibly: just anywhere but Kilburn.

But going in to the Spaniards, though – you can easily get crushed by a bus or a lorry or something, if you're not jolly careful crossing the road. It's on a sort of a dogleg corner that you just can't see around, total blind spot, so in the end you just close your eyes and make a dash for it, really – hoping for the best. Anyway – we're here now, and already I'm worried about what to order to drink, because I never quite know. Most other girls seem to be into lager and lime and even gin and lime sometimes, if they've got the money for it, but I don't even like lime, let alone all the other things: hate lager – and gin, well . . . I only tasted Yvonne's that one time ages ago, but oh

God, that was worse, that was worse by miles: just so horrid. But lime, I love the colour – it's just that it's so sour, but in a really kind of sweet and sickly sort of a way: hard to explain. And anyway, that bottle of orange I had on the Heath was easily enough for me: I don't actually like a lot of volume, can't take it – don't understand how boys can go on drinking pint after pint without getting completely bloated . . . although they do spend a lot of time going to the lavatory, I've noticed. Yes, but if I say I don't want anything George will say well he's very sorry and all the rest of it but in fact I've got to have something, you see, because we're in a pub, okay, Dorothy? And it's what people do in pubs, isn't it, Dorothy? They order a drink. So I just can't face going through all of that again – be becomes so cruel, and he won't ever stop – so I'll just ask for a pineapple juice, I think. Those little Britvic bottles – they're terribly tiny, so that will do, although they are most awfully expensive for the little bit you get. Once I asked for a Babycham, which I do quite like actually, but I never heard the end of it from George – it's clichéd, it's suburban (of *course* it's suburban), it's pathetic, it's just so typical of you, Dorothy – so I'm not falling for that one again in a hurry. I wouldn't mind Tizer, actually – always loved Tizer since I was little, although I only ever got it on birthdays and at Christmas: that's maybe why. And even on those special occasions, my mum, there she'd be at the head of the table to tell me that it would rot my insides and kill me, but if that's what I wanted – to be a fool to myself – then I must go right ahead with it, and that would be my funeral then, wouldn't it, and I mustn't come crying to her when my teeth drop out. Terrible thing to say to a child, really – but then she was, my mum, pretty terrible all round. Still is, of course. And still I'm with her – same house, same room, same everything, just putting up with it all, and handing over half my wages for the privilege. Can't see a time when I'll ever be rid of it. Because I'll never be with George, will I? Not properly, I mean. Living together, and everything. He'll never ask me – because he would have, by now: if he wanted me to be with him properly – living together, and everything – well he would have asked me, wouldn't he? By now, he would have, of course he would. And do you know . . . I've been thinking like this for just so long . . . wanting and wanting it, yearning for it to happen . . . but I don't even know if I do any more. Want it so badly . . . or even at all. Because it would only be the same – wouldn't it? He would be the same, we would be the same, but I'd have it always, instead of just some of the time. And so do I want that . . .? Do I really . . .? You know . . . I don't actually think I do. After the way he's been today . . . I don't really think I do. And I never, never thought I'd be saying anything even remotely like that. Because George, he's all I've ever wanted – since the moment I saw him, really. Since that very first night when I walked out of the bierkeller with him, and went to his horrible room in Kilburn. Oh well. There it is. Have to work it all out some time, I suppose: work out what I do want. But just thinking about the other thing, though . . . it's just occurred to me: nowhere seems to sell it any more, Tizer – unless you want to buy a huge great bottle in the newsagent's, they have it sometimes, but you never seem to see it anywhere else: maybe they're the only places you could ever get it, I really don't know. It's the colour I love as much as anything, I think – that wonderful orangey red, like liquid rubies, or something else very warm and lovely. And I just hope George isn't going to do all his Oh God I've come out without any money thing, what a stupid thing to do, how in the world did I manage that . . .?

Because I'm completely flat broke after buying everything this morning. Total waste of time and money, as things turned out. And still I'm lugging it all about in this great big heavy bag, like a packhorse or something – seems like I've been carrying it around for just years. And that mess of melted and gooey Mint Chocs: that's half-a-crown right down the drain . . . and I'm not sure that the Thermos isn't leaking. Oh dear. Makes me feel so stupid. I just feel so utterly and completely stupid.

I terribly didn't want to leave the Heath – I was really, really happy there, and I thought that everything was going to be wonderful: that this picnic I'd suddenly invented in a panic could actually turn out to be something just brilliant. As soon as we stood up and I started putting everything together, I noticed this other couple who had been just sort of squatting next to a tree quite a bit away from us, and they suddenly looked at one another as if to say, Oh good: those people are going, we can move over there now. Yes, because we'd got the best spot of all – a weeping willow, lots of sun, a bit of shade, thick green grass and absolutely the most perfect view of the beautiful bridge, glowing in sunlight and gorgeously reflected in the water, just as if it were a mirror. But the Skol was finished, you see, so we had to up sticks and leave all that to walk a mile to a blessed pub. Harp, I should have said – not Skol. Because I'm so completely useless, I bought far too little lager, and it wasn't even Skol.

Anyway, now we're here I'm going to make a beeline for the Ladies because there was quite a breeze while we were walking, and I can feel that my hair must just look a total fright – it doesn't feel like it ought to, and also I'm going to wash my hands which are actually quite sweaty now after carrying that bag, and the handles were digging in a bit. George, he'll be going straight to the bar, if I know George, so I'll just try to get away quickly before he asks me for any money, and see if I can find the lavatory – not quite sure where it is, whether it's on this floor or maybe upstairs. George has now taken to saying 'toilet' instead of lavatory, but only because he knows it upsets me. I can't think why it does, it's only a word, completely silly of me, I know it is . . . but for some reason it just does upset me, so there we are: nothing to be done about it. But from the moment George picked up on the way I react, he has continued to say 'toilet' quite relentlessly. According to him, to call it anything else is *suburban*, of course – and never mind that he always used to call it lavatory. I must start saying 'loo', if I can remember.

George, now . . . he's raising his arm. Why is he raising his arm . . .? He's smiling – he's waving. Why is he waving? Who on earth can he be waving at? Oh . . . my goodness! I don't believe it . . .! What an amazing coincidence – I just don't believe it: it's Sammy, of all people. Sammy is here . . .! He's just got up from that table in the corner and George has gone over to meet him and now they're into all that backslapping thing and sort of mock boxing that boys seem to do, and George . . . he seems so happy. All of a sudden, he just seems so terribly happy. Oh. I see. Oh God, yes – of course. How very stupid I am. Because it's not, is it? No, it's not. Sammy being here, it's not a coincidence at all, of course it isn't. That's why George was so eager to get here. Not a whim, not just a casual idea – they'd made a date, they'd arranged a time. George had calculated just how long he thought he could bear to be alone with me on Hampstead Heath, found some idiotic reason to end it, and now we're in the Spaniards with his friend, so finally he can begin to enjoy himself. Well that's very nice. Isn't that nice? And I, the packhorse – I've been just left at the door, and forgotten. I just stand here, blinking stupidly. Like a mule. How very stupid I am.

'How was your walk . . .? Hi, Dorothy! Come over! Come over and have a drink. What would you like?'

'Thanks, Sammy. I'm just going to go to the lavatory, actually. Loo. Be back in a minute. Nice to see you. It wasn't a walk – it was a picnic. Or meant to be, anyway.'

And then I just walked away. Leave them to it.

'What's wrong with her . . .? She didn't seem very happy. What have you done to her this time, Georgie?'

'Oh Christ, Sammy. It's just the way she is. It always goes like this. Bit getting to me, actually. Can't explain, really. Is that lager? I'm gasping.'

'It's draught Long Life. You don't often see it. Pint?'

'You bet. Got any fags? I've done all mine.'

'Yeh. As usual. Here. Okay – I'll get the drinks in. What do you think Dorothy will want?'

'Christ knows. Mother's milk. Lucozade. Christ knows.'

'You shouldn't be so hard on her, you know. I've told you before. She doesn't do anything wrong. I can't understand you, Georgie.'

'I know. I know. She doesn't do anything wrong at all. Always doing everything right – and I don't actually mean that in a sarcastic way, or anything: she does, she does – she does do everything right. She's always thinking of me. I know. Like today – she'd done this most amazing packed lunch. All sorts of good stuff. Salami. Ever had it? It's great – really groovy. Not much lager, but still. She's very good like that. She thinks of everything. Even brought along the most amazing radio – her mum's, apparently. Wish I had a radio like that.'

'Well what's wrong then, you silly bastard?'

'I don't know, really. Nothing, I suppose. Except, well . . .'

'Except what?'

'Oh . . . sod it. Get me a drink, will you Sammy? Gasping.'

'She seemed quite surprised to see me . . .'

'Yeh . . .'

'What – didn't you tell her we were meeting?'

'No, I . . . no.'

'Why not?'

'I just didn't, that's all. Drink, yeh . . .?'

Good old Sammy – I'll just nick one of his Bensons while he's gone. Fantastic jacket he's got on – so gear. Midnight-blue corduroy with buttoned patch pockets and epaulettes. Terrific. I haven't seen it before – new, obviously. Probably Lord John – looks like it. He's always got new stuff. Why couldn't I have a mum and dad like Sammy's? Instead of my two. It's right, though . . . what he says about Dorothy, it's right what he's saying. I don't know why I treat her like I do. I know what she wants, I sense it all the time – and it's never much, she's not at all demanding. The odd little comment on her hair, or what she's wearing . . . like that cardigan she had on today, for instance. I saw that. I really liked it – suited her really well, the colour and everything. I thought it had to be new. But I didn't say anything. Why didn't I say anything? Don't know. Can't explain it. Because I was sort of really wanting to. It's weird. And even when she asked me – even when she was forced into asking me, poor bitch, whether I liked it or not, I just . . . what did I do? Grunted, or something. Why did I do that? And I was going on about the lager being Harp and not Skol – I can't even tell the bloody difference, if I'm honest: it's just the usual piss – they're all the same to me. But I just had to put her down, didn't I? Just had to. I think there must be something wrong with me. Like that time the other week when she told me she had her period and I said yeah I thought so, because you do look pretty shitty.

Not nice, is it? To say that to a girl. Not really what she wants to hear when she's already feeling pretty bloody lousy. And today on the Heath, she looked really lovely, actually – with the sun on her hair, her gorgeous bare legs and that little flowery skirt and everything. I should've taken a picture of her when she asked me to. I wanted to. I wish I had. And I'm really sorry about the Mint Chocs. I'm really sorry that they melted – because she only bought them because she knows I like them, and they're not cheap, you know: they're not at all cheap, and she hasn't got a lot of money. I even felt bad as I was watching her heaving that bag across the Heath. So many times I nearly said to her – here, give it, give it to me: I'll carry it. Yeh, but I didn't. Did I? I've really messed up this picnic – and I was so looking forward to whatever it was that she'd planned: really pleased when she told me it was a picnic, can't remember the last time I went on one of those . . . and yet I didn't say a word. Not a bloody word. Was enjoying it, yes I was . . . but still though, I was pleased that I'd arranged to meet Sammy here. Because although it was nice in one way, sitting in that really lovely spot next to the water and that great old bridge which I never even knew existed . . . and I was with my girlfriend, and there was sunshine, decent grub and everything . . . still though after about ten minutes of that, I'd had enough. Like I knew I would. Why? Don't know. Can't explain. I think there just must be something wrong with me. I can't say any of this to Dorothy – what I'm thinking, what I'm feeling. I've tried – once or twice I've sort of started to when I can see that I've begun to upset her again like I always seem to do, but when it actually comes down to it, I can't, I just can't, I don't know why. I can't even bring myself to tell Sammy about it either, which is even more weird actually because Sammy, I talk to him all the time about anything in the world, tell him absolutely everything. Except for this. So now they both of them, Sammy and Dorothy, think I'm a complete and utter shit, and that I'm too stupid and insensitive to even know it. But I do know it, I do – and that's why I also know that there has to be something wrong with me . . . I just can't imagine what it can be.

'Here we are, mate – one pint of Long Life. Good luck to you.'

Sammy's boots as well – haven't seen them before either. Cuban heel, centre seam, chisel-pointed toe. Just like The Beatles – probably literally: Anello & Davide, I should think, knowing Sammy. Christ. I can't stand it, really. I can't stand any of it.

'Thanks, Sammy – life-saver. Oh god, yeah – lovely. Why did it take so long? You were gone ages.'

'Oh – some ancient old bugger at the bar started on at me. You know the type – moustache, badge on his bloody blazer, stinking pipe in his rotten old mouth. Fought the war for the sake of unwashed little bastards like me and I want to get my hair cut because I look like a bloody *girl* . . .'

'Stupid old bastard. They should be killed, I think. Old men.'

'I didn't get Dorothy anything. Thought I'd wait till she got back and ask her what she wants. Where's she gone, actually? Taking a hell of a while . . .'

'Christ knows what she gets up to. No idea. Lavatory, didn't she say . . .? Or "toilet". I always say toilet, now – or I do if she's ever around, anyway. Drives her crazy.'

'Well why do you say it, then? If it drives her crazy.'

'Oh . . . I don't know. Something to do. Sometimes I quite like to annoy her. Wind her up. Get a reaction. Because she's not *always* perfect, you know. You only ever see what she wants to show you. Like – last night, after we left you, yes?'

'What about it?'

'Well – I wanted her to come back with me, didn't I? Only natural. Christ – she is meant to be my *girlfriend* . . .'

'And, what – she didn't, then.'

'No she bloody didn't. Had to get home to her crackpot bleeding mummy. Jesus. It wasn't even late . . .'

'Well it's your fault she's got to traipse all the way back to wherever it is every evening. Edgware, is it? Where she lives?'

'Edgware, yeah. Why's it my fault?'

'Because you don't want her staying with you. Do you?'

'I do . . .! Well no – not in that sense, no. I mean . . . I want her to stay with me, yeah . . . but then I want her to go. Don't you? Don't you feel like that? Can't stand it when they want to hang around afterwards – all talking and stroking, and stuff. Just have a fag and fuck off, no? What – have her with me all the time, do you mean . . .?'

'That's what she wants. You can tell. It's obvious.'

'Yeah . . .? Well she's not going to bloody well get it, matey, I can tell you that. What – you mean have her *living* with me? With all her stuff, and everything? That what you mean? Night and day? Christ no. Drive me mad.'

'Well then you can't complain if she's got to get back for her Führer mother's curfew. Can you?'

'Suppose not . . .'

'No but you do, don't you?'

'Do what?'

'Complain.'

'Yeh . . . I do. I suppose I do. Anyway – last night, okay? I was really fed up with her for going. You know? Really pissed off. Because I was properly in the mood, yeah?'

'So what did you do?'

'Shi-vawn.'

'*What* . . .? What the hell's that? Pass me a fag, can you?'

'It's not an "it", it's a "she". Irish name. That's how it's pronounced. Christ knows how it's spelt. Daughter of the people downstairs. Paying a visit from Bogland, apparently. Yeah I think I'll have a fag as well . . .'

'What . . . you mean you . . .?'

'Yeh. Why not? I gave her the option didn't I? Dorothy. And Shi-vawn – she was willing enough, I can tell you. Hot little number. Lovely bird, actually – noticed her once or twice before when she's been over, but I never did anything about it. Long blonde hair. Skirt you can hardly see. Difficult to know what she's talking about with her Christawful accent and everything – but Jesus, who's listening? One of her eyelashes came off while we were doing it. Huge thing, like Dusty's. Didn't even twig they were fake till it happened. She brought along a bottle of Jameson's. Not too bad at all. Bit of a result.'

'You little devil. Dorothy doesn't know, does she? She on the Pill, by the way? I meant to ask you. My latest is. Trixie.'

'Trixie . . .? Blimey. You haven't told me about Trixie. Yeh, course she's on the Pill. I'm not going to be using johnnies, am I? Well I suppose she is, anyway – never really asked her. And Christ no. I'm not going to go and *tell* her, am I? About Shi-vawn, you mean? Not that much of an idiot. I mean – it's not that I feel bad about it, or anything. Why should I? Not married, are we? I've made no promises. Haven't even known her that long – only a couple of months, bit longer. And I asked her, didn't I? I asked her to stay, and she wouldn't. Not my fault. Yeh well. Look, Sammy – I would get us in another, but I seem to have come out without any money at all. Don't know quite how I managed to do that, but I did. Sorry.'

'Yeh well – probably the same way you managed it last time,

I expect. Okay, Georgie – here's ten bob. You do it, can you? And you'd better get more fags while you're at it, rate you're going through them. Should we get something for Dorothy . . .? Maybe we should.'

'She'll probably want Tizer, or something.'

'You see – you're doing it again. Always putting her down . . .'

'No I meant it, actually. It's the sort of thing she likes.'

'Well just get her a Coke, then. That should be okay.'

Straight away at the bar I clocked the old git who had just given Sammy an earful. Face pretty red, but blotchy with these brown sort of spots, and his moustache all yellow. Chain on his waistcoat across a big fat belly. He glared at me, and I glared right back. He didn't say anything, though – I was ready for it, I tell you . . . but after, I was really quite glad that he hadn't because I'd had a couple of full pint mugs in my hands at the time, and I would've happily smashed them right into his big red stupid and ugly face, I'm telling you. Got a Coke with a straw for Dorothy, wherever the bloody hell Dorothy's got to – had a sort of a look about, couldn't see her – and twenty Bensons and a couple of packets of crisps. Bit hungry again. I had to top up Sammy's ten-bob note with a bit of my own – because I wasn't completely out of money, I never am: always carry a little bit, just to be on the safe side. It's not that I'm mean . . . I don't think I'm mean, anyway. Not how I see myself. It's just that Sammy, he's always got money – he's always got everything. Doesn't even have to go to work – just some parent-funded course, or something, which is only a couple of days a week . . . and then they give him all of this dosh on the top of it. So I'm just helping him out, really – helping him get rid of a bit of it . . . because there will always be more: they're never going to let him go short, are they? His parents. It was tricky, balancing the tray and carting it all back over to the table, because the place had really filled up a lot, by now.

'Couple of lovely birds up at the bar – did you see them? Could be au pairs, or something. One of them was sort of looking at me, so I gave her bum a little squeeze. She liked that. Was giggling, you know? They were drinking shandy. Didn't want to leave them, really – seemed a bit of a waste. Oh yeh, Sammy – did you see in the papers?'

'See what in the papers, Georgie? Lots in the papers, isn't there? They weren't at the bar when I was there. Didn't see any girls . . .'

'About the mods and rockers. Kicking off again this weekend, apparently. Tomorrow, I think. Margate or Brighton or somewhere. Well they must have just come in, then.'

'I think they only do it because it gets in the papers. Why would they do it otherwise? Sorry I missed those birds – good, are they?'

'Cracking. I said. Well those rockers, you know – pretty vicious people.'

'And the mods aren't . . .? Maybe they'll still be around later. Chat them up. Yeh but you're with Dorothy, remember? Wherever she is.'

'Yeh I know. I do know that. But yeah, the mods can dish it out, no doubt about that, but they're a lot less nasty, I'd say. More into the clothes, aren't they? All the Fred Perrys and Crombies. And they like those sort of American button-down shirts, don't they? They're pretty cool, actually. You've got some of those, haven't you Sammy? Ben Sherman, are they?'

'Yeah. English, actually – not American. Well what are they fighting for, then? The mods. Mess up the clothes, won't they?'

'Why they wear those horrible parkas on the top, maybe. I

don't know. Obviously I'd rather be a mod than a rocker. Those Vespas are the gear.'

'Bit of a comedown from an E-Type . . .'

'Well yeh – I'll take the E-Type if you're offering, Sammy. Crisp? You want a crisp . . .? . . . where the fuck is Dorothy? Been gone for ever . . .'

'Well I hope she's okay . . . should we check, do you think? Think I will. I'll have a look about.'

There's another good example: that's what I'm thinking now, as I'm watching Sammy push back his chair and set to having a wander about the place. So many nooks and crannies, it'll take some doing. But what I mean is, I was a bit worried too, if I'm honest. About Dorothy. Maybe she's sick. But I didn't say it, did I? I just said 'where the fuck is she?' – like she was just being a bloody nuisance, or something. But Sammy – he's gone to look for her. She's my girlfriend, supposed to be – but it's Sammy who's gone off to look for her. Because he's a good bloke, Sammy . . . and he probably thought . . . he was probably thinking, well look: someone's got to – and it's not going to be Georgie, is it? No it isn't – because Georgie, he never does anything decent. Just sits there – fuming, moaning, sponging money and smoking my fags. And he's right, that's the trouble. I think there must be something wrong with me.

'That was quick. Any luck? Did you find her?'

'Well . . . yeah . . .'

'She okay?'

'Well she – yeah. Seems fine, actually.'

'Well what the fuck is she doing? Where is she?'

'She's in one of those little alcoves round the corner.'

'Yeh? Well what's she bloody doing there? She coming over?'

'Well I'm not sure that she is, actually, Georgie. She's with some bloke.'

'What . . .?

'Yeah . . .'

'What do you mean . . .?'

'Christ. What do you mean what do I *mean* . . .? I told you: she's with a bloke.'

'What "bloke" . . .?'

'Jesus – how do I know? Some bloke, that's all.'

'Right . . .'

'Now listen, Georgie . . . don't do anything . . . stupid, okay? It's maybe an old friend. Relative, maybe . . .'

'What are they doing?'

'What . . .?'

'The two of them in the little bloody alcove. What are they doing?'

'Well they're not doing anything. Talking. Having a drink.'

'Oh right. So we can dump the Coke, then. What's she having? Tizer?'

'Christ, Georgie . . .'

'Did she see you?'

'Did she see me? Yeh – she saw me.'

'And she didn't . . . move, or anything.'

'No. She didn't do anything.'

'Right, then. Okay. Think I'll have another fag.'

'So you're not . . .'

'Not what?'

'Going to – do anything.'

'No. Don't think so. What should I do? If that's where she wants to be . . .'

'I'm amazed.'

'Yeh?'

'I'm completely amazed. This isn't like you, Georgie. Not like you at all. I thought you'd be round there with a hammer, or something. Shouting and screaming.'

'Yeh? Well that just goes to show little you know me then, doesn't it Sammy? Because I'm not going to do any of that. Here – drink your pint.'

'So . . . what? That's that then, is it . . .?'

'Yeh, Sammy. It is. That's that.'

'Incredible . . .'

'Is it? It's not really. Jesus, Sammy – she's only a *girl*. Isn't she? Only another bird. Lots of birds around. Aren't there? Just look at Shi-vawn. Those two up at the bar. So maybe it's a good thing. Maybe it's time.'

'You're nuts if you think that, Georgie.'

'Maybe.'

'No maybe about it. You're crazy if you let her go. She's not just another "bird" – she never was. She's really good, Dorothy. I've said it before. You don't want to let her go.'

'Well I'm not so sure about that. Maybe I do. Maybe that's exactly what I want. What say we walk across the Heath and have a last one at Jack Straw's Castle?'

'You really just going to walk away . . .?'

'I am, yeah. Look at me, Sammy: I've stood up, yes? And I'm walking. See me walking? One foot in front of the other. And now I'm just walking away. Let's see if those two birds are still there. They might be in the mood for a bit of a stroll, who knows? So . . . you coming or not?'

CHAPTER FOUR

OTHER WAYS OUT

I don't want to go anywhere. And if I do go somewhere – if I find myself attending some damn dinner or charity bash or whatever the hell I agreed to just so bloody long ago as to be completely insanely positive that the date would never actually arrive – then all I am thinking is Christ, why did I do this? Why did I come here? What am I doing, sitting in this chair? Eating food I do not choose to. Trying for another drink when there is no more. Uttering words I am barely able to form to people who nod, and are grinningly unhearing. How soon will it be before I can get out? And if, as sometimes happens – though never nearly often enough – someone cancels at the very last moment, oh . . . I hug that cancellation to me as if it is the very most precious gift. When that happens, it's actually close to thrilling. Jesus, though – what a difference from the way I was. How I used to be. Hardly believe I'm the same person – doesn't seem possible. Out all the time, when I was young. Loved it. Being in, staying at home – I thought it was the same as being dead. Amazing to think it now, but I did, I really did. Being in, it was just like the night, but without any sleep: the grogginess of insomnia overlain by the black and crushing shame of having failed – wide-eyed and semi-delirious, unreasonably maddened by fractured fantasies of all the abandoned fun being riotously enjoyed by just everybody else on earth, except me. But if I was in, if that was my fate, if I absolutely had to be, well then I'd need to have somebody over. Lots of people, preferably – didn't matter too much who, exactly . . . just so long as they were there. Drink, smoke, talk, records. Never got tired of that. Drive me mental, now. Because these days, well . . . I yearn for a day of nothing, all on my own. Yes . . . yes but I dread it too, dread even the thought of it – terrifies me, frankly . . . which is why I suppose it never really happens: why it never actually can quite come off. But in my mind, anyway, that's what I want. Yearn for. That's the theory. A day of nothing, all on my own. I never would actually go through with it, though. Even the thought, it makes me shiver. Because you see . . . well, the God's honest truth of the matter is that I'm not at all sure that I could, in the end . . . sustain, or entertain me.

I don't look at women any more, because they don't look at me. So why should I? Went through a phase – how long ago? Five years? Less than that? Something. Went through a phase – or they did, anyway – when yes they were looking, they still were looking, but they were looking at me differently. Not how it was. Can't explain – just sensed it. Well no, I didn't sense it, actually – I didn't bloody sense it at all: I saw it perfectly plainly, it was right in front of my face, insolently hanging there. What it was, you see . . . well how can I . . .? Well they just didn't look in the way that a woman should rightly be looking at a man. Like women used to look at me. There was no squeak of contact – no earthy whiff of mutual recognition. No glimmer in the eye. No spark of what might once have taken light. But, well . . . at least they were looking, though. Now they don't. Look at all. Don't even register that I'm there. And how much of that is to do with me? I have asked myself that. Do I shrink, from within? Do I stare downwards, or even up? Are my eyes just two dead blanks? Don't know. But if so, if I am all bricked up, then none of it is conscious. I am how I am, that's all. I don't rehearse. I am not posturing. I am how I am, that's all. But anyway . . . they don't look. At me. Any more. So I don't look at them. Why should I?

They say you're as young as you feel. That's what they say. They say a great deal of stupid and really fucking annoying things, don't they, on the whole? And that is just one of them. So all right, then: how do I feel . . .? I feel fine. As The Beatles have so very memorably sung to me, and how many thousands of times . . .?. No but I do – I feel fine, averagely fine. Considering. I feel . . . spry. Christ – what a word. What does it mean? Young people don't ever, do they? Feel spry. Only broken old sods like me can ever get to feel spry. Used to be a sort of cooking fat, Spry. In the Sixties. One of the so many brands I just can't help remembering. Like a Wall's Neapolitan Family Brick . . . Old Spice, Omo, 1001 Carpet Cleaner . . . Esso Blue paraffin. And Cadbury's Lucky Numbers – Christ knows why I should remember those of all things, because it was Mint Chocs I liked the most. Clarnico. But I ramble, as derelicts will, God curse it. But yes – Spry. Lard, it was. Probably got it from dead old men – which I would have been very much all in favour of, at the time: hated old people, hated them. Still do, in many ways: my actually being one of them hardly can alter the fact: old people, they are so very aesthetically distressing. Lard, yes. From dead old men. Useless blubber, rendered down. God, oh God. Still I do feel it, though – what I was saying: spry. If it means what I think it does. What can it mean, exactly? Full of vim, all things taken into account . . .? Still able to get up the stairs? Striding about a field or shoreline with an elegant and well-preserved white-haired woman, and grinning maniacally like some stupid old fucker in a life assurance ad or a commercial for a cruise, or even a retirement home. Life in the old dog yet. Well preserved, yes. As in virtually embalmed. Sprightly, Christ save us. Another thing that young people aren't. Not sprightly. Young people . . . they're just . . . *alive*. And that – along with love – is all you need. Me – I'm dead inside. And that's where it counts. On the surface, I can be whatever you want me to be, really . . . yeh, but I'm dead inside. That's the trouble. Dead . . .? Or merely comatose? There's a difference. Big difference. Because being dead, well . . . that's irreversible, we all know that. But people do – awake from a coma. A coma, it allows for resuscitation. Just need the right sort of stimulus. All it needs. So where do you get that from? I wonder. Anna . . . well, when I'm around Anna, that lifts me up. Yes but that . . . that's just a father's joy – still a far cry from, I don't know . . . the thump of a meaningful heartbeat. Recovery. Salvation. Living again. Remembering how to. All that.

Woman, really – it's got to be a woman. Every man will know this. To get everything pumping again. Not your wife – not Enid. Well of course not Enid – you've just got to take one look at her. And nor anyone elegant, well-preserved and white-haired, for God's sake. No – I'm talking about something that is actually and truly recognisable as a young and fully-fledged woman, you know exactly the sort of thing I'm talking about. A centrefold made flesh. Flesh, mm. And no I'm not ashamed, as a matter of fact – I'm not remotely ashamed of thinking such things: and I'd voice them too, were there any point in speaking. Good news, I'd say – that I feel that way. For isn't this the much-required evidence, actually? That there is still, maybe, just a shudder of hope . . .? Yes and I've been thinking that for quite some time now, as a matter of fact. Just a question of how to go about it. I was actually intending to pursue the thought this very day . . . but just that little memory of Anna, there . . . the realisation that my dear little Anna is back at the forefront of my mind – and she's never that far away, not really – means that I'll have to dwell on that, think of her now, for just a little bit, anyway. Because I'm concerned, you know. I sense that all is far from well. Anna . . . I know her, you see . . . and there's something . . . well what can I say? Clearly, there's something she's not telling me. Hurts me, really. Because we used to talk, Anna and I – we used to talk all the time. She would confide in me. First port of call. Trusted me, you see. There's nothing we wouldn't discuss. It's that bastard she went and married – it's he who bloody well messed up everything. Of course I was passionately against her marrying him in the first place – knew he was no good, fucking Max, the minute I set eyes on him, the bastard. The bastard, bastard. Anna, she wouldn't listen. All I did was make her more determined – the force of my opposition, it just made her even more determined. Saw very little of her, once she was with him. Felt bereaved. I consoled myself by thinking that, well . . . she seemed contented enough, or so I could only suppose. But why should Anna, my only daughter, be no more than merely contented? She's worth more than that. Far more. She could have had anyone, my Anna. She could have had her pick. Beautiful, intelligent, capable, loving . . . she could have anyone she wanted. Instead, she goes and marries this fucking spiv, who two minutes later ups and bloody leaves her . . .! And his child – his son. Left him. Just walked away. Never looked back. What sort of a man can do a thing like that? And it wasn't a question of irretrievable breakdown, or whatever they call it – no discussion of any kind, so far as I could gather. It just ended.

Anna, she'd come over one evening – never forget it, never forget that evening – and I was delighted to see her, of course I was. Surprised that she'd just suddenly turned up out of the blue, no announcement – but delighted, quite delighted. And over dinner I could see that she was far from easy. I know her, you see, and I detected that much more or less immediately. Something nagging at her: something on her mind. Enid, she was rattling on about, oh Christ . . . all the bloody twaddle that will just constantly spill out of her, if ever she does us the goodness of actually speaking at all. She notices nothing, senses nothing, Enid. Open to no nuance, deaf to an atmosphere, unseeing even of any gaudy alarm. She just sat there, blind. Yattering on. I love her – I really do love that stupid woman, but Christ . . . at times she can come very close indeed to driving me absolutely mental. Sometimes . . . I shouldn't say this, I really shouldn't . . . but sometimes, she's so desperately, unfathomably bloody *boring* that I wish to Christ she'd take a drink again. I know, it's an awful thing to say, quite awful – even to think it, it's just so terrible . . . because I'm quite positive it would kill her, it would literally kill her, if she ever went back to it. But it has to be said that back in the day, she was a hell of a lot more fun to be with. Selfish attitude, I'm aware of that – but there it is. Anyway – back to that evening when Anna came round: kid was asleep, I think I'm right in saying. Upstairs, maybe. Somewhere else, anyway – because he wasn't around, that I do know. And after practically no sort of probing on my part, Anna . . . she put down her fork and knife – and she'd only been picking anyway, I'd noticed that, and normally she has a very good appetite, always been one for her food – she just quietly put down her fork and knife, looked up and then said to me:

'Daddy . . . I think he's gone. Left us. Not completely sure . . . but it looks like he's not coming back. It's really very odd . . .'

I looked back at her. I just was staring at her, really – gaping, more or less, I suppose I must have been. Wasn't even positive that I understood what she was actually saying to me. Glanced over at Enid: blank, as usual. Eating Brussel sprouts, as I recall, for all the world as if she was on a solitary picnic in a soundproof booth.

'What . . . do you mean, Anna? Husband we're talking about, yes . . .?'

'Mm. He seems to have gone.'

'Business, maybe . . .? Often does that, doesn't he? Didn't he tell you where he was going?'

'He doesn't, usually. Just goes. Then he comes back. But this time . . . he hasn't. Come back, I mean. Been a few days. No call, or anything. Took more with him than he generally does. Two big bags. Most of his clothes – all his best things, anyway.'

'Well . . . he'll turn up soon, of course he will. I'm sure you'll hear from him before too long.'

I said that while feeling sure of no such thing. I was actually hopeful that what she said was right – wishing to God he'd stay away.

'Don't think so, Daddy. Money, you see: it's all gone. Everything.'

Well that just did it for me, quite frankly. Went mad. Didn't mean to. Wanted to remain quite calm and measured and quietly in control: wanted to be the brick for her to rely on. Wasn't. Went mad. Subjected her to the most appalling I Told You So rant, grilled her over every detail – made her cry: last thing I wanted or intended, but Christ – I was just so unbelievably . . . *furious*. Well, there it was. All history now. But as a result of this unspeakable fiasco, Anna – she has to leave her child with some or other woman whom she pays, and then she goes to work. I just can't believe it. How many times have I told her she doesn't have to? Won't listen. Independent, you see? Headstrong – self-willed. Like her father, I suppose. I admire it in her, of course I do. But I vowed to myself on that very evening that I'd track him down, this useless bloody so-called husband of hers. Straight away put a private detective on to it – and it quickly became clear that wherever the fucker had run to, he was taking very great care not to be found. I mean – let's make this quite clear: I don't want him to come *back* – of course I don't want that: never want Anna to set eyes on the cunt again. Don't even care about screwing out of him punitive financial damages – don't care about any of that because I can perfectly happily take care of Anna, take care of the boy and everything. Education, and so on. And anyway – I doubt he's got any money: spivs, they don't, not for long. No but still, I do remain committed to tracking him down, wherever the bastard has gone to earth: that detective, I've still got him on the case. This man must be found . . . because simply . . . I need to do him harm.

And now my little Anna . . . something else is wrong in her life, I just know there is, but she doesn't choose to talk to me about it. Well, maybe she will. Given time, maybe she will. Because I yearn to help her, whatever the problem might be. And as I've been just sitting here . . . going over all of this in my mind . . . I suddenly am aware of Enid. She's put down whatever is the latest embroidery she's been horsing around with – she's a devil for embroidery, the house is jammed with the muck – and she seems to be more or less eying me. Is she now going to say something, do we think . . .? No . . . it doesn't quite look like it. She's just going to continue looking at me narrowly then, it surely would seem. I know that expression, oh Lord yes – that particular one, I know it very well. It's among the elite, that one is – that's one of the expressions which clearly she cherishes above rubies, along with, say, the other indomitable classic that involves the supplicatory upturning of eyes, this mawkish affectation contrasting so very perfectly – sweetly, you might say – with a sour and downturned mouth . . . all to convey the fleeting wince of a deep-felt and regularly recurring hurt which first had been unwittingly inflicted upon her at some point during the Crusades, conceivably – possibly the Napoleonic Wars. But this one, this rather vulpine shrinkage in the eye department, matched to a pursing of the lip – this is one that harks back, actually (though in diminished form, and heartrendingly shrivelled) to the very first time I met her. All those eons ago. Which was an extremely odd circumstance, I think we can all agree . . . and one that I am unlikely to forget. I do, it is true, tend to forget, oh . . . rather a lot of things, these days – but largely only the nonsense of a couple of weeks or minutes ago, nothing really load-bearing. The old stuff, though . . . that seems to cleave to me: all the old stuff, it stays for ever.

Just leaving this restaurant, we were, and the woman turns to me and she says . . . but wait just a minute: how old can I have been? Back then. How many years ago was this, actually? Thirty-five, it could easily be. Thirty-five years ago – actually rather more. Forty, might be. Half my life, and then some. Two-thirds, nearly. Anyway, we were just getting on our coats after a pretty decent dinner somewhere down in Soho, no way I can remember the name of the place (but it will have been pretty good because by this time I was starting to rake in more or less proper money and was getting to know a little bit about food and wine) and the woman, she says to me Oh no, George – that waitress . . .! The waitress – I don't believe it! – the waitress, she's just gone off with my umbrella . . .! What, I said – are you sure . . .? And then she's saying to me Well no, I wasn't sure – not at first, but now I am . . . because I was just actually thinking, George, that it was rather odd for the waitress to be leaving before the restaurant has closed, and then I thought oh look: what an amazing coincidence – her umbrella is exactly the same as mine. So I yawned elaborately and said to her well there you are, then – just a similar umbrella, that's all. No, she said, that's not all – is it, George? Because it isn't similar, I didn't say similar – it's identical. And mine isn't here, is it? It's gone – because that bloody little waitress has just walked off with it . . .! And another thing – it was Dior: how can a waitress have a Dior umbrella? I just looked at her at this point and said in I imagine a thoroughly stupefied manner: *Dior . . .?* What do you mean 'Dior' . . .? How in Christ's name can an umbrella be *Dior . . .?* It's an *umbrella,* for Jesus' sake. And she said oh God George you're just so completely *ignorant* when it comes to just anything at all like this: just take my word for it – it was Dior, and bloody expensive and now some moronic little waitress has just as calm as you like gone and swanned off with the wretched thing . . .! Before our very noses! So what are you going to *do* about it, George . . .? Well groan out loud, if you really want to know – because this, all this, I was honestly finding it most awfully tedious. So I sighed very heavily, I hope theatrically, and then I sort of conveyed to the manager of the place the simple bones of the thing, once some minion had eventually dredged him up – hadn't seen the little bastard from one end of the evening to the other – and he said well that's really very unfortunate and I am so desperately sorry and all the rest of his craven and weasel apology . . . and then he goes on to say that she's left, the waitress: she's left. And I was getting mighty fed up with the whole damn thing by now, as well as this fucking little snivelly manager person, so I said to him really quite forcefully that I *knew* that she'd left – we'd seen that she'd *left*, we are both very well aware that she's *left* – but what in God's name did he intend to do about it? No, he said – you don't understand: I mean she's left, left the company, she no longer works for us, this was her very last shift. Well phone her, I said. Well sir, he's going – in the circumstances I don't really think that I can do that, you see, because as she is no longer in our employ, we have no jurisdiction, as it were. And I could have ranted on about how it's his responsibility, he's the manager, it's his restaurant, his ex-member of staff, the whole damn thing . . . but all I did say was well give me her bloody number then, and *I'll* ring her. So he did that – glad to be shot of me. And the following morning, I went through with it – telephoning a waitress about a fucking umbrella. And the woman, while we were still in the restaurant, all the time I'd been talking she'd been hissing at me *Now*! Ring her *now*, George – Christ's sake do it *now* – what's *wrong* with you at all? And I said no. I'm not doing it now. No intention of doing it now. I'm tired. I want to go home. I want to go to sleep. God Almighty – I don't think she's going to fence it overnight, this bloody umbrella of yours. Little danger of her, I don't know – having it resprayed and shipped out in a crate of apples to Bogotá or some other godforsaken corner of the bloody universe . . .! I'll phone her in the morning. Now let's just find a bloody taxi, for God's sake – and in Christ's name will you please just stop *moaning* about it, all right? It's only a sodding *umbrella* . . .! No sex that night, needless to say.

So. Following morning:

'Oh, hello – um. You don't know me, but I was at the restaurant last night. Restaurant you work in. Used to work in. Soho. Yes?'

'You're George, aren't you?'

Well that bloody threw me, I can tell you.

'Er . . . yes. Yes I am. How did you, er . . .?'

'I heard you talking. I heard her say your name. Nice name: George. I wasn't deliberately eavesdropping, or anything – but it's difficult in that job not to, you know . . . hear things. Bits and bobs.'

'Right. Well anyway, the thing is . . .'

'I knew you'd call.'

'I'm sorry . . .?'

'I knew you would. I just knew you'd find out my number and call me. Because of this *thing*. There was a *thing*, wasn't there?'

'There was a *what*? A *thing* . . .? What *thing* . . .? Umbrella, you mean . . .?'

'Between us. A thing. I know you felt it.'

'*Between* us . . .? Honestly, I have not the slightest idea what you're *talking* about. I'm phoning about the *umbrella* . . .'

'Oh yes. I know. That's why I took it. I thought, well – if he's too shy, this will give him a reason. An excuse. To get in touch. Because I knew the restaurant wouldn't. Call me. Not after sacking me, they wouldn't. Pleased to see the back of me, I expect. And that woman you were with, whoever she was – she wasn't going to either. She would see it as completely beneath herself, wouldn't she? Talking to a waitress. Probably gets you to do everything for her, doesn't she, George? Poor George. So you see – I knew it would be you.'

'Look, whatever your name is . . . I think you've rather got the wrong end of the stick here, if you'll forgive my saying. You seem to be imagining all sorts of frankly completely crazy things that just aren't . . .! Look: this is stupid. Never mind all that. Any of that nonsense. Let's just focus, shall we? The umbrella, yes? You admit you took it, then?'

'Of course. I've just said so.'

'Right. Well do you intend giving it back?'

'Oh God yes. I hate it. So vulgar. Don't you think so? I mean I ask you – who in their right mind would pay a fortune for an umbrella from Christian Dior? Preposterous, isn't it really?'

'Well maybe. Not the point. The point is that if you do intend to keep it, well then I shall have no alternative to bringing in the police. Do you understand?'

'Oh *I* understand – I understand perfectly, George. It's you who doesn't seem to understand. I've *told* you, haven't I? I don't want the beastly umbrella. It's vile. Come and collect it.'

'Well . . . I don't really see why I should have to go and . . .'

'No. You're right. Okay then – I'll meet you. Tell me where and when. I can be anywhere. Any time. Now I don't have a job any more . . .'

'Well . . . can't you just, I don't know . . . post it, or something . . .?'

'You wouldn't trust me to. Would you, George? I'll say I'll put it in the afternoon post, but you'd never believe that I'd actually do it. Why would you trust a common thief? And another thing – you wouldn't really want to give your address to a complete and utter stranger. Would you, George? No: it's better all round that we meet, I think. Then at least you'll be sure. Won't you? Of getting it back.'

'Well . . . all right then. I suppose. Are you near Victoria Station at all?'

'No. But I can be.'

'It's just that I happen to be in the area.'

'Fine. An hour?'

'An hour, yes. Or less, if you like – otherwise I'll be hanging about. Half an hour, say . . .? That suit you?'

'Fine. And then you can finally get to talk to me. You know – properly. I know how much you want to. And I do – I do too.'

'*Talk* to you? What about? I don't want to *talk* to you – I just want to get this sodding umbrella back and then I'm off, I do assure you . . .'

'Well . . . that's what you say. I suppose you have to, don't you really? Say that. Keep up a front. Whereabouts in Victoria?'

'Oh . . . well there's a hotel on the concourse. Grosvenor. Know it? What do you mean a "front" . . .? I'm not keeping up any bloody *front* . . .'

'I'll find it. See you in half an hour, then. In the foyer?'

'Foyer, yes. And Christ's sake don't forget the bloody umbrella.'

'No. Otherwise you'd be in trouble, wouldn't you George? With Little Miss Bossyboots. She's not right for you, you know. That woman. Not right at all. You need someone much more sensitive. To your needs, you know? Someone a whole lot more loving.'

'Uh-huh. And you'd know all about that, wouldn't you? Look – this is stupid. Completely ridiculous. I'm hanging up. I'll see you in half an hour. And don't be late.'

'Won't be. I know you don't want to be hanging around.

Gosh – how terribly exciting – an assignation . . .! A tryst . . .! I really am so terribly looking forward to meeting you, George. Are you looking forward to meeting me too . . .? I just know you are.'

'*Jesus* . . .! Look – just be there, all right?'

'I will be. Half an hour. Promise. And oh – I'm Enid, by the way.'

For yes indeed: that was Enid.

And she was late, of course. Christ, I was fuming. Went to the bar, eventually. Couldn't hang around in the foyer any longer: person behind the desk there – he kept on sort of looking at me. So: in the bar – just sitting there, in a place I had no intention of ever being. Just sitting there waiting for a waitress called Enid to come and return a bloody Dior umbrella that she had brazenly filched from . . . well that's why I've been calling her 'the woman', you see – that person I'd been dining with. Because I can't remember her name, and I'm not even going to try and have a stab at it. 'Helen' is banging around in my mind, but it could just as easily be Harriet or, let's face it, Hortense or Henrietta – not to say, of course, some other bloody name beginning with a different letter entirely. I hadn't been with her for terribly long, I don't think. No very lasting impression. Certainly she annoyed me to bits – but then most of them did, really, after a pretty short while. She had wonderful legs, I do remember that much – no one wore very high-heeled shoes with such arrogant elegance and quite sinuous grace and downright boiling sexiness, even if it did mean that she rather towered above me. But why did I *obey* her . . .? I know that that was a feature of our relationship, and normally, of course . . . well: I'm not like that at all. But on this very occasion, for instance – why did I hurry to pursue some waitress simply because she had *told* me to . . .? Unfathomable, now. Anyway – it's just as well I did. Otherwise, well . . . I never would have met her, Enid. The mother of my children. So it's just as well I did. In one way.

'Where in God's name have you *been* . . .? Jesus. Half an hour, we said.'

'What's that you're drinking . . .?'

'What? It's a . . . look – what the hell does it matter what I'm drinking? Where have you *been*? Have you got the umbrella? You'd better have that umbrella . . .'

'Well it matters because if I like the sound of it, I thought I might have one too.'

'Oh *did* you? Well that's very, um . . . something of you. Can't think of the word . . .'

'Presumptuous . . .?'

'Presumptuous, yes, Exactly. Where's the umbrella? I don't see it.'

'May I sit down?'

'What?'

'May I sit down?'

'Yes I heard what you *said* . . . what do you want to sit down for? This isn't a social occasion. This isn't a *party*, you know. Just give me the umbrella and you can go.'

'You're not being awfully polite.'

'Well why should I be? I'm talking to a waitress who stole my girlfriend's umbrella.'

'Ex-waitress. So she's just a girlfriend then, is she?'

'Oh God yes. Nothing more. Why am I telling you this . . .?'

'May I sit down?'

'Oh Christ. Yes. Yes – sit down, if you want to.'

'And that drink is . . .?'

'Hm? Oh – the drink, yes. Campari. With tonic. Better than soda, I think.'

'Lovely. That would be lovely.'

'What . . .?'

'Well it looks like you'll be ordering another in a moment. That one's just more or less ice, now. Isn't it? So you might really just as well order two. Don't you think?'

So what could I say, really? She sat. I ordered drinks. I ordered more. She was pretty, very. In a simple and very straightforward sort of a way. Refreshing, is what she was. To my eyes. Hardly any make-up. Hint of lipstick, maybe. The ironic light that sprang into her eyes. The way they glittered as she cheekily narrowed them down. The wrinkle of her nose when she chucked up her chin as she laughed. Which she did quite a lot. And I did too – Christ knows what about. Within an hour . . . I was captivated. An hour? No – less. Much less than that. When she walked in the door, really. And oh yes: she hadn't, actually, brought the umbrella. She said she was going to – she had it in her hand, it was honestly her intention – but then on an impulse she had handed it to a homeless woman who had been covered in bags and rags and didn't, said Enid, look at all pleased with it. I so didn't care. How could I care about that? Already I had decided that I wouldn't be seeing 'the woman' any more. Would be taking no more orders from her. Legs, or not. How could I care about her? Let her sue me for the cost of the umbrella. Because now, well . . . I was captivated. And Enid, she had divined it: there truly did appear to be a *thing* . . .

Hard to believe. So impossibly hard to believe that the woman before me now – that woman who is narrowing her eyes in presumably more or less precisely the same way as she always has . . . same eyes, after all . . . same muscles that are brought into play . . . it is just not even feasible that here is the Enid of the Grosvenor Hotel, from all those dusty decades ago. Christ. Oh Christ. It's all just so terribly sad. Do you know what I wrote to her? Soon, very soon after, I wrote to her in a letter – and I'll never forget it, of course I won't: how could I ever forget it . . .? I wrote to her, 'I will love you unto the door of death, and then eternally beyond.' It's all just so terribly, terribly sad . . . and I think I may quite need to cry, now.

'Do you want tea?'

'Tea? No, I don't think so, thank you, Enid. Got a drink, haven't I?'

'Well I think I'll make myself a cup. Are you sure . . .?'

'Quite sure, thank you.'

'Well I'm going to make some anyway.'

'Fine.'

'But you don't want it? Sure? You're sure?'

'I have said . . .'

'Right, then. Well I'll just make a cup for myself.'

Yes I will – and you can continue to wallow, George, in whatever is the newest rot that you're conjuring up now, in that bloated, biased and ultimately quite thoroughly inconsequential little mind of yours: a stew of hate, and utter wrong-headedness. I daresay you'd be really rather surprised, wouldn't you George, to know that I am capable of perception, or even to feel such things, let alone articulate: adequately express them – rather as I used to. He thinks I'm stupid, and that's why he hates me. One of the reasons, anyway. Ugly too, I suppose – old and ugly are two debilities he could never even pretend to bear. He forgets that we're more or less the same age, and neither of us ugly, actually – but never mind:

men – because he is hardly alone – men, they see things differently. They see things as they want them to be: he needs to see me as old, I think, because then he can easily justify a certain disgust. But stupid, he certainly thinks me that – though he never used to: he didn't think I was stupid when he married me. Nor ugly. I was really quite beautiful, actually: he said it to me constantly. All the time he touched me – wherever we were, and whatever we were doing. His hurrying fingers, they were always all over me. He said he simply couldn't help it. And then . . . a hundred years went by. He liked me more when I was drinking, that I do know. I was not stupid and ugly when I was drinking – that was my skewed understanding of it, anyway: probably I was both, and very embarrassingly so. I think he was genuinely concerned about me – certainly I did need help. And then when the drinking was no more (I found it so much harder than I imagined, or ever would have said) he snapped back immediately into holding me in complete contempt. One time he said to me: I cannot believe that Anna is actually your daughter – there's nothing of you in Anna. And clearly he saw this as a very good thing indeed – for why would he wish the taint or even aroma of a broken, stupid and ugly old woman to infect anything so saintly as bloody Anna, his true and magnificent daughter.

David, of course, he doesn't even recognise as being quite properly alive. David is dismissed as an irrelevance. In George's eyes, he just simply isn't at all the sort of son he thought he ought to have had. Well it is true, of course, that David . . . well, he can be very undemonstrative, and he's had more than his share of setbacks, shall we say. He is maybe overconfident, initially he is – and that's just how he was at school, his housemaster was always saying so in his reports and at meetings

– but then, this was the sad thing . . . never really quite brave enough when it actually came to it. But I'm sure he does his best. I'm sure it can't all be his fault. If only he'd gone ahead and married Barbara, that time. Would have been just so good for him. One thing George and I really did agree about – though God knows what really was going on in his mind: you never really know, with George. But then of course, David . . . well, the dear boy really had no say whatever in the matter, did he? Barbara – one day she was here, the next day she was gone. Pastures new, I suppose. George said well can you blame her? Wonderful woman like that – beauty, brains – what would she want to spend the rest of her life with David for? Look at him – *look* at him, Enid. It's cruel, the way he goes on. No man could ever measure up to *him*, that's all he's saying. And Anna, she very much appears to agree with it, more's the pity. But even when he's praising her to the heavens – and when is he not? – all it is is the merest variation on his rampant egomania: he thinks she's quite fantastic because she reminds him of himself. I hate when any parent praises a child in public, because that's all it ever is: self-adulation. But I hope she's not, Anna – just like him. I do hope she's better than that. I myself couldn't pass an opinion. I don't really know her all that well.

So now I find myself in the kitchen. I'm going to make some tea. I don't really terribly want to drink it – it was just a reason to get out of that room. I find his presence oppressive, more and more I feel that. Far too early to go to bed . . . so I thought of tea. Lapsang, maybe. I have so many – teas, infusions, tisanes . . . but generally it does tend to come down to Lapsang. In the old days I used to use it, tea. To camouflage whatever I was really drinking. George was entirely unaware that even if I wasn't drinking openly, still I was drinking. Tea, coffee . . . orange juice . . . even water: they would all have something in them. Brandy or vodka, depending on the colour. You become so terribly good at it: disguise. You become so completely adept.

I wonder what he really thinks of Lilian, the poor little girl he orders around so much. Oh it's David again I'm thinking of now: my mind, it is inclined to hop and wander. I find it difficult, more and more so, to actually properly focus on a given subject, and hardly at all on a passing idea. I think that the drink, it affected my brain. The balance, the concentration. Certainly I feel less, am aware of less – in every sense, I mean. Physically more or less numb. I scalded myself on the cooker just the other evening, and even as I could smell the burn of my finger, watch its swell and reddening, I barely felt a thing. And I find that increasingly I drift away whenever people are talking. But then, I can drift away even if they aren't. I don't really . . . care, that's the trouble. About the outcome of just about anything. Not just domestically, I don't mean – not just in terms of the house and family – but in any realm at all: wars, inflation, a general election . . . even the weather: I just can't care. It's a worry in one way, but then . . . I never really was what you might call a powerhouse of emotion. I never have experienced all the . . . *feelings* . . . all those grand sort of operatic *feelings* . . . I never had any of that. When you see these people in a film . . . undergoing passion . . . or the need for vengeance. The fury it would take to attack and kill a man. Morbid and all-consuming jealousy. Lust that turns your mind. I never had any of that. Even at the times in my life when there have been more than ample grounds for enormous resentment and disappointment . . . I would await the deadly crush of pain, but still it never came. No more than a passing discomfort. The way I am now, the position in which I find myself . . . the way that George is treating me – the fact that he just sees me as old and ugly and stupid and simply in the way . . . I ought to feel mortified. Profoundly depressed – or even suicidal. But I don't. Or else I should be filled with a righteous anger at the sheer and blatant injustice of the way things are and will always be . . . but no: I'm not. I am an empty drum, not even resounding. And yet . . . I do understand that something – don't know what, but something – really must be done. And it is I, of course – it is I who will have to do it. And maybe rather soon.

I can't in all honesty remember the details of David's business, David's venture, David's newest big idea . . . whatever he chooses to call it, these days. Or even its general nature. All I do know is that it isn't really going too well. Why he hates to come here, of course – because he knows how George is going to behave. He must at least be earning enough, though, to be paying the rent on his flat, anyway – and that rather nasty little office of his. Eating properly, I hope. There's Lilian's wages, of course, which he'll have to be paying – won't be terribly much, I don't expect, but still: it all mounts up. Does he know that she's in love with him . . .? Is that why he treats her so badly? Is that, after all, his father's sole bequest to him? His father's twisted gene? I haven't met the girl really all that often, but you simply have to see the way that she looks at him. Well she doesn't just look at him – she does far more than merely look at him: Lilian, she *beholds* him. She's really quite sweet. A little plain. But clearly devoted. I wonder whether David sees it? Men don't, sometimes, if it comes from an unexpected source – or else, of course, if they require it to be from elsewhere. Could be that he sees nothing else, while giving off quite another air. One day – I've just remembered this, this has only just occurred to me – one day not too long ago, David, he said to me: why did you do it, Mum? Do what, David, I said to him – knowing perfectly well exactly what he was asking me. Marry Dad, Mum – why on earth did you do it . . .? Well now . . . that's a question. That really is a question. Because he was rich . . .? No: he wasn't, at the time. A good catch . . .? Not really – not especially. Because I fell in love with him . . .? Well . . . very remarkably, yes: that's exactly what happened. Might seem extraordinary, I know: not to Anna – but certainly to David, who didn't believe me. Thought I was making it up. Simply couldn't believe it might even be *possible*. But it's the truth. George . . . I knew that I was in love with him, from the very day we met.

I had them then, did I . . .? The feelings? Well no – I had just the one, a feeling, only one feeling. Because it wasn't a passion, oh no . . . it was more of a deep-seated conviction that this was *right*. That this just had to *happen*, and if I failed, if I didn't ensure that it did – if I let it simply just drift away, well then instead of a lifetime of fulfilment, all I would be left with for the rest of my days on earth . . . was a vacuum, a hollow-eyed void, and all of my own creation: an eternity of emptiness, and all as a result of simply doing nothing. Large language – but that's what I felt. I well remember the startling unfamiliarity of just any of this: the spark that had been ignited, the thrill I was feeling. So very strange that I was actually aware of this, because I was still so, oh – just so terribly young. My life up until then had been, well . . . what can I say about it, really? It was nothing. Nothing at all. It's not just that it wasn't exciting – who ever expects exciting? – but it hadn't even been of interest. Not since I'd left school, where I did, I suppose, reasonably well compared with the average – not hard, because it wasn't a wonderful school: the academic level was far from high. So much so that I can't actually imagine anyone having failed to find a place there. And as soon as I'd managed a handful of O levels – can't even remember how many, and yet their superhuman importance was constantly being dinned into you – I left and did a secretarial course. Not Pitman. My father, he looked at what it was going to cost him, and pretty much spat out his open derision. Not in a month of Sundays, were his actual words: what did I take him for? A mug? As a parent myself, I still find it inconceivable how one could talk to a child like that . . . but George, I suppose, comes very close with David. Well, let's face it – he surpasses it, doesn't he? If we're being frank.

Anyway, it was my mother – truly deserving of that hoary old term 'long-suffering': she truly did suffer, my mother, long and hard – it was she who found an alternative, much cheaper, and a bit out of town. The classes were held in what might have been a small converted factory – garage, storeroom, depot, something of the sort. Large double doors, and mostly bare brick walls. Freezing in the winter, and in summer we broiled because the roof, it was flat, and made of corrugated iron. The teachers were commendably strict, but otherwise extremely so-so. I learned most of it from books (Pitman books, actually) and I practised every evening and most of the weekend at home on a deadweight hulk of a typewriter – ancient even then – called a Royal. My mother had bought it for me: she had followed up an ad on a postcard in the newsagent's window. Shorthand too – I became rather good at it. Can't remember any more how many words a minute, but I think it was impressive. I did corrupt the absolute purity of Pitman, though, with the addition of a bit of what was then called Speedwriting – a new idea, though basically all it came down to was the omission of vowels. Jobs were so very easy to obtain in those days, and in less than a year (and the course was for twice that long, so you can imagine my mother's pleasure) I was easily qualified for a middling sort of secretarial position. Which, I had long ago decided, I very desperately did not want. Not at all. I'd only kept up with it all for my mother's sake, really. Because the thought of being the bright and nicely turned-out young lady in twinset, pencil skirt and spectacles (I wore none of these things, but you see what I am getting at) and being ever available to take a letter on the whim of some man in a three-piece suit – a chain-smoker with a ginger moustache is how I always imagined he would be – I just absolutely could not even begin to face the prospect of that. And so my mother, poor soul, went from happy to sad in the space of an instant. Something I was to subject her to time and time again, though never once intentionally.

There was the time I borrowed her keys and promptly lost them and my father was insistent that we had to now have the locks changed and I said but look, that's completely ridiculous – if anyone's found the keys, they don't know where we live . . .! No good, of course: he was adamant. And he held my mother to account for letting her useless daughter anywhere near her keys in the first place. I lost count of the number of times he told us both how much this was going to cost him: my mother, she just sat there, her fingers writhing within her lap, and always hovering on the verge of tears. Then there was the time I took the car, and crashed it. Not seriously, I don't mean – I wasn't actually hurt, or anything. It just rolled away down the street with me inside it. Such a curious sensation. I couldn't drive, you see. Never even taken a lesson. I had just been watching people do it, and it all appeared so natural, it seemed so easy . . . I think I must simply have assumed that I'd be able. Stupid, really. And it's not as if I was ten years old, or something, and peeping over the dashboard – it wasn't just a prank or a bit of childish folly. I must have been, oh . . . I don't know – eighteen, or somewhere near it. Unworldly. My mother, she said I was unworldly. You don't want to hear what my father called me. But I was, I suppose – unworldly. Still am. I think I still must be.

So then I got a succession of jobs as a waitress. Was it what I wanted . . .? Well – I didn't *not* want it. That is the nearest, really, I ever came to anything: ambivalence. Never enthusiastic, though if any given situation or opportunity were not actively repugnant, or else quite evidently beyond my so very limited powers . . . well then I didn't really mind. It would do: I wouldn't say no. And so given all of that, what makes my subsequent behaviour so wholly astonishing to me (because still it does, it really does) is that that is precisely the state of mind that blanketed me when first I encountered George – by chance, of course: everything in my life has been quite by chance. I'm not sure I have ever made an actual plan. I was, as I say, ambivalent. Careless – careless, yes, though in no sense abandoned. I simply went along with people and things – not because I was nice or even frightened to say no, but simply because I couldn't ever see a reason not to. I did not object. I was unobjectionable. Yes but when I saw George that evening – that evening in Mario's when he was dining with the woman – well, the whole thing, you know . . . it was really most awfully extraordinary. I felt it, I felt it move within me – I almost heard it: this grinding wrench, nearly a screaming, as if after so many years, rusted points on forsaken rails were suddenly being quite frantically manhandled into some sort of urgent and desperate submission, or else the gorgeous and unmissable train would thunder through and just leave me standing there.

In the other places I had worked as a waitress – surprisingly many in so short a time: either I simply left on the merest whim, or else the bosses had regarded my almost robotic complacency, my unfathomable equability, as somehow unaccountably suspicious, and needed quickly to be rid of me. Yes . . . so in all those other places, I barely had even registered the undulating to and fro, the constant coming and going of all those hundreds and hundreds of customers: even their individual genders. I looked down without interest upon patches of baldness gleaming amid the Brylcreem . . . ill-treated roots . . . a dusting of dandruff. Occasionally I was aware of a scent that had me reeling, an ugly hand gripping the menu, the enquiring eye sullenly revolving towards me, some small piece of covetable jewellery – but never had I latched upon a whole and separate person. Not until George. And he, well . . . he just took me over. I don't know what it was – there had been no eruption of bustle, nor exclamations – no tipped-over glass or raucous laughter. The restaurant had been rather full, as it generally was – such a novelty, in those days: an Italian in Soho, one of the first with the red gingham cloths, the dripping candles in raffia-covered Chianti bottles – and we always had lots of people from Hampstead and Chelsea and places like that, who I think saw it as suitably bohemian, and consequently very much enjoyed being seen there. So tables full of diners . . . and why should I come to notice just one man in particular . . .? But no – that wasn't it, not at all: I didn't just *notice* him – his presence was suddenly quite totally overwhelming. I knew, with a blind and utter conviction, that I had to claim this man, that I just had to make him mine. And also make it right, you see? Because that is exactly where we each belonged: together – with one another, for always. To say I had never actually experienced anything of this nature would be so totally ridiculous an understatement: before, I had seldom even been brushed by a fleeting attraction. Men, to me, were just like everything else, really: neither to be desired nor shunned. But immediately I was behaving in a thoroughly uncharacteristic manner: I was deliberately and appallingly rude to my boss, without having a clear idea of what it was I was actually saying – wanting the sack, because I had to be away from there – and then I just walked straight out of the door, showily twirling the woman's umbrella. It was a gamble, actually – would she even care? I thought she might though, because this umbrella, it was clearly quite stupidly expensive. Some very famous designer, I think – so long ago, can't really remember the name. Anyway – he rang me. The following morning. Quite disappointing, I remember that being – I had been sitting by the telephone for the whole of the night. And then – oh, the sheer and utter thrill of it! – I went to meet him in the Grosvenor Hotel. Not the Park Lane one, the other one – where is it . . .? Victoria, yes – just next to the station. I can't exactly recall why it should have been there – but anywhere, anywhere would have done for me. Don't actually know what happened to the umbrella – I think I just threw it away: it was irredeemably vulgar. But that – that had been a tool, merely the device. To get him to see me. Because I knew, I just knew that when he saw me, when we talked . . . once we were together, and sharing a drink . . . well, that that would be that, really. And . . . so it was. George . . . he was quite as smitten as I – which was wonderful, of course, though completely unsurprising to me. And from that very first moment, truly we were both in love. So . . . it is a shame, really. Such a terrible shame.

A waste – it all seems really such an awful waste. This, I suppose, is why I have been thinking back on all of this nonsense, I think it must be. Because there I conjured up for me the just too beautiful beginning of us . . . but then, at some long ago and distant point, I just lost myself completely. After the birth of Anna? After the birth of David? Or did neither of them have anything remotely to do with it? I can't ever be sure. But, whatever the cause, I just simply imploded. Became not me. Why I am so very terribly lonely – now that I have lost me for seemingly always, who else ever can I possibly be with . . .? Because I never did have friends, not really. At first it was because . . . well, with George, I didn't feel I needed them, to be perfectly honest: George, you see, he was . . . oh, just my everything: all I ever wanted. After that . . . some years on, I wouldn't have minded. Did actually strike up one or two relationships, if you can even call them that, with other young mothers whom I met at parent's evenings or one of these play dates, or whatever they called them then . . . though it soon became clear that George, he didn't at all approve, I didn't quite understand the reason – except that of course from very early on I had perceived that he was something of a bully: 'controlling', I believe they call it now. So I stopped them, those occasional coffees and shopping trips – it wasn't really a hardship. And then, so very rapidly and almost without my even seeing it, I apparently slipped into becoming a caterer, the manager, a mediator between the children – certainly between George and David . . . but most of all, I can see quite clearly now that I fitted so snugly into a mould of my own creation: I was a careful rendering – pastiche really, is all I had become – of a loyal, supportive and safely stupid wife. He was always generous – with things, anyway: things and money. Always urging me to buy all these terribly expensive clothes, shoes and handbags that I so much didn't want (I already possess so embarrassingly many) – to go for beauty treatments, massages, facials . . . health farms and spas. Maybe I should have . . . because now, in George's eyes, I am old and ugly. And also, he hates me. Sad. That is sad, isn't it? And why something now really has to be done. But there is only one thing, isn't there? Only one thing I can do. Nothing else is in my power. Yes. And so . . . I have to go. After so long a time. Leave. I must be apart now from nothingness, just existing, though actually living absolutely nowhere . . . though I doubt if even maybe there is some other place I might possibly be.

And now . . . the phone is ringing. I shall wait here in the kitchen for just a little longer, staring deep into the shimmer of my cooling and abandoned Lapsang. He might just answer it, George. He won't answer it. Or maybe, the phone, it will simply stop ringing. It won't stop ringing. Will it? So I shall see to it, I suppose. It is the sort of thing I shall continue to do . . . though not, I am afraid, for very much longer.

'Hello . . .?'

'Hi. Me. You okay . . .?'

'David, darling. How lovely to . . .'

'Dad there?'

'You want to talk to your father . . .?'

'Yup. He there?'

'Well yes, but . . .'

'I won't keep him long.'

'Is there something wrong, David? What is it? What's wrong?'

'Nothing. There's nothing wrong. Why do you always think there's something wrong?'

'I don't. I don't always think there's something wrong. How can you say that? It's just that I can't remember the last time you called and wanted to speak to your father. That's all. You never want to speak to your father. Do you?'

'Yeh well. So can you just put him on, then? I would've called his mobile, but he always goes crazy whenever I do that. Christ knows why . . .'

'I know. He does that with me as well.'

'Yup. So . . .?'

'All right, then. I'll tell him. Hello . . .? Are you there . . .?'

'Of course I'm *here* – what on earth are you talking about . . .?'

'Well you just went silent, that's all.'

'Well I was waiting, wasn't I? I was waiting for you to . . . oh – just get him, can't you?'

'All right, David. No good getting upset with me, is it? I'll tell your father you want to speak to him.'

'Fine. Jesus . . .'

'I'm quite well, by the way.'

'What . . .?'

'Well you didn't ask, but I just wanted to reassure you that your mother, she's perfectly fine.'

'Oh. Right. Yes. Sorry. It's just that . . .'

'Quite all right. As your father says, you're a very busy man. I'll get him for you.'

It's at times such as this that I completely understand George's constant and seething impatience with the boy. So terse. So completely self-centred. Well, there you are. I don't suppose he'll ever change, not now: man, isn't he? Grown-up person. And whatever he says there will be something wrong, of course there will. He hardly ever phones – can't remember the last time. And to talk to his father . . .? He does his level best to avoid even so much as looking at him when for some unusual reason the two of them are in the same room.

'Oh, George – there you are. I've been looking all over the house for you. I thought you were in the living room.'

'No, Enid. I'm here. In my study, as you perceive. Where have you been hunting? Loft? Larder? Boiler room?'

'Yes well it's just that when I left you, you were in the living room, weren't you?'

'Yes. I was. And now I am here. A state of constant flux.'

'David wants to talk to you.'

'David . . .?'

'David, yes. Your son.'

'Yes *thank* you, Enid – I do know who you're talking about. What – that was him on the phone, was it?'

'He's still on the phone. Wants to talk to you.'

'Talk to *me* . . .?'

'That's what I said to him. Do you want to take it in here?'

'Have you . . . have you actually told him I'm in . . .?'

'I have, yes. He says he won't be long.'

'Right. Okay. So what's wrong, then?'

'He says there's nothing wrong. I asked him.'

'Yes but there will be, won't there? Why else would he be calling?'

'Well why don't you find out, George? I'll leave you to it.'

'Right. It's just that I'm actually rather busy at the moment . . .'

'He said it wouldn't take long.'

'Right. Okay, then. You run off, Enid, and I'll see what the bloody boy wants.'

What in Christ's name can the bloody boy want? Something, obviously. Because this – his calling me, it's not just unusual, it's close to unprecedented. Oh well – let's see to just how elaborate a degree the bugger's gone and fouled up this time.

'David . . .?'

'Christ. *Finally*. Thought you'd *died*, or something . . .'

'Sorry to disappoint. I'm afraid you'll just have to hang on just a little bit longer for that most joyous occasion, David. Sorry I won't be able to be a part of it. Now – how can I help you? I'm assuming you want my help . . .?'

'*Jesus* . . .!'

'Well do you or don't you?'

'Look. This isn't easy for me . . .'

'So very little is . . .'

'Christ, Dad – why do you always have to *be* like this . . .?!'

'Look, David – I've really no time for more of your very tiresome histrionics. I am right in the middle of something rather important, actually. Say what you have to say, yes?'

'Well okay. You see . . . I'm in, I'm in . . . something of a temporary hole.'

'A *temporary* hole, I see. Well in terms of *your* life then, David, I'd say things were decidedly looking up, no . . .?'

'I'm going to ignore all of your fucking snide and nasty comments, Dad. Because . . . well look – I do need help. I hate to ask you. But . . .'

'But . . . there's no one else. Right?'

'Well. Yeh. Right. I hate this, I just hate it . . .'

'It's no bunch of roses for me either, David, I do assure you. So what is it this time?'

'You say it like I'm *always* asking you . . .'

'You don't always ask me. But you often need to ask someone – and they, this time, are not eager to comply, it would appear. It must be that this "temporary" hole of yours is just that much deeper than the last one. God's sake, David – just speak.'

'Well look – I need a short-term loan. Is what it is.'

'Uh-huh. How large a loan? And how short-term?'

'Just a few thousand. Pay you back in a month. Yes? Hello . . .? You there . . .?'

'I'm here, yes. And I am deeply concerned. How can a bona fide businessman, which is what you always are claiming to be, David, be in need of just a few thousand? In business, a few thousand – Jesus, that's petty cash. And how can you require an entire bloody month to pay it back? What's going on?'

'Well . . . it's actually a bit more than just a few thousand . . .'

'Really. How much?'

'But I will pay you back. I swear it.'

'How much, David?'

'Honestly – if there was anywhere else I could *go* . . .!'

'How bloody much, Christ's sake?'

'Seventy grand. Give or take.'

'I see.'

'Right. So there it is. Will you help me . . .?'

'There is no point, I presume, in asking you what exactly it is for? This seventy grand. Because I remain unclear as to what it is you are actually engaged in, David. Your business. The Big Idea. And this "temporary" hole, as we must learn to call it – this will allow you to pay back seventy thousand pounds within a month . . .?'

'It's a certainty.'

'Now I'm worried.'

'With interest. Any interest you like.'

'And now I'm *really* worried. There are no certainties, David. Not in business – and nor in anything else either. And people who offer any rate of interest on borrowed capital tend to frighten off a potential investor, you see.'

'Look, Dad . . . I'm desperate. You have to know that. You have to know that if I could raise this money in any other way, I would . . .'

'Which is also rather concerning. Why have the banks turned you down? Are you overextended?'

'It's . . . it's the banks who want the money.'

'Ah. They have threatened foreclosure. Liquidation of assets, if assets there be. Bringing down the curtain. Well possibly, David, now is the time to ask yourself: would that maybe be the better option? Offsetting debt? Even formal bankruptcy. Not such an awful thing, these days – some even see it as a legitimate business ploy. Can you really contemplate flinging more, yet more good money after bad? My money, at that.'

'I can't let the business go. Can't. I just can't . . .'

'But is it truly a viable *business,* David? Hm? Businesses – they make money. It's what they're *for* . . .'

'Oh Jesus. Oh Jesus Jesus *Jesus* . . .!'

'I think you must consider every option.'

'*Look* . . .! Are you going to help me out? Or not? Simple question: yes or no?'

'I have to reply as I always reply to any proposition set before me: I should like to think about it, if that's quite all right with you. And of course any accounts – facts and figures that you felt able to show to me would very much help me come to a decision . . .'

'You heard me, Dad: yes or no?'

'Well, dear boy – if you are determined to hold a gun to my head . . .'

'Yeah . . .?'

'Well then the answer just has to be no. Obviously.'

'I see. Right. Well I'm sorry to have taken up your time, then.

You can get back now to whatever was so bloody important. *Thanks*, Dad – thanks a fucking *lot* . . .!'

'David . . .? Hello . . .? No . . .? Gone. Right, then.'

So. What infantile behaviour. What petulance. So completely typical. Is this really what you expect from an adult man? Dear God – this generation! So anyway: I don't often, you see, receive a telephone call from my one and only son. Just as well, on the whole – don't you think?

Yeh well – what else did I expect? When did he ever stick up for me? Support me, like a father's meant to? The bastard. Oh *Jesus* I so wish I hadn't called him now. Why did I call him? What was I bloody thinking? Why did I put myself through all that appalling humiliation? Because I knew – I just *knew* that that's how he'd be. Well of course I knew – because that's how he always bloody is. Days I've been trying to reason with the banks – stave them off a bit. It took me that long to realise that you just can't do it, reason with banks. Nor can you ask them to have a heart: well – you can ask, but all you're going to get is one fat belly laugh. Dad – he could have told me that straight away . . . but I knew it myself, really: it's just that desperation, well – it makes you crazy: has you hoping against hope, clutching madly and wildly at just any stupid thing that's flying around your head. So it was only after it became perfectly clear to even me that what I was doing was attempting to negotiate with a solid brick wall, that I started trying to think of other ways out. Agonised for hours and hours: will I call him? Won't I call him? Yes – I'll call him, because what other chance is open to me now? No – I'll be *damned* if I'll call him, the fucker. He's not going to help me, is he? When did he ever? So what's the bloody use in asking him, then? Maybe . . . I don't know – but how about this: I can go over there. Do it face to face. Or – as Dad would put it 'man to man' . . . yes, and then he'd smirk: that scornful and crooked expression that is wholly reserved for me, and me alone. But no – that would be worse. Because then I'd have to look at that smug and unbearable face of his, wouldn't I? And I'd only lose my temper. I'd only end up stamping out of there and slamming the door behind me – like I've done, oh Christ, how many bloody times before? And upsetting Mum. Again. As well as knowing that after I've done that he'll just be sitting there exactly as I'd left him, pursing his lips and widening his eyes – inviting an invisible audience to silently marvel at the lunatic scene that had just been enacted, the antics of a simpleton – while slowly wagging his fucking head from side to side, of course more in sorrow than in bloody anger . . . though actually just thinking what a useless little cunt I am, can't even keep my tinpot business afloat: how can I call myself his son? How can I even call myself a man? On and on, yadda yadda, into eternity. And wishing that it was Anna he was dealing with, and that I was dead.

It was my fault too, of course. It generally is. I started off on completely the wrong foot – hissing out my impatience that he had taken so bloody long to just pick up the phone. I was going to ask how he was. Not because I gave a flying fuck, but because I hadn't with Mum, and I should have, and I could tell that I'd upset her. But when there's something on my mind, I just pitch right in, you see. Can't think of anything else: my mind, it's just completely consumed. So – no small talk, no levity . . . but any of that sort of thing, well – I find it practically impossible, with him. And even when I was asking the man for money – not that much to him, but a fucking fortune to me, pretty much life and death, God damn it – still it must have sounded like an assault. Because that's the trouble with me – one of them, anyway. Even with people I'm fond of – not Dad, I don't mean, but people I'm fond of – even when I'm all out to get something, still I'm just this rude and angry person, eyes blazing, I shouldn't wonder, and always on the attack. And then of course I have to go and put the tin fucking lid on it by dishing out a fucking ultimatum . . .! Twice I said it: will you or won't you? Yes or no? Pretty much a death wish, really – an act of sabotage upon my own little flimsy supplication. So of course he said no. Of course he did. Who wouldn't?

'Who were you calling? Was it your father?'

'Hm . . .? Oh. No. Nobody. It was nothing.'

'It was your father, wasn't it?'

'I just told you no, didn't I, Lilian? What's wrong with you?'

'You're worried. I know that.'

'You *think* . . .?'

'It would be completely natural for you to ask your father for help. It's nothing to be ashamed of.'

'No – it's me *he's* ashamed of. Maybe with reason.'

'So you did call him, then?'

'I *didn't*! I bloody *didn't*. How many times?'

'And you shouldn't go saying that about yourself, David. There's nothing about you to be ashamed of. Nothing at all.'

'Well . . . good of you to say so, Lilian, but . . .'

'Look – why don't you?'

'Why don't I what? What are you talking about?'

'Oh . . . don't drink any more, David. You've had an awful lot this evening, you know. I mean, why don't you call your father? You never know . . .'

'Christ! Are you my mother now? I'll drink as much as I bloody want to drink. Jesus . . .'

'Ring him, David, It's worth a try.'

'No. No point.'

'Nothing to lose, is there?'

'Oh Christ I *did* ring him – I *have* rung him. That's who I was on the phone to. Of course I rang him. Who else? He's the only person I know who's got any money . . .'

'Ah. Because I thought you said . . .'

'Yes well I did say. I did. What else was I going to say? And he said . . . well of course he said no. Is there any more of this . . .?'

'I'm . . . not sure.'

'Is there or not?'

'I think there might be another bottle in the kitchen, but . . .'

'Yeh well get it, can you?'

'David – I really don't think . . .'

'Just *get* it. Okay?'

'I hate it. I hate it when you talk to me like that.'

'Like what? What do you mean? Don't know what you're talking about.'

'You do know what I mean. You know exactly what I mean. I'll get the bottle, if you want it.'

'Oh . . . Lilian. I'm . . . sorry. I shouldn't, I know. Say these things. Talk like this. And whenever I do, I sound like him. It's the only thing I've ever got from him – this . . . vileness, all the condescension. Being a bloody awful bullying pig. Christ. I actually hate *both* of us . . .'

'Don't say that. Look – I've been thinking. I've been over and over the figures, and really, you know, it's only a little over half the full amount that we've got to find immediately. The rest can wait a bit. If we can just somehow manage to get together half, everything will be okay. For now, anyway. And listen, David . . . maybe, I can help a bit . . .'

'You . . .?'

'Mm. A bit.'

'You've got half? You've got thirty-five grand? Not on what I bloody pay you . . .'

'No. No of course I haven't. But when my mother died, she left me a little. Few thousand. And then there are those earrings I've got . . .'

And I look at her. I just slump there on the bloody sofa and look at that sweet little face. And my whisky-rimmed eyes, I feel them filling up with such hot and stinging tears. Christ oh Christ. How in God's name can it ever have come to this . . .? Everything . . . everything was meant to be just so bloody wonderful – so why isn't it, then? Hey? Why bloody isn't it? My father – hah! I was going to show him. My God yes – I was going to show him exactly how it's done. Because that man . . . Jesus, ever since I can remember, he could always, I don't know . . . it was a knack, a real ability to just simply make things happen. Has the gift – always did. Doesn't even seem to be trying. People do what he wants – but it's not about charm, of course: he pays them, and he bullies them. Doesn't matter, though – it works. And that's the point. Sixty-four he is now, and still the unchallenged supremo in his unendingly successful company, money to burn, don't know how he does it. And I am aware . . . look, I am completely aware that it's got nothing whatever to do with it, but listen: he's even still got all of his hair . . .! Nothing thinning, nowhere receding . . . I mean okay it's practically white, but still. Yeh and look at me! Just you take one look at the top of my head, if you can stand to. As if blind and ravenous goats have been let loose on it. I'm not even elegantly bald – a finely rounded and possibly suntanned cranium, glossy thick and wavy hair at the sides and just over the top of the ear, and maybe even a cluster of curls touching my collar. No – my entire skull, it's like it's been laid to waste. Frayed old rope on a warehouse floor. Lilian, she said I ought to consider a conditioner. I shouted at her, of course, but I suppose she meant well. Well of course she did: she always does. So terribly supportive, she's been. And particularly at the beginning, when I so much had to believe in all my big and stupid ideas. Her still being around me, her endless and apparently perfectly sincere encouragement in the face of frank disaster . . . now of course it means more to me than ever. Because who else is there? I need her – I need her, you see, because everyone else, well . . . they're gone. Mum and Anna, well – they were never really there, but Dad, he's gone. Barbara. Oh Christ. Yes, Barbara – she's well and truly gone. Jesus. So it's all down to Lilian, really. And I need her. Wouldn't actually tell her that, naturally enough. Yes of course I should, anyone would . . . but still I know I won't. It's because . . . I think it's because I still have to idiotically maintain the illusion, do I . . .? That she is merely my employee, my P.A. . . . and that I am – don't, please God, laugh – the boss. Oh Christ. She constitutes my entire workforce now, Lilian – unless you want to count Freddy and Ginny, more or less gophers on minimum wage. Which they're lucky to get. Myself – I haven't had one, a wage, for . . . Jesus, I don't know: seemingly years. I can barely support myself, it's got to be faced. Personal loans. Overdraft right up to its limit. On all three accounts. Can't go on taking out new credit cards: I'm amazed that I can still get away with it, actually. But banks, they do that, don't they? Keep wanting to give you money . . . until the moment comes when they decide that they want it all back. And then there's this scrubby little flat – I hate it. I hate it so much. Whenever I walk in here – when I come to turning the key in the lock, the sight of the rubbed and shabby panels of the door, my heart hits the floor. And I can barely afford it. It's cheap, as it bloody well should be, but still, I can barely afford it. The office, that will have to go. I suppose I can just about do everything from what the landlord likes to call the spare bedroom. More of a vertical coffin. That's if I still am left with a business to deal with. Which looks to be not so much unlikely any more as completely out of the question. Now that Dad won't help me. Can't blame him. Of course I can't blame him. I wouldn't – I wouldn't help me. What – I would lend me seventy grand in the absolute knowledge that I'll never see a penny of it again? I hardly think so. Still hate him, though – for not giving it to me. Still hate him for it. For not feeling the need to help me. He's my father, isn't he? And no matter how crushingly disappointing a son may be, I truly do believe that it's just what fathers should do.

Which came first, actually . . .? Which of my magnificent big ideas was the trailblazer? Do you know, I'm not even sure now I can honestly remember. It wasn't concierge service . . . no, it was buy-to-let, of course it was. Serviced offices, that came later. In each of these ventures I have been effortlessly superseded, more or less totally annihilated – and in next to no time – by the big boys: that is to say, those people who actually have the first idea about what it is they are doing, and have taken care to assemble suitable expertise while amassing the capital to back it. Which, on all counts, I signally failed to do. Those two flats I bought in Kilburn . . . oh Jesus, what a fiasco. My calculations, such as they were, were completely predicated upon their letting immediately at a higher than current market rent – and they weren't even that well kitted out. Why did I even for a moment imagine that might be possible? Panicked, of course, when still they were empty after a couple of months: cut the rent. Then I cut it again. Might even have done it a third time, I'm just too ashamed to recall. Anyway – the flats found tenants then, of course: everywhere will, if it's cheap enough. Trouble was, the rental income wasn't covering the bloody mortgage I'd taken out so that I could buy the fucking things in the first place. And then there was not just the rates but eternal maintenance: Freddy, he was round there pretty much every week, it seemed to me. Blocked drain, fuse, leak in the roof . . . on and on. Even paying him an insulting pittance was becoming a struggle. So eventually I got shot of them, sold them, the flats. Yes of course at a loss. Property prices only started going absolutely crazy about six months later. Six months later, I could have sold them for nearly forty per cent more than I did. Six months later, I could have had a queue of people mad keen to rent them for twice what I'd been asking. Yes, but the flats were gone by then, weren't they? Bought by someone with a brain.

So serviced offices, then. That's what came next. That's how now I was set to establish for myself an elaborate fortune. I took a short lease on four of them in a newish and quite attractive small block quite close to West Hampstead Tube station: good area for this sort of thing, I'd surmised – and no, I wasn't wrong. The idea was to undertake for the subtenant all cleaning, maintenance and security, whereupon I would receive far more than I was paying the landlord. Was rather good, at first. Freddy was coping with all the odd little jobs – though he had to bring in his brother-in-law when it came to technology – and then he used to sit in the foyer until long past dawn. That, God help us, was the security side of things.

Christ knows what he would have done if there had been any sort of trouble. Screamed, I expect – or else maybe fainted, because he's only small, Freddy. Although he was probably always asleep, now I come to think of it – because when else would he be? And Ginny, his wife – they're not actually married, but I call her his wife – she was cleaning and seeing to the rubbish, and so on. That sort of thing. It jogged along really rather surprisingly well for quite a good while. Lilian, she told me that after just seven months we were showing a profit. Great, I thought: here we go then . . .! I'll buy four more – expand the business: growth, it's the only way. Except that the bank, they wouldn't extend me the money. They blamed the 'climate'. I don't think they were meaning the weather, but they might very easily have been. So I went somewhere who would. And yes, the interest was so almost criminally high that in my many weaker and more terrified moments, it actually made me laugh out loud – a high-pitched and strangulated din I was making, and it frightened even me. I paid it with a smile. And then I didn't: pay, or smile. I certainly wasn't laughing any more, even hysterically. The landlord informed me that he had accepted an offer for the freehold of the entire block, and so although the fag end of my lease would of course be honoured, within a few months the building was to be subject to complete refurbishment, whereupon the office rentals were set to soar. Yes well. I salvaged a few thousand out of that debacle. Paid Lilian. Hadn't, for months. Christ knows how she managed. And that's when it came to me: the greatest idea of them all: a concierge service . . .! I called it that, you know, long before it became an actually recognisable phrase. I might even have invented the concept, who knows? Roped in Freddy's brother-in-law – he does have a name, that man, though I'm not sure I ever did know it – and he rigged me up a website. The Art of the Possible was the name I bestowed upon this particular venture. Not the most sophisticated website (very strange fonts, rather depressing colours) but I thought it would do. The idea – well, you know the idea, everybody does these days: to relieve the pressure on those extraordinarily fortunate people who have the money to indulge themselves, but not the time or inclination. Or possibly they have all the time in the world but are just too bone bloody idle to be bothered with it. So: finding cleaners, odd-job men and babysitters, booking holidays, theatres and restaurants, locating the perfect gift for the man who has everything – all that sort of rather nauseating baloney. The further spoiling of already very horribly spoiled brats – though all in exchange for money, of course.

At first I used as a source of information, clout and contacts actual concierges – not from the grand hotels (I did try quite a few, but not one of them wanted to know: they all abide by some sort of a code, I think) but the middle rankers were eager enough to play ball. In exchange for money, of course. Personal shoppers in department stores came in rather handy (keen on the commission, you see), as did straightforward employment agencies, florists, wine merchants, all of that. Publicising the service, that was the tricky bit. Freddy said he would get it up on eBay. I said why, and he said if you're not on eBay, you're dead in the water. I said okay: I didn't understand the first thing about it (as should be appallingly clear), so he could have been talking complete and utter nonsense, who's to know? I placed a couple of largish ads in the *Evening Standard*, which pretty much took up most of the pitiable float I had very optimistically budgeted for the whole of this caper. Printed two-sided coloured and glossy flyers so that people could angrily screw them up and chuck them into the bin. The whole affair was just about jogging along for a while, I suppose. But then it was the usual thing: the backhanders to the concierges, those ads, paying Freddy, keeping Lilian more or less alive and treating myself to the odd meat meal . . . well, any money I was making just simply was vaporised. Then, of course – again, again – the professionals moved in. The people who had thought about it deeply. Planned it. Staffed it. Financed it. Those people. 'Quintessentially' – I think that could well have been the first, but there are loads of them now. And they were just offering *anything*: a poolside table at an A-List sold-out media happening in Acapulco? Of course. The Birkin bag in orange crocodile? Naturally. Jennifer Lopez to sing at your birthday party? Nothing easier. A couple of transvestite hookers tricked out in little except Spandex and whipping cream? No problem whatsoever. So eBay or no eBay, I was dead in the water.

Further problems arose, of course – in the wake of what was only, after all, my very latest debacle. I had to keep any detail whatever entirely secret. From Dad, I mean – and that meant Mum and Anna as well, because they always seem to tell him just everything. But imagine: if he had got the slightest whiff of the extent of my continued idiocy and seemingly inevitable failure, oh Christ – he would so have been in clover. Whatever business you are currently engaged in, he used to keep on saying to me, pack it in and get a job. Get a job. Over and over he said that to me. I was amazed, actually, that he even considered me employable – because I very much doubt if I am, in all honesty. Lilian, she says I could do anything – that any company would be glad and lucky to have me . . . yes, but that's Lilian. Soon have to find out, I suppose. Closer to my heart, however . . . was the matter of Barbara.

I was in awe of her. Of course I was. And as for Dad, well . . . you could see it in his eyes – Mum's too, though she'd never let on. Not just that he completely adored her (and not always in a thoroughly wholesome manner, it seemed to me: something about his gestures) but there was this outright astonishment, you see: genuine bewilderment that a woman such as this would want anything to do with me. A view I shared. Why I was in awe of her – and also, rather wary. Because I was always thinking, well Christ – how the bloody hell has this lot come about, then? Can't last, can it? Got no real hope of lasting, this – has it? It'll end. When will it end? How will it end? But it will end, matey – no bloody doubt about it. Amazing it ever got started in the first place: how did it get started in the first place . . .? See what I mean? On and on, round and round. I had met her in a wine bar – she was with a party of people, eight or so, some sort of a leaving do, I thought it might have been. No – not a wine bar: they don't exist any more, do they? Anyway – some sort of a bar (Chelsea, rather nice) and it was certainly wine that we were drinking. It's all I ever used to have in the old days: Rhône, Beaujolais, always red – couldn't ever run to the sorts of Bordeaux that my cherished father favours, though I wouldn't at all have minded. He only ever seems to open the really good ones when he is alone with Anna – and she honestly couldn't care about it either way, as she'll happily tell you. Oh well. Whisky now, is what I drink. It's quicker. And quite cheap at Tesco, if you buy it by the litre. Which I tend to do. Two at a time, actually. Lilian, she looks at me, when I'm rather overdoing it – a fairly regular occurrence just lately, I'm afraid. Doesn't often say anything – but the look, it's more than enough. Her eyebrows are forming a concentrated thicket while she continues to stare at me pointedly, compressing her lips until they are practically white – it's rather as if she is willing her thoughts to enter my head: just you remember what happened to your mother – and I read somewhere, David, that it very often can run in the family, that sort of thing, you know. Yes well. Unlike my dear old drunken mother of old, I know what I'm doing. I can control it. I'll be just fine.

But Barbara, though. I was in this bar . . . I was there because . . . I can't remember why I was there. Chelsea – off my beat, rather. There must have been a reason. Chasing some non-existent contact, or something. Pinning all my fevered hopes on the latest false promise: launching myself headlong down another blind alley, just one more dead bloody end. I had gone up to the bar to get myself another glass of whatever I was drinking – it might have been a Languedoc, never bad value in places like this – and also to ask the girl there if they had any crisps or nuts or something. She idly pointed to a stand-up menu which was full of things like, I don't know . . . lambs' tongues and olives and chicken skin and artisanal bread, whatever artisanal bread might be. And I said no – I don't mean that: I just want some crisps. Or nuts. Or something. She shrugged and looked away. Possibly didn't speak English – so many of them don't, these days – though more probably she had simply smelled my odour – the rankness of defeat that I seem to trail behind me, and which instantly alerts just everyone around to the blatant truth that I am worthy of nothing but contempt. And so I said to her well just make the wine a large one then, can you? And while I was fishing out some money . . . that's when I saw her. There was the instant. Amazing I hadn't noticed this absolute vision well before this – and particularly because she appeared to be looking straight at me. Maybe she was adding her pointed censure – heaping disdain upon this, simply my most recent humiliation, and this time at the hands of a dumb and stupid barmaid. That was my first thought. But then I did that thing of glancing quickly behind me to see who she might really be looking at . . . but no, no one there: it did actually seem to be me. The rest of the room . . . I laughed later on at my memory of this moment, because if it had been a scene in one of those . . . what do you call them, that sort of movie . . .? Romcom, is it . . .? The American ones – usually they're American – and though they're clearly quite squarely aimed at women, I still do rather enjoy them. Well if it had been in one of those movies, everyone else in the bar would have become instantly blurry, the din they were making muted to no more than a murmur – all their actions maybe even reduced to slo-mo. And she in a spotlight – because this woman . . . she was literally outstanding. I'm telling you: this woman, she stopped all the clocks.

Did I go over to her . . .? Are you kidding me? Of course I didn't bloody go over to her. She was with people, wasn't she? They were drinking champagne. Why would I want to cross the floor and infect the whole of this happy and oblivious party of friends with the miasma of despair which habitually clung to me – see them catch its damp aroma, watch it spread like a poisonous vapour, and cast each one of them down? Far better to scuttle right back to my dark little hidey-hole in the very farthest corner, drink quite quickly, and hug to me the bitter truth that I would for ever remember this fleeting frisson, that dazzle of beauty in the wine bar – curse myself eternally for doing absolutely nothing about it, while almost fondly sympathising with my mortal incapacity. So I did all of that. And then, seemingly instantly . . . she was there, and standing over me.

'Have I seen you in here before . . .?'

'Don't think so. No. Impossible. Never been. First time.'

'Aha. Well that rather sounds as if you'd prefer to be left alone.'

'What? Oh Christ no – sorry. Wasn't meant to. Christ. So rude.'

'Almost as rude as you not asking me if I'd like to sit down . . .?'

'Do you want to? I didn't think you would.'

'I just thought I'd seen you in here before, that's all. Maybe somewhere else.'

'Oh quite possibly somewhere else. I've been to . . . other places.'

And she laughed at that. It was quite funny, I suppose, but I didn't at all see it at the time. I was fairly used to people laughing at most of what I ever had to say, so this one, well . . . I just took it on the chin. Added it to the heap. And then I struggled on:

'Party, is it . . .?'

'I'm sorry?'

'Friends from work? Party? Birthday, maybe?'

'Oh . . . no. Not really. I'm Barbara, by the way. No – we just tend to do this, you know? End of the week. Blow off steam. Spend our ill-gotten gains.'

'I see. Are you a criminal, then?'

And as I said this, I had meant to smile – even rather roguishly – but I somehow completely forgot to, so it came out straight. I think we may agree that every word I had so far uttered to this woman made me out to be a complete and total moron. So why didn't she run? While she still had the chance.

'Some would say so. I'm a lawyer. Is it any good, that wine . . .?'

'It's all right. Oh God I'm so sorry . . .! Would you like a . . .?'

'No. Got champagne. See? I'm fine. And your name is . . .?'

'Christ. Sorry. David. I'm David, yes. Lawyer, eh? Well . . . there you go.'

'And what about you? What do you do? You work round here?'

And I know it was only chat – of course I know that: it's just what people say, isn't it? You run into someone for the very first time and sooner or later you're going to ask them what they do. For a living. Only natural – even if you don't give a single devil's damn about whatever it is they're going to come back with. It's just that it was always the question I most dreaded on earth – still is, really. Because I don't have a bloody answer. Do I? So I lied. Constructed an absolute fantasy, right on the spot – chock-full of inference and allusion. Wilfully oblique and hinting at an essential secrecy, while effortlessly conveying gracious and perfectly charming modesty concerning my outstanding if necessarily mysterious capabilities, all very strongly underpinned by the quite vital and potent implication of virtually limitless wealth. Oh dear Christ in *heaven* . . .! So there, anyway, was the basis of it: mud and clay, soon to become a quicksand.

I still will always be confounded by all sorts of astonishment that she was moved to approach me in the first place. Well . . . I did actually ask her about that, one time. So wish I hadn't. She said it was because I had, in that noisy little bar, looked so very lonely and sad, and terribly lost. Yes. So she thought she'd find me. Jesus. Anyway . . . a couple of nights later, we met up again. Probably at her instigation. And as soon as I had been mesmerised by her quite totally unbelievable body – Christ, even thinking about it now . . .! – I was taking her to all of London's finest and most cripplingly expensive restaurants . . . and I hired, I actually rented a bloody silver Porsche. Believe that? In which we drove off for a seemingly endless succession of weekends at some or other five-star palace with a couple of Michelin stars. Lilian . . . oh Christ: she wanted to know where all the money was going. Contacts, I said: pursuing leads. Well she didn't want to sound unduly alarmist, is what she whispered to me (and so very caringly), but she thought I ought to know that the float was long gone, and so now was all of the working capital. I knew that. And on the top of it all, I had by this time three personal loans as well as overdrafts and maxed-out credit cards. Nightmare. Yes . . . but oh Christ, I so much loved every single second of that time . . .! I was living the life I'd always dreamed of – one that once I honestly believed I would have earned with ease – and I was with the sort of woman that I thought I would never in a million years have the tiniest chance of getting . . .! And other men – oh my God. When we walked into a restaurant, the atmosphere was palpable. No one – no other woman ever outmatched her. She was . . . oh, all the usual words. Just stunning, really. I was constantly drunk with lust, just even standing beside her. Yes. And then I lost it all. Everything. She found out the truth – not all of it, obviously, but enough. Various horrible scenes – but the end came quickly. She said it was the lies. She said that the thing she could never forgive me for, the reason she could no longer so much as contemplate spending even one more minute in my company, was knowing I was such a blatant liar: how could you, she said, have told me all those lies . . .? Yes – but it wasn't the lies, of course. Not really. What she couldn't stand was the fact that I wasn't the man I had so very diligently pretended to be: that the sweet life could no longer continue. Had I been as rich and fabulous as I had suggested, I think I could have lied to her until doomsday, and she would neither have known nor cared. But I was relieved, in some ways: so sick of all those bloody restaurants, to be honest – the oleaginous maître d's, the sauces, the courses – attempting not to flinch or shriek at the sight of the bill. Not to say the constant strain of the continued pantomime. Dodging all the creditors, day in, day out. And my father . . . to this day, he will very loudly and pig-headedly not remotely understand how I could ever have been so very criminally stupid as to let her go. Let her go . . .! Christ.

I fuck Lilian instead, now. Serviceable . . . I mean, it's got me out of a jam, but oh God . . . so not anywhere close to everything I came to more or less depend upon, with Barbara. I was in a boil of desire just all the bloody time: the very sight of her – that was enough. Sexual intoxication. Yes well: that's that. But what now about the creditors? The banks? Well – they've simply had enough, plain and simple. I haven't even been servicing the interest. Because if you barely are eating and subsist almost wholly on Tesco whisky, it's rather hard to. Amazing they left it so long, really. Amazing they lent it to me in the first place. So . . . before I throw in the towel utterly, sink without trace and make my father's day, I'm going to try just the one more phone call. I don't want to – of course I don't want to, but this is quite literally the very last chance I've got. Just sent out Lilian on some fool's errand, so now I have the flat to myself.

'Well . . . this is a surprise.'

'A surprise? What do you mean a surprise?'

'Can't remember the last time you called me, David. How are you?'

'I'm sure it's not that long ago, Anna. Oh – I'm fine. Well. Not fine, actually.'

'Dad again?'

'No. Well yes, but that's always the case. With me, anyway. I know it's not the same with you. No look – I was just wondering. Long shot I know, but . . .'

'I'm quite well, David, thank you for asking.'

'What? Oh yes. Sorry. Good – I'm glad you're, er. Look, Anna – that husband of yours. Max, yes? Well I know he was in the diamond business – there was always a lot of cash and everything for you, wasn't there?'

'There was. For a time.'

'Right. Well I know it sounds awful, but I was just wondering if, er . . .'

'David, if it's money you're after, you have so come to the wrong person. I won't sort of go into it all, but . . . I'm just not in a position. Really not. But listen – what about Dad? Have you asked him? Because I'm sure he'd . . .'

'No. I haven't. And I'm not going to either. Not the slightest intention. No no – not to worry. It's nothing serious, or anything. Little cash-flow hiccup, that's all. No no – sorry to have, er . . . so anyway: everything all right with you then, is it? And the boy?'

'His name is Troy, David.'

'Yes I know that. I do *know* that, Anna. Well look – I won't delay you. Sure you've got things to see to. Bye, Anna. Sorry if I've been, um . . . Bye.'

Well . . . goodbye then, David – and yes I do, as a matter of fact. Have things to see to. Packing bags, actually, and I'm rather in a hurry. Not, you know, as neat or methodical as I would be normally. Because packing – I usually have a system of folding and rolling, perfected over the years . . . yes, but not today. Today it's more a question of ramming as many essentials as I possibly can into just two bags, because

I know that with Troy, that is all I shall be able to carry. Before you called, you see – not that much more than an hour ago, possibly . . . seems like seconds and years . . . someone rang my doorbell. Yes . . . I had a caller. I wasn't expecting anybody – I never do. I don't remember the last time I had what you might even jokingly call a social life. Not since . . . well, not since Max left. And that really only came down to expensive dinners in famous and glamorous restaurants with a succession of rather glittery other couples whom I did not know and never saw twice. Contacts, he called them. As usual, I didn't ask – just blithely went along with it. As to any other sort of socialising . . . well no, not really. I have never been one for coffee mornings with the girls – joining a book club, tennis club, any of that sort of thing. Could never see the point. All other women ever appear to need from you is scandal – real or fabricated, they don't really seem to mind. And then it can be tweeted, retweeted . . . oh, all the rest of it. It tires me out. I do actually find it quite exhausting, just the thought of it. So certainly I don't have people popping round unannounced – unless it's to read the meter, or something. In the old days, when still I was more or less me, I would have just swung open the door, my face already bright with the smile of welcome. But now, I am far too . . . what am I . . .? Circumspect? No – just bloody untrusting. Of everyone. So I peered through the spyhole. A man was there. Big man, he seemed. I spoke loudly through the panels, because I don't have an intercom. It was one of the things we were going to have done. But we didn't.

'Hello? May I help you?'

'Open the door, please.'

'Who are you? What do you want?'

'Just open the door, ay? We don't want no fuss.'

I don't know anyone who would ever say, 'We don't want no fuss.' The voice was deep and thick with a touch of gravel. Not threatening, exactly – but what I think people mean when they say 'quietly determined'.

'I'm very sorry but if you won't tell me who you are and why you are here, then I'm not opening the door. And anyway, this is not a convenient moment. I'm very busy.'

Troy was having his nap just next door, and I was suddenly aware that I was speaking loudly enough to wake him. But I knew, of course I knew, what this must all be about. The thing that I hoped would just blow over. Go away. Knowing, of course, that it wouldn't. These people, whoever they are: they don't forget. I think we know that.

'Listen, Anna – let's be nice. Ay? I don't want to have to ask you again.'

'I think you'd better leave. Or else I shall call the police.'

I said that more or less automatically, while quite idly thinking: he knows my name. How does he come to know my name? Oh but yes . . . I suppose he would, wouldn't he? Still though, I wasn't exactly scared. And then . . . oh God: then I was. There was a moment's silence – and then this most terrible cracking noise as the door just imploded with thunder into the hallway, and the side of my face was glancingly struck by a jagged section of the splintered frame. He stood there, quite impassively. He was huge. Some sort of iron bar was hanging loosely from the fist of a large red hand. He was smiling. He looked quite kindly.

'Sorry about that,' he said. 'All this mess. The damage. I can recommend somebody to put it right, you interested. Good little chippy. And he's ever so reasonable. Would've saved trouble, wouldn't it? If you'd just gone and opened the door. Little mark on your cheek there, look. Does it hurt? Bit of Savlon, could be, you want to put on that. I don't reckon it's needing an Elastoplast, though. Don't look too bad. Not . . . what can I say . . .? Life-threatening. Come in, will I . . .?'

God I was rattled, and shaking so badly – truly a violent trembling, as if I were mortally cold. All my limbs were juddering, and my stomach was repeatedly convulsing – the whole of me was simply uncontrollable. But even so, I did somehow manage to stutter out a few words – I did at least manage to say, oh . . . I don't know . . . something like . . .

'Well it rather looks as if you're in already. Doesn't it?'

He smiled. Almost shyly. Blue eyes, though nearly lost amid the puffs and creases of an enormous face. His bulbous neck appeared to be uncomfortably red and strangled by a high-collared shirt and an extraordinarily colourful tie.

'Thing is, if I'm honest a cup of tea wouldn't be a bad thing. What you say to that? Then we can sit down, the two of us. Yeh? Have a little chat. The lock . . . your actual lock, look – it's not harmed at all. I take care, like that. Detail, isn't it? All in the detail. So it's only the bits of wood. Door still solid. My mate Jon-Jo, he'll have this little lot fixed up in no time. Did I say that were his name? No? Well it is. Jon-Jo. Ever so good with his hands. Right, then – through here is it . . .? Nice flat, I must say. I like the colours you chosen. Classy. And a biscuit wouldn't go amiss neither, if I'm honest. Chocolate, you got it. I'm Stanley, by the way.'

'Do you mind if I . . . don't make tea, actually? I'm just a bit . . . you know.'

'Well of course you are. Only natural. Bit jittery – course you are. I just come busting into your life like this, what you supposed to think? Nah – it were thoughtless of me. Got a drink then, maybe? And I'll just sit here then, will I?'

'Yes. A drink. There's . . . Scotch. Wine, if you want it . . . in the fridge, I think.'

'Drop of Scotch be lovely. Hit the spot. You know, Anna – you're a very nice lady. A very nice lady indeed. Don't know what you saw in him, your bloke. Myself, I only met him the once or twice – but nah, didn't deserve you, you want my opinion. But it's funny, isn't it? Human nature.'

'Look, Mr . . . um . . .'

'Stanley. My name's Stanley. I told you.'

'Right, yes – Stanley. Of course. Well look, Stanley – what exactly do you, er . . .?'

'Want? What do I want? Why am I here? That what you asking me? Well I think we both know that, don't we? You want me to get down to it, well: the problem is, Anna – your bloke, he gone and offended quite a lot of people. Sort of people you don't want to go offending, if you see my meaning. Now – he gone . . . and, well . . . we got to find him. See?'

'Well I don't know where he is. He just left us. I haven't a clue where he is. Haven't heard from him since the day he went.'

'You're quite sure about that, are you my dear? Not mistaken in any way?'

'No! No – I'm telling you . . .!'

'Yes well you see that is rather unfortunate then, isn't it? For you, I mean. Because the people he upset, well . . . way they see it, it's down to you, then. If he done a runner, they'll get to thinking you got his stash, see? Which weren't his stash in the first place, of course. And now they want it back.'

'*Stash* . . .? What on earth are you talking about?'

'That drink coming, is it?'

'Oh – look, it's just behind you on the table. See it? Do you think you could just, I don't know . . . help yourself . . .?'

'Thank you. That's very kind of you. And for yourself, Anna?'

'Oh . . . no. Well – I will, actually.'

'Clever girl. Good decision. Calm your nerves. Settle you down. No – thing is, clearly you're not in the picture. Mind you – intelligent woman such as yourself, educated woman like you . . . I'm guessing you're not in the picture because you don't want to be in the picture. Am I right?'

'You – could be.'

'Yeh. Thought so. Head in the sand, ay? Well who can blame you? Messy business all round. Here you are – a good stiff one. Get that down you. Knock all the edges off. Macallan. I do like a nice malt. But you see the trouble is, Anna . . . my bosses, they don't seem to believe it, you see. That you're not in the picture. I do. I do – of course I do. See it in your eyes. You get to be good at judging people, my game. But my bosses, they got an altogether different way of looking at things. Way they see it . . . you owe them. Quite a lot, if we're being honest. What with the stones. The cash. Yeh – quite a lot, really.'

'But . . . but . . . I haven't *got* anything! I'm completely *broke* . . .!'

'Could be true. Needn't be . . .'

'It *is* true! It's *true,* I tell you. I go to work. I can't pay my bills. I'm owing on the rent of this place, along with . . . Christ, just about everything else. I don't have a bloody *bean* . . .!'

'I see. Right. Well . . . it's unfortunate you say that. On the whole. See . . . if you was just to hand it over to me now, nice and sweet, it would all be over. You could be about your business. I go. Send Jon-Jo round to see to the broken doings, and that's the end of it. Weight off your shoulders, that would be.

Wouldn't it? Get back to looking after that little boy of yours. Troy, isn't it? Yeh – Troy. Unusual name. I don't dislike it. But if you're saying to me you haven't got it . . .'

'I haven't! I'd give it to you if I had it. I haven't!'

'Yeh. I hear you. Well that's what I'll have to tell them, then. But listen to me, Anna – I like you, all right? Like I said, you're a very nice lady. And so I shouldn't really be saying this to you, but I'm going to, yeh? If I was you, I'd be thinking in terms of a nice little holiday. See? See what I'm saying to you? Because they're not about to let it lie. They never do. How they come to be in the business they're in. And what'll happen next is, well . . . they'll send me back to pay you another little visit, see? Find out if you suddenly remembered something you forgot. And that time, well . . . not going to be like this. Won't be a little fireside chat with a nice glass of whisky. And I hope you know I'm being straight with you, Anna, when I say that I'd take not one iota of pleasure in anything to do with any of that. But hand on heart, it would get a bit . . . well. Know what I'm saying? Yeh. Good. Word to the wise then, ay?'

Yes well. And he left the flat very soon afterwards. So now I'm packing. Getting out. Don't know where to. Just away from here, that's all. Take Troy, and anything else I can carry. Because otherwise . . . well it's perfectly plain from what he said and the way he was looking at me: Stanley, he's going to come back here. And when he does, he's going to . . . hurt me. Then . . . when he still doesn't get whatever it is he's after . . . well then it's just obvious, isn't it? There's going to be, oh God . . . a different sort of pressure. He didn't . . . that man, he didn't mention Troy just by accident, did he? Oh Christ – I just can't . . . I just can't think of it. I'm weeping now, in fear – I'm shaking, with the horror of it all. But when he sees that I'm telling the truth – by the time he knows for sure that I have absolutely nothing to give him . . . well then . . . then he's going to kill me. Kill us both. It's what these people do.

CHAPTER FIVE

SHABBY AND TATTERED PARTS

Sammy lately, he keeps on telling me I'm being a right little miserable bastard these days, and that I ought to just go and see her – talk to her, for Christ's sake. I say to him I don't know what he's bloody talking about – and go and see who, exactly? I'm fine – I'm completely fine. Got a new girl, haven't I? No shortage of girls. And anyway . . . I don't know where she lives.

'You know where she works though, Georgie. It wouldn't be hard.'

'Don't know where she works. How could I? Temp, isn't she?'

'Not any more. I told you. Don't pretend you don't remember. I told you.'

'Yeah, well. It's been months now. Over two months. And anyway – I'm fine. I'm completely fine. This place though, Sammy . . .! Can't get over it. It's . . . amazing. I never thought I'd be here. Read about it so many times. Never thought I'd be here, though. Bag O'Nails. I'm actually sitting and having a lager in the Bag O'Nails . . .'

'Yeah. It's not so great at this time of the day, though. Gets much better later on. And you never know who's going to be playing. Somebody was saying they had the Rolling Stones not too long ago. They get great groups – and lots of American acts as well, apparently. Jazz too – lots of jazz. Not really my sort of thing. And you see the most amazing people late at night, Georgie. Just, you know – hanging around and having a drink. Oh God yes – just remembered, I meant to tell you: you'll never guess who I saw in here last week. You'll never guess.'

'Who? But listen, Sammy – how can you come here all the time? And late, and everything. It's a club, isn't it? You can't just walk in off the street, can you? Got any fags . . .?'

'Well no, not technically. But it's my dad, you see. You want a fag, just take one. He's really into negro jazz bands and stuff, and so he's a member, you see. Also goes to that other place, what is it . . .? Quite near here. Oh yeh – Ronnie Scott's, that's it. And I just sometimes tag along, that's all. I've never been in here this early in the evening, though. Pretty empty. Quite surprised they were even open, actually. But it was just so handy, wasn't it? Just round the corner from where we were. It's really good I just saw you standing there.'

Yeh – because I'd just met him accidentally, Sammy. And although it's great just being here in the Bag O'Nails and everything, I still pretty much wish he hadn't, actually – just seen me standing there. I'd come straight from bloody Smith's – got away a bit earlier for once, and Thursday is late-night shopping in the West End: lots of places don't close till seven – so I went straight to Carnaby Street, of course, because I sort of needed my fix of just, I don't know . . . breathing in the place, really. I'd live here, if I could – I really would: above John Stephen or His Clothes, that would be just bloody marvellous. Not Vince Man's Shop, though – I've heard that's for queers, don't know if it's true, but you do see some pretty funny-looking people going in. It's a bit of a funny street all round actually, now I come to think of it – because although there are all these fantastically groovy boutiques and everything, there's also a really old-fashioned tobacconist with all jars and pipes and cigars and stuff in the window: dark wood and dimly lit – it's like something out of Sherlock Holmes. Couple of doors on is a stinky old ironmonger with metal buckets and mops outside and an Esso Blue Paraffin tin sign, and two others that say Brasso and Aladdin Pink. Then suddenly you're outside this shop with these gorgeous tall and thin mannequins of girls with huge eyes and Vidal Sassoon-type wigs, all in a row and wearing this same just tiny little lacy dress that's full of holes and coloured bangles and there's all this great music that they play really loudly – Animals, Manfreds – so that you can hear it in the street, and some people even sort of dance a bit, right on the pavement. Just so groovy.

So I was staring into the window of Lord John, as per usual – and I'm even more broke than ever now because Magsie, she's the latest, oh Christ, oh bloody hell: she always wants to go to things like Italian restaurants and bars instead of pubs and although she's got a really good job in some sort of an art gallery or something, I think she said it was, she never bloody offers to pay for anything because she says that girls, they never do. Well – some girls do. One, anyway, used to. But she's pretty sexy, I've got to say, Magsie is . . . she wears loads of black around her eyes and false eyelashes and thick pink lipstick, but the trouble is she's always saying not to touch her face or kiss her or anything because it messes it up and it takes just ages to do it all over again. Last weekend I got one of those enormous yellow plastic hoops that she wears all tangled up in my jumper and she was screaming that I was tearing her ear off. She always wears a miniskirt, obviously, but when you try to put your hand up it she says mind my tights – they're new and they're Mary Quant and they cost an absolute fortune. It's only really when she's taken all her clothes and make-up off completely that I can ever get to be near her . . . yeh, but she isn't nearly so sexy then, if I'm honest. Bit bony, you know? And her face . . . really very ordinary. I do it, of course . . . but it's not that great.

So anyway – there I was in Carnaby Street, and I'm gaping at this amazing grey herringbone jacket with a half belt at the back and five black buttons up the front of it and it's exactly like one I've seen Paul McCartney wearing in a picture in *Melody Maker*, getting out of his Mini. And I was thinking okay, right then – if I dump Magsie and don't eat a single bloody thing for maybe about a month, or could be as long as a year, I could just about possibly afford that. And then from inside the shop, there's somebody flapping his hands about at me. Sammy. I actually did think of turning and running away, but I knew that he'd seen it was me. It wasn't that I didn't want to spend time with him – I always like to be with Sammy – but I just knew, didn't I, what he'd been doing in there. What I didn't know, you want the truth, is whether I could actually stand it. The envy. Not again. Not any more. Eats me up like acid. Anyway – he'd come to the door by now.

'Hi, Georgie . . .! How great to see you. Come in – I'll only be a minute. Just got to pay. What are you doing round here? Something you're looking for? They've got just piles of new stuff – have you seen? Girl here's been telling me that they got a delivery only this morning. Amazing. None of this was here last week, I can tell you that. Hey – you know what would really suit you, Georgie? This shirt. See? You like? I've never seen mustard-coloured shirts before. And the tab collar – isn't it great? Rounded. Double cuffs. Really good with a black knitted tie.'

'Yeah. I love it. Did you buy one?'

'I did. And I got it in blue and this sort of really pale pink as well. Girl was saying that soon they're expecting them in with polka dots, and also a pattern that's all made up of tiny little flowers . . .! All different colours. Can you imagine? I'll definitely be getting one of those.'

'What else have you bought?'

'Belt – silver buckle. Cord waistcoat – quite nice. Oh and a jacket. Grey herringbone – really cool. Saw it in the window – why I came in, actually. Fits perfectly. Doesn't need any alterations at all. What do you want to look at?'

'Oh – nothing, really. Don't really need anything just at the moment. Got so much lately. Only passing. Anyway – I've got to get back.'

'Really? Oh – okay. Time for a drink?'

'Well – maybe. Could do with a fag, actually. Where shall we go? There's that pub, the Shakespeare. We could go there.'

'We could. But I've just thought of somewhere better. Round the corner.'

Yeh. And that's where we are now: the Bag O'Nails.

'So who? Who did you see in here last week?'

'You'll never believe it.'

'Well tell me, Christ's sake.'

'You simply won't believe it.'

'You're annoying me now, Sammy. Who was it?'

'Okay then: only Cilla. That's all.'

'Cilla? Cilla Black? You are *joking* . . .!'

'Not. Not joking. Sitting right over there.'

'But . . . she's number one at the moment! "You're My World" . . .'

'I know. But listen to this, Georgie boy: it gets better. Guess who was with her . . .'

'Oh God. I can't. Not . . . not . . .'

'No – not quite that. But close. Brian Epstein . . .!'

And I just sat there. I just sat there. It was like he'd said, I don't know . . . Jesus, Joseph, Mary and all the Saints, or something. The only thing that would've been better than that is an actual Beatle. I was elated. I was floating. Just last week, Cilla and Brian Epstein had been sitting right over there . . .! Believe that? I was elated. I was floating. And then . . . well then . . . I just wasn't. I came down really hard. My eyes were practically closed, but still I couldn't miss this great big bunch of Lord John bags that were stacked just anyhow around Sammy's feet (chisel-toe Chelsea boots in midnight blue). I looked around at the so completely fabulous Bag O'Nails, where Sammy's dad is a member and he sometimes tags along. I thought of stupid Carol, who I'd been seeing for a bit, few nights, before bony Magsie, who is bleeding me dry and never makes me laugh, or even happy . . . and then what came crowding in on me was my job at W. H. Fucking Smith's. And then I just thought . . . oh Jesus. My life . . . my life now . . . it is just such a crock of shit. I've got to do something. I've got to *be* something. I've just got to . . . get out of this place.

And now I'm on the bus, heading back to Kilburn. My lousy little pit in Kilburn – yeh and that's another thing, one more, that's just got to go. I'm up on the top deck, right at the front, having a fag as usual. Ten No. 6 I got earlier. I would've offered one to Sammy, but he'd probably turn up his nose at No. 6. Well no – he wouldn't, actually. He's too nice to do that. Might be the school he went to, Westminster, taught him all that sort of behaviour – it comes completely naturally to him, he doesn't even have to work at it. And his dad, I shouldn't wonder – he probably learned by example. What a dad to have. No – he would've taken it, my No. 6, Sammy – of course he would – and then he would've smiled, smoked it, and not said a word. Pretty classy, you see. Yes ... and all of that would've made me feel a whole lot worse. So I scrounged another couple of Bensons from him, and then I just pushed off. Where are you going, he said: you haven't finished your drink. And I said yeh well – just, you know, got to go. Because I did. I suddenly did feel that I just had to go. I was excited in one way, which is really a bit weird. What I mean is – I mean, I was depressed as hell about, Christ ... everything, really ... but at the same time I was feeling, well ... just a bit ... well it is excited, actually, that is the word, because now I'd decided I was finally going to do something about it all. My life. That's what I was feeling, more or less. Kind of filled me up.

Yes ... but now I'm on the bus, front of the top deck as usual, and we've stopped at the lights and I'm looking down like I do at the tops of people's heads as they're all just rushing about ... and the shops are shutting now and I think it must just have begun to rain ... yes it has: couple of umbrellas, and the window's suddenly covered with all these silver little pinpoints. There's that stupid saying painted on those shutters over there, look: Kilroy Was Here. And his nose poking over a wall. Who the hell is he, this Kilroy? Why does everyone think it's so funny, whenever they see it? I don't – I don't think it's funny. It's just stupid. Annoys me. But what I really mean is ... I'm down again. Yes – that's the point. Back down on the ground, and fed up as hell. The excitement, if that's what it was – well any trace of it, that's all gone now. Because it's all very well me saying I'm going to change things – blow everything up – but how do I think I'm going to do that, then? Pull off that little number. Hey? How the hell? Look: I hate my job, right? So I chuck it in. Then what? No money. So I get another crappy job. The room – the shitty room in Kilburn. I tell the landlord to find some other mug to go on paying his rent, to fill up his bloody electricity and gas meters with a million shillings a night. And then I'm on the street. Looking for another hole to go and crawl into. Say to Magsie, Christ I'm so sick of you, Magsie. You're really boring and you're mean and once all your kit is off you're a right bag of bones with a face like a loaf of bread and you never make me laugh, or even happy. Well . . . there's always another girl knocking around somewhere. That's not hard. But it'll only be another girl, won't it? And I'll have to buy her a drink and give her a fag and ask her all the bloody questions I don't give a fuck about the answers to: you live round here? What do you do? You got a boyfriend? Then say all the stuff I don't believe – all the stuff that just falls right out of me without me even thinking about it: you look lovely. You're different – you're really interesting. So much more intelligent, sensitive, thoughtful than anyone else in here. I love your hair. When all it comes down to is this: look, girly – I'm in between birds, okay? Bit drunk – hour to spare. You want a shag, or what? And if yeh, do you promise to fuck right off straight afterwards and not make coffee and then start getting to know me?

It's a circle, isn't it? Or maybe it's a cycle, I don't know. Even if there's a difference. But whatever a thing it is – the big question is this: how do I break it? Shatter it to pieces, and just start again. Not just go on shuffling around the same few shabby and tattered parts, not settle for something just because it's different when it's just as bad as the thing before – but somehow invent, I don't know . . . a brand-new game . . .? Well . . . I haven't a clue, really. Not a single bloody idea. Useless. She'd know what to do, though. She'd help me. Encourage me. And all the time she'd be loving me, too. Christ – she's the only bloody one who'd even understand what the hell it is I'm actually talking about. So I think, really, that that's where it's just got to begin. With her. Jesus, though . . . I should've done this, oh – just bloody ages ago. Sammy, he was always telling me. He knew – he knew I was just so completely buggered inside, but of course I'd never let on to him. Why wouldn't I do that? Why haven't I talked to him? He knew – I knew . . . so who was I pretending to? Yeh but the real truth is, I should never have let it happen in the first place. Obviously. That day . . . that wonderful hot and sunny Saturday, when she'd gone to all that trouble and spent Christ knows how much money to arrange for me such a completely fabulous treat: the picnic on Hampstead Heath. Oh God . . . my guts, they're just so wrenched around when I think of it – I really hurt now, like I always do – because I just can't stop remembering the way I treated her, for the whole of that afternoon. Or any other afternoon, really. But Sammy . . . he'd told me, hadn't he, that she was sitting in a little tucked-away booth in the Spaniards, and talking to some bloke. He was amazed, Sammy, when I didn't do a damned thing about it – when I just went on sitting there, and talking balls about a couple of girls who were up at the bar. Who yeh – we did pick up, actually. Quite easy. Took them to Jack Straw's Castle. They were au pairs or nannies or something from some or other stupid bloody country – Sweden, Denmark, somewhere. Blonde hair, hardly any English – pretty much perfect for the mood I was in. But of course I saw her . . . I pretended I was on my way to the Gents, because I just had to see her, didn't I? She was sipping something fizzy through a straw – the bloke, he had his back to me, but his hair was quite long. Quite Beatley, actually. But it was her face that struck me. I sort of convulsed, the second I saw her. She just looked so fantastically beautiful to me . . . I can't really quite explain it: I had just never before seen her looking anything like as beautiful as this. And so soft. And so very tender. This beauty, it punched me right in the face. I was transfixed, and so damn screwed up inside: my guts, they were really churning. I don't know if she'd seen me or not – I was skulking like a criminal behind a wooden beam – but if she had, she gave no sign. And then – feeling the way I did – I just turned away and went back to Sammy and the two bits of skirt at the bar. And even as I did it, I was screaming at me to stop. To stop and go back. To get her – to get her away from that bloke. And on I went. I have no words to explain this. I think it was the single most stupid thing I have ever done in the whole of my pretty useless little life. So off we went to another pub, Sammy, me and the two little foreign birds. They didn't understand what we were saying, and I didn't even listen to anything that they might have been stuttering out. At the end of it all, they said they had to go home. I got a bit aggressive with one of them, and then I just thought oh sod it: they want to go home, let them go home – who fucking cares? Yes. So anyway . . . that's how I just came to leave her, with the heavy bag with all our picnic things in it, alone in a pub – but not alone, actually . . . because she was talking to a bloke with hair like a Beatle. Christ. Oh Christ. No wonder she'd had enough of me. I know the feeling. Every night when I go to sleep, I've had enough of me. I wake up in the morning, and there's more.

Back in my room. After the Bag O'Nails, I'm back in my

shitty little room. Nothing in the fridge – not even a Skol. Not even some Pork Luncheon Meat. Half a bar of Cadbury's Dairy Milk, so I'll have that with a No. 6 and a mug of that bloody awful cheapo coffee I keep on buying, some bloody reason. Thought I'd got some Golden Wonder Cheese and Onion, but there's nothing in the packet: had it last night, I think – can't remember, but I must have. I wonder . . . I wonder what she's doing now . . .? Right this moment. I do that quite a lot. Supper with her mother in Edgware, I expect. If . . . if that's where she's still living. Yes well of course it is – where else would she be? Whatever she thinks about her bats old mother, I don't think she'd ever actually leave her. Wouldn't be allowed to. Sammy, he somehow got a bit of information about her. Typically decent of him. I pretended not to be listening while he was telling me – did a load of extravagant yawns – but I never actually told him to stop talking. Permanent job now, apparently. Secretary. Which she never really wanted to do, but still. Well which one of us is doing what we want to do? Apart from people like The Beatles and Cilla and Brian Epstein. Sammy, of course – he's always doing exactly what he wants to do. Some sort of agency she's in that finds jobs for secretaries, if I got it right. Could be the same place that was getting her temp work, I don't know. Got the address, though – somewhere in Baker Street. Sammy, he wrote it down for me. I screwed up the paper and tossed it over my shoulder: shan't be needing *that*, is what I said to him. He told me I was a fool, and fucking ungrateful as well. I laughed, knowing that that was just about dead on. When he'd gone, I picked up the piece of paper, smoothed it out, put it away. Why did I put it away? Why didn't I *do* something with it? Why didn't I go straight round there and batter down the door so that then I could just finally get *back* with her . . .? Yeh well. Okay look – you know what they say: better late than never, right? So tomorrow . . . tomorrow's Friday, and that's exactly what I'm going to do. First thing. Whenever the office opens. And as for Smith's, well – I just won't be turning up, that's all. That spastic fucker at the door – what's his name? Timpson, yeah – he won't be able to check me off on his bloody little clipboard with one of his bloody coloured biros that are all lined up in the pocket of his bloody brown work coat: that alone will be enough to drive him mental. Timpson, he's been there man and boy. How do I know that? Because he bloody tells me, doesn't he? Every single day. Like he thinks it's a good thing, or something. He says to me that I'm a sound lad at heart, and that if I stick at it, then one day in the distant future, who knows, I could even rise to take over his position. Believe it? He's actually *proud* of having done completely bugger all for the whole of his bloody life. Jesus. Old people. They deserve what they get. So yeh – fuck Smith's: they don't like it, they can do the other thing. Couldn't give a shit. Shan't be working there for much longer anyway – fed up with being just pushed around every day and getting tuppence ha'penny at the end of the week. Won't still be living in this poxy little room either. Because everything now . . . just the whole bloody lot: it's all got to change.

And now I'm on my way to somewhere in Circus Road – flat, or something – and that's in St John's Wood, I've just been told. Why am I going there? I'll tell you: because the girl in the office in Baker Street said to me that that's where she could possibly be. The office, it was up a couple of flights over some sort of a café, restaurant could be. Jewish, I think – had that sort of a funny name with a 'stein' at the end. I thought I'd just cruise straight in as casually as you like, see her immediately . . . and sort of, I don't know . . . smile. Just smile. Not actually speak. And she, she'd be just so completely amazed at the sight of me – even completely overcome, quite possibly. Because suddenly, after all this time, there I'd be, just standing in front of her in the middle of the place she's working . . .! I thought – because I'd been thinking about it all the way there – that she maybe might have just dropped whatever it was she'd been doing and rushed towards me. Held me. Crying with sort of relief, or something. Yeh but it didn't turn out like that. There were three girls in the outer office – it was all pale green with an enormous plant and a Beatles calendar on the wall, which could only be a good thing – and you could hear the racket from the typewriters halfway up the stairs. The girls, they all stopped and looked up at me as I walked through the door. Two of them went right back to their typing, but the nearest one to me was sort of smiling – bit of a raised eyebrow.

'I'm looking for, er . . . I was told she worked here.'

'Who, exactly . . .?'

'Oh God yes – sorry. Dorothy. I was told she, um . . .'

'Oh Dorothy, yes. Yes she does. That's her desk over there. And you are . . .?'

'Cousin. I'm her cousin. Said I'd look her up when I was in London.'

'Oh right. Well she's off today, I'm afraid. You could ring her at home . . .?'

'Yes. Right. I'll do that. Edgware, isn't it? With my aunt, of course.'

'Think so. But she could be in Circus Road, I don't know.'

'Circus Road . . .?'

'Yup. She seems to be there quite a lot. She hasn't been too well lately, actually – why she isn't in this morning. I don't think it's anything serious or anything but a couple of times lately she's phoned in to say she isn't feeling too great, but she says she likes to be near so that she can come in later if she's feeling a bit better. She's so conscientious . . .! If it was me, I'd just take the day off and be done with it.'

'Uh-huh. Right. I see. Sorry to hear that she's, um . . .'

'Yeh – but like I say, I don't think it's anything to worry about.'

'No – of course not. So . . . Circus Road, you think . . .?'

'Yup. It's possible. Here – I'll give you the address. It's quite near, actually.'

She was nice, the girl – didn't ask her name. Long blonde fringe and legs in black tights. Cheeky little face. Probably about my age, bit older maybe. Any other time, I would have been going through all of my stuff with her, of course I would – but do you know what? It didn't even cross my mind. Just said thank you, and legged it back down the stairs. The address . . . it turns out to be a large and rather smart block of flats. Redbrick, with a big sort of glass-covered entrance. I don't know what I've been expecting, but it isn't this. I'm really pretty jangled, actually – because this is just such a weird day. I should be at work, but instead I'm haring about bits of London I never even go to, and not really quite knowing what in fact is going on: what the hell it is I think I'm up to. The hall, foyer – it reminds me a bit of the Odeon: really thick carpet and pinkish mirrors – feels like, I don't know . . . before the war, somehow. Cream-coloured leather sofa with an ashtray on a stand. Magazines like *Punch* and the *Illustrated London News* on a shiny black coffee table. It's never going to be 1964 in here – nothing modern about it. Sort of building where old and rich people live, I should think . . . so listen: can this actually be right, then . . .? What on earth can Dorothy be doing in a place like this? There's a desk over there where it looks like some sort of porter should be, but there's nobody actually sitting at it, so that's one explanation I can get out of, then. A notice by the lift – more of a plaque, actually: marble, with engraved gold letters, like a gravestone – it tells you what floor the flats are on: I'm heading up to third, apparently. There's a mirror in the lift. As the doors are hissing shut, I'm catching a sight of me. But only for a second, because I've turned my back to it now. I was looking really odd, I think – my eyes, I don't know. Staring, and quite scared-looking. Like a hunted creature.

The doors have pinged open, and still I'm just standing here. I feel so . . . I don't really know . . . what do I feel? I'd love a drink of water, that I do know. And a fag, of course – but not right now: I'll have it a bit later on. Only just put one out. I feel quite . . . well – *scared*, I suppose, is what I'm actually feeling, but that's just so completely stupid, isn't it? What have I got to be scared about? I'm only going to talk to a friend of mine. If she's there. If she wants to talk to me. Though I don't know why she shouldn't. Can't be any harm in it surely? Just talking. And now, Christ, I've got to really quickly wedge myself in between these hissing doors because I've been just hanging about for so bloody long, they're bloody shutting again now. The landing is sort of like in hotels that you see in films – I've never actually stayed in a hotel, nowhere decent anyway, so I wouldn't really know. But that's what it seems like. More soft carpet. Royal blue. More mirrors. They really do go in for mirrors in this place. Another great big plant in a pot on the floor. Total bloody silence. Christ Almighty. And now I'm standing right outside the door: 304. That's the number. That's the number I've got on this bit of paper. And there's the bell. So I'll ring it, I suppose. Yeh well of course I'll ring it: not going to stand here for ever, am I? So . . . I've done that, I've rung the bell . . . and I'm thinking Jesus, what am I going to say? I haven't got a plan – what the bloody hell am I actually going to say . . .? Yeh but I'm really needing to run now: I just want to run the length of the corridor and get back into that lift and then streak through the lobby, foyer, and back into the fresh sweet air of Circus Road and then clear out of this area altogether and go back on the Tube to my room in Kilburn and put on a Beatles record and maybe have a Skol and about forty or fifty cigarettes.

'Oh . . . my *God* ! Oh my God . . .'

'Hello, Dorothy. So pleased you're in. You look awful.'

'I just can't . . . what are you doing here? How did you . . .?'

'Yeh well I just thought I'd like to, you know – see you again, and so I . . . well. You know. Anyway – I'm here now.'

'Well look, George . . . it's not really . . .'

'Yeh well I know you're not well, and everything. I can see that. You look absolutely awful.'

'As you keep on telling me. Look – can you, I don't know . . . telephone me, or something? If you want to talk.'

'Well I could, I suppose. Except I don't have your number, do I? Or I would've. And look – I'm here, aren't I? Standing right in front of you. So we can talk, can't we? Right now.'

'Look: I really don't feel that great at the moment, George. Okay? Why I'm not at work. And don't for God's sake tell me I look awful again . . .'

'No I won't. I shouldn't have. Sorry. Actually . . . you look really, really *good*.'

'Oh God, George . . .'

'But look – let me come in, yes? Just for a minute. Whose

place is this anyway? Your mother win the pools, or something? So bloody posh . . .'

'It's . . . a friend's. Well look – all right, George. Come in, then. But just for a minute, okay? You said just for a minute, yes? But everything's . . . all right, is it? You're okay, are you? Not ill, or anything? Why are you here? I don't understand you, George.'

'No well. I don't understand me either. But you probably do, actually, Dorothy. You're the only one who ever did. Hey – cool pad . . .! Wow. I love this sort of rough stuff on the walls. Like sacking, or something. So groovy – that is just so groovy.'

'Hessian. It's called hessian.'

'Yeh? And Jesus – look at the size of that sofa . . .! Like a boat.'

'Sit, if you like. Do you . . . want something? Drink? Coffee?'

'You haven't got a lager, have you? I don't mind if it isn't Skol.'

'I . . . no . . . I don't think so. Got coffee, as I said. Do you want some coffee? Or . . . what else have we got . . .? Tea . . .? No – you don't drink tea, do you? Coke? There's Coca-Cola, I'm pretty sure.'

'What's all that on the sideboard?'

'Oh . . . I don't really know. I don't drink any of that. Maybe we'll just forget it, yes? You're only staying a minute. And I'm not really feeling that wonderful . . .'

'But what is it? I can't see from here.'

'Well there's . . . let's have a look. Um – Bacardi, it says. Don't know what it is. Gordon's. That's gin, isn't it?'

I can't really believe this. I just simply cannot believe that any of this is actually happening. George. George is here. Sitting on the sofa. And I'm offering him a menu of drinks . . .! How on earth can this *be* . . .? Two minutes ago I had my head hanging over the lavatory for the second time this morning . . . I was just about to make myself a cup of camomile tea . . . and now there's George, in the middle of the room. George – who I haven't seen or heard from for, oh . . . just months and months. And look at me . . .! I just caught sight of myself in the mirror, and oh my God – just look at the state of me . . .! No wonder he said I looked awful. I look so much worse than awful – what I look is practically subhuman: white and green, virtually a walking corpse. My split ends sticking out from under an Alice band. And wearing this ghastly candlewick dressing gown, which I would only ever put on if there was no one around to see me. I wouldn't even have opened the door, but I assumed it had to be Mike. Because although of course he's at work, who else was going to be ringing the bell? And he did say he'd be popping over at some point to see how I was getting on, although I'd told him that he didn't have to and that I'd be perfectly fine. I now see, silly fool that I was, that it couldn't possibly have been Mike, because Mike's got a key, hasn't he? It's his dad's flat, for goodness sake, or I wouldn't even be here in the first place. I really am in a bit of, what is it . . .? Turmoil, now. I'm just standing here, looking and feeling awful, and George, he's come over to look at the bottles on the sideboard, like he's in a bar or at a party, or something. And my mind, it's just . . . I don't know – I'm just so completely . . . oh, I can't even think of the word. Haven't set eyes on him since that day – that lovely hot and sunny day when I damn well nearly killed myself over all that stupid, stupid picnic business, and he just left me in the Spaniards. I'd watched him watching me, although I was careful not to let him see that. When I'd come out of the Ladies, still hauling around this really heavy bag with Mum's radio in it apart from loads of other junk (and I just knew she'd be going mad about that by now – already I was dreading all that I'd be in for the second I stepped through the door), this boy just sort of came up to me and asked if I wanted a drink. He said he liked my dress. He said he liked my hair – which probably wasn't true because I can never get it to really go right, and it's nowhere nearly long enough: I hadn't had time to iron it that morning, and I'd been perspiring quite a lot since then heaving all the picnic about and so now it was back to being not exactly frizzy, but still not remotely how I like it to look. I'd tried to do something with it in the Ladies, but it didn't work. And I – pretty stupidly, I suppose – asked him, this boy, if he liked my cardigan, because it was new . . . and he, he said he did. So I told him I'd have something like a 7Up or a Canada Dry, one of those, because they don't have Tizer and cream soda in pubs, and he said are you sure that's all you want, and I said oh yes, quite sure.

So we were sitting in a booth where I knew that George would be just bound to see us, and my heart, oh God – it was pounding like anything: I could actually feel it, hear it thumping. I was so scared – not by the boy particularly, no. What it was . . . don't know, not sure, but I think that I was actually scaring myself: I was scared by my bravery for even thinking of this, let alone doing it. George, he'd be bound to go mad, I thought – but at the same time I really did hope he wasn't going to make some sort of a ghastly scene or anything, which of course he's completely capable of. But when he saw me, he'd realise how rude and beastly he'd been – this is what I was hoping for: that he'd realise how much he needed me, how much I cared for him, loved him, and then he'd come and get me and pick up the bag and tell me we're going home. But he didn't. He walked past twice – to get some drinks, the first time, I suppose with Sammy's money, as per usual . . .

and then the next time, it looked like he was almost hiding, or something. Behind a sort of wooden pillar, as if he was a spy. And while he was doing all of this nonsense, I was acting up terribly – smiling like mad at Mike (because it was Mike, he said his name was Mike) and pretending I really, really liked him and laughing at just about everything he was saying, and I wasn't actually properly listening to even a single word of it. He seemed perfectly happy though, because boys, they like it when you do that. But it was only because of George: that's all I was doing it for. And then suddenly – I could hardly believe it – he was just gone. George and Sammy, I noticed them talking to a couple of girls who I'd seen before standing at the bar – blonde hair and fringes, the sort of girls that boys like best – and then next time I looked over, they'd all just vanished. Couldn't believe it. I started to cry. Didn't want to, of course – amazed when it happened. Mike said, what's wrong? I said nothing – nothing's wrong. Then why are you crying, he said. He even looked as if he cared, a bit. I'm not, I said. You are, he said – you are, you're crying. Well it's nothing, I said – honestly, it's nothing at all. And then, more to change the subject than anything, I told him I liked his name: my favourite pop star is called Mike, I said. Mike Smith. Dave Clark Five. And he said oh really? Well I don't play the piano, keyboards, organ, whatever it is he plays – but I am a drummer. I mean – it's not my job, or anything. Just a hobby. Only a small group. Maybe you'd like to come and hear us, some time. And I think I was only properly looking at him for the first time, now. He had lovely eyes, really kind. And his hair was beautiful – thick and wavy, but not too long. Just over his collar. Quite Beatley, actually. He seemed really nice.

Then he asked me if I wanted another drink and I said oh

goodness, I've barely even touched this one, and he said he was having another, and was I sure. And so I asked for a sherry, sweet sherry, and even now I can barely believe that that's what I did. I was going to say Babycham, but George's scorn was ringing in my ears – it's just so bourgeois and common, apparently, and I didn't want to shame myself. So instead I said sherry, sweet sherry. It's what my mother drinks with a box of Keiller chocolate gingers on Boxing Day when she's watching the Black & White Minstrels. Bristol Cream. I didn't even know if I liked it or not, because I'd never even tried it. So he got me that – and while he was gone I was straining to look over towards the door, expecting George to walk back in at any moment – yearning for it, actually – with a smarmy grin on his face and telling me it was all just a joke, and give me that bag, Dorothy . . . I'll carry it, because now we're going home. But he didn't. The sherry, it was quite nice, actually. And then Mike said that the group, his group – they were called The Hornets, but none of them really liked the name and they're trying to think of something better – they didn't have a gig booked for weeks, but he did have some . . . what did he say they were? Acetates, I think. Not sure. Demos, demo discs, that's what he meant, anyway – and they were back at his father's place, if I'd maybe like to hear them. Your father's place . . .? No mother, then? They divorced, he said. And I said oh. Where is it – your father's place? Not too far – St John's Wood: know it? No, I said, I don't – how do we get there? Only I've got this hulking great bag. Well, he said . . . I've got a car outside. And I said gosh – really? Wow. So we went.

Honestly, it's the prettiest car ever – a Triumph Herald. Pale baby blue, mostly – but the boot and bonnet are a sort of a whitey-creamy colour, and it really does look so terribly sweet.

He said he needs it for his work, which is something to do with houses – property . . . estates, did he say? Not quite sure, but something like that, anyway. I think it's got to be his father's business: that's the impression I'm getting anyway, but Mike, he doesn't really ever talk about it, and I don't ask because I'm really not remotely interested in it: not my concern, and I don't want to seem nosey. He told me that it used to be his mother's, the car, but she gave it to him when he passed his test. She's got a Mercedes convertible now – and he laughed when he told me that, and so I asked him why. Because, he said, she did pretty well out of the divorce – just ask my dad! He's twenty-one, nearly twenty-two, terribly mature – just come down from Oxford, didn't ask what he'd been studying, but I should do, really . . . and he's got a younger sister called Lisa, and she's up at Oxford right now, first year, so they both are obviously awfully clever, not like me. I've never met her, Lisa. Never met any of his family, actually. His mother he hardly sees because she's got another place in France, or is it Italy – and although this is his dad's flat, there's no real sign that he actually lives here, or anything. Some really lovely suits hanging up in a huge wardrobe in the main bedroom – sliding mirror doors, never seen anything like it – and there's a pile of cigar boxes in the living room, but that's about it. The family's obviously rather rich and what you might call 'free-living', I suppose. Not bound by all the usual sorts of English prejudices and embarrassments that have practically buried my mother alive, so far as I can see. In one sense, George would adore all that – so uncommon, so not bourgeois – but on a deeper level he'd hate them, of course, because they've got everything he hasn't. Same with Sammy. Mike, he's terribly handsome, I think – those soft brown eyes and a dimple in his chin, just like Cary

Grant – and he dresses really nicely. Fashionable, but not like a pop star, if you know what I mean.

Anyway – we got back here from the Spaniards that Saturday in the Triumph, and I was awfully impressed with the block of flats, but I tried not to show it too much: didn't want him thinking I'm just some sort of a gawping little kid. The porter in the foyer – he's called Adrian: didn't know that then, of course – he stood up as we walked into the hall . . . practically saluted! And the flat itself, oh wow . . .! It's just so . . . well I don't really know what the word is. Never been anywhere like this – never seen anything even near it, except in films and magazines. Sophisticated, could be: that could be the word. Really grown-up, but not all old and fusty like it is at home. The sort of place John Steed in *The Avengers* would live with Cathy Gale. It's all a creamy beige and brown with orange shades on big brass lamps that look like Roman columns. Huge glass coffee table and squishy sofas with piles of little round and square cushions – all different colours on one side and black on the other, and each of them has got a button in the middle. There's a pair of small silver cannons on the mantelpiece and a clock that chimes the hours. Chinese-looking vases and really bright and modern pictures on most of the walls that are all in a Picasso sort of a style – and that other one who does blobs in primary colours with black lines and crosses, can't remember. I don't really know much about modern art, so I couldn't tell you if they're originals, or anything – probably not, because they'd cost just hundreds, I expect. The curtains – and they go all the way down to the floor – they're really thick and puffy, more like an eiderdown really. Fitted carpets everywhere, also in that creamy beige, and really deep and soft. My mother wouldn't dare walk on them because she'd be afraid they'd show the dirt.

There are always fresh flowers in tall glass vases and stacks of new magazines – I don't know who keeps bringing all this stuff in, because it isn't Mike. Porter, maybe – Adrian, he maybe does it. *Town, Tatler* and rather boring-looking ones called the *Spectator* and the *Economist*. The pictures in *Town* are *amazing* – George would just love that magazine, it's just so groovy: all men's clothes, cars and dolly birds: his idea of heaven.

So Mike, he played me those records that The Hornets had got made somewhere, he did tell me, HMV in Oxford Street, it might have been . . . and I thought they were pretty good, okay, but not really that great, if I'm honest. I mean – I can't see them at number one in the charts with The Dave Clark Five and The Beatles! I didn't say any of that – I told him they were fab, and that the drumming was the fabbest: it's what boys want to hear. He said I'm afraid we don't have any sherry here, but there are other things – and I said oh God no, I don't want anything else, thank you: that Bristol Cream, you won't believe it but it's gone right to my head. We were sitting on one of the sofas, and he started fiddling about with my hair a bit, and I completely instinctively pulled right away from him. He looked quite shocked. Even hurt. But look – I was still so filled right up with *George*, wasn't I? Who I hadn't told Mike anything about, obviously . . . and I was finding all this, oh God . . . just so weird: I couldn't believe that George had just . . . *left* me . . . and even more than that, I couldn't believe that I was here at all. What on earth was I *doing* here, actually . . .? And also I knew that my hair wasn't really looking that good, and so why would he want to touch it? And still I was holding on tightly to this damned big bag I'd been dragging around with me, full of my mother's radio, empty Harp tins, bits of salami and a packet of Mint Chocs, mangled and melted at the bottom.

It was only then that it really dawned upon me . . . and I think I must have been blushing horribly, because I could feel my cheeks, and it's as if they were blazing. Look at it: I was a pick-up. Wasn't I? I'd been seemingly alone in a pub on a Saturday afternoon – he'd offered me a drink, and I'd said yes. Then I sat with him, laughing away at everything he said, and after that I accepted another drink, and this time it was alcoholic. He'd asked me to his flat, and I went. In his car. And that's where I found myself – recoiling from his touch, while he was just sitting there, looking amazed. Oh God. What on earth did I think I was *doing* . . .? I told him briefly that I had to go, and he said why? You've only just got here. I said that this had all been a huge mistake, and that I was sorry. He said he didn't really know what I was talking about – but if I truly did want to go, then he'd happily drive me wherever I liked. He meant it, you could tell. He wasn't angry with me, as a lot of boys would have been, I suppose. George would, that's for sure. He'd be raving by now – and chucking me out into the street, not even caring what happened to me then. I said to Mike that it wasn't that I didn't like him – I did like him, I liked him a lot – but it's just that he'd caught me at a really difficult moment, and that I was feeling all a bit confused, and I hope he could maybe sort of understand that . . .? He smiled – beautiful smile, with his eyes all crinkly – picked up that blessed bag and asked me where I would like him to drop me. Well I wasn't going to say Edgware, obviously, so I just said oh the Tube station, that would be perfect, thank you – but I can just as easily walk. Then he asked me what line I wanted, and he drove me all the way up to Hampstead. So sweet, really. It was in the car that I said I was sorry again, and that I hoped he didn't think me most awfully rude. He said no, not at all – and then he said that when I was feeling a little less confused (I was blushing again, I could feel it) he'd really like to see me again. And I said well if that's how you really feel, this is my phone number: best to ring in the evenings, when I'm in from work. He said he'd call me, which I know they always do. But he did. The very next day. And we went and had supper in a really nice place in St John's Wood called Zia Maria (I asked if I could keep the menu, and they said of course, with pleasure, *bella signorina*). There were lots of candles and red tablecloths – terribly Italian, with those giant pepper grinders and lovely wine in funny sort of raffia-covered bottles. I must have drunk two whole glasses – I was terribly giddy, and laughing like anything. We walked back to the flat after that – it was really near – and I let him take me to this lovely bedroom with the most enormous bed I have ever seen . . . because I really did want him to. He was amazingly gentle . . . I've never known anything like that before. I sighed and cried . . . but really because I was just so very grateful for all of his niceness, and care. His tenderness. We began seeing quite a lot of one another, after that. I'm really so terribly fond of him – and Mike, he tells me he loves me: he tells me all the time. Like I always used to do with George . . . who never ever said it to me in return. Not ever. Not even once. So anyway . . . soon after that, the agency I'd been temping for asked me if I'd like a permanent job in their very own offices in Baker Street, and I absolutely jumped at that: after I got my very first wage packet I bought a wonderful orange- and cream-striped polo-top at Bazaar – before I handed over half of the rest of it to my mother. And . . . George never called . . . Mike never stopped . . . so that's how it's all happened, really. And now, suddenly . . . after all this time . . . George is here. In the flat. In this flat. *George* . . .! I simply . . . I simply just can't believe it. I really do wish I hadn't opened the door. I feel just really awful and pretty groggy too from these pills I've been taking that Becky in the office had told me were really good . . . and I'm just not sure how I'm going to be able to cope with all of it . . .

All this time, while I've just been hopelessly standing here, George has been picking up the bottles on the sideboard one by one – reading the labels so ridiculously carefully, as if he's . . . I don't know . . . going to be quizzed on them later on, or something. The Gordon's gin he actually sniffed – winced away from it and put the cap back on. He's now pouring Bacardi into one of the big crystal tumblers that Mike always uses for his whiskies and soda.

'Got any Coke? I think you said you'd got some Coke . . .?'

'Look, George . . .'

'Because it's rum, this stuff. I didn't know that. Not the usual sort – not the stuff that sailors get in their grog. It's not that sort. White rum, this is. And do you know what? The Beatles drink this. Rum 'n Coke. That's what they drink when they're in places like the Bag O'Nails. I've been there. Go there quite a lot, as a matter of fact. One night when I was there – you'll never guess! Brian Epstein and Cilla were at the very next table. Yeh. Tables were practically touching. You been there?'

'George . . . I don't know what you're talking about. Why are you here? You can see I'm not well. Why don't you go? Why are you here?'

'Well I've come to see you, Dorothy Obviously. I was missing you. Really have been missing you. Have you seen *A Hard Day's Night* yet? You haven't? Really? I'm amazed. It's been out for more than a month. I've seen it three times. Going again at the weekend. Got the LP, of course. Absolutely great. Best ever.

Heard it? Well, you will have heard the single, obviously. The title track. Number one for weeks. Still watching *Ready, Steady, Go!*, like we used to? Big telly over there in the corner. Even bigger than Sammy's. Record player too, I expect. Radiogram, probably . . .'

'George . . .'

'Don't suppose you've got any fags, have you . . .?

'No. We don't . . . no, there aren't any, I'm afraid.'

'Okay. Not to worry. Get some later. But when they went on tour – did you see? Did you read all that? They took this bloke called Jimmie Nicol to be their drummer because Ringo wasn't well. Tonsils, I think. Couldn't believe it . . . couldn't believe they could do that. Looked so . . . wrong. Anyway, Ringo's fine now. He's all right again. Back with the boys. So that's okay.'

'George – for God's *sake* . . .! You haven't been in touch for *months* . . .! You can't just . . . you can't just turn up like this . . .'

'I know. I know I've been bad. I've been awful. I am awful. I do know that, Dorothy. I do know it. And I'm sorry. Really sorry. I know you think I don't give a shit . . . um, is there any Coke then, actually . . .?'

'My God . . .'

'Okay, okay – forget about the Coke. Forget all that. But listen: I know you think I don't give a shit about you, because of the way I've behaved – but I do. I do give a shit. I give lots of shits.'

'George . . . please go. If there's anything you want to say to me, I'll . . . I don't know . . . phone you. Or you can write, or something. Or ring me at work. But please go now – I'm begging you, George. Please . . .'

'Ring you at work, yes – well I know you've got a proper full-time job now, of course. Well that's good. Isn't it? What you wanted. Maybe not being a secretary, but still. Soon you won't have to be living in Edgware any more. How is she? Your mad old mum? You didn't commit matricide, then? It's funny – when I was younger, the very first time I heard that word, I didn't at all get it and I was going well Christ, that's a bloody stupid word, isn't it? Because why would anyone want to murder a mattress . . .?'

'*George* . . .!'

'It doesn't really taste of anything, this Bacardi. Bloody strong, though. I daresay it could be all right, when the Coke's in it. This flat . . . you're living here now then, are you?'

'It's none of your business any more, George. What I do.'

'No. No I know that. I suppose that's fair. But I'm asking, that's all. You live here? Or not?'

'No, I . . . no. I don't. So now you know. Please go, George.'

'That's all you've said to me, you know. Since I came. You've just told me to go. Like I'm a stranger, or something.'

'You made yourself a stranger, George.'

'Is that what you think? I see. Right. So what you're saying is . . .'

'I'm saying go. Go, George. What's wrong with you . . .?'

'Well . . . I don't know. Quite a lot, really. But mainly it's you, I think. It's you that's wrong with me. Not . . . having you any more.'

'Yes, well. Should have thought of that before.'

'I should, yeh. But I'm thinking of it now, Dorothy. I really do . . . need you, you know. I really do . . . and seeing you here . . . just being able to look at you again . . . Christ, it just cuts me up. You look so . . . beautiful.'

'Oh Christ's *sake*, George . . .! What are you *talking* about . . .?! I look absolutely *ghastly*. And I feel absolutely ghastly too – and I'm asking you to *leave* . . .!'

'To me you don't. You don't look ghastly to me. To me, you look absolutely . . . beautiful. I know I should have told you before. I never did tell you, but I always thought it. I did. I really did. And . . . I need you. I really do, you know . . .'

'I do know. I've told you that how many times? But now . . . well now I'm afraid it's just too late. You've left it too late. Sorry, George, but . . . all that, it's past. Don't . . . don't . . . oh God please, George – don't start *crying* . . .!'

'Not crying! Not. Just a bit . . . sad, that's all. Well look . . . all right then, Dorothy. You've been very plain. Honest with me. You've said what you think, and I suppose I can't blame you. And I expect you've probably got somebody else by now. Well of course you have – why wouldn't you? Beautiful girl, after all. So yes – there will be someone, of course there will. Better than me, I should think. Wouldn't be hard. Lives . . . here, I expect. Nice. Lucky for some. Well look . . . I will go, actually. Feel a bit stupid now, you want the truth. Thanks for the, er . . . you know. Drink. Bye then, Dorothy. Goodbye. I hope you feel better soon. You know – I mean, whatever it is that's wrong with you. And sorry to, um . . .'

He's picking up his coat, and now he's turning away from me. I don't know what it is I'm feeling. Shivering relief, in one way – and yet I'm just so cold with pain for him. How sad he seems. How very terribly sad. Not all filled with vanity and anger . . . but simply . . . I don't know . . . just so small, and crumpled. I don't really want to think that I'm the cause of that . . . but still it's good that he's going. He's got to go, and at least he can finally see that. He's right in front of the door . . . and now George – oh no, oh please no – he looks as absolutely astonished as I am when suddenly that door, it's flying right open, and oh my God in *heaven*, why oh why does this have to happen . . .! Because now . . . well now there's Mike in the room. Just standing there, and staring at the two of us. And he's going to say something, I know it. I think I should have said something first, but I sort of feel quite sick again and I really can't think of a single thing – and anyway Mike, now: he's talking.

'Oh. Hello. Hope I'm not, um . . . All right are you, Dotty? Just popped in to, uh . . .'

'*Dotty* . . .?'

'Quiet, George. Mike, this is George . . .'

'*Mike* . . .?'

'I said to shut up, didn't I? George is a . . . friend. Old friend. He'd heard from someone that I wasn't too well, and so he's just come round to, um . . .'

'Yes. I just came round to see her. I'm a friend. Old friend. I should have brought flowers. Grapes, maybe. What they do, isn't it? Not sure why.'

'Right. I see. Well hello, George. I'm Mike, as you heard. Can I get you a, um . . . ah – I see that Dotty's already given you a drink. Good. Good good.'

'Dotty. Right.'

'It's . . . what I call her. So, Dotty – feeling okay? Not too bad?'

'I'm fine. I'm perfectly fine. George, he was just about to leave when you . . .'

'Yup. Just going. Must be off. Nice, um . . . place you've got here.'

'Oh, well – you know.'

'Yeh. I do. Well bye again then, Dorothy. It's what I call her, Mike. I call her Dorothy.'

'Right. Okay. Fab. Well – maybe run into you again sometime, George.'

'Well maybe. You never know.'

No. I suppose you never do. That's what I'm thinking. I'm gazing at my bloody face in the mirror in the lift again, and that's all I'm capable of thinking, at the moment. It's the only thing I do know, right now. That you never know. You never can. Maybe a good thing, actually. Otherwise – why would you get up in the morning? And if you did get up, why wouldn't you, I don't know . . . just get hold of a gun from somewhere and blow your bloody brains out? Yeh well.

Now . . . if I was sensible, I'd go back to work. I haven't even phoned in – and that bastard Timpson, he'll be going completely nuts, silly bastard. Where's *George* . . .?! Where is he . . .?! Anyone seen *George* this morning? By God – he's been late before, but this is just beyond the pale. That young man – he's cooked his goose this time. Crossed the Rubicon. Yeh. This is how he talks. Not one original thought or phrase has emerged from his big and solid skull since the day he was born – or at least since he took a job at W. H. Smith's Wholesale. And now a hundred years have passed, and he's a fucking robot. He'll dock my wages, of course, for the whole of the morning . . . and I'm just so broke. As bloody usual. Well he can just fuck off. They all can. They can all just fuck off. Sack me, with a bit of luck. Because I've got to get out of there anyway – just got to. If I get myself out of there soon – no, not soon, not soon: right bloody *now* – if I don't do that . . . well then before I know what's happened to me, I'll be old and I'll have turned into bloody Timpson . . .! And I'd rather be dead, than that. I'd rather be dead than old anyway. Hate old. I'm never going to be old. It's disgusting. When I'm forty, I'll end it. Thirty-five, actually – yeh, when I'm thirty-five, there'll be no fun left in anything for me, so why hang about? Do I want to be another old and ugly and stinking waste of bloody space and telling young and beautiful people how useless and *ungrateful* they are . . .? No I bloody well don't. So I'm not going to do that – go in to work, I mean. No. I'm going to a pub. I need that now. I really do need it. The Bacardi – filthy, really – that didn't even take the edges off. So I've got to find a pub, and bloody quickly. Only thing that works. Only thing I know, anyway. Apart from . . . yeh well: I've lost that, haven't I? I'd have to be even more boneheadedly stupid than I already am not to realise that. She's gone. She's just gone. To Mike, apparently. Mike. Who calls her Dotty. Mike. Who's tall and fucking handsome and older than me and loaded and he's got an amazing flat in the centre of town and probably he's got a bloody car as well. Yeh – bound to have a car. Could be a Rolls-fucking-Royce, for all I know. E-Type, more likely. Mike . . . fucking Mike . . . whose hair is really quite Beatley . . . and that bloody suit he was wearing: Christ. Beautiful. Just so beautiful. Midnight-blue mohair, red lining. Made-to-measure, looked like. Die for that, I would. And talking of his bloody Beatley hair . . . well I've seen it before, of course. Saw the back of it, didn't I? In the Spaniards Inn. When he was talking to Dorothy. And I walked away. I just walked away and out of there with Sammy and a couple of foreign bloody dimbo slags, and just left him . . . talking to Dorothy. And now he's been talking to Dorothy ever bloody since. Dotty, he calls her. Yeah . . . and not just talking, either. He's had her. He's got her. She's his. Oh Jesus. Christ I need a fag . . .

What's this place . . .? No idea which direction I've been walking. Raining a bit. So what this place called . . .? The Volunteer. Right. That'll do. Not really a suitable name for me – no, not a bit, but it'll do me very well. Because I never volunteer. Everything . . . it all seems to happen to me: I just get dragooned. So yeh . . . this turns out to be the sort of pub I really do like, actually. As if nothing in it's changed since the day it was built. I love old pubs – the only old things I've got any time for, really. All the dark polished wood and cut glass and big brass pumps and little cubbyholes – yeh, love all that. Makes me feel safe. Protected. Stupid, really.

'Is there a phone here?'

'You want a drink?'

'Course I want a drink. Why I'm here. Just want to know where the phone is.'

'What do you want to drink?'

'Christ. All right then. Pint of lager. What have you got?'

'You blind?'

'What . . .?'

'Right in front of your face, aren't they?'

'Right. Okay then – Harp, that'll do.'

'Pint, you say?'

'You deaf?'

'You taking the mickey?'

'Bloody hell. And what whiskies have you got? Oh yeh – in front of my face, right?'

'Right.'

'Okay. The lager, and a Bell's. Okay?'

'No Bell's. Can you see Bell's? No you can't. Teacher's, Vat 69, Haig . . .'

'Haig. Great.'

'Single?'

'Double.'

'Right.'

'Oh God yeh – and fags. Gasping. Twenty No. 6, yeh?'

'Not got that. Benson's, Gold Leaf, Player's.'

'Gold Leaf.'

'Twenty?'

'I said twenty. And where's the phone?'

'Over in the corner. Behind the curtain. You going to pay?'

'No – I'm going to pull out a bloody gun and rob you.'

'I've had about enough of you, squire . . .'

'Course I'm going to *pay*. Look – I'll pay you now, all right? How much? I'll pay you right now. Jesus.'

'Comes to nine-and-eight.'

'Really? Blimey. Okay – here's a quid. And a packet of crisps.'

'Only got plain.'

'Plain's fine. And some pennies for the phone.'

'You want the lot, don't you?'

'Do you like your job . . .?'

'Fuck off.'

'Because you're no bloody good at it, I can tell you that.'

Yeh: nothing like a quiet little drink in a friendly old pub. Now then . . . light up a fag . . . oh Christ yes: drag it down, drag it down: that feels so good. Thought I was dying. Quick couple of gulps of lager, and now I down the whisky. You ask for a large one, but it's really bloody small. Ooh . . . lovely, though. That was lovely. A lot better than your bloody Bacardi, matey. But The Beatles, they drink that too – Scotch 'n Coke, they drink that too. I'll just stick the glasses on this table here – not sure why I bought the crisps, not even hungry – and now I've got to make that phone call. Step one in my brand-new life. Step one.

'Hello. Hear me . . .? Yeh. Is Magsie there . . .? Magsie. I know. I know. I know she's not allowed calls in working hours, yeh yeh yeh I know that, but . . . yeh. I know. But this is an emergency. Family emergency. All right? I'm her brother.'

Can't really be bothered with the lager, now. It's whisky that gets the job done. I've worked out that I've got about enough for three, maybe four more doubles, if I don't mind walking home. From wherever the hell I am. So I'll have the three or four more, then – and then I'll walk home. Or die on the pavement, whatever comes sooner: who cares?

'Magsie . . .? Hi. Me. George. Yeh. I know I'm not your brother – I do know that, Magsie. Well I had to say that, didn't I? Or they wouldn't have put you on. Yeh – I'm fine. Look – it's about tonight. No well it *isn't* a bloody family emergency, of course it isn't. Christ Almighty – what do I know about your bloody family? Listen to me, Magsie, all right? Just listen to me. Tonight, okay? Can't make it. Yeh well. That's how it is. When . . .? Well not ever, actually. Not again. Got it? Finished. Can't be doing with it any more. Up to my neck in boredom. You never make me laugh, or even happy. So that's it. Sorry you're crying, Magsie . . . but there it is. I'm not . . . I'm not a bastard . . . no good calling me a bastard, is it? All right then – call me a bloody bastard, I don't care. But it doesn't change anything, does it? And I'm not. Oh look – that's the pips. Don't have any more coppers – sorry. Yeh. So bye then, Magsie. Bye.'

So that's that done. More Haig now. Have another fag.

What I've got to do . . . well, let me think, then. Let me think about this. Okay. What I've got to do is . . . well, I've got to get rid of all the deadwood. In my life. Yeh . . . trouble is, that's all I've really got now, deadwood. Okay – Magsie's gone, so I won't get any more bruises from banging against her sticky-out ribs, the restaurants won't completely bankrupt me and I won't have to listen to her droning on and on about cats all the bloody time. Because that was her thing: cats. Had about six of them, apparently, and she carried around pictures of them in her handbag, if you can believe it. Would you like to see them, she said to me – they're all so really, really cute and gorgeous . . .! I just looked at her. Okay – so she's gone, she's out of the way, she's on the scrapheap . . . and my job, well . . . one way or another, that's gone too. Silver lining, I think that is – because I'm lazy, you see. If something like this hadn't happened – if all this hadn't arisen, I have this awful feeling that I'd just have gone along with it for ever and ended up with a brown coat and coloured biros and a clipboard doing bloody Timpson's job: I know me – that's what easily could have happened, you know. Needed a kick up the arse. Well – I've certainly had that – one or two in the face, as well. So when I get out of this pub (not yet, not nearly yet – need more Haig) I'd better get an *Evening Standard*, I suppose: see what's on offer in the classified section. But it's got to be something more than a 'hey-you-boy' sort of a job, this time. Shop, maybe. Somewhere classy. Bond Street. Jermyn Street. Somewhere like that. Or some sort of a position in an office, maybe. No – not an office. Go mad in an office. Oh look – I'll find something, I expect. Have to be soon, though: got no money. And if it pays well – and it's just got to pay better than W. H. bloody Smith's, bloody pittance they give me – well then I can move out of Kilburn. Maybe Belsize Park, that would be nice. Near the Odeon – somewhere round there. Because I'm a bit fed up of Kilburn, if I'm honest. Right outside where I live, the other night there was blood on the pavement. Not nice, is it? And the Irish downstairs, they're always making such a hell of a noise whenever they're drunk, which is usually – and particularly on Tuesdays when they all get the dole.

Yeh . . . but all that, all that's nothing. Isn't it? That's just nothing compared with the heart of the thing. The very heart of it. Which is Dorothy. I've been trying really hard not to think about everything that's just happened to me in that bloody fabulous flat in Circus bloody Road, but it's all just crowding in on me now, of course it is. Can't keep it out any longer. Oh Jesus . . . if only I'd listened to Sammy. Because he was always telling me, wasn't he? How many times did he say to me that she was just so amazing? How I should look after her better – think about her more, take into consideration what it is that she might be wanting. Not go on just taking her for granted, and generally behaving like the bloody pig I am. Said she was a keeper. Yeh – and he was right. Sammy, he always is. Why I love him, I suppose. One of the reasons, anyway. But I didn't, did I? Keep her. No. I bloody lost her. I bloody gave her away. Christ – I *pushed* her right out of my bloody life, and Jesus . . . oh Jesus . . . just look at me now.

I wish I could wipe it. That scene, that scene in the flat. I wish I could rewind it, like on Sammy's Grundig tape recorder, and do it all over again. Because everything . . . everything I did, it was just so wrong. Well – even being there. I mean, knowing she wasn't well (and she did look peaky: not as awful as I kept on saying, but hardly beautiful like I told her later) . . . yeh because look, this is what I mean: I knew she wasn't well, didn't I? So of course I shouldn't have gone charging round there. Shouldn't have been there at all. Seems obvious now, seems completely plain – but at the time, Jesus, I just felt so . . . I don't know: driven. Almost mad, I was feeling, as I was running full pelt all the way to Circus Road: must have looked like a crazy person. And I had the address – I could have just written. Bought a nice card, or something. And written. Not about everything I was feeling and going through – Jesus, that would take a book – but just, I don't know . . . suggesting a meeting, or something. In her own time. Day or two – whenever it best suited her.

Coffee bar, or somewhere – she likes coffee bars. Or . . . oh yes, I know: afternoon tea with all the scones and cakes and things in a smart hotel. She would have loved that, I just know it. But not a pub, is what I'm meaning – which she doesn't like at all, and that was the only place I was always dragging her. Then she would have had a bit of time to get used to the idea of seeing me again. And so would I. I could've thought about what I was going to wear . . . what I was going to say. Brought a few flowers, maybe. Instead, well . . . oh Christ. She opens the door, and *bam*! There I am. Right out of the bloody blue, and for the first time in months. What can she have been *thinking* . . .? And me . . . all the crap I was coming out with. Didn't try to . . . hold her. Didn't even touch her hand. Just went blathering on about that sacking stuff on the walls – what did she say it was called? And bloody Bacardi and where's the Coke and *A Hard Day's Fucking Night* . . .! Oh Jesus, oh Jesus, oh Jesus. And lying – lying too. Suddenly I'm, what? A really close friend of not just Brian Epstein but Cilla Black as well, who I'm seeing just all the bloody time in this really exclusive nightclub. When I'm not having a steak and chips with my mate Paul McCartney. Hessian . . . yeah: that's what she said it was.

Well . . . I don't know why I did all of that. I think, maybe, it was the only way I could keep myself together. Because looking at that flat, well . . . I knew, didn't I, there just had to be a man behind it. But looking at her . . . I saw nothing. In her eyes, I mean. Pity, maybe – yeh, I maybe saw pity. Which was hard to take. Contempt. Bit of alarm. Bloody annoyance, that's for sure. Yes – all that, all the negatives. But nothing I wanted to see, that's what I mean. Because once she loved me. And with a love like that . . . yeh well. She doesn't any more. I'm afraid not. No no: that's gone. When bloody Superman Mike showed up, she actually told me to shut up. She never would have done that. Her – tell me to shut up . . .? Joking. And me? I would have gone insane. So it's all very different. See? It's all . . . very different. What I should have done – I mean, if I was there in the first place, which I shouldn't have been, as I now know bloody well . . . but I was there, wasn't I? So what I should have done is told her that I realised now how very wrong I'd been in the past. About everything. How it was all going to be just so great from this moment on. That I'd seen the light – and better late than never, right? I am a new man. That I needed her. Maybe . . . I did actually say that bit – can't quite remember. But I didn't tell her I loved her. I didn't tell her that. I never have. I never ever said that to her, in all the time we were together. I did, though. Love her. Whether I knew it or not. And that's why . . . that's why I'd really like to be able to wipe the tape. Wipe it clean. And play it out again. Well: too late. There was only ever going to be just the one shot at this, and a long shot at that. I knew there could never be a second chance. And I really, really messed it up.

I feel . . . I don't know . . . very young, quite suddenly. As in like a kid. But I don't mean all just sort of giggly and happy and carefree, oh Christ no . . . what I mean is hopeless. Useless – bloody useless. Out of my depth. Can't cope. No experience. No knowledge. Just guessing, really – that's all I'm doing. And guessing wrong, of course. Really badly wrong. A man, a proper grown-up man, he would have known exactly what to do. Yeh but a man, well . . . he wouldn't have been so bloody stupid as to get into such a fucking awful mess in the first bloody place. What would Sammy do, I wonder . . .? Well he's never been in this position, because he's never really had a long-term girlfriend Always wanted it – can't imagine why he hasn't got one, actually. He says that after a while, sometimes just a week, girls will end up telling him that he's just too nice. Which no one has ever said to me, I can promise you. He's amazed by that, but I think I can sort of understand it. He accepts the situation – not much he can do about it, really – but if he ever did need some sort of, I don't know . . . guidance, say . . . well then he's got his wonderful dad, hasn't he? Who would probably take him out to lunch somewhere really fine, and talk to him. Find out what the problem is. And then he'd help him, in whatever way he could. That's what fathers are for – or should be, anyway. My father . . . huh! No one ever told him that: he was bloody useless for years, and after that . . . well then he was just gone. I was well rid of him, selfish bastard. And that's why I'm never going to do that, have children. It's too much, too much to take on. Because if you end up not . . . loving them enough . . . well then that's just as bad as killing them.

And . . . now I've seen her again . . . now I've watched her move and heard her voice, I miss her more than ever. Now that I know she's gone, I can't stop thinking of all the days and months we had, the two of us together, and wanting them back. Wanting to have more of them. She won't, though. Well – obviously: she's made it just about as plain as she could. And the time we did have together, well . . . I enjoyed it more than she did. I can see that now. All about me, really. Wasn't it? Yeh well. Too late. All too late. And Christ . . . here's another thing that is really getting to me badly: I so much wish I hadn't seen him. Superman. That encounter . . . that really very strange moment when he appeared, when suddenly he was just standing there in the flat . . . I think that's what people call being 'civilised', isn't it? Because everyone was aware of the awfulness of the situation, and yet we all were behaving so terribly well. Civilised, yes. Sensible adults. I was the intruder, of course. In the Spaniards, it had been him – he was the intruder then, and I should have gone over and hit him, probably. Sworn at him, at least. Seen him off. But I didn't. And in the flat, I did actually wonder for a moment if he was going to hit me. I hoped not, because he was tall and quite muscly-looking, and I think that Dorothy thought little enough of me as it was, without my being battered and bleeding all over the floor. Although you never know with girls . . . she might have hated him, Mike, for doing it to me. Anyway, he didn't. None of that happened. Sensible adults. Still, though, I so much wish that I did not know he existed. Superman. Because . . . not having her, that's hard, that's very bad . . . but knowing she's with someone else, well – that's just close to being absolutely unbearable. That's what I'm feeling, right at this moment. And every night, now . . . I shall see his face, next to hers. Her, just looking at him . . . the way she used to always look at me. Her body . . . and his. And then his hands . . . just all over her. Oh dear God. And even if I was a proper and grown-up man . . . could I really be dealing with all of that? What do they do, grown-up men? How do they do it? Just swallow all the pain, like cowboys in a film? I wish there was someone . . . I wish I had somebody to tell me, because I don't know – I just have no idea. The way I am, though . . . I can't. Deal with it. That I'm sure of. I can't. Unable. I just . . . can't.

So . . . how much money have I got left . . .? Not much, Very little. Less than I thought, actually. But certainly enough for another large Haig. Which will be small, but still. There's what looks like a *Standard* on that bench over there. Think I'll nab that. Oh hang on . . . it's not the *Express*, is it . . .? No – it's the *Standard*. Yesterday's, but that doesn't matter. Okay then – let's take a look. Haven't seen a paper since . . . well I just can't remember the last time I looked at a newspaper, frankly. We had to, at school. Current Affairs. All those stupid old politicians with Brylcreem and baggy grey suits banging on about young people with long hair like the Rolling Stones, and how they were going to spell the end of civilisation – or else foreign countries that nobody's heard of. I don't see the point of foreign countries, never have done. Like here – look at this, page five: some bloody bit of Africa that used to be called something, and now it's going to be called something else. Zambia. Well who cares? I mean – people in Zambia, I suppose. But why is that in the *Evening Standard*? London paper, isn't it? So who wants to know about bloody . . . what is it . . .? Zambia. Some bunch of niggers in a place that no one's ever going to go to. It's just stupid. It's not that I hate them, sambos, like some people do. Never met one, actually. Anyway . . . never mind all that: let's just get to the jobs section. Oh bloody hell . . . look at this . . .! Ian Fleming's died. Oh dear. That's a pity. I love those books. Read all of them, I think. Pan paperbacks – nicked most of them from Smith's. Won't be any more, now. Shame. Seen the two films, obviously. Ursula Andress – oh my God. New one out later this year – *Goldfinger,* pretty sure. Ian Fleming, he was fifty-six, it says here. Well that's long enough, isn't it? Too old, really. I don't ever want to be fifty-six. Can you imagine . . .? Better off dead.

I've got another whisky now. And a lager. And a fag. There's practically nobody in this pub. Some old cretin in the corner there . . . woman who looks like a prozzy up at the bar, laughing like a drain . . . and that's about it. I suppose because they haven't been open long. Not yet lunchtime. Right, then – let's look at the jobs: see if anything decent's going. Well . . . a lot I don't want, that's for sure. Street sweeper. Office boy. Trainee dustman. Trainee dustman . . .? There are lessons, are there? In heaving a load of rubbish up on to a cart? Christ. Bus driver – that wouldn't be too bad. Not as good as a cabbie, but they all have to do that exam, don't they? You've got to know the whole of London inside out. Well I'd never manage that. Anyway – can't drive. What about this . . .? Managing Director of an export company. Offices in the city. Private secretary. Chauffeur-driven car. Competitive salary, many fringe benefits and generous expenses. Sounds great – I could do that. Yeh but you need all these qualifications, it says here. Wouldn't you know it. Experience. Knowledge. In other words, you've got to be old. It's a sort of a . . . what-do-they-call-it, isn't it really? Conspiracy. All the old people ganging up – making sure that the young ones can't even get a look in. Laughing at us all. Knocking back the champagne in the back of a Rolls-bloody-Royce and just laughing at us all. The young – we've got no hope. Unless you're a pop star, or something. Fashion photographer. That's the only way. And I know I'll never be one of them. Got to face it.

I'm going a bit . . . woozy, now. Room is beginning to look sort of funny. I quite like this feeling, actually. Can't often afford it. Gets worse later on, but it's still pretty nice at the moment. And what I'm thinking now is . . . well maybe . . . it's not really that great, is it? Being a young person at all. You keep hearing it is. How it's meant to be. All so fab and groovy and all the rest of it. We are the Sixties – we are what it's all about. But look at me: I'm not, am I? What it's all about. I'm about sod bloody all. Can't even get my clothes in Carnaby Street, and it's me who's meant to be wearing them. Not just Sammy – it shouldn't be just Sammy: it should be me as well.

And all these bloody politicians with their slicked-back hair and stupid moustaches . . . all the managing directors of export companies . . . they can afford all of that, and they don't bloody want it. All the big fat men with shiny faces and bloody cigars stuck into the middle of them – they can afford an E-Type, and they probably couldn't even fit inside one. Not fair. Not bloody fair. And girls: they like them the best – they're the ones they go for. If you're not on *Top of the Pops*, or something, then it's the rich old men, they're the ones they like the best – the ones who can take them to all the flashy clubs and restaurants and go on aeroplanes, and things. Buy them stuff. Mink coats and diamond bracelets. Not fair. Not bloody fair. So unless you're a Beatle, what's the actual bloody *point* in being young . . .? Not bloody much. Street sweeper. Office boy. Trainee fucking dustman . . .

Oh Jesus . . . I'm depressed. I'm feeling really lousy now. What a bloody day I'm having. And I haven't got any more money – counting it: just pennies. A thruppenny bit, couple of coppers – that's it. Thought I had another tanner, but I haven't. Oh Christ. Well I think I'll go home, then. My fabulous penthouse pad. I don't even know where I am. So how do I get there? Got enough for a bus, just about . . . but I haven't a clue what number. Because I don't even know where I am. Tube – I'll take the Tube, if I can find the Tube . . . but I'm going to be really wobbly, when I make it to my feet. I'll ask the bastard at the bar to tell me where the Tube is. I suppose I could get a taxi to somewhere close and then say I've just got to pick up something and I'll be back in a minute and then just bugger off round the corner and leg it. Done that before. Not sure I could make it today, though: think I'd fall over.

'Same again . . .?'

'No no. Had enough.'

'Yeh you have, by the look of you.'

'Where's the Tube?'

'Ay?'

'Tube. Where's the Tube?'

'You joking?'

'Am I laughing? Why can't you ever just . . .?'

'Tube? You want to know where the Tube is?'

'Jesus Christ . . .'

'Up the road, isn't it? Up the road.'

'What road?'

'What road? You trying to be funny?'

'Oh bloody, bloody hell . . . why can't you ever just . . .?'

'This road. Just up the road. What's wrong with you?'

'Well which way's up?'

'I can't believe you. You taking the mickey, or what?'

'Just *tell* me, Christ's sake. Which way's up?'

'Well it's not *down*, is it?'

Jesus Christ, what a moron. No wonder the pub's completely empty with a fucking idiot like that behind the bar. Sod him – I'll find it on my own. Yeh and I'm outside now, and the light, it's blinding. Pretty hot, but it hasn't stopped raining. And I see it now, the Tube. It's just there, more or less across the road. Why couldn't he just have said that? Why did we have to go through all of that bloody rigmarole? Why couldn't he just have told me that the Tube, it's just across the road. Because I wasn't to know, was I? I'm not from round there. Here, I mean. Not from round here. Christ, I can't even think straight any more.

Just turning into my street. I can't imagine how long this bloody journey's taken me. All sorts of lines in Baker Street – it turned out to be Baker Street, which I could've worked out if only I'd thought about it – and of course the state I'm in I got on the wrong one, didn't I? Wrong train, wrong direction. And I was feeling like absolute hell by this time, and just bloody aching for another shot of booze. Might have fallen asleep at one point. Because I found myself sort of rubbing my eyes, and people were looking. This creep's onions were falling out of the Wimpy he was eating, and he just kept on staring at me. Needn't have been a Wimpy – just some bun full of muck. So did a woman, putting on lipstick – she was staring at me too, Christ only knows why. Maybe I'd been snoring. There was a bit of dribble around my mouth, and I wiped that away with my hand. And I must have dropped my fag, because there's this bloody black burn mark on my trouser leg. Anyway, I've somehow got to Kilburn eventually. Seems like I've been on the Tube for bleeding years. One of the Irish is hanging about in the street outside our door and waving around a bottle of Guinness, while I'm fumbling for my keys and trying to light a cigarette. Big red face, reddened knuckles and a closed black eye: that one, she gets into a lot of fights. Next thing I know, I'm talking to a policeman. He's saying my name, and asking me if it's my name or not. I suddenly laugh, and I'm sounding like the barman: are you joking, I say to him. Trying to be funny? Taking the mickey, or what? Like me, though – he's not even near to laughing. He wants me to accompany him. Why, I'm saying: where are we going? The Irishwoman, she just can't believe her luck – be all over the street, this, in ten minutes tops. Don't tell him nothing, she's screaming at me: tell him you got rights – get your phone call, demand to see your brief. She knows more about this than I do – probably more than the copper too. Station, he's saying now, this policeman – I want you to accompany me to the station. But why, I say: why? And I'm rattled, I don't mind saying it. What's going on? Don't feel drunk any more. Wish I did. He says it is in connection with an allegation made by a young lady. And now that I'm sort of babbling all sorts of questions at him, he adds on that that is all he is at liberty to say. And so I'm thinking: allegation? *Allegation* . . .? Young lady? What's all this? What's going on? What the bloody hell is this? What has Dorothy done to me . . .? No . . . she wouldn't – she wouldn't do that. Dorothy? No. Never. She'd never do anything like that.

'What young lady? What are you talking about?'

'Come along, sir. Won't tell you again.'

'What young bloody lady . . .? What's going on . . .?'

'A Miss Margaret Simpson. Come along now, please sir.'

'Miss Margaret Simpson . . .? Who the hell is Miss Margaret Simpson? I've never even *heard* of Miss Margaret . . . oh hang on: *Magsie,* do you mean . . .? Oh Christ – you talking about *Magsie* . . .?'

'Car's round the corner, sir. Come on. And put out that cigarette.'

'Magsie . . .? This is Magsie . . .? Well what's this "allegation", then?'

'You'll find out soon enough.'

'Oh Christ just *tell* me, can't you . . .?'

'Alleged sexual misconduct with a minor. Very nasty.'

'A miner . . .? She said she worked in an art gallery . . .'

He's got his hand around my upper arm now, and he's hurting me a bit. My mind, it's just all over the place, and the Irishwoman – she's having a field day. Don't tell them *nothing,* she's more or less shrieking at me. But the policeman, he's walking me round the corner to the car, now – because he's determined to take me to the station. And . . . no matter what I think or am feeling . . . well look, there's just nothing I can do about that.

CHAPTER SIX

TO BEING CLUELESS

Enid, she's gone out. Don't know where – can't say I care very much. I'm only even remarking upon it at all because always, if she's off somewhere, well then she'll say so. I don't ask her to tell me – I do not require this: it's just that over the years it has become something that she invariably does. Leaves a note, sometimes. On some of our own very fine headed paper, actually – something I insist upon; it had been her habit, from time to time, to scribble on a jaundiced Post-It which she would stick on the fridge, but I told her quite firmly that I most certainly wasn't having any of that. Paper and print, these are the things that over the years have provided the money to furnish every single one of your nonsenses, I told her, and I would ask you please to respect that. But if she tells me face to face that she isn't going to be here for some damn reason or another . . . well then I don't even listen, of course – so I haven't for centuries ever known even vaguely where it is she'll be going to, nor what time she'll be back, and never have I found that a hardship. 'Just off to the . . .' she'll say, sometimes even rather gaily, and my mind, it simply closes down. 'Going to call in on . . .' she'll sing out to me, and the rest, it tails away. I grunt: generally, that's what I'll do. An acknowledgment that sounds of some sort have been uttered by Enid, and that a stirring has been registered in the air around me. Today, she's been gone rather longer than usual, and I don't at all mind that either – just so long as she's back to cook me something.

I like it when the house is completely my own – and I have been using the time. Some invisible witness would doubtless protest that all I have been doing is sitting at my desk, twiddling about with this rather splendid Montblanc Meisterstück (just so fat you can barely hold it) and gazing out of the window . . . where the leaves on the trees are turning to bronze. Ah but they'd be wrong – because my mind, you see, it has really been rather active. For I have been thinking about sex. Not idly, I don't mean – not just as in a series of everyday reveries of arousal: these quite curious fantasies, inevitably spliced with the glorified recollection of some lusty triumph of Christ knows how many decades ago. No – I'm thinking quite specifically. About sex, yes, and my current utter lack of it. I am really rather puzzled as to quite how this situation has come about. I haven't had what might be termed a serious relationship for too long a while. Affairs, they may always be relied upon to add immeasurably to the quality of life – provide the zest, give one a reason to get up in the morning – until, of course, that ever-looming moment when the sweetest of fruit will turn to sour. And then all of the retribution, and petty tears. Threats, occasionally – more of a problem, but generally not too difficult to handle. In addition to all of that, there has always been the odd girl at work, or one whom I will encounter at a trade fair – something of that sort. These young women tend to be quite openly mercenary, a thing I have come to admire. At first they doubtless see before them a reasonably personable man, offering them a drink – a man, though, who undeniably just has to be in his early sixties. This, they rapidly compute – and you can so easily trace that flickering of calculation amid the glitter of their eyes – is nearly forty years their senior, and, therefore, quite laughably out of the question. But then, very soon afterwards, this attitude of utter though polite disregard will altogether alter. Maybe they do a quick bit of instant research on their damned bloody phones, which never leave their fingers – or possibly there comes a whisper from an in-the-know colleague. I then am instantly perceived to be – in eyes that now are dealing with a different arithmetic – a handsome and mature gentleman of very considerable means, hugely respected within the industry, known for his generosity, his style, and with a Bentley in the car park. And so . . . off we go again.

But all of this, it's rather fallen away, just of late. Don't know why. I think because I haven't been bothered to pursue it – worrying in itself, actually, because I can easily recall a time when I would have chewed my way through a solid brick wall if it meant that there was to be the scent of cunt on the other side of it. But one does grow weary – because these young or youngish girls, you know, they can really be most terribly tedious. During the unavoidable nonsenses of the lead-up, I mean – when you have to ask and reply to the same and dusty eternity of stupid questions, not caring a damn about any of it. They like to talk, you see, but mostly have absolutely nothing to say. Or else, when they are talking, I have not the slightest idea even as to the nature of the topic about which they seem to be so mystifyingly animated. And because they are gainfully employed, subsequent meetings have to be structured around their working hours, and that is a pain in itself: late morning suits me best, followed by a damn good lunch. So what I am thinking now . . . well I have thought it before, of course, but always for some reason the trail was abandoned . . . but what I am thinking now is that it is high time I investigated the professionals. The women who look so much more extraordinarily beautiful than any chance encounter ever will. Who are skilled in the art of doing for me precisely what I want, exactly when I want it . . . and immediately following that, are perfectly happy to go to hell. And all in exchange for far less money in the long run than even a half-cocked quasi-relationship is inevitably going to cost you – and believe me, I've had a few of those.

Never been with a whore before. Well – not quite true. There was that one very terrible occasion – and how would I ever forget it? Oh my God . . . how old can I have been? Don't think I was twenty, you know. Maybe living in Belsize, was I by this time . . .? If so, it was very soon after I finally got out of that bloody awful hole in Kilburn. Yes, I'd been living there for, Jesus – far too long. My life, such as it was, had gradually entered something of a trough, it's fair to say. Only eighteen, nineteen, and already for quite some time I'd been feeling such a failure. Wouldn't have told anyone that, of course: one can't ever be seen to be weak. Don't quite remember the exact chronology, but I know I'd broken up with Dorothy by that time. It's funny – I was thinking about this just the other day – but even now at my age, I still think of things, my life, in terms of being pre-Dorothy, during Dorothy, and after Dorothy. Ridiculous, really – you'd think, if anything, it would be Enid. But no – it's Dorothy. And she was how many women ago . . .? Christ, I only knew the girl for . . . I don't know: three or four months? Not much more. But I just had thought it was time to move on, really. Can't recall the actual circumstance when I broke it to her – I hope I did it gently: one never wants to hurt people unduly, times like this. I do remember very vividly that she was in the most terrible state about it – and that was half the trouble, I think: she'd become so terribly clingy, and when you're a young man just starting out in the world, well . . . last thing you want, isn't it really? Begged me to stay with her – crying, screaming, telling me how much she adored me, how I mustn't leave her, how she'd die without me . . . yes well: that's girls for you, isn't it? They always become so terribly emotional. Nice enough Dorothy, though, I suppose. Very nice, actually. I loved her, really. But still: sometimes you just have to make a stand.

So that was her out of the picture . . . and I think it must have been around that time I also gave in my notice to Smith's. They were pretty sad to see me go – offered a promotion, as I recall, but I had to let them down. And that was when I first got into printing – lowly position, of course, but it was at Smythson, wasn't it? Top of the tree – Bond Street, Royal Warrants. Funny to think that these days they're my only serious rivals – apart from, I suppose, that little place in Mount Street. I was stuck down in the basement – packer, basically. But very nice people – and for those days, even the starting pay was really rather good. One hell of an improvement on Smith's, anyway – but I think I could have got more from begging on a street corner than I ever did from Smith's. And it must have been on the back of this new job, I think, that I was able to take on a set of rooms in Belsize Crescent – altogether so much nicer I could barely believe it. The real point, of course, was that finally I'd got out of Kilburn – and Belsize, well . . . it wasn't just all drunks and kebab shops. That little flat . . . well I daresay it would seem a slum to me now, but I remember thinking at the time that I was living in a palace. Youth, you see? Christ, it was an age ago.

I used to walk on Hampstead Heath quite a lot – most

weekends. But I was lonely, though – I do remember that. If it hadn't been for The Beatles, I don't know what I would have done: put a Fab Four LP on the record player, let all the familiar songs and harmonies wash right over and into me: just so wonderful – they never let me down. I felt I knew them, really – they were just so much a part of me. I still feel that now, maybe oddly, and two of them are dead . . . which I do find very sad: just not meant to happen. Dead . . .! I simply can never take it in. I did still have the odd girl on the go, of course – Christ, one of them accused me of rape, if you can believe it . . .! Yes, but that's another story. And apart from Dorothy, I'd always had Sammy in the past as well, of course . . . but that . . . well that rather went too. But anyway – it was around the time when all of that was going on that I did it: the tart. King's Cross. Complete accident, of course – nothing about it was planned. Christ Almighty – I was scared half witless. Looking back, it all seems highly comical . . . though I doubt that it did at the time. Anyway – that was then: I think we can do a little better now.

I'm nervous. How completely stupid is that? Sometimes, I utterly amaze myself, I really do. Sitting in front of my laptop, perfectly aware of the sort of thing to look for – all that I've got to key in . . . and look at me: I'm nervous. Because that's one of the things about me, you see: I'm not nearly so suave and accomplished as I think most people believe me to be. I'll throw out an arm to a cruising taxi with all the easy insouciance of a practised veteran, but still I'm always anxious that he's just going to sail on by – pick up someone more deserving. Why I stick to restaurants where I'm known, to be honest: couldn't bear the worry of not being able to catch a waiter's eye, or the maître d' not treating me with respect and attention: somewhere new . . . it's just not worth the risk. Extraordinary, really . . . to be feeling just any little part of that, at the age of sixty-four. And now I find that I'm wary of dickering with a laptop. What do I imagine the machine is going to do to me? Realise with a shudder that I am delving into murky waters and snap down shut to chop off my fingers . . .? Jesus – people do this sort of thing just all the time. More or less what the internet is for. That and email and the odd thing from Amazon – what the hell else do you want it to do? I mean . . . I myself use the pornography sites, well of course I do. 'Porn' – that's the universal abbreviation, these days – but I hate it: the word, I mean. Pornography, that sounds rather comfortingly like a serious academic subject: geography, ethnography, topography . . . you see what I'm meaning. 'Porn', well . . . just sounds coarse. Which, I suppose, is half the point. Often, when I go to one of these sites though, I simply sit there and gaze at it. Sometimes in a state of excitement, occasionally in disgust – but always with a curiously light-headed sort of quasi-amazement that any of this can actually be here at all. So in that sense we have come rather a long way from smuggling into school a copy of *Parade* or *Health & Efficiency*. In *Parade*, I remember, there would be these really quite cute and fresh-faced young girls with pert little breasts, and some or other prop very carefully arranged to hide from our wide and greedy eyes anything more intriguingly intimate. A parasol, say, or an edifying novel. Far more worrying was *Health & Efficiency*, which I think purported to be dedicated to the health-giving benefits of naturism, ho ho ho. So tennis featured a fair deal, so far as I can recall. The truly disturbing thing – God, you know, this really did give me nightmares – was that the woman was fully nude all right, but between her legs there was nothing but a large expanse of white unblemished flesh. I agonised over this for hours and hours – not actually from a sexual point of view, but wrestling with my sheer inability to explain to myself how females – women, girls, nuns – ever could manage to go to the lavatory. Oh dear God . . . it's amazing we ever grow up at all really, isn't it? When you're young, you're just so very alone, stranded amid an ocean of ignorance – and regarding old people as another race completely, viewing them half in envy, and half with unspeakable revulsion.

I quite like to see . . . what I like best is when women are wholly subservient – yes, but willingly so. I don't care for any sort of coercion. Adoring subservience, yes – which initially I had innocently believed would be difficult to find: Christ – internet, it's awash with it all. Actually seems to be pretty much the normal thing, and I'm not quite sure whether that pleases me or if it doesn't. Yes but this new idea . . . taking the thing to a whole new level, to use the jargon of the day . . . one where I am to be physically and actively involved with an actual paid-for woman . . . well that I really do find rather nerve-racking. Escort agencies, they call them. Escort . . .! Dear dear. The opposite of what it used to mean, then. An escort was a guide, a protector, a chaperone. Not now though, I don't think. And although I'm perfectly aware that without any sort of commitment or outlay one can browse to one's heart's content (if the heart has anything to do with it) . . . still, there is something . . . I don't know . . . there's just something that's holding me back. It might not be the way to go, is what I'm thinking. This might not be the best way to set about things. There could easily be a better and more satisfactory method altogether, of getting what I want. And that's why I've decided that I'm going to call Saul. Saul, he'll know. Very much a man of the world, young Saul – and I say young, because he can only be in his forties.

Met him a year or two back at some big trade do in Paris: got thoroughly plastered on one of the evenings – were talking about all sorts of things, things I'd never really spoken about before to anyone at all, really. Lives in Chelsea, wife, couple of children still at school. It was Saul, actually, who put me on to that detective who's still trying to track down dear Anna's quite criminally useless husband. Not doing awfully well, but still. Which reminds me – I have to ring him, the gumshoe: find out what the hell is going on. Yes . . . but in the meantime, I'll call Saul. He'll know what to do about this little predicament of mine. He'll understand completely.

'Saul. Glad I've caught you. George.'

'George . . .?'

'Yes – you know: George . . .?'

'Oh *George*, m'dear – yes of *course*. How are you? Been far too long.'

'I was thinking exactly the same thing. So how about . . . I don't know – lunch, or something? Good idea? Evening, if you prefer.'

'Sorry, George . . . just getting into a taxi. You broke up a bit there. What saying . . .?'

'Oh right. Hear me now . . .? Yes? Well I was just thinking – spot of lunch, maybe.'

'Oh yes – absolutely, George. I tell you what – you don't happen to be free today by any chance, do you? Lunching at my club – you'd be very welcome. Decent crowd, should be.'

'Oh well I . . . well that's awfully decent of you.'

'Not a bit of it. About twelve forty-five suit you . . .? Quick couple before we go in?'

'Yes, I should think so.'

'Jolly. See you there, then. You remember where it is . . .?'

'Yes yes. Fine. Perfect. Bye then, Saul. See you soon.'

The Savile, his club is. Mayfair – just up the road from Claridge's. Very nice place indeed, actually – been there a few times, though I've never been moved to join. Well . . . never been asked, to be fair – but I mean any club, really: not really sure if it's me. I daresay over the years if I'd subtly put it about to one or two people that I'd quite like to be a member of – well, the Savile, say, or the Reform or somewhere, it probably eventually would have come to pass . . . but I've never been quite sure about it all, quite frankly: the whole club thing. Because you don't just join, you know: you don't simply plank down your sub, and then you're in. Can take bloody years. And during all of that time you have to be repeatedly paraded at the expense of your proposer as if you are livestock up for sale, or something . . . and the membership, they are constantly judging you – judging whether you are worthy to become one of their number. Not sure how it's done, exactly – how it all comes about: they maybe have to sign your page in a bloody great ledger, I've never really gone into it. And . . . well, I'm really not at all sure that I could face all that. Cope with it. It's just the old insecurity again, I suppose – although, as I say, I am entirely convinced that no one I ever encounter would suspect me of being victim to any such thing. But just imagine . . . if one did come to be put forward for one of these places . . . just imagine the terminal embarrassment, the complete and utter mortification, if word came down from the gods on high that you just didn't come up to snuff . . .! Sorry matey – nothing personal! Except that it would be, of course: quite wholly personal – couldn't be more so. Well Jesus . . . one just could never show one's face again. Couldn't live it down. On the other hand, though . . . it's all rather vexing, in honesty, because deep down . . . I very much like the idea. In principle. Band of brothers, all of that – though not to the almost comical extent of the Freemasons, nothing of that sort. And nor am I at all averse to the air of superior entitlement that members of some of the more eminent clubs will effortlessly display, though without ostentation: I've watched them – I know. White's, say – but that's just chock-full of aristocrats, so what can you expect? Or the really rather elegant swagger of the Garrick – actors, writers, doctors and lawyers, I'm given to understand. Well I've enjoyed one or two very decent lunches and evenings there as a guest. And that extraordinary pink and green tie that they love to show off – it's a perfectly ghastly tie, in one way, and yet really rather fabulous, all at the same time: the connotations, I suppose, like the MCC's egg and tomato: bloody awful design, well of course it is, but nonetheless profoundly covetable. Well I'd love to sport the Garrick tie – salmon and cucumber, I think they call it – but I'd never get in, of course, and nor would I put myself up for the humiliation of attempting to, and failing. Egg and tomato . . . salmon and cucumber . . . maybe I should form a club of my own with an all-orange tie, and then we can call it the fish and chips. Enough nonsense: the point is that, all in all, clubland isn't really me . . . which maybe has rather a lot to do with why I resolutely stick to my carefully nurtured repertoire of four or five favourite restaurants where I may be sure of excellent treatment. Places where I am bound to be appreciated. Cuts out all of the anxiety, you see. Because look: at my age, I hardly need nor deserve any sort of stress, and I absolutely refuse to put up with it. Why should I? It's my life. What's left of it.

Anyway . . . it's terribly pleasant here – and now I'm back, I remember it utterly. Little bit later than I agreed with Saul:

wasn't sure initially quite what door it was – because there's never any indication, obviously. But it's an extraordinary thing – in the better parts of London, though particularly Mayfair, you find yourself ambling down an unbuggered-up street, and the occasional handsome Georgian doorcase will emerge from an unbroken redbrick terrace wall. You barely give them a second glance – and truly, you have absolutely no idea that behind every one of them there lurks – so very discreetly – a veritable palace in miniature. How could one imagine such a thing? Not that the Savile is as miniature as all that. Lovely and welcoming traditional entrance hall – black-and-white marble floor, deep-fielded panelling, the twist of an elegant staircase – and the bar, oh my goodness: that is just about perfect. Dark wood carvings, very Grinling Gibbons, low leather upholstery, and quite the most wonderful coffered ceiling. And oh yes – I'd forgotten about that: a charming Parisian sort of enclosed courtyard just outside, there it is – high walls lined with architectural trellis rather in the chinoiserie style, it looks like from here: quite ideal for the enjoyment of a decent cigar – because there are just so few places left where one can have a proper smoke in comfort since this bloody stupid ban came in. I mean, yes okay – outlaw it if you like in restaurants and theatres, fair enough . . . but in London's gentlemen's clubs . . .? Appalling – quite appalling. Ah – there he is: that's Saul, waving a paper around. Sitting with a couple of chaps, and looking rather dapper, I must say.

'George, m'dear . . .! Welcome, welcome. Come and meet the boys. Stephen – this is George, friend of mine. Oh and this is Georgie. George – Georgie. Coincidence, no? Try not to get confused, won't you? I can't have you both forgetting which one of you is which. Now – far more to the point: what can I get you to drink? We're on Chablis, at the moment.'

'A glass of Chablis would be perfect, Saul. Thank you. Sorry I'm a little late. Always such a pleasure to be here. So good of you.'

It's the old fellow Stephen who's about to talk to me now: Jesus, he's ancient – makes me look like a bloody teenager. Yes – he's leaning forward in his armchair, and I can see that he's cranking up to it.

'Ah. So you're not a member of our merry little band. Thought I hadn't seen you before. John, is it . . .?'

'George. I'm not, no.'

'I offered to put him up, one time. Turned me down flat.'

'Oh God, Saul – I *didn't*, of course I didn't. Wasn't like that at all. It's just that . . .'

'No no – just kidding with you, George. Georgie – could you grab a glass for George . . .? Georgie's in theatre. Vastly successful, though far too modest to say so.'

This Georgie person – and it is quite a coincidence, actually, because I'm not sure I've ever met another George – he's sliding over the Chablis to me now. Pleasant-enough looking sort of a fellow – about Saul's age, I should think. Mid-forties, thereabouts.

'I have much to be modest about, I do assure you. Good to meet you, George. Not your first time here, I'm assuming?'

'No no. Always a delight though, as I say. Good wine, Saul – thank you.'

'Glad you approve. I've just actually been elected to the Wine Committee, so I hope it's good – we've laid in cases and cases of it! Now Stephen here – he will tell you that this is a *proper* club – won't you, Stephen . . .?'

'Well it *is*, Saul. A proper club. Not like the way some of them have gone. This is a *proper* club, John.'

'What he means is – and it's George, Stephen: he's called George. What he means by "proper" is that we have no lady members. Right, Stephen?'

'Perfectly correct. It's not that we dislike women, or anything . . .'

'Absolutely not. Quite the reverse.'

'. . . but there are certain times and places where they are simply not required. One never used to have to explain this. Sensible women will understand it immediately. It's only these rabid bloody feminist harpies who are determined to break down the door. And then they would only destroy all that they would find here. Look – it's simple logic. Just as we would be wholly and quite properly unwelcome at a . . . what do they call them . . .? Where all these ghastly females get together . . .?'

'Hen party . . .?'

'Hen party: quite so. Thank you, Saul. They wouldn't want us, would they? And we, of course, would very much not want to be there. So there it is, really. An old-established club is best left alone. Do you agree . . .?'

'Answer carefully, George. Could be a trap . . .'

'Well I do, as a matter of fact. I agree wholeheartedly.'

'Good man – we'll make a member of you yet. Because you see . . . women, well . . . perfectly acceptable as a guest from time to time. Nothing wrong with that. We make them most welcome, ladies – don't we, Saul? They always do seem to be most appreciative. But otherwise, you see, their presence, well . . . on anything approaching a permanent basis, it would alter the character of the club irretrievably, do you see? Perfectly obvious, really. The feeling – the *feeling*, that would be quite lost. Which would be a truly terrible thing. And we – we would have to be on our guard. Best behaviour. Minding our P's and

Q's. And that is not at all what you come to your club in order to do. Is it? You want to be yourself. Among your friends. And I further think – and this is absolutely key – that it is the duty of the younger members such as you and Georgie, Saul . . . to bear this in mind. It is a legacy. We must – it is absolutely vital that we preserve it for future generations of like-minded men. Otherwise . . . well: just look at the Athenaeum, if you want an example of just what can happen the moment your back is turned. Overrun with women members now. All over the bloody place. Last time I was invited there, well . . . didn't know where to put myself. Couldn't get out fast enough, I can tell you that. Reform's the same . . . but then the Reform, well . . . hardly a club at all . . .'

'Thank you for that, Stephen. We'll have it engraved in marble and hung above the bar.'

'No laughing matter, Saul . . .'

'Not laughing, Stephen – honestly not. We'll go up to the trough in a minute, George – but maybe room for another drop of this, do we all think . . .?'

'I'm not allowed to get us in another bottle, am I . . .?'

'You most certainly are not, George. I'll just see if I can get the chap's attention . . .'

'No I'll get it, Saul – just about to, actually.'

'Oh jolly – thank you, Georgie. And there he goes – as good as his word. You'll like Georgie, George. Good chap, isn't he Stephen? Yes – I think you'll get on.'

And we did, as a matter of fact. Went up to lunch soon after the second bottle, bringing with us all that was left of the third. Stephen had buggered off somewhere with a pack of similarly archaic cronies, and I found myself sitting between Saul and Georgie at the club table. And it was Georgie who very politely reminded me how to write down what I wanted to eat on one of these curious little notepads that are set at each place – and they even supply royal blue Savile Club pencils, perfectly sharpened. I was warming to the place more and more – and who knows? Maybe I ought to completely reconsider my attitude to the entire business of clubs. Saul, he seemed to be rather engaged in earnest conversation with the man on his right, so it was Georgie I found myself talking to during most of the meal: nothing terribly specific – just little bits of this and that, no topic at all you could really put your finger on. Afterwards – and it had been a more than decent lunch of something prawny, entrecôte and proper Stilton with rather a lot of claret – the two of us found ourselves sitting outside on that extremely lovely terrace . . . whereupon Georgie from absolutely nowhere produced a couple of Upmann coronas, cutter, long matches, the whole caboodle. Extraordinarily considerate, and entirely welcome. And oh God: look at this – large malt whiskies as well.

'I do feel now that I am rather imposing upon your hospitality . . .'

'It's my great pleasure, George. Honestly. I do enjoy a cigar after lunch, but it's so much better if you have someone to smoke it with.'

'Well I'm very grateful indeed. Not sure where Saul has vanished to . . .'

'I think he said something about a bit of club business. He's on the Committee, you know. Not the Wine Committee, I don't mean – the actual Committee. Daresay he'll reappear. Have you known him long, George?'

'No, not really. Hardly know him at all, actually. We're in the same line, that's all. Meet occasionally.'

'Oh yes – that's printing, isn't it? Don't know much about it. Sounds interesting.'

'Well – hardly. Not like you. A theatre producer! That must be very exciting indeed.'

'Only rarely. Mostly it's just endless planning, raising money – and that gets harder and harder, as I'm sure I don't have to tell you. Waiting around for years, being let down continually . . .'

'That's not all though, surely . . .? This cigar is quite sublime . . .'

'Oh God no. Otherwise one wouldn't be in it at all. When things do eventually come together . . . that can be a wonderful moment. Twenty-hour days, though – when you're in the thick of it. But that's one of the things I most like about it, actually. No children, or anything – so nothing to rush back home to. Oh and, um . . . I maybe didn't say – I'm a widower, you know.'

'Oh really . . .? I'm so sorry to hear that. I had no idea. But you're so young . . .'

'Yes well – so was she. Even younger, actually. I'm forty-five, but she . . . Susan . . . she was only thirty-nine when she went. No age, is it? Awful, really. Nearly a couple of years ago, now. Hadn't actually been married that long. Came to it quite late. We were planning the whole family thing, you know? Both wanted kids, but . . . well. Hit me pretty hard. My mother too – she was terribly upset, of course. Very close, you know? And it wasn't that long after Dad died, so she was really going through it, poor old Mum. Heart attack, it was with Dad. Bolt out of the blue. But with Susan, well . . . usual thing. Cancer. Well. There it is.'

'I really am so terribly sorry. And so . . . there's no one else . . .?'

'No. Well . . . no. Not in the proper sense. I see women, of course.'

'Ah. So . . . just sort of . . . girlfriends . . .?'

'You could say that. Think we might need another whisky. Look – club rules, yes?'

'I'm sorry . . .?'

'I mean – nothing leaves these four walls. Yes?'

'Oh God – *got* you. Yes – oh yes, of *course*. Naturally.'

'Well – there are these women who are . . . professional. You know? I just . . . I don't know . . . I just find it so much easier.'

And I think I just must have been gaping at the man.

'Are you . . . shocked? It's not actually all that unusual, these days. People of my age . . . people I know . . . they don't think anything of it. Saves time, you see.'

'Shocked? No no – not at all. Bit stunned, that's all. It's just that . . . well you won't believe this Georgie, but . . . well earlier today I was . . . well to be perfectly frank with you I have been thinking just recently on exactly the same lines – and that's one of the things, actually, that I wanted to talk to Saul about. Why I rang him, really. Why I'm here. I thought he'd . . . know.'

'Saul? Oh I doubt it. Quite happy with his mistress, I gather. But I do. Know. I know all about it. Another Macallan . . .? What do you reckon? I think, you know, we might owe it to ourselves.'

And I laughed out loud at that. Not actually quite sure why – wasn't particularly funny, I suppose . . . I think that largely it must just have been the man's delivery. Completely deadpan, and then just the merest twinkle of the eye. More of a knowing sort of a blink, really – but anyway something that I very much responded to. We connected, you know? I liked his style: a man's man, clearly . . . though equally clearly one who was hardly a stranger to the ways of women. Am I like that . . .? I think I might be. Don't know. But I think I might be. Anyway, we did that, had another whisky – bloody enormous measure – and I was very eager now, of course I was, to get well stuck into this new and rather exciting topic which had suddenly and so very unexpectedly arisen. Well – from an unexpected quarter, is what I mean – because it was meant to be Saul . . . but Saul, well . . . I had already completely forgotten about him, isn't it funny? By this time, the occasional chap was approaching our table – hello Georgie, is what they were saying, and amicably raising a hand. Each time it happened . . . it really made me feel so strange: I automatically would look up in expectation, my face – I could feel it – wholly receptive, and spread wide with a welcoming smile. Wasn't me they were talking to – of course it wasn't, I was wholly aware of that: none of them was remotely concerned with the interloper George: it was Georgie, the member. My new chum. Don't even know why I even was moved to look up in the first place – because Georgie, well . . . no one's called me Georgie since . . . well now let me think about that. Since Sammy, I'm pretty sure. Might have been one or two women along the way who would say it playfully (Georgie-Porgie, pudding and pie – you know the sort of mawkish drivel they can be given to) . . . but other than that, no: no one else since that friend of mine from a million years ago. No one else, since Sammy.

'Look, George . . . we're never going to get any peace to have a chat. It's like that here. Lovely and friendly and everything, but it can be absolute murder if you actually want to have a conversation. I'll tell you what – how are you fixed for time? Not in any rush? Oh well that's good – because what we might do, you know, is push off to my other club, if you fancy the idea. Altogether . . . looser, there.'

'Your other club . . .? Good heavens.'

'It's not too far. Ten minutes in a taxi.'

And that's just about how long it has taken to get us from the Savile to the Chelsea Arts, not much more. I've heard of the place, of course – a noble if rather raffish reputation – but I've never actually been here. Well why would I? Not my sort of circle, really. Wish it was. And I'm feeling . . . I'm feeling two things really very strongly almost immediately after Georgie has led the way through the tiny front door, which rather surprisingly was bang on the pavement – he's swept a gizmo of some sort in front of a winking eye (I'm telling you – everything's like this nowadays). The first thing I'm thinking is, my goodness – you could hardly find a club more different from the one we have just come from . . . and that now, quite simply, I just felt so terribly at home. Difficult to . . . articulate, really. I had loved the Savile, really loved it – knowing as I always have done that if ever I were to join a club of any sort at all, then this is the type of thing I'd be aspiring to. And yet here . . . here in this plain and even rather scruffy large room with a vast snooker table dominating the central space, a piano rammed into the corner . . . the walls haphazardly hung with unframed canvases – each of them a rather forceful example of what I believe might well be called expressionism . . . or conceivably not . . . here I just am feeling so terribly at home. Which is not at all the appropriate comparison, actually, because I never feel at home when I'm at home. Haven't for years. But I am utterly comfortable and at my ease, is what I'm meaning here. Which is really very odd. Because, well . . . the Chelsea Arts Club, it's just not me, is it? It's not me at all. But I don't know, though . . . maybe it is: maybe it exactly is. Because look: if this is what I'm feeling, well then it must be . . . mustn't it? It must be me, if that's what I'm feeling. Or am I just hopelessly befuddled by booze, and I don't even know what I'm thinking? Well . . . there is certainly an element of that at play here . . . but I feel sure it's not all of it: nowhere near. The feeling of peace, even happiness, that has washed all over and into me: it is real, I just know it.

The plain wooden bar – oak, is it? I used to know a bit about wood, think it's oak – well that's quite wonderfully rudimentary. Like bars used to be, before everything got out of hand and they were all tricked out with marble and leather and downlighting and all the bloody rest of it. Georgie – who's received a fine and generous welcome from the few people who are scattered about, as well as the barman – he's ordering something or other for us, can't quite catch it, and now he's asking me if I'd maybe like to sit in the garden . . .? Nice afternoon – and there are a few little corners, he's saying, where we can hide away and be left to ourselves. A very large man with a bright red face – truly not much short of tomato – he has suddenly arisen from somewhere and is clapping Georgie about the shoulders with a force that would have had me sprawling. Green teeth – and his darker green corduroy jacket, it looks as thick as carpet. Two rather elegant old ladies, wafer-thin with pale and powdered skin, thin crimson lips and violently colourful garb, are sitting at a small round table: speaking quite earnestly, and sipping pink fizz. I like it here. I really do like it here.

And the garden . . . you talk of clubs, you don't really think about gardens, do you? Terraces, yes – like at the Savile – but this is much more the proper and traditional thing: an extraordinarily inviting old-fashioned English cottage garden, what a terribly lovely surprise. A little pond . . . lichen-encrusted cherub, spitting intermittently . . . a curve of lawn . . . sort of gazebo thing, I suppose it is . . . and Georgie, he's taking me now towards the back bit, where I can see there's a small round table, three or four chairs, all set deep into an alcove that seems to be formed wholly out of some sort of a brambly bush affair, not too good on horticulture: garden, that's always been Enid's side of things.

'Glad it's not taken. People sit here, they don't ever tend to budge. Drinks'll come in a minute. Service is pretty good. Also asked for another couple of cigars. That all right?'

'Very all right – thank you, Georgie. But are you sure I can't, um . . .?'

'No no. My club again, isn't it?'

'Well I'm exceedingly grateful, I must say. Next time I insist we go somewhere on me. Lovely here. All terribly, um . . .'

''Tis, isn't it? I tend to come here more in the summer.'

'Very nice too. Been a member long?'

'No, not at all – couple of years. Some people here – been members since Whistler's time, I reckon. He founded it, you know. Whistler. Painter. Nineteenth-century. Know him?'

'Of him, yes. Think so.'

'It's my mother's club, really. Comes all the time. She who got me in, actually. I take her to the Savile sometimes, but I'm not sure she's really that keen. Always polite about it, of course, but I don't think it's really her thing. Loves it here, though. Comes all the time, when she's not working. Ah – here we are! Champagne – all right? Only the house, but it's actually pretty good. Nice after lunch, I think. Refreshing. And it goes with a cigar rather better than people might think. To be completely honest with you, I'm actually a fake – a bit of a fraudulent member, really. In the arts, it's true – theatre, and so on – but I'm not what you call a "plastic" artist, you see. That's what they really want here. Just pour it will you, Emily darling . . .? I'm sure it will be wonderful.'

'"Plastic" . . .?'

'Mm. Actual painting and sculpture and so on.'

'Ah. I see. Mmm . . . you're right: very refreshing indeed.'

'Glad you approve. I'll just cut the cigars, shall I . . .?'

'Please. And so your mother, then . . . she is a . . .?'

'Is, yes. Painter. Rather good, actually. Photographer. Works in clay. All that.'

'Mm. Not like my mother, then . . .'

'No?'

'God no. My mother, Jesus . . . she wouldn't have known art if you'd hit her round the head with it. Sounds mean, but – well: it's true. Anyway: enough about her. Well look: cheers then, Georgie. Hail fellow, well met. A very opportune encounter. Wouldn't you say? Extraordinary though, isn't it? I often think that. About, you know – things that just come out of nowhere – out of the blue. I mean to say . . . this morning . . . this morning . . . when we both got up, just as we normally do – dressed ourselves, made for the Savile Club . . . well: neither of us had the faintest idea that the other was even alive. That we even existed. And look at us now . . .! Chatting away – in a place I have never before set foot in . . . having a drink . . . like we've known each other for ever. Odd. Very odd. In a good way, of course. But it's very strange, this sort of thing. Don't you think it's strange? Because we think we know, don't we? We think we're in control. We actually do imagine we can predict what's going to happen next. Nonsense, of course. We don't have a clue. We don't really have a clue about bloody anything at all . . .'

'Well let's drink to that then, George. To being clueless . . .!'

'Clueless . . .! Oh dear . . . oh dear me. You really are a most amusing fellow, you know.'

'How's the cigar . . .?'

'Good. Very good. I prefer these fat ones.'

'Mm. Better flavour. Altogether more rounded, I think. Let me just top you up with bubbles. So then, George – you want to know all about London floozies, do you?'

'*Floozies* . . .! There's a word . . .!'

'Well . . . they're not, of course. Like floozies. Not the ones I'm talking about. Nothing crude or showy about them. Nothing you'd be embarrassed about being seen with, if you know what I mean. Quite the reverse, in fact. Because if you actually, you know – take them out somewhere – restaurant, party, nightclub, you know the sort of thing . . . which I do, as a matter of fact, time to time . . . if I need a lift, if I want to impress . . . well I'm telling you: they just make you feel a million dollars. A zillion dollars. That's the absolute truth. They are so worth whatever they cost. Ten times over, in everything they deliver. And God – you walk in somewhere with a woman like that on your arm . . . oh, the look on all the other men's faces . . .! That's worth the price of admission on its own. They are simply . . . the ones I'm talking about, yes? They are simply . . . well – the best.'

'The best, yes. Well . . . that . . . all that . . . that's exactly what I want.'

'Of course you do. It's what we all want. Every man on earth, that's wholly and utterly what he wants. And I just can't tell you, George . . . what a fantastic *relief* it is when finally you just *admit* it to yourself. Wonderful, undreamed-of sex, exactly how you like it, when you want it – and with a phenomenally beautiful woman who actually knows what she's *doing* . . .! Can you *imagine* . . .? Christ. It's great.'

'Jesus. It sounds it.'

'It's not marriage, of course. It's not like being married.'

'No. Doesn't sound it.'

'But if you can't be married . . . if the wife you love just goes and bloody *dies* . . .!'

'Christ, Georgie – you okay . . .?'

'Yeh. Sorry. Yeh – completely okay. I just sometimes . . . oh, it's the drink, I expect. Always does this, a bit of drink. But look – what I mean to say is . . . if you can't any more be with the woman you love . . . well what's the bloody point of getting to know someone you don't? No point at all, is there? I don't want to know *any* woman . . .! I mean – I meet actresses all the time, of course I do – there's hardly a shortage of candidates. But I'm not . . . ready. I hope I will be again soon . . . but at the moment I'm not. Not yet. So in the meantime, all I want is just . . . to see one, occasionally. So – the best, right? Why not? Why not the best?'

'Why not indeed? I have no answer. It's exactly . . . it's exactly what I meant.'

And I just am sitting here now, drinking in the dream. It had been no more than the merest idea before, a fancy that had just occurred to me, but now . . . well now, just the thought of *not* going through with it all, well . . . seems almost criminal. Got to be done. Simply got to be done. And I can't bloody wait.

'George . . .? George . . .? This is Jane. Jane – George.'

'Oh . . . hello . . . sorry . . .'

'Oh *please* don't get up, darling. My – what an utterly *perfect* gentleman you are . . .!'

'So sorry – I think I must have been dreaming. Didn't see you arrive.'

'We drift upon the lawn like ghosts . . .'

'Well, George – this is all beginning to look as if it was *meant*. Because everything I've just been saying, yes? Well, Jane – she can tell you all about it.'

'About what, darling . . .? What have you two naughty boys been talking about . . .?'

'Floozies, as a matter of fact. Or *not* floozies, actually.'

'Oh you *are* naughty, aren't you? May I have just a soupçon of your *divine* champagne, darling? I've just lit a Gauloise and I always do find that they are just perfectly *divine* with champagne . . .'

Now she's sitting down between us, I can properly take a look at her: a very striking face indeed – the high and defined cheekbones of a model, or something . . . wide green eyes, sparkling, yet set rather mournfully into painted hollows . . . long and marmalade hair, as loved by that Rossetti person . . . an extraordinary assemblage of coloured scarves . . . a deep and musky quite all-conquering scent that could catch your throat. And do you know . . .? She needn't be that much off my age. Christ – could even be older. Looks bloody marvellous, though – in a rather gorgeous and extravagantly faded sort of a way: a bit like the muted gold and dusty velvet in the gods of an old theatre, still with just enough of its once quite blinding glamour, and seductive opulence.

'My sweet . . . in my prime, I myself was a *belle dame*. Was I not, Georgie?'

'Not just a *belle dame*, my dear. I have heard that you were the finest of the finest . . .'

'Why *naturally*, darling . . .! My fame was quite extraordinary.

Oh darling – the men I have lain with . . .! The *crème de la crème*, each and every one of them. I could have brought down governments, toppled whole countries, reduced the whole of Hollywood to quite abject and pitiable surrender . . . not to say most severely embarrassed to the core our very own monarchy. But I was a lady, you see – we all were, in those days – and so none of that awfulness could possibly occur. It would not have been . . . how can I say . . .? Polite. It would not have been polite. It would have been ungrateful, and ungracious. Do you see . . .? Gentlemen, they knew that they could depend upon us: our word was our bond. It did not do to *chatter*. Chartreuse, this was my *nom de sexe*. In many corridors, the name will still resound. Chartreuse, yes indeed – do you care for it, darling? Does it *thrill* you utterly . . .? Such a name was seen to be vital, of course, because nobody really wants you to be called Jane, you see. Nothing dull. Never anything remotely *wifely*, if you see what I am saying. The exotic and the erotic . . . such good bedfellows, don't you agree? We all of us had quite the most outrageously silly names – part of the fun. All part of the *carnival*, darling. Belladonna – *such* a good friend, though alas no longer does she walk this earth. My poor, sweet Belladonna . . . the angel succumbed when still quite horribly young. I have no doubt that Saint Peter still is delighting in her company. Scheherazade . . . Salome, but of course. Delilah. Dolores – that was eternally popular, I can't say I quite understand why. Sounds a little common, to my ears. But I chose Chartreuse. People did find it so very intensely amusing . . . because *green*, darling, I most assuredly was not, you must please believe me. Oh . . .! Yet one further soupçon of champagne! How very captivatingly *divine* you are, darling . . .! So George – do tell me everything you are longing to know. Because I like you terribly – and when I like someone terribly, I am most immensely *generous*. I promise you, George – I shall give you my *all* . . .'

And she did, she did – she was perfectly true to her word, Chartreuse, Jane, whatever I was calling her by then. I now know everything I need to – and so much more that has astonished me. But oh my Lord – I'm not thinking about any of that *now*. I'm at home, back home . . . and still I am shivering. Trembling. Actually *quivering* with the totally unbelievable *thrill* of it all . . .! The journey back in a cab – that just passed me by in daze. The driver, I remember – he had to ask me twice if this is where I lived, and I had idly glanced through the window at the house and said What . . .? Oh yes – yes. What a thing . . .! Oh my God in heaven what a *day* it's been . . .! I still just can't believe it's *true* . . .! Nothing to do with women . . . nothing to do with Georgie or Chartreuse . . . it's all about what happened to me *after*. Christ. You see . . . the hours had passed – getting dark in the Chelsea Arts garden, rather chilly – and Christ alone knows how much I'd had to drink by that time: the bottles, they just kept on appearing. Eventually, the moment came when I knew, just knew, that if I didn't get out of here right now, then I would enter into a state of careless lassitude, and after that I'd lose my reason. Not something you want – and particularly when you are not on home turf – but it happens, as you get older. I have noticed and cursed this before. You forget it, you see – you forget that no longer are you the young and invincible man who can go on drinking till dawn, and then later on that very same morning feel no more than a little bit groggy, just slightly fatigued. It fells you for days – for the past few years, it's been a complete and utter killer.

So I was tottering through the bar . . . look, I'm yearning, just yearning to scream out now just what happened to me next . . .!

But let's just get the whole thing in order, yes? For the sake of my own just hovering sanity, if for no other real reason. So . . . I am tottering through the bar . . . can't recall whether or not I had said a formal farewell to Georgie, my host – or even if he was still around. You lose perspective, you see, as well as your footing. Jane, Chartreuse . . . I think she had drifted away, pretty sure, quite a long time earlier – very probably to drink someone else's *divine* champagne, if maybe she had sensed that ours might soon cease to flow. Other people, I think, had come and gone . . . laughter, lots of laughter, another great raft-load of booze . . . but none of this, none of this matters the slightest *jot* . . . because as I continued to weave my way towards what I thought I remembered might be the door that led out of this place, vaguely calculating that in Chelsea, at least, a taxi was not going to be remotely difficult . . . my eye for some reason strayed to the very corner of the room . . . and there, there, all on his own, wearing a great big grey herringbone tweed overcoat with the collar pulled up high . . . there, holding a glass and looking into it . . . was . . . oh Jesus *Christ* . . .! Even now, I am – I am, I am *quivering,* I tell you . . .! Because just a few feet away from me . . . was Paul McCartney. I am not joking . . .! Oh my God. Oh my *God.* I've just got to sit down, now. Just thinking about it – as I have been, just over and over – I've just got to sit down again. I've been pacing about ceaselessly since the moment I got home. My eyes – I can feel them bulging in amazement. In the short time I've been here, I've played *Revolver* twice, and now it's *Band on the Run* I'm listening to. That voice! Those harmonies! The unmistakable thud of those extraordinary things he does with his beautiful violin-like bass guitar . . .! And there's more – that's not all of it: it gets even *better* . . .!

I knew it was him . . . I sensed it was him, before I'd even gasped at the profile. And yet I grabbed at the sleeve of the nearest person to hand and was gabbling quite manically at him: Is that *Paul* . . .? Is that Paul *McCartney* . . .?! Yeh, he said – he comes in here a bit: he likes it, because nobody bothers him. I was nodding. Gaping at Paul, and nodding. And I knew that I couldn't. Leave it alone. I wanted to – I wanted to be adult about this . . . but how in Christ's name could I suddenly be that, when already I had been reduced to the state of a shudderingly tearful and demented teenage girl from 1964 . . .? Thank God I was so helplessly drunk. Had I not been, I would have walked straight out of there, and cursed myself for the rest of my life. And . . . only when I was so close to him that he could hardly avoid looking up, and at me . . . did my heart practically leap from my body. His wonderful eyes were dipped, very possibly in sympathy. How many times in his life must he have been confronted by middle-aged people making a complete and utter bloody idiot of themselves . . .? He understood, though . . . I just knew that he understood. I wanted to tell him that I had adored him and his music for the whole of my life. That I could not have survived my teenage years without The Beatles, along with all the decades since. I wanted to say that I still had a scrapbook full of all the Sixties cuttings, along with a painstakingly gathered and peerless collection of very early memorabilia . . . that I still had the original mono LPs . . . that I had yearned to dress like him, have hair as great as his hair . . . that I had wanted to *be* him . . .! I wanted to talk to him for the rest of my life, and ask him a million questions. And in his eyes, during the space of what can only have been seconds, I saw that he got it. He completely got it. He reached out his hand – his left hand, the hand that had done . . . oh Jesus, just *everything* . . .! And instinctively I reached out to grasp it. And as I was touching Paul . . . his look . . . the look he gave me . . . it was just so deeply and very desperately reassuring, that I was instantly flooded with . . . I don't know . . . warmth . . . and a surging of love, pure love. And I had not uttered a single word.

I've put on *A Hard Day's Night* . . . and although I love it every single time . . . it's suddenly different now. So much more . . . personal. Because look: I've met Paul McCartney. Just now. Touched him. He looked at me – Paul McCartney, in the Chelsea Arts Club, he looked straight at me, and then I touched him. I'm listening to the music, and all I'm seeing is him as he used to be, back in '64 . . . the way he held the Hofner bass, the way he arched his perfect eyebrows – his mighty left hand with the dangling bracelet, plucking out the notes. I touched it, that hand. Just now. I touched it. Jesus. Because I went through the whole of the Sixties not meeting anyone, not a single soul – not just Beatles, I don't mean. Anyone. Anyone at all. Never even saw a pop star . . . film star . . . nobody. Couldn't afford the concerts – lucky to get the LPs. Once . . . my God, how astounding, the silly little things you remember . . . once, I'd been to the Bag O'Nails with Sammy. Very groovy place, at the time – you read about it everywhere: never thought I'd actually go. Sammy, yes . . . he went to them, he went to the concerts. Rich dad. Nice for some. Anyway – Sammy, he told me that the last time he'd been there, the Bag O'Nails, he'd seen Cilla Black at the very next table. Even that had given me a kick: that I was somewhere that on another occasion entirely there had been sitting in a different chair somewhere else somebody famous. God, I must have been just so completely useless in those days. And she was there with . . . who had she been there with? Not a Beatle – I'd certainly remember that. Brian Epstein, I think.

Yes – it was Brian Epstein. When must all this have been . . .? Oh yeh – '64, of course. Year of *A Hard Day's Night*. So just four years before poor old Epstein died. This must have been around the time I broke up with Dorothy. Shame about that. I maybe shouldn't have got rid of that one quite so quickly. She was . . . good. She was . . . wonderful. Never really into The Beatles, though – well she was, everybody was, but not like me: she didn't feel what I felt. Some other group she liked more, if you can believe it. Can't remember. Not Gerry and the Pacemakers . . .? Couldn't be, could it? Might have been.

Anyway . . . all I'm good for now is just to sit at my desk, and glance through emails. Not really concentrating on any of them . . . my mind, it's still just fizzing. Fizzing with Paul. I don't even feel drunk any more. Oh but look . . . I've only just realised, you know . . . yes: this is odd. Bit peculiar. I knew when I came into the house that something wasn't right . . . something wasn't normal . . . but Jesus: after today, I ask you – what's *normal* . . .? But the house . . . I'd left the taxi . . . gave him an enormous tip, because of the way I was feeling . . . but the house . . . it was all in complete and utter darkness. Driveway lights not on. Groping about in the porch. Because Enid . . . well: she's not here. No note. Been out all day. And no email either. Just been through them, and there's nothing here from her. Give her a ring, maybe. Yeah – think I will. Hang on – what's this? What's this, now? Ah . . . here's an email worth reading. From that detective. Finally. About bloody time. Anna's husband . . . yes . . . he's *found* the cunt. Well good: bloody good. Dave Clark Five. That's them – that's the group that Dorothy was always going on about, some reason. Oh well. Do you know what? I'd love to be able to ring her up – right this minute. 'Dorothy . . .? Hello. You won't remember me, I expect – it's been a very long time. George. George, from way back. When we were young. When we were beautiful people. You loved The Dave Clark Five. I loved The Beatles. And you too, actually, now I come to think of it: loved you as well. I just don't think I ever said it. Anyway. So how are you? Keeping well? Oh good – glad to hear that. Hey listen: I've just met Paul McCartney . . .! I always wanted to hold his hand – and now I have!' It's funny . . . when you suddenly think of people you haven't seen for, what . . .? Not much short of fifty years. Can that be right . . .? It is right, you know. Nearly half a bloody century. Jesus. Wonder what she looks like now. I suppose she could be dead. Paul, though . . . he looked the same. Paul, he's just eternal.

Just rung Enid. No answer. Bit odd. I'll ring Anna – maybe she knows what's going on. I can tell her I've just met Paul McCartney – because Anna, she's the only one who could ever come close to understanding everything it means to me. No answer. Bit odd. I also could have told her that at last I've tracked down that bloody no-good crooked bastard of a husband of hers. The cunt. But I wouldn't have said . . . what I'm going to do to him. Wouldn't have told her that. Don't want to upset her. Anyway . . . that's that, I suppose, for the time being. It is strange that I can't get through to Enid, though. Or Anna. Very odd. So what am I expected to do about dinner, then? Has anyone thought about that? Maybe something in the fridge. Music's finished . . . I've got to put on another record. *Help!*, I think. Yes – that's exactly the thing, longing for it now: I need *Help!*

* * *

'That was your father, wasn't it?'

I look at her as she says this to me. The cup of tea she continues to hold as she has been doing for seemingly days: it is hovering just above the saucer, though never, not once, has she attempted to drink it. Stone cold by now. Her face . . . completely impassive, just as it always does seem to be, these days. No discernible emotion in this mother of mine – ever, about anything. Apart from when she called me . . . and how long ago was that? Hour or two ago? Then she most certainly sounded extremely agitated – I registered that much before I began even listening to the words. But all we have from her now is just a completely simple enquiry – no guile, no inquisitiveness, certainly no hint of reproach or accusation . . . not the slightest trace of even the vaguest loading or undercurrent. I am left to make my own mind up as to the nature of her question. And why do I notice? Observe all of this? Why do I actually care? Because I've so much else to *think* about. Everything's happened, oh Jesus . . . just so quickly. Oh look – I am dizzied by this. The whole situation. I don't what is going on – with her and Dad, with me and Troy. I just don't know what is going on. Even what I'm doing, sitting here – just foolishly sitting here, in this stupid room, in this stupid place. I'm not meant to be here. When I absolutely knew that we had to get out, that we just must go, I had no idea about what I was actually intending, but I surely wasn't meant to be here. I should be somewhere else entirely.

'It was, Mum, yes.'

'Mm. He just called me as well. I don't suppose he's remotely anxious, or anything. It's just that his routine has been interrupted. That's all. He probably wants his dinner. And has just noticed that the idiot who makes it for him is not in the kitchen, as she should be. Why didn't you speak to him? I'm surprised you didn't speak to him. You always want to speak to him, your father, don't you? So why didn't you speak to him?'

'I . . . I don't know.'

No I don't, not really. I had glanced at the phone, registered the caller – went to reach out for it, but then I held back. And Mum's right – I never do that with Dad . . . but at the moment, the way I'm feeling, well . . . I would've done that whoever had called, because I'm just not ready to actually *say* anything. You see. To anyone. Nothing to say. Haven't worked it out. Don't understand. I feel . . . hunted. I feel that, yes – because that's exactly what I bloody am. They were coming for me. Whoever they are – they were coming for me. That is true, and very chilling. So I had to get out. It's all I could really take in. But I wasn't thinking that it was . . . look: I didn't think, oh God, this is all just so *unfair* . . .! Because it probably isn't. I married the man, didn't I? Asked no questions. Yes well – my fault too, then. Three cases and a holdall thing, that's all I managed to pack. As much of Troy's great piles of junk as I could manage – I think all of his favourite toys, oh Christ I do hope so – and all the time cooing to him about what a lovely little holiday we were going to go on, just you and Mummy: won't that be nice? Threw all the stuff into the back of the car. Remembered passports, might need them – and just that one single thought, it simply terrified me. Stopped off at a cashpoint and took out of my account quite literally everything I have . . . which is really so frighteningly little. And then I went back to where I had parked the car and just sat there, hands on the wheel, staring dead ahead of me and thinking nothing except that if I didn't move soon I'd get a ticket. Troy, he wanted to know where we were going. So did I. And that's when Mum called.

'Anna, dear – is that you . . .?'

'Of course it's me, Mum. My phone, isn't it? This isn't really a good, um . . . very busy just at the moment – can I call you back?'

'Well no. Not really. Need you, you see. Need to speak.'

And I just sat there, gaping at the phone. Amazed. Never – never heard anything remotely like that, not from Mum. What was this? She *needed* me . . .?

'Why? What's wrong? Is everything okay? What's wrong?'

'Well no, clearly everything isn't okay. Is it? Or else why would I be needing you?'

'Well what's wrong, then? Tell me. Is Dad all right?'

'Don't know. Expect so. Generally is. It's not about Dad. It's about me.'

'About you . . .? Well what about you . . .? What's . . . ?'

'Can you come and see me? I'm not at home.'

'Where are you?'

'I'm at the Holiday Inn in Brent Cross.'

'You're *what* . . .?'

'Mm. It was handy. I've got a room. Large. Two rooms, actually. More of a little suite. Quite nice, apart from the orange curtains. Will you come?'

'Are you . . . ill? What's wrong? Why won't you tell me? What in God's name are you doing in a room at the . . .!'

'Will you come?'

'It's so, oh . . . really *difficult* at the moment, Mum. You just have no *idea* . . .'

'I'm going to say it just one more time, Anna. Will you come?'

And now I'm here. Troy's asleep on the sofa next door – that took a hell of a while. And we're drinking tea. Or at least I am – Mum, she just keeps on looking down into hers, and then suddenly, straight up at me. Her eyes are wide. She seems surprised by her situation, as well she might. And soon we're going to get to the bottom of it all, are we? I don't know, I have no idea. I've just for the moment got to try to keep my mind off all that's going on in my own life, if I can do that: and I've also got to be sure to say absolutely nothing about it.

'Okay, Mum . . . so . . . so far, you've said absolutely nothing. About why you're here, or anything . . .'

'Well I did say. It was handy.'

'No – I don't mean that. I mean . . . why are you in a hotel at all? What's the idea?'

'I . . . well I had to get away. That's all. Be somewhere else. I thought it might make me feel, I don't know . . . more like me. The other me, I mean. The old one. I thought . . . I think what I thought was that if I wasn't any longer under the sheer, oh God I don't know – *weight* of everything, I thought then that I might possibly . . . emerge. As the old me. The other me. You see? But I'm not actually sure now that there is another me, because all I feel is just like the me I've been for, oh – just decades, really. The only me left, I suppose. I just am what I am. And that is . . . something of a disappointment, really . . .'

'Mum . . . what are you . . .? I just don't know what you're *talking* about . . .'

'No. I suppose not. I'm only really understanding a very small part of it myself. I don't say very much, as you know – but when I do, well . . . it doesn't seem to make an awful lot of difference . . .'

'Have you had some sort of a bust-up? With Dad? Is that it?'

'Bust-up? Ooh no. No no. We don't do things like that, your father and I. Bust-up? Heavens no. That would involve . . . well, it would involve communication for a start, so things could never really be expected to get that far. No look, Anna – I can see that this, all of this . . . it must be most terribly perplexing for you, and I'm sorry really to have involved you at all, of course I am, but . . . well you see . . . in my life, there's no one else. Is there? To turn to. Some women – well most women, I suppose . . . they have friends, don't they? A network of friends. Confidantes. You keep reading about it – you see it in all these terrible American films. Yes, well I don't. Never have done. And I know I've never turned to you before . . . but, well – I am doing so now, I'm afraid. I did think of David, I did think of ringing him . . . but David, well . . . it seems to me that, poor David, he can hardly manage to keep his own little life together, to say nothing of his business, whatever that is, so I hardly could expect him to . . . but you, Anna . . . well you, you're always so dreadfully capable. Aren't you? You're the only one, I thought, who might really be able to help me . . .'

Oh God. She just looks so very desperately sad. Lost, quite lost . . . and even a little bit crazy, too. But of all the times to 'turn to me', as she puts it, wouldn't she just have to choose now . . .? This very day . . .? And she's done so because she thinks I'm 'capable' – well Jesus, how insanely funny is that? Christ – if only she knew. I don't know what to do. About anything at all. So why is she asking me? And what can I say? I don't even know what's wrong, what the problem is, why in Christ's name she's even here – because for all this talking, she hasn't actually *said* anything. And now . . . she's looking directly at me. Her eyes, dipped at the corners, and just a little milky: not too far from supplication. On any other day, I think I would be touched – moved, even. So I suppose I'll just have to tell her something: I must, whatever it is that's bothering her . . . be reassuring. I wonder . . . I wonder . . . could this be an idea, maybe . . .? Yes . . . that might just about be possible: yes . . . that could be good, actually. Because what I'm asking myself now is whether this really very odd situation that I never could have seen coming in a million years . . . whether it might just be turned into sort of an advantage . . .? For all of us, I mean. Some sort of a solution – temporary, obviously, but a solution for now, anyway.

'Are you having more tea . . .? Do you want . . .?'

'No, Mum. I'm fine. Listen: how about this . . .?'

'It's cold, of course – but I can easily ring down for more . . .?'

'No, Mum. Just listen, all right?'

'Or something to eat? Have you eaten? I bet you haven't eaten anything, have you? Are you hungry? I should have asked you before. Don't know what I was thinking of . . .'

'No, Mum. I'm fine – I'm fine. Listen: how would it be if . . . we stay here with you. Okay? Troy and me. For tonight, anyway. If you're really sure you don't want to go back home, for whatever reason . . . I really can't imagine . . . well then we can stay here with you. Okay? Plenty of room. And then we can . . . talk. If you want to. About it all. All right? Is that all right? What do you think?'

'Oh . . . *yes*, Anna – thank you. If you mean it. That would be . . . lovely. Oh but I can't ask you to do that – you'll be wanting to get back, the two of you.'

'No, Mum, honestly – it's fine, it's fine.'

Well . . . this is certainly something of a transformation – really quite astonishing, actually. Mum, she's gone from being a sad and distracted old lady to just someone else completely: a hostess at a party – keen, happy, and actually . . . very nearly vivacious. So what I'll do is . . . what shall I do . . .? What shall I do first? Well go and see to Troy, obviously – Mum has gone in already, but he's sounding just a little bit panicky: waking up in a strange room, doesn't know where he is – and then I'll go down to the car and bring up just whatever we're going to need for the night, and just hope to goodness that the rest of it will be safe. I actually even feel a whole lot better myself – which is lunatic really, because I've absolutely no reason to. Nothing is going away, is it? No – nothing. None of it's changed: God knows what's going to happen. Anyway. My problem, isn't it? And after that, I've just got to ring Dad. I haven't the slightest idea about what's actually going on with him and Mum, but I do know I have to ring him. Tell him we're all safe and sound. For now, anyway. Because he will be concerned, of course he will. People don't get him: he's not nearly as selfish as everybody seems to think. Oh look . . . my phone is ringing now: I bet that's him – I bet a million pounds that it's him. It happens quite a lot, that: if ever I'm thinking of Dad, my phone will go and very often it'll be him at the other end. We've got this sort of thought thing going.

'Dad – hi! I knew that would be you.'

'Where the hell have you been? Why haven't you been answering? Can't get hold of your mother – Christ knows where she is. What's wrong with everybody today?'

'It's okay, Dad – everybody's okay. I'm with her now. She's just next door. And Troy's here too – we're all fine. Sorry I couldn't pick up earlier.'

'Well how long is she going to be? Bloody starving. Bugger all in the fridge . . .'

'Well look, Dad . . . it's all a bit hard to explain, but . . . well, the thing is, the three of us, yes? Mum, me and Troy . . . we're staying overnight somewhere. Okay?'

'Overnight . . .? What in Christ's name are you talking about . . .?'

'Mum forgot to mention it to you. Planned it ages ago. Little treat for ourselves.'

'Little *treat* . . .? What – not someone's birthday, is it? Where the hell are you, then?'

'Hotel. We're in a hotel. It's just for the night. We'll . . . we'll all come round and see you tomorrow, okay? Can you manage in the meantime?'

'Well . . . I *suppose* so. If I must. Bloody odd thing to do . . . Well now look – listen, Anna: never mind all that. The most *extraordinary* thing happened to me today. You'll never guess in a thousand years! I still can't believe it myself . . .!'

'Really? Listen, Dad – Troy is crying next door. Got to go, okay? But we'll talk tomorrow, yes? I'll come over in the morning. Promise.'

'Yes no but *listen*, Anna – you'll never *believe* who I met . . .!'

'Tell me tomorrow, Dad – I'll hear all about it tomorrow, okay? Got to go. Got to. Sorry. Bye. Love you. Bye.'

It's not Troy that's crying – it's Mum. She's shrieking – she's screaming and shrieking like someone gone completely mad . . .! And I've just dropped the phone and I'm running across the room and throwing open the door and my eyes, I can feel them all screwed up so horribly tight in sheer and utter terror of whatever it is I am now about to be confronted with . . . but I've already decided that if something unspeakably terrible has happened to Troy, well then I shall just completely lose my mind and pray to God that my life now must just be *over* . . .

'Mum . . .! What's . . .?! Troy . . . Troy, baby . . . you okay? Yes? You are . . .? You all right . . .? You are all right, aren't you? What is it, Mum? He seems fine – Troy seems completely okay. But look at you – you're as white as a . . . what's *wrong*, for Christ's sake? Tell me! Tell me! *Speak* to me, Christ Jesus . . .! You're shivering. Oh my God – you're *shivering*. Sit down, Mum. Sit down and tell me what's wrong, will you? Your phone. You're looking at your phone. Is that it? Yes? Did someone call you? Who called you? What's happened? What *is* it . . .?!'

'It's . . . oh my God – we have to go. We have to go *now*, Anna . . .!'

'Go where? Go where, Mum? What's happened? *Tell* me . . .!'

'That was Lilian. We have to go. Quickly, Anna – can you drive?'

'Who . . . who is *Lilian* . . .?'

'Lilian. *Lilian* . . .! *David's* Lilian – who do you think? You know Lilian. They're at the hospital. We must go now . . .! Oh my God. Oh my *God* . . .!'

'David? Is he all right? Oh my God . . .'

'He's not all right. He's very . . . they're seeing to him now. But apparently it's . . . apparently it's . . . oh dear God. Lilian, poor Lilian, she sounded so desperately *upset* . . .! Come on, Anna. Pick up Troy. We have to go *now* . . .!'

'He's ill? Is David sick? Was he in an accident? What's happened to him? Come on, Troy – there's a good boy. We're all going off in the car again, yes?'

'It wasn't an accident. No it wasn't.'

'Well what, then? What?'

Her face is taut – rigid with amazement, and plastered in tears.

'Oh Anna, darling . . .! Your brother . . . I can't even say it . . .! I just can't bear to say it . . .! David, my dear sweet little boy . . . oh Anna . . .! He's dying . . .! He's *dying* . . .! According to Lilian . . . he's practically *dead* . . .!'

CHAPTER SEVEN

EVERYTHING I'VE BECOME

I like it, sitting on the top deck of the 13 bus – right at the front, left-hand side – quietly dragging down a Benson & Hedges (no more No. 6 – I've gone up in the world) and wishing I could be listening to The Beatles. I used to bring my transistor with me, but it's hopeless even at home – and on the top of a bus, Christ . . . it just sounds like somebody's frying chips, or something. That's Luxembourg, of course – BBC's okay, not too bad, but they only play stuff like Mantovani and the bloody Black & White Minstrels. Anyway, here I am – and really enjoying looking down at all this loony scurry of people rushing about on the pavements below me. More of them than usual, and particularly in Oxford Street, which we've just turned into – because that's exactly what people do, isn't it? When December comes. They all flock to the West End, like a flapping migration of really stupid birds . . . they've been saving up for the whole of the year, and now they buy loads of stuff for presents that nobody even wants – and then in January the same old junk is marked down to half price in the sales, which just must make them feel sick, and really half-witted. They still go on doing it, though. And all those presents – the only thing people want to know is whether they've kept the receipts, because they're only going to take them back anyway. The reason being that most presents, well – they're crap: bath cubes, handkerchiefs, Basildon Bond . . . book tokens for people who want record tokens, and record tokens that aren't even enough to get you an LP. Like my useless auntie in Southend, Auntie Louise – a ten-shilling record token every birthday and Christmas: they won't give you the change from a single, so you've got to add to it to get two, or else an EP: I don't even write and thank her any more – it's all more trouble than it's worth. And then the shops . . . all this useless stuff that gets returned to them – the shops, they probably bung it into storage somewhere, and then the next Christmas heave it out and sell it all over again and cut anything that's left to half price in the January sales, while the first great load of it is being carted back for a refund.

My mum . . . she always used to take me down here to see the lights. Dad, he'd never come – which was just as well, because nobody wanted him. Never went anywhere if he thought he'd be expected to smile, or spend money. Which meant he never went anywhere, full stop – which was fine, because nobody wanted him. Regent Street lights were always better than Oxford Street – still are – but my mum . . . she didn't really think we were Regent Street people: that's what she always said. Didn't know what she meant, and I still don't, not really. The Selfridges windows are always great, though . . . I can see them now: looks like Alice in Wonderland this year – there's always a theme to it. I remember when they did Santa's workshop in Lapland – that was just marvellous: I'd wanted really badly to be an elf, so I'd get first dibs on all those amazing toys. We used to queue for bloody years to get into Santa's grotto – but it was Uncle Holly I liked the best: a giant, he seemed to me, in a green top hat – and he gave out badges. I've still got all of them, somewhere. And oh my God look . . .! It's still there – that barrow just around the corner where my mum always used to buy her festive wrapping paper because it was so much cheaper than even Woolworth's. And then when she got it home she found out that it was practically transparent: all the Santas and robins and holly, you could see right through them and clearly read the writing on the box of whatever was inside. So she put on three or four layers – crazy really, because all she ever gave to anyone was a pound of Milk Tray. Except for my toys, of course . . . but I knew what they were going to be because I'd always told her what to get. She gave my father socks, a Brylcreem dispenser and a hundred Senior Service – always – and received in return Terry's All Gold, a Yardley's English Lavender gift box and a twin-set from the British Home Stores. Always. And then the following year we'd come back to Oxford Street, Mum and me, queue eternally for Santa's grotto – and, although quite visibly parched and near to dropping, she would firmly refuse to buy a cup of tea and a bun in the cafeteria at those quite ridiculous prices because she wouldn't want to give them the satisfaction, and anyway, George, we'll be back home and cosy, very soon. Then we'd cross the road and she'd buy more rolls of exactly the same wrapping paper as the year before from exactly the same barrow because it was so much cheaper than even Woolworth's. Old people, they really are pretty bloody stupid.

Like the boring old creep who's sitting right behind me on this bus. Smoking something stinking in a dirty old pipe – I'm practically choking. And he's saying to this stringy and ancient woman who's next to him, probably his wife, Jesus just think of it . . . they could've been married since the First World War, or something. Boer War, could be. I had a squint at her earlier, and I'm telling you: she looks like she's died, been left to hang around for a couple of years, and then just rammed through a mangle. She looks like, I don't know . . . well just literally like a load of old rubbish, actually, that's been put out for the binman. And I bet she smells really bad. If it weren't for her great big fat and stupid husband's pipe, I just know she'd be reeking – filling the whole of the top deck with her horrible decay, and an indescribable stench. And he's been saying to her, the husband, how fast the time goes. Old people, they're always saying that: they shouldn't have any more time – it should have been taken away from them just bloody ages ago. He's telling her it seems only two minutes since Home took over from Macmillan, and now it's bloody Wilson: bloody Labour – what a Christmas present, ay? Well I don't know a thing about politics – can't understand why people even care about it: just old men in suits, can't see the difference between any of them. If I had a vote, I'd vote that they were all taken out and hanged. And anyway, listen: who cares about Harold Wilson when The Beatles are back at the top of the charts . . .?! 'I Feel Fine': fantastic . . .! And . . . I do, actually, feel quite fine. Yes – I feel pretty good, considering: hell of a lot better, anyway. And time . . . well I don't think it passes that quickly. Seems absolutely ages to me, since the summer. Maybe because, well . . . I've done quite a bit, I suppose. Moved on. Life . . . it's all right, sort of. Actually, it's really really good. Apart from the one big hole. And all that is the result of the most amazing . . . well, accident, I suppose you could call it . . . yes, that's one word – but everything now is changed. Back in the summer, though . . . Christ . . . it could hardly have been worse: I wondered at one point if I'd ever get through it.

Breaking up with Dorothy . . . that had been the worst of it.

Never felt so low . . . but I've now managed to more or less convince myself that all in all it was a good thing. A positive step. I mean . . . I still do miss her, I can't deny it. And I realise now that it wasn't just sex and playing records and going to the pub with Dorothy . . . it was everything else. Which I couldn't even describe. Just so nice . . . having her around, really – knowing that she loved me. In the days when she did. But being without her, it has sort of triggered me into *doing* things – partly in really a pretty stupid attempt to fill up the one big hole, it's partly that, it's got to be – but also because I just was feeling so completely useless: that everything I did was a complete and utter waste of time . . . and so something, something just had to be done. Because up till then, well . . . I'd just let things chug along as they wanted to, really. No . . . that's not true – not with Dorothy, anyway: I never let Dorothy just chug along as she wanted to, did I? I had to be in charge of everything, bloody idiot that I was. And then I acted like I didn't want her any more . . . I did want her, I did, but I hardly showed it – gave her to Mike on a plate. I still . . . hate to say his name, or even think it. I'd pay money to be able to just blank out his bloody face, but I can't, just can't. Whenever I think back to Dorothy – and I still do that, I do that quite a lot – I can't not see his bloody face, hanging there handsomely, and right next to hers. So maybe, subconsciously . . . I wanted to be set free, did I? No – too deep, just rubbish thinking in that way. Psychology, is it? Rubbish. I messed up, simple as that – took her for granted, just as Sammy was always telling me I did. Anyway. I did phone her, the day after that awful morning in the flat in Circus Road. Rang her at work. She was polite enough, I suppose, though not actually saying anything at all. And me . . .? Oh Christ, I can't even recall. Probably bullying, then whining – shouting, then pleading. Makes me cringe – and all of it was hopeless, well of course it was. Didn't even ask if she was feeling better. Second time I rang I'd got it all worked out: what I was going to say to her – nice light tone, and perfectly calm. How I was going to ask her out to lunch or whatever she wanted at this really nice-looking sort of Italian restaurant that I'd spotted in Camden Town – that avenue just opposite the Tube. Yes . . . but they wouldn't put me through. Whoever answered the phone, they wouldn't put me through. I can sort of see her in that little office up the stairs in Baker Street – green walls, big plant, Beatles calendar on the wall – and a whispered and hurried conversation with the three other girls: 'If he rings again, just say I'm out, or not at work today – all right?' So they did that – three or four times I got that. Then when I rang again, the girl, she said that Dorothy didn't work there any more – so sorry but she didn't leave a forwarding number, and no – not an address either. Could be true. Needn't be. Most likely not – but did I go round there to find out for sure . . .? No. Writing on the wall, I had to face it: sometimes you've just got to give up. So I did. Felt dreadful. Well Jesus – I'd only just got over the Magsie thing. That bloody little bitch: Christ, what she put me through – I simply couldn't believe that any girl on earth could just go and *do* something like that . . .!

When that copper had picked me up in the street – just as I'd pretty much crawled back to Kilburn after all that booze and sadness, when all I was yearning for was just to flop down on to my bed, tip into unconsciousness, and never wake up again . . . well at that point I was still really pretty drunk, of course. So drunk – much drunker than I realised, because Christ knows how much whisky I'd had in that Baker Street pub, what was it called . . .? Volunteer, or something – yeh, it was called the Volunteer: the place with the spastic barman. So all the way to the police station in the back of a Panda, I'd actually been unbelievably cheeky – and that, just that, it frightened me to death, when I thought of it later. Because I remember reading somewhere that the police, if they take a dislike to you, well . . . you can accidentally fall down the stairs, or walk into about a dozen doors, if you get what I'm meaning. But actually, the older copper who'd been dumped with dealing with me – sergeant he was, Sergeant Dunphy – this geezer, he turned out to be really pretty decent. Saw things the way they were.

'So. Got yourself into a bit of a scrape, haven't you laddie?'

I nodded – but then I shook my head quite hard, because what I meant was: *yes*, I'm clearly in a bloody mess, but *no*, I haven't actually done anything wrong, and he's got to understand that. I was a bit more sober by this time, which meant I felt a whole lot worse. The room was really small, and nearly the green of Dorothy's office. We were on opposite sides of a table, the sort of metal that buckets are made out of, with a big old black phone on it – just like the one Mum and Dad used to have in the hall. Sergeant Dunphy, he'd shoved across to me his packet of Embassy and a box of Swan Vestas – I must have been on about my fourth by now – and the ashtray was a tin lid that said Cadbury's Drinking Chocolate on it. Much later on he told me that actually he was a Player's man, untipped, always had been, but it was his wife who made him get Embassy because she had her eye on a hostess trolley in the gift catalogue, which was typical of her, he said, because she'd never done any hostessing in the whole of her life, and it needed about a million coupons and that by the time they got the bloody trolley he'd be lying there dead of lung cancer, so the only good she'd get out of it was to heave him up on the top and wheel him to his grave. He was a pretty funny bloke, this Dunphy. I got the impression that in his time he'd seen the lot, and couldn't give much of a fuck any more.

'It's not like she said, Sergeant. It's rubbish, what she said.'

'You don't know what she said, son. I ain't told you, have I?'

'Okay – well what did she say, then?'

'What they always say. You jumped on her when she weren't looking, basically.'

'That's bloody nonsense.'

'Yeh. Usually is. They just happen to find themselves with no clothes on in some bloke's gaff after a boozy night out and they don't how that could have come about and they bloody amazed when this bloke, he turn round and give her one. Dear oh dear. But this is the way of it. Some girl point the finger, we got to act on it. They can say anything they like, you see, and we got to act on it. Often cobblers, but what you going to do? Now in this case, I not saying she right or wrong – but I got to ask the questions, see?'

'Right. Okay . . . go on, then.'

'Not just the one time, was it? How long you know her?'

'How long? Don't know. Not long – month or so. Bit more. Told me she worked in an art gallery. Think she said art gallery. Wasn't really listening, tell you the truth.'

'No, well why would you? So, tell me how it were. You take her for a drink . . .? Have a couple, back to your place, one thing leads to another . . .? That it?'

'Yeh. Pretty much. The first time, anyway. She didn't complain.'

'No, well – trouble is, she complaining now. Why you're here.'

'Yes. Bitch. So . . . what do we . . .?'

'Well – can't do nothing at the moment. She not long left school, see – so I got someone finding out when, exactly. Finding out her age – a bit important, that. You all right at the moment, but if it's bad news, well . . . you might want to get yourself a brief then, son. Could be tricky. We don't like to go to the parents, at this point. May not have to. Quickest way, of course – but they get funny, parents, when they find out their ickle girly ain't the angel they thought she were. But if it turn out she telling the truth and she what we call a "minor", well . . . could go badly for you, son, can't lie to you. Not saying it's right – but that's the law, see? I mean, look at you – you're only a kid yourself. Can't see why we're spending time on it, between ourselves. Not like we got nothing else to deal with, blimey – you look at London lately, have you? Enough bother going on out there to last us a hundred year. But still – we go through the motions, ay? Jump through the hoops. What I'm paid for. Girls today, though – "dolly birds", that right? Way they dress – skirts up to their bums. Way they go on . . . get what's coming to them, you ask me, don't quote me. Not a problem for me, though. My missus and me, we only had boys. Three of them. Lovely lads. I'm blessed in that way. The eldest, he training to be a solicitor, but you can't have everything in this life.'

Then the phone rang – made me jump. The little tin lid was rattling on the table.

'Yeh . . .? Hello . . .? Sergeant Dunphy, yeh. You what . . .? Can't hear you too good. That traffic, is it? Shut the door of the box, what's wrong with you, you dozy article. Oh yeh – that's better. Yeh. Okay. Oh really . . .? Well well. Oh dear. She said that, did she . . .? Yeh. Yeh. I'm sure she did. Right. Okay. Well that's that, then. Thank you, Constable. Yeh – see you later on, back at the shop. You done good, lad. Ta.'

He replaces the receiver, and now he's looking right at me.

'Want another fag, son . . .?'

'What did he say? What is it? Was that about me . . .?'

'You don't want another fag . . .? Sure . . .?'

'Yeh. Yeh I will. Thanks. So what . . .?'

'Yeh you might as well. Help yourself – matches there, look. Hurry up the wife's bleeding hostess trolley, ay? No listen, son – I won't keep you hanging about no longer. You in the clear. All right? That little mare – turns out she nearly seventeen. Having us all on. Waste of bleeding time. Then she tries it on with a rape charge instead, you believe it. Well – like my constable told her, sod that for a game of soldiers. Up to me, I give her a good little slap. What it all were about was just to get back at you for dumping her, apparently. Dump her, did you . . .?'

'Oh Christ . . . that's just wonderful . . .!'

'Yeh it is. Nice result. So did you? Dump her, did you?'

'What . . .? Oh yeh. Yeh – I did. I did, yes – just today, actually. Not long before I was taken here. So it's . . . all right, is it . . .?'

'Well you done the right thing, dumping her. Well shot of that one. Don't know why you want to take up with her in the first place. Well stupid thing to say, that was. Bit of a goer, I expect. So anyway, George – yeh, all over now. What a carry-on, ay?'

'Well thank Christ for that, anyway. So . . . I can go . . .?'

'Yeh – off you go, son. Have a nice little drink. And keep your nose clean.'

'Drink . . .? Christ – I've still got a hangover.'

'That's what I mean – nice little drink, you'll be in clover.'

'Thanks, Sergeant. Thanks for everything. And the fags.'

'Nah – nothing. I got boys, remember. I were a boy myself,

one time. So listen, son – get yourself a nice girl next time, ay?'

'Yes. Hope I will. Had one, once . . .'

Well I didn't go and have a drink – just the thought of it, nearly made me retch. And anyway, I was broke: and I mean completely broke. So I went back home – and the Irishwoman, she was still just hanging around the hall, swigging at Guinness, and really surprised to see me. Said she thought I'd be breaking rocks in Dartmoor by now, or even Sing Sing, because those fascist bastard English police, they all were agents of the devil, may the saints preserve us. I told her that, actually, Sergeant Dunphy wasn't really like that. She said he was, he was, sure he was – because they're all of them like that, may God strike her dead if she's telling the shadow of a lie. Her niece was over from the Emerald Isle, is what she was telling me next – Mary Clare, lovely girl, big tits, you'll just fall head over heels for the little darling, Georgie, and sure couldn't she be doing with a night on the town . . .? Yes well, I said – not tonight: sorry. Then she wanted to know what sort of a man is it that I'm calling myself, to be sure. God it's wearing, the way they bloody go on and on, the Irish: always the same old crap – if it wasn't for the dole, they wouldn't even be in England in the first place.

So what I did instead of getting hammered all over again and then drunkenly fucked by the big-titted darling Mary Clare was wait an absolute eternity until yet another bloody Irishwoman was out of the dim and dripping little bathroom down the passage – and when I finally got in there, it stank of fags and Lifebuoy. I jammed the chair under the doorknob because the lock had been in pieces for months, and then just sat on the lavatory for a hell of a while, trying hard to sort my thoughts out and kind of wincing at this bloody awful headache that I'd suddenly got. Splattered water all over my face – though I had to take care not to get my hair wet because then I'd either have to ask the Irish for the loan of their hairdryer, or else hang it in front of my poxy little gas fire and that always took an age and sometimes singed it – not to say costing about two bob in the meter. There was sod all in the fridge – cracked egg, bit of Dairylea – and I was right out of fags . . . so I thought I might go out after all and meet up with Sammy, maybe. I mean . . . it wasn't just about the fags, I did want to anyway . . . always like to talk to him, Sammy. I thought I'd be able to fill him in on all that's been happening – see if by any possibility he might have some ideas . . . because Christ, I needed them. He was at home when I rang, which was a bit of luck – said he didn't fancy going out, it was raining, so why didn't I just come over . . .?

'Christ, you look awful . . .'

'Yeh, well thanks, Sammy. You'd look awful too, if you'd had a day like I've just been through. Can't believe it, really. Everything that's been going on . . . you'll be amazed, when I tell you. You just won't believe it.'

'Well come in, God's sake – getting soaked out there.'

'Already soaked. Walked here. Rain hasn't bloody stopped for a single minute. Would have got the bus but I'm broke. Usual thing. But I'm going to change all that. One of the things I want to talk to you about, actually. Sick to death of living like this. Can't go on. You haven't got a Scotch, by any chance . . .? First lot's worn off. Feel a bit shivery, actually. Where shall I stick my coat? Dripping all over the place. Up to your room, are we going . . .? Great. Christ I need a fag. Lovely and warm in here. Central heating. No bloody shillings in the meter for you, ay, Sammy? Jesus I envy you. You don't know how bloody lucky you are. Well . . . you probably do, actually. Fucking fool if you don't . . .'

And for the whole of the rest of that day, Sammy . . . oh Jesus, he was just wonderful to me: I was with my friend – the very last person on earth who could actually give two shits about whether I lived or died. He listened. He really did listen to all the muck that was tumbling out of me, and pretty unstoppably. He listened when I got angry – he listened when I became actually almost completely incoherent . . . because his dad's Scotch, Sammy made sure that it kept on coming. And most of all he listened . . . even when I cried. Talking about Dorothy. When I told him that I thought it might be over. No – that I *knew* it was over. And about . . . Mike. The flat in Circus Road. He held my shoulders, and he said that he was really, really sorry. Not that he'd told me so – not that I was the biggest of bloody fools for having lost her . . . no: just that he was really, really sorry. Then he did a great job of being totally appalled when I told him about Magsie – and quite right too: I'd better never run into that little slut again, I'm telling you – or else I don't know what I might do to her. And after all that, when I'd pretty much worked my way through his twenty Bensons . . . he just so completely surprised me. It wasn't maybe a bombshell – nothing like, anyway, the bombshell he was destined to drop on me a good while later on . . . but pretty bloody explosive nonetheless.

'Look, Georgie . . . don't take this the wrong way or anything, but . . . well look: let me just say it. Until you get back on your feet, okay . . . maybe I could help you out a bit, yes . . .? I mean – a loan, if you like. It's just that, well . . . I had a birthday lately and my dad has been really pretty decent. Says it's time I stood on my own two feet, had a room of my own somewhere, and

I sort of agree. I mean – it's great here, obviously . . . but still I'm living with Mum and Dad, you know? My course – well that's nearly over, and then I'm due to take on this job that's lined up, and the room, this new room . . . well that's pretty much set up too, actually, and so he gave me this cash to kind of get it sorted, if you know what I mean. But the thing is, I won't need nearly all of it, so . . . well, until you get a new job, and everything . . . I thought you could maybe do with a little help. That's all. You'd be very welcome . . .'

I just looked at him. Nearest I've come to truly loving him, really. And then I said:

'I'm sorry I forgot your birthday . . .'

'Oh Jesus – that doesn't matter . . .!'

'No well it does, a bit. You always remember mine.'

'Telling you, Georgie – couldn't matter less. All done. It's over.'

'I should have sent you a card . . .'

'Don't want a card. Now how about it . . .?'

'Or bought you a drink. I should at least have bought you a drink. Christ – the number you've bought me . . .'

'Are you hearing me, or what? Few quid? Help you get set up. Yes? No?'

'Well . . . yes. Obviously. But it has to be what you said – a loan. Yes, Sammy? Okay? Because I'm absolutely determined, now – I'm going to get a really good job. Don't know where yet, but it's going to be really good – not like the last one. Christ, that was just so awful. Proper pay. And somewhere decent to live. And then I promise you, Sammy – I'll pay back every penny. I swear it. I absolutely swear it.'

And here's something interesting: any time in the past, any time before that single extraordinary day, if Sammy had told me he was about to leave home and get his own place to live – yes and it wasn't just going to be a room, was it? It would be a proper flat that his dad was buying him – well then what is the very first thing I would have said to him . . .? Exactly. This is how it would have gone: Oh well *listen*, Sammy – how about I share it with you? How about that, ay? We'd be great together – wouldn't we be great together, Sammy? The Two Musketeers! What do you think? What do you say . . .? Yes – that's exactly how it would have gone. But I didn't. Say any of that. Didn't even occur to me. Because I didn't want it. Not at all. Just sitting there with Sammy, for the first time ever – and even through the haze of booze – I knew that the time had come for me to actually . . . well: *start*. Just . . . to *begin*. Everything had sort of pushed me against a wall, and there was nowhere else to go. Is how I saw it. That after all the bloody time-wasting and sheer fucking nonsense that made up the whole of my existence on earth, here was finally the time to *start*. Oh Christ – just to bloody *begin*. My life – start my life all over again, if you like. Big thoughts – boozy thoughts, I suppose . . . but there was no doubt that there was something behind them, if only need, a bit of self-disgust, and something else that was actually quite frightening: desperation, pretty much. It's just that I didn't want to be a . . . kid any more. Now, from now on, I was going to be a man, a grown-up man, who would one day have everything – *everything*. On my own. Because who else would I be with? I was going to do it all on my own, yes I was: just you stand back and watch me.

I stood up then – it was time to go. Felt a little dizzy. Sammy said – are you okay? And I said yeh, oh yeh . . . I'm just a bit, you know. And then he said: do you want another drink? Last one? For the road? Where are you going now? Home? Are you going home now, Georgie? And I said no, no more drink: had too much. Don't know quite where I'm going – haven't worked it out. Possibly home. Yeh – I'll probably go home now. Well look . . . maybe just a very small drop, yeh? Like you say – one for the road. And a fag. Hope to Christ it's stopped raining.

It had stopped raining – quite bright, now: the bushes and things in sort of urns at the front of Sammy's house were all just dripping quite heavily. And then I saw the Spitfire – this low and beautiful Triumph Spitfire: couldn't believe I hadn't noticed it before, when I'd just rolled up here. Bright red. Covered in all these glassy raindrops, shimmering in the sun. Black hood, wire wheels . . . just fabulous.

'I know . . .' Sammy was saying to me now, lounging against the open front door and looking down at his shoes, which he was kind of rubbing on the mat as if there was something on them – which there wasn't, so far as I could see. 'Bit embarrassing, really. My dad said that I'd need to be getting around, so . . .'

'What, you mean . . . it's yours? This car is *yours* . . .?'

'Well . . . my dad's really, I suppose. But yeh, it's . . . for me. To, you know – use. I only just got my licence . . .'

'You've got a driving licence? Bloody hell. You've got a licence? I didn't even know you'd been taking lessons.'

'Yeah. Had about ten. BSM. Didn't I mention that . . .?'

'No. No you didn't, Sammy. I'd have remembered if you did.'

'Yeh well. Just passed, actually. Last week.'

'So first time then, presumably?'

'Oh . . . it's not actually very hard, the test. Anyone could do it, you know.'

'Yeh right. Okay then, Sammy. Well look . . . thanks. For . . . you know. And I'll be seeing you, yeh?'

And I haven't even mentioned his clothes . . . but I was thinking about them afterwards. I remember . . . I remember just walking quite aimlessly along the pavement – holding on to the occasional wall, my useless mac still quite clammy – and just marvelling in a pretty drunken way at all that I'd heard, all that I'd seen. And all that he'd given me. When I'd been slumped there in Sammy's room – sprawling all over one of his so cool denim bean bags, and feeling the wet of my elephant cords clinging to my shins and ankles, the black of my crinkled-up boots going white with all the rain they'd been wading through. And I needn't have worried about splashing water on to my hair when I'd been trying to wake myself up by slapping it all over my face, because the state of it now . . . oh Christ. It was just hanging in front of my eyes in long and lank sodden lumps. I just felt so dirty. But I often did, in Sammy's room. Everything there is just so perfect. And that goes for Sammy as well, of course. His hair . . . it looked like it had just been cut and blow-dried. His mum goes to Vidal Sassoon somewhere in the West End, and sometimes she takes him too and he gets it done there. Today it looked like Paul Jones's from Manfred Mann, and also the singer in the Walker Brothers. Pale grey flannel hipsters, which I hadn't seen before. He was often wearing things I hadn't seen before. The flowery tab-collar shirt that he'd said Lord John was getting in soon, with a really slim dark blue leather tie. A gold identity bracelet that said 'Sammy'. Probably another birthday present – this one from the cat, maybe. Black patent slip-ons with a big silver buckle right in the middle of them, just like P. J. Proby – and pretty much matching the one on the three-inch-wide belt on his hipsters. So yeh, I was thinking back on all of this, as I pretty dizzily just stomped my way along the road, not knowing remotely where

I was going, and caring not at all about that – because why did it matter? There would be a Tube station – there's always a Tube station – and then I'd get on a train and go: didn't much care where, exactly. Not Kilburn, though: I wasn't nearly ready to go back to Kilburn, that I did know.

But Sammy . . . well, he's just about to leave all that behind him. His wonderful little flatlet in his parents' house on Hampstead Heath, with the panelled fitted wardrobes and full-length mirrors and the specially built window seat with orange cushions piped in white . . . a huge black fluffy rug and a swivel chair and those big blue denim bean bags. He'll be taking his Ludwig drum kit and his Rickenbacker guitar and his television and his radiogram and his Grundig tape recorder and all his hundreds of acres of clothes . . . he'll be putting all of that into a van, I suppose, and then driving to his brand-new flat, wherever it is . . . hadn't asked him – but obviously somewhere just so fab and amazing, if his quite fantastic dad has got anything to do with it . . . yes, he'll be driving to his brand-new flat in his brand-new bright red Triumph Spitfire . . . and he will already have spent a lot of his father's money on pictures and scatter cushions and spotlights and . . . well I don't know what people need in a flat, how would I know? Towels and sheets and pots and pans. Maybe he'll put hessian on the walls – seems to be what all the groovy flats are wearing, these days. But do you know . . .? I didn't resent it. Didn't mind. Not really, I didn't. I mean – I remember thinking it doesn't make me the happiest person on earth . . . I couldn't say I was bloody *thrilled* about it all . . . but what I mean is, well . . . not long ago, okay? Not too long before that time, Christ – it would've burned right into me. I'd be seething. No – worse than that: I would have boiled right up into a state of sheer bloody crazy. And . . . if Dorothy had still been around, I would have roared at her. Like it was all her fault, or something. Gone on and on and on at her about the *injustice* of it all: why Sammy . . .?! Why him . . .?! Why does it always have to be *him* who gets everything *wonderful* . . .?! Because that's exactly what I used to do, bloody fucking pig and idiot that I was. Just scream and bellow at her, until she just looked at me so totally helplessly . . . and then she'd start to cry. Oh Jesus. Oh Christ. How did I do that . . .? Why did I *do* that . . .? Anyway . . . can't think of it now: can't bear to. So . . . to get back to Sammy . . . I honestly did feel pretty okay with it, really. Because soon, you see – soon I was going to have it too. All of it. And better than Sammy – more than Sammy: all of it. Just all of it: soon it would all be mine.

So I did – I went on the Tube to Jesus knows where. Might have fallen asleep. Well I *did* fall asleep, because I was suddenly woken up by a booming announcement on the platform: my mouth felt the worst – my limbs and stomach, they felt bad, but my mouth, it felt like hell. Didn't make head or tail of what the person was saying – you never understand them, announcements on the Tube. So I just looked up, saw I was in King's Cross, and I'd got off the train before I'd even decided to. And then . . . well then I'm walking in a kind of a trance. Is the only word I can think of for this cloudy and not-quite-there and airy feeling that was filling up my head, and a bit sort of all over my fingertips. I didn't hate it, this sense of more or less floating – but it did feel really strange. Wasn't just down to all the whisky, I don't think . . . not sure, though: could have been. Thinking back on it all now – because this was just months ago, but it's not an experience I'm ever going to forget, let's face it . . . so looking back, it was probably more a tremendous tiredness than anything else. Couldn't remember the last time

I'd actually been asleep – or even at peace. Because look at it: this really had been one hell of a day – and Jesus, I didn't even know then the horror and sheer amazement of all that was going to happen to me next. But already there'd been Circus Road . . . and Dorothy. Fucking Mike. That pub . . . that pub, with the stupid barman, where I'd gone and phoned Magsie. And so then because of that there was the bloody police, God help me – and that was pretty scary I can tell you, until I knew that it was all going to be okay. But the whisky . . . so much whisky. Sammy, then . . . and yet another great vat of the stuff: Christ, it's a wonder I was even standing.

After that I was thinking well okay, then: now I'm just . . . somewhere. King's Cross, apparently. And really all I'm doing is putting one foot in front of the other, solidly and actually quite carefully, because I did feel a little wobbly. So clomp clomp, plod plod – and this eventually will take me somewhere else, I suppose. That's more or less the way I was thinking, though I don't actually believe that I was thinking at all. It had got quite dark by this time – I remember the brightness of the lights in all the shops, the streaks of red and yellow reflection in the blackness of puddles in the street, as all these endless streams of buses were fizzing right past me. It was only when I rammed my hands into the pockets of my sticky wet coat that I thought oh hang on . . . what's this? What's all this? What's this lump of stuff I'm feeling . . .? Completely confused for ages – seemed like a week, but it can't have been more than a second or two. Then I remembered the wodge of money that Sammy had put there, while I'd still been vaguely pretending that I didn't want it, wouldn't take it. Not quite sure how much – didn't count it, or anything . . . but more cash than I've ever actually had, it's fair to say: got to be fifty quid, minimum – it's all in fivers.

And yeh, although it's meant to help me achieve everything I now know I've just got to have – because I hadn't lost that drive: all this crazy meandering hadn't affected my complete determination, which was actually quite bewildering in itself, as well as a bit shocking . . . still, there's got to be a few spare bob that I can maybe spend on . . . well, don't know, really: what do I want . . .? What do I actually feel like . . .? Maybe just another drink or two, actually . . . because suddenly, just standing stock-still in the middle of the road, I'm feeling really ill again. My eyes are closed – feel threatened, they're screwed tight shut against anything beyond them – and I'm shaking now, and really badly.

'You all right, sweetie? Seem a bit lost. Not from round here, ay?'

Woman's voice. A bit sing-song. She said lost like lawst. Don't feel like opening my eyes, though: too risky.

'You don't want to be standing in the road like that, my love. Get hit by a bus, won't you? Ay? Because this here – this is where they goes and turns. See? So come over here, luvvie. Be safer over here. That's right. That's it. Toss away that fag – nearly burning your fingers, look. Why don't you open your eyes – what's wrong with you? You shy? That it? Lonely, are you? Bit out of sorts? Do with a little company, could you? Fancy coming in out of the cold?'

'Not cold . . .'

'No but your clothes – they's all wet. Aren't they? Ay? Wet through, you are. How you get to be so wet? You're all shivery, you are. We don't get you somewhere nice and cosy, you're going to come down with something – that's what's going to happen to you. Catch your death, you will. My name's Lola. What's your name, then? You got a name? Want to come with me, do you? Get you a nice little drink in the warm, yeh? That sound nice? And then I make you feel all better. That sound nice? Think I'm pretty, do you?'

'Drink . . . yes.'

'Yes? Fancy a drink, do you? All right then, my love. Let's go, yeah? It's just around the corner. That's it. You just hold on to me, and you'll be right as rain. Had a few, have you? Out for the night, that it? So you got a name, sweetie? I'm Lola, like I says. Think I'm pretty, do you? Like what you see? What you called then, ay?'

'George. I'm George. Where are we going . . .? Who are you . . .?'

'I'm Lola – remember? You think I'm pretty, don't you? Like what you're seeing. Not too far now. So you're George, ay? Well that's a nice name, that is. George – I like it, George. Like the Queen's daddy, isn't it? Don't suppose you old enough to remember him, though. Only a young lad, aren't you? Well don't you worry about nothing no more then, Georgie. Call you Georgie, will I? Lola, she going to look after you really brilliant, isn't she? Ay? Really special. Yeh – that's right. That's it. That's it. You just hold on to me. Not too far now. Just around the corner, look. There in two shakes of a lamb's tail.'

It went quite suddenly from really a bit chilly to absolutely stiflingly hot. We were inside, then: must be. Wasn't aware if she'd been talking to me as I'd been staggering along a seemingly endless succession of streets and turnings: she was holding my arm really tightly, I remember that – lost all feeling – and there was a sort of a cooing noise coming out of her, though it could have been her actually saying things to me: I was in no state to know. The room seemed really small – angled ceiling I saw, when I glanced up from the chair I was slumped into: my neck, it was loose and useless – couldn't hold up my head. So . . . attic then, probably . . . but I didn't remember any stairs. There was this really strong perfume, quite choking . . . and a gas fire hissing, and really pumping out the heat: my face felt red and was sweating. She'd given me a drink, thank God – don't know what it was, not whisky I don't think, but still pretty strong, quite raspy on the throat, and it was making me feel a little better. Not so numb. Or maybe more numb, hard to say. But I was understanding what she was saying again – I could make out the words now.

'Feel nicer now you got that wet old coat off of you? I should say so. So tell me then, Georgie – what you after, my love?'

'Sorry . . .? What am I . . .?'

'After. What you after? What you want?'

'Oh. Everything. I want everything. And I'm going to get it too.'

'Well that's the spirit, Georgie! I like it. No but look – how much money you got? Know what I'm saying? I don't like to come right out with it, sort of style – but business is business, ay? See what I mean?'

'Money . . .? Oh. Loads. I've got loads. Going to get much more.'

'Loads, ay? Well if you ain't the little millionaire! So listen, Georgie – since you so very wealthy, milord, how about we say couple quid, yeh? That sound okay to you?'

'Couple of quid . . .?'

'All right then, seeing as it's you – always a sucker for the pretty ones – we can call it thirty bob. Fair enough?'

'Well . . . um, I'm sorry, but I've forgotten your name . . .'

'Lola. I'm Lola, Georgie. You remember Lola, don't you? We old friends.'

'Lola. Right. Well look that's really very kind of you, but I don't actually need thirty bob at the moment. I would have taken it this morning – I was broke. But I'm not now. But thank you anyway . . .'

There was a bit of silence – very welcome really, because I so much wanted now just to go to sleep – and then there were all these shrieks of laughter. Terrible sound. Made my head hurt.

'Oh you are a right laugh you are, Georgie . . .! Quite the comedian. Well come on, dearie – let's stop messing about, will we? You give the money now, yeh? Then we can go over to that lovely comfy bed in the corner, look . . . and Lola, she make you feel all nice. All right, Georgie? All right, my love . . .?'

I didn't really need to be asked again. It was her mention of a bed that did it – because oh Christ Jesus . . . I was so amazingly *tired* . . .! So she sort of dragged me up out of the armchair and bundled me over to the edge of this, oh God, just so blissful bed and I fell on it as if I was dead. The springs were creaking badly as I just sort of bobbed up and down there – and my stomach, that wasn't good.

'Let me do your trousers, Georgie . . . and you fish out that little bit of cash, yeh? Then we can forget about all of that and just get down to seeing to you proper, all right?'

'Cash . . .? Oh yes . . . cash. In my coat. Oh my God I'm just so *tired* . . .'

'Oh it's in your coat, is it? That wet and smelly coat of yours. Well Lola will just have a little look then, okay sweetie? You just stay there, my darling, and I'll be back before you know I gone.'

My eyes were closed, and I maybe just waved her away – though it was also possible that I just thought of doing that, because both my arms, they simply weighed a ton. She could be gone for as long as she liked – did she not get that? Just so long as I was allowed to *sleep*. Yes . . . but it was horribly plain that she just wasn't going to let me do that. Her voice . . . her voice, it was coarse, I think I'd only just realised, and it was seriously annoying me now. Why couldn't she just shut up? Why can't women ever do that? Why did she have to keep *talking* . . .? Why wasn't I allowed to just *sleep* . . .? What was *wrong* with the creature?

'Blimey. You wasn't joking, was you? All the money in the world in here. Well well – who'd have thought that? You haven't got no quids though, Georgie . . . no ten-bob notes neither. So we call it a fiver, yeh? Nice round figure. Seems fair, don't you think? You'll hardly miss it, will you my love?'

This time I did wave an arm – lifted it anyway, moved it around above my head. Couldn't speak. I think I just wanted to get across to this bitch that she could do anything in the world she bloody well wanted, if only she'd just leave me *alone*. Yes but then . . . then I was aware of a change, a sort of a shifting, in the noises in the room. Her shrillness, this woman's shrillness . . . and what was her stupid name again . . .? Christ alone knows – and who could actually care? But her usual shrillness, bit like a parrot – that had dropped down now to hardly even audible, and I was distantly hearing the muffle of another voice too now – all very low: practically whispered. I forced open an eye and saw them: her and this man, big man he looked like, both of them standing at the open door. Couldn't focus, though. Couldn't think straight. Who was he? Husband? Father? Landlord? Why do I care? Where am I? What am I actually *doing* here, in the name of Jesus . . .? And then suddenly, something happened that kicked me into the very nearest I was going to get to being even a little bit alert: I was aware of a rustling, a crush of paper, and I saw the woman holding out my coat.

My coat! Christ Almighty – my coat! My coat – I had stupidly and drunkenly told her about my coat – with all of Sammy's money in it! How could I have *done* that . . .? That money, that's meant to be for my future – in that coat is the whole of my new beginning! Oh God, what had I done! What was I *doing* . . .? I tried to get up, but the pain and sheer exhaustion were simply terrible: I felt as if the whole of my body had been very badly beaten. I stood, though . . . I did make it – and I saw her panic as she turned and looked at me. She had thought I couldn't move – she had thought I was completely unaware . . . that's what she had thought, but she was wrong. And I was staring right at her, seeing just now what a hideous old crone she actually was, oh god Jesus . . .! More than forty years old, her bony face painted nearly all white with a smear of red lipstick and this stupid bright green muck all over her eyelids. The man, he was looking at me too, and I stood there completely transfixed, utterly motionless – it was rather as if I was watching a distant and grainy film of a man, big man he looked like, slipping my roll of fivers into a brown and battered briefcase. He turned then quickly and walked right out of the room. I *roared* . . .! I heard that roar, and it sounded quite terrible – it was frightening me to death, and I had felt the roughness of it rising up in my throat. Howling now – I was howling as if I'd been injured. Then I was across that room, and the bitch, the ugly old bitch, she put out her arms to try and stop me – and I didn't at all mind hearing her whimper and then cry out as I just was knocking her sideways.

The landing was dark and bare, and the man . . . he just stood there. His eyes, they were simply quite terrifying: black, and yet on fire – defiant, you know? As if they were daring me, egging me on almost, to even think about making a move.

I reached out a hand, and he hugged the briefcase up high to his chest. I just went for it then – I made a lunge at him, and he swung up that case and my brain was jangled and booming as the corner of it banged hard into the side of my head. Fingers, I could feel them – frantic fingers were clawing at my back, trying to haul me away, so I elbowed and struck out at all of that, and the woman gasped, but still she just continued to shriek at me – and now the man had turned towards the stairs: he was making his move, so I just flew at him, and still I could hear myself making these awful sort of animal noises. He looked at me once with sheer and complete contempt and I pulled hard at the case and I'm sure then he was about to hit me – but quite suddenly there was alarm in the dead cold blackness of his eyes as he staggered against the handrail: he knew that his legs had become twisted, and that he was losing his footing. He cried out as he tumbled – a thick kind of gargle, really – with his one free hand just clutching at anything, even at me, but the headlong fall, we both of us knew it, was just absolutely about to happen. He pitched clumsily to the side and then forwards as if he was as drunk as I was, his flailing body completely capsizing – he was thudding, and then just thundering down to the bottom of the stairs amid a splintering of all those wooden rods attached to the banister, as the crazy woman just continued to scream. I threw her back from me for the final bloody time and ran down and away from her – didn't know what I was doing – and then I just stood there at the foot of the stairs, staring down at the man. He didn't move at all – I didn't even know if he was breathing. The woman now was banging down the stairs and screaming like a mad thing – other doors were opening, and now I was feeling that the whole of the house was just alive with *danger*. I prised the handle of the briefcase from the grip of his slimy fingers, bolted down another flight, and two more after that. Fumbling with the lock on the big front door in a cold and pitch-black hallway, as the rumble and anger of people behind me was getting close, so very close, and all I could do was tug at this fucking bloody door as I was weeping with terror – and then it sprang open in my hands and I was out, out – back out into the street, and haring down it as fast as I could possibly go. The blaze of street lights made me squint away from them and the rain was splattering hard on my face – was hitting the tears that I knew I was just covered in. I took all sorts of turns – I ran and ran and ran . . . it was just ages before I dared to even think of slowing down. The few people who were around barely even gave me a glance – horror of their own to deal with, is what I was later thinking: it's that kind of area. Filth in the gutters – some woman howling, way in the distance: this was a very bad place. When eventually I just fell to my knees – virtually collapsing at the side of a row of bins in an alley outside the back of what was maybe a Chinese restaurant . . . my heart, my heart . . . I felt it was practically exploding. I crouched there in silence. Still my limbs were feeling as if someone had set about me with a scaffolding pole. I stayed there, listening – listening so hard for I had no idea what . . . just any hint of threat: any more *danger*. Don't know how much time went by. I just was sitting on the hard wet ground, my breath punched out of me in desperate bursts, before very slowly it became a little more even. I continued to sit there, not making a sound. Still there was silence. No one was about. These rough brick walls, the glistening tarmac and the pounding of the rain. That was all. My knuckles were bleeding – that happened on the staircase, I think: banged my hand on a broken spindle. The rain was washing the blood into a pinky colour. My clothes . . . they were just in sodden ruins. Still I didn't quite dare to move – just hunched there in the cold and dark and wet, clutching really tightly a battered brown briefcase. No noise. No movement anywhere. And so gradually, very gradually, I came to think that this thing, the whole of this thing . . . it did now seem to be over.

It was an unbelievable hell, trying to get home. Had no real idea where I was, so I just wandered around looking for a Tube station or a bus with a number I could sort of recognise – but none of them really went to Kilburn. I was squelching in my horrible shoes, and crouching low, avoiding the eyes of everyone who was staring at me: still I was frightened of an attack from around just every corner. The first thing, when eventually – oh Christ, after how long? – I got back to my room . . . the very first thing I did was not just strip off everything and hope to Jesus that the bathroom wasn't full of Irish and that I still had at least three shillings in the tin for the meter. I just sat in a chair, amazed. Put the fire on – I was completely frozen: it really did feel like that – as if the wet and cold had gone as deep as my bones. It was more or less dawn by now – the room was covered in a dull grey light, and looked just about the worst and most depressing I had ever seen it . . . which admittedly isn't really saying a lot. Another day then, thank Christ. And had it not been for the battered brown briefcase on the floor over there, I might even have been dreaming. And then I shivered – not actually with a fever or something, but just at the thought, the possibility of my being . . . undressed in that place. What if that ghastly woman had undressed me . . .? What if, when I saw her passing Sammy's precious fifty quid to a man who by now, I suppose, could very easily be dead . . . what if I had been completely naked, and stranded in her stinking bed? What could I have done then? Nothing – I couldn't have done a thing, because how could I ever have got away, and out of there . . .? It didn't actually bear thinking about. Scared me rigid. And then . . . then I went to bed, just as I was – sopping shoes and all. When I woke up, I felt as bad as ever I have done in the whole of my life on earth. It seemed a bit darker . . . so what can be the time, then . . .? Seven, just about. Evening. So I'd been out of it for more than twelve hours. The fire wasn't on any more, obviously – that would've conked out just ages ago. I felt so filthy. I did peel off my clothes, eventually – stuck them all into a Tesco carrier that I'd bung in the bin when next I went down to the scuzzy little pit outside the front door that we all called a yard. Out of all of them, I'll only miss the elephant cords. Put on pyjamas.

In the fridge there was nothing, of course there was nothing, and I was ragingly hungry. And then all over again I felt suddenly exhausted. Slept a bit more in the chair. Then I found a Mars bar in a jacket. Ate that. Felt ill. The Irish downstairs were playing 'Pretty Woman' again and again and again. And then I picked up the briefcase, and stared at it. I supposed that once I'd rescued my fifty pounds that I'd better, I don't know . . . dispose of it. Because it was evidence, wasn't it? The briefcase. This could be linked with me. Mad, really – but it was all those echoes, I think, of TV programmes like *No Hiding Place* and *Highway Patrol* when things like this were always somehow traced back to the people who'd taken them. I could fill it with bricks and drop it into the canal. More likely though I'd just jam it into the bin along with my bag of disgusting clothes. It was heavy, the case – I'd noticed that before, of course. I'd been heaving it around for, Christ – seemed like days, and it was quite a weight, I can tell you. So I unbuckled the straps, and there on the top was my roll of fivers. Well good. But can you believe the bloody nerve of these shitty little creeps? Just to *take* it . . .! Then there was what could be a sandwich in that paper, what do they call it – grey paper, greaseproof, yes. Mm – it's a sandwich all right: brown bread, possibly Hovis. *Evening Standard.* Scarf. And under that . . . money. Oh yes. More money . . .! Bloody piles of it. Couldn't believe it – hadn't crossed my mind, which I suppose was pretty stupid of me. Tipped it out. Loads and loads of cash. Pound notes, ten-shilling notes – and lots and lots of fivers. Great handfuls of half-crowns, clinking around at the very bottom. I was trembling. Not fear, though – not this time. This was excitement. Oh yes – absolute excitement. Because this . . . all this, this is just exactly what I needed – everything I'd been talking about. This . . . it was meant to be. I started to laugh. I was laughing so hard it actually hurt. And then I ate the sandwich. I was ravenous. It was cheese, with a bit of pickle and some shreds of wilted lettuce: quite nice.

Then . . . well then I really did want that bath, but one of the Irish bastards was just about to barge his way in there – this one, I think he's called Sean, he clearly intended a lengthy session, because he had under his arm a roll of Bronco, a copy of *Tit-Bits* and a couple of bottles of Double Diamond. Big bloke, red face, can never understand a single word he's saying, what with the accent and him being completely drunk or doped all the time. I said I'd pay him to go away, because I really needed a bath. He stared at me, his eyes sort of rolling around in different directions – was goggling at me as if he'd never actually encountered a human being before, and was trying his hardest to work out exactly what sort of a thing this could be. He obviously didn't believe me about paying him, so I told him to stay right there exactly where he was and I shot back to my room and then came back with four half-crowns which I held out to him as I quickly jammed my foot behind the bathroom door because he was already halfway inside, the bloody bastard, and was fooling about with the bolt which he was just too stupid to understand. He blinked, took the money and scarpered. Dropped one of the bottles of Double Diamond and nearly fell over trying to pick it up as it was tumbling about the landing. I put three bob in the meter – normally it's never more than a shilling I can afford, so this would be a really good deep bath. It's the old-fashioned sort – is it Victorian? With lion's feet? Christ – in this house, it could be Tudor. Anyway – huge thing, and you need the stool to get into it. We all call it the stool but actually it's only a pretty rickety orange crate, with a bit of red-checked vinyl on the top of it, fixed with drawing pins. It was a lovely bath . . . never enjoyed one so much. Someone had left their packet of Radox under the sink, which had never happened before – so that was a bit of a bonus. Just lying there, the warm and milky water right up to my chin, I was beginning to feel . . . really rather great. Because here was the start: here was only the beginning. Downstairs, the Irish were playing 'Little Red Rooster' again and again and again – not a record I love, but I didn't even mind. Washed my hair with Vosene, which stung my eyes as usual. Sponged all the grime off me with this sliver of Palmolive which I'd had since . . . well since Dorothy, of course: she couldn't stand Lifebuoy, even the smell.

Got dressed in whatever I could find that was reasonably clean, dried my hair in front of the fire (the back wouldn't comb down right – it had gone a bit funny) and some time later on I went round the corner to the Greek place that does

English breakfasts all day and night and I ordered the works, because now I was actually weak from hunger. Two fried eggs, bacon, three sausages, mushrooms, black pudding, baked beans and chips. With three slices of Wonderloaf and butter to mop up the leavings, and an awful lot of coffee – which was very strong and pretty disgusting, but never mind. The waiter – I think he's the son of the person who owns it – when I told him what I wanted, he said to me, 'Hey sonny – this a lot. You sure you got money pay me, yes?' And I put a ten-shilling note on the table and suddenly he's going, 'Okay, okay sir. I get now. Thank you sir.' See? Ten bob to the Irishman, ten bob to the Greek . . . a wave of the magic wand, and now I was getting everything I wanted, exactly when I wanted it. It was then I realised that that's what money is: the magic wand. This, I thought, is definitely the way to go. Because here was the start: here was only the beginning.

I've never been the sort of person to make lists – that was always Dorothy's way of going about things, and she was forever saying how it would be good for me to do it. As soon as you've written something down, she kept on telling me, then you can put it right out of your mind because you'll never forget it again – and if you do, well: you've got it on your list, so you're completely okay. And as you do all the things on your list, one by one . . . well then you can cross them off: it's really good, she said, crossing them off. And her eyes were sparkling as she tried to . . . oh, I don't know . . . make me even a bit enthusiastic about the idea – make me see how much it would help me, how wonderful and easy my life could be. I probably just grunted, if I reacted at all. Asked her why she couldn't just shut up about it; told her she was being stupid. Why did I do that? Why did I do that . . .? Christ, oh Christ,

I miss her. Well – can't think of it . . . so instead, the morning after my Greek English dinner breakfast, I thought well okay, then: let's give it a go, this list thing. Because it's the first time, actually, I had a number of things to be listed: things I now just had to get done. The night before, I'd slept like I was dead again – felt really good when I woke up at about eight-thirty, quarter to nine. So pleased – thrilled, almost – that my throat wasn't clutched with fear about how terribly late it was: that I didn't have to clock in at Smith's and be looked at by Mr Timpson. Mr Timpson, he was a thing of the past – I'd never have to set eyes on Mr Timpson again . . . and I actually did laugh out loud when I thought that: sheer joy, really. Before anything though, I did check the briefcase . . . had this sudden panic that I'd imagined it all and I still was near-homeless and broke – or else that it had been stolen back by the King's Cross bad man who had risen from the dead and followed me here with bloodhounds. But no – there it was in the chest of drawers, just where I'd carefully put it.

Okay, then: the list. On page one of a notebook, nice thick paper, that she'd given me for just this purpose. It's got a cloth cover with all sort of swirly leaves and flowers on it in green and a mustardy colour with just a bit of red, and she said it was – I remember she told me – she said it was a print, a fabric or something, by a very famous designer called . . . a very famous designer called . . . no: can't get it now. Somebody, anyway – some famous designer or other. She knew all about this stuff. I wish I did. I will, one day: it's another thing I want. Like reading books – she loved to read, Dorothy . . . and me, since I left school, I don't think I've even picked up a book, not a proper book, anyway. The odd thriller, that's about it – and I take an age even to get through one of those. Looked at *Lady Chatterley*

– couldn't see what all the fuss was about, really boring; *Forever Amber*, that was okay. But I'm going to do that now: read all the great classics and know about art. They're both going to go on my list. Music I'm fine about, because I've got The Beatles, and I'll never need more than that in the whole of my life. John Lewis, could it have been . . .? The famous designer? Or no – that's a shop, isn't it, John Lewis? Maybe where she bought it. Don't know – confused: can't remember . . . doesn't matter anyway. I've found a Bic in the drawer with no top on, but it seems to be working. I've written the word LIST in capitals with a couple of lines underneath, which I suppose is actually pretty stupid, but still: I'm not used to all this, and I had to head it with something. Okay, then. Item 1: *Find New Place to Live*. Yes – that's first, because I can easily afford to now: first month's rent in advance, deposit, no problem at all . . . and I just can't stand this hell-hole for a minute longer: just look at it, just look around you – no, I simply can't bear it any more. Item 2: *Buy New Clothes*. Not mad, actually – because I'll need to look good, I'll need to look smart for when I get to Item 3: *Get Job*. If I'm properly turned out, if I put myself over in just the right way – which I know I can do if I really put my mind to it – well then at the interview, well look . . . the job is as good as mine, no? What job . . .? What sort of job . . .? Don't know. Item 4: *Buy Evening Standard*. Yes – then I can see what's going. Or maybe go to one of those agencies – the sort where Dorothy was working. Or are they just for girls? For secretaries? Don't want that sort of job – don't want a girly sort of a job. Anyway – can't type, can't do what-do-they-call-it: shorthand. Can't do any of that. So something else: I'll find something good – not worried about that at all. Item 5: *Pay Back Sammy*. Which I could do right now, of course . . . but I want it to be out of money I've earned. As opposed to stolen from a King's Cross pimp. Jesus Christ. But I want to be able to say to him – okay, Sammy: thanks so much for that loan, I really needed it, as you know. And now I've got somewhere groovy to live – just like you. I've got a really good job, earn loads – just like you. Oh and hey: look at all my gear, the clothes, yeah? What do you think . . .? Fab, yes? Really pretty cool, no? Just like you. So look – here's the fifty quid I owe you: I earned it. It's mine. And here's a bottle of whisky on the top of it: little present. Yes: that will be a good moment – something to look forward to. Not John Lewis . . . no, it isn't John Lewis, of course it isn't . . . it's Morris, John Morris – *William* Morris, that's it. Yeh: William Morris. Of course.

And now . . . well now it's what . . .? Five months later, more or less. Five months . . . well yes, that's quite a long time, I suppose – but not really, not when you think how completely different my life has become. Last summer . . . well obviously I wasn't thinking about Christmas – who would? – but if it had occurred to me to even wonder how and where I would be spending it, I suppose I would have very miserably assumed that I'd still be stuck in that filthy little Kilburn room of mine, still every morning clocking on at Smith's . . . and still abusing Dorothy, who I'd still be expecting to go on taking it for ever – and still being told by Sammy to take it easy, to take more care of her . . . and of course not listening to a single word he said to me because I was just too eaten up and crazy with envy for everything he had and everything he did. I didn't really see it then – but actually, that's all I ever thought of, and it messed up who I was, I think. Dorothy was always telling me that, and I said to her she was stupid. And now . . .? Well: just look at me. The clothes – you like? I think you probably do. All from Carnaby Street – His Clothes and John Stephen mostly, and a little Lord John. Except for the boots, of course: Anello & Davide. I know . . .! The very same place where The Beatles get theirs! I tried some from Dolcis, but they just weren't any good: clunky, and they didn't have the centre seam, which you really do want.

Now ask me where I live. Go on. Say to me: Oh tell me, George – are you still infesting that reeking rat-hole in Kilburn above a raving nest of mad and drunken Irish . . .? Ah, well it's funny you should ask me that, my dear chap, because the answer is no, actually – no I am not. I now have a proper bedroom as well as a sitting room with a sofa, a bathroom and a kitchenette all of my own, in a really nice house very close to the Tube in Belsize Park. Use of the garden – and there's this old woman who lives upstairs, I think she might be the owner, who sees to all the flowers and things, so it really does look very good indeed, even in winter. Electricity is included in the rent, so no more fumbling for shillings for the meter in order to stay alive. The furniture isn't really too bad, though not a bit trendy – but the bed is big enough for two (always handy, and something I'm not used to) and actually pretty comfortable. I still haven't got over being able to use the bathroom whenever I like – because it's mine . . .! I've got a Remington shaver in there and Palmolive soap and an Old Spice roll-on deodorant and I've switched shampoo from Vosene to Drene, which doesn't sting my eyes. I've even been cooking a bit – nothing much: fried things . . . did a chicken casserole the other weekend, which just fitted into this Baby Belling I've got. The recipe was in a Sunday paper I took home from work, and it was okay, actually – chicken a bit chewy, but that was down to the supermarket, I reckon: I'd got a frozen packet of thighs.

Anyway – Rose, she had no complaints. And I laid on a bottle of Chianti as well. Rose – I met her at work. Ah yes: work. Got a job really quickly at Smythson, in Bond Street. Bond Street . . .! Never thought I'd even go there, let alone work there every day – I thought it was just for the Queen, and people like that. When I first saw the name in the advert in the *Evening Standard*, I pronounced it Smith-son, and that was a bit too close to W. H. Smith & Sons for comfort, I can tell you that – thought it might even be an offshoot of the same bloody company. But in fact it's Smythe-son, that's the way you say it – and oh God, it's just millions of miles away from anything to do with that. Twice the wages, for a start – because I've already been promoted, and that came with a bit of a raise. And I'm sure it was because I was dressed so fashionably and smartly for the interview that they gave me the job in the first place. Blue mohair suit, mustard-yellow tab-collar shirt with cufflinks and a black knitted tie (Beatle boots, obviously). I was really polite and I was smiling quite a lot because I'd remembered that Dorothy had told me once that when I smiled, it was like light bulbs going on and everyone would give me just everything I wanted: seemed to work.

At first I was just packing things in the basement – but even that wasn't nearly as grim as it sounds, because it was really okay down there, decent lighting, warm, proper stools to sit on, and everyone there was very nice to me (there was no one remotely like Mr Timpson) and the boxes and ribbons we were given to wrap everything up in made it really rather a nice thing to be doing. Then in no time I was put on to the sales floor, given a little bit of training – though all the really important customers are still looked after by Mr Wallace and Miss Parker: he wears a black jacket and waistcoat with striped grey trousers and always has a white carnation, and Miss Parker . . . she's very upper-class, and I think she must have been working here since the Wars of the Roses. Now I tend to be mostly in the print shop, selecting papers and even setting type: they say I have a flair for it, but I wouldn't know anything about that. Smythson, they sell such beautiful stuff: the stationery, of course – but all sorts of leather things as well. Terribly expensive, but the quality, you can really see and feel it – and people, the right sort of people, they don't seem to mind the prices. And do you know what? They've just given me – all nicely gift-wrapped and with a bow, the way they do things there – a 1965 diary: Christmas present. Dark blue leather with pale blue paper – very smart indeed. I doubt if Sammy has got one of those. It's funny I should think of Sammy, actually . . . because tomorrow I'm going round to his flat – which he doesn't yet know about, because I want it to be a surprise. The thing is, I haven't actually seen him since that day . . . that weird and totally unforgettable day when everything in the world just suddenly happened to me, and he lent me the fifty pounds. This was a deliberate decision, not to be in touch with him. He'd rung me a couple of times on the phone in the hall when I was still in the rat-hole – got some garbled messages from the Irish, but I never rang him back. Not because I didn't want to speak to him, but because I'd decided that when I saw him the next time, everything in my life just had to be right. When he sees me, I want him to be amazed. I did send him a notecard – a Smythson notecard, actually, in a purple tissue-lined envelope (there's usually a boxful of slight seconds which they'd only throw away) and I was purposely pretty vague in what I wrote. Just that I was alive and well . . . and that I'd see him before the end of the year. Also that I missed his company – which was true, because I did. I do. When I see him, I want him to think that I'm as good as he is. If I'm honest . . . I actually want him to think that I'm better. He's just got to, you see . . . be amazed.

'George, darling . . . can I ask you something . . .?'

This is Rose. She calls me 'darling'. I don't why she calls me 'darling' – I don't call her 'darling'. She's very posh, Rose – very upper-class. Went to Roedean. A bit older than I am – twenty-two or twenty-three, don't know, never asked. She dresses like the 1960s never happened – it's really quite funny, actually. Tartan skirt down to her knees, Alice band, flat shoes – carries an alligator handbag and she seems most awfully proud that it comes from somewhere called Mappin & Webb, is what I think she said it was. Never heard of them – but look: if it pleases her, who cares? She's got a lovely face though – otherwise I don't think I could be bothered. She's well named, I must say: truly an English Rose – quite lovely, really. And she's a clever person, clearly . . . but we don't really have a lot in common. She's very into horses and dogs and things, and her parents are something quite high up in Buckinghamshire, is what she was telling me. Whatever that means. She's asked me to their place for Christmas. She says there's always an enormous crowd and I'll be so terribly, terribly welcome and Mummy and Daddy are going to completely adore me, she just knows they will. I said okay. I say okay to everything, really. She was the one, actually, who first suggested we go for a drink after work . . . and I said okay. Not because I've suddenly become obedient in my old age – not because I'm scared of her or anything, Christ no. It's just that, well . . . I don't much care, you see. One way or the other.

'Ask me whatever you want, Rose.'

We're in my flat – just back from having a Wimpy, and she's sitting on this really groovy Casa Pupo rug I just got last weekend – all swirly orange and red with a great big floppy fringe – and she's looking through all of my LPs. I've got quite a lot now – it's a pretty good collection. Kinks, Marianne Faithfull, Rolling Stones, Who . . . not the bloody Dave Clark Five, though: they always were rubbish. But it's *Beatles for Sale* – that's the one I'm just playing all the time: it's on right now – 'Eight Days a Week', absolutely fantastic. It only came out a week ago, and I must have played it a million times. At nine o'clock on the morning of its release, there I was standing outside HMV, the exact money ready in my hand: it was great – there were loads of us there, singing all the oldies like 'Please Please Me' and 'She Loves You'. Laughing a lot, and all of us pretty excited. Rose, she's not really into all that, which isn't too surprising. She plays the cello, she was telling me, which is at home in the country and she rather misses it. I've imagined her whole family there in a thousand-year-old mansion – she's got more brothers and sisters than you could believe – all clustered round a harpsichord during the long winter evenings, doing embroidery, reading out Keats and knocking back the cocoa. She's been at Smythson for about a couple of years, I think – shares a flat in Chelsea just off the good bit of the King's Road with one of the sisters, as well as an actress who does rep but has been in an episode of *Danger Man*, and two air hostesses with BEA . . . and one of them is absolutely gorgeous, I can tell you that. Lorraine, she's called – only seen her once, and she's absolutely gorgeous: looks like Shirley Eaton.

'Well it's just that . . . oh look, George – I hope you won't take it the wrong way or anything, I hope you're not going to be angry with me, okay . . .? And I don't want to be rude or anything, but . . .'

'What? What is it? What do you want to ask me?'

'Well . . . you're not . . . queer or anything, are you? You know – homosexual? I mean, I wouldn't terribly mind, or anything. I know it can be dreadfully unfortunate and it's just something that people can't actually *help*. But it would be, you know . . . quite nice to know.'

I'm just staring at her. I'd been looking through my ties, wondering which of them to wear when I go round to Sammy's in the morning. I've more or less decided that it will probably be the black knitted, though – because it usually is, and it goes with all of the shirts that I've marked out as possibles . . . but I've forgotten all of that now, and I'm just standing here. Staring at her.

'You are joking, yes . . .?'

'Well . . . it's just that you never . . . I mean, we've been with each other for quite a time now, haven't we George?'

'Couple of weeks . . .'

'More than a month, actually.'

'Okay: more than a month. And . . .?'

'And . . . well – you don't seem . . . particularly interested in me. That's all.'

I'm nodding. Because yeh – that's why I didn't go crazy and talk through all she's just been saying. I know what she means, you see – I've actually thought it quite odd myself, from time to time. Because under those stupid frilly blouses she's always wearing, under the bloody twin-sets, she's actually got a great pair of tits that I have had fun fooling around with, once or twice. Great legs too, when you can see them. Fab face, like I say. But it is true . . . apart from the odd bit of snogging when

I've been rather drunk, I haven't really gone any further. And girls today – they maybe expect it, do they? Suppose so. Well Rose clearly does anyway. Trouble is . . . oh well Christ, it's obvious, really. All this with Rose . . . it's just a fill-in, isn't it? Means nothing. Not to me, anyway. Same with all of the girls. Because I've been planning something for quite some time now – but like with Sammy, I've been biding my time. Waiting till things were right. And they are now – I've got everything in place. So bugger Mike – sod *Mike*. What – you think I've forgotten him . . .? Well I haven't. And what I'm going to do – I've got it all worked out, I've had it all worked out for ages – what I'm going to do right after I've seen Sammy and made all of that okay, is get myself back to bloody Circus Road, barge right in there and just let Dorothy see, oh . . . just everything I've *become* . . . and then I'm going to take her back. I've got to. Get her back. It's just driving me insane. She *belongs* with me, Dorothy – and I'm *worthy* of her now. Now I am – yes. See? I finally do deserve her. Won't take no for an answer. And as for Mike . . .! *Mike* . . .? Well he can just fuck off. I might even hit him, the bastard.

'Well are you, George? Queer? Yes or no? I mean, don't worry – I'm not going to *judge* you, or anything. It's just that I would quite like to know where I stand, that's all. I mean – it is quite confusing. I do feel quite confused, George. Because look – I've seen the way you . . . look at me. I mean – you do like touching me, don't you George? I know you do. You do find me attractive, I can see it. Or maybe I'm wrong. Maybe you don't find me in the least attractive. Do you, George? Think I'm attractive? Do you? Maybe all you need is, I don't know . . . some sort of a *cure*, or something . . .'

'A cure.'

'Something you *take* . . .'

'Rose. I'm not a homo. Okay? And even if I was, I'm not sure there is a "cure", as you put it. Don't think you can just bring along a prescription to Boots and get a Queer Cure – could be wrong, of course. Look, Rose – it's just . . .'

'What, George? Just what?'

'Well . . . things on my mind. That's all. It's not you, Rose – course it isn't. You're – well, you're lovely. Beautiful. Of course you are.'

'Well then . . . why don't you . . .?'

So I'm doing that now – right here on the floor where she'd been sitting. Save me an awful lot of time and chat in the long run. And it's actually rather good – haven't done it in ages. And Christ – look at this: she's become someone else, Rose. I'm right on top of her now, pounding away – and look at her . . .! Just look at her face . . .! All red and shiny, her eyes like diamonds. Her legs are clamped around me so bloody tightly it feels like my ribs are about to crack. Well who'd have thought it? That's an English Rose for you: you learn something new every day. Ah. Ah. Yes. Done now. Very good. Mm . . . that was very good. Very nice. I just hope the Casa Pupo rug's okay.

'George . . . oh . . . George. That was . . . oh, George . . . just so heavenly. I really do love you, you know. George . . .? George . . .? Are you listening to me? Did you hear what I said . . .?'

'I heard you, Rose. I'm going to make some coffee. Want some?'

I had this sort of idea that the rest of the evening was going to be tricky, and I wasn't remotely wrong about that. Rose, she was all sort of pouty, but still she couldn't seem to be able to keep her hands away from me. She was all stroking my arm and coming up behind me and covering my eyes and saying 'Guess who?' in a baby sort of a voice – which is pretty moronic, because who else was it going to be? – and then sucking on my ears, and things like that. I've noticed this before with girls – that once the dam is broken, if you know what I mean, well then there's just no bloody stopping them. I actually do think that once they get going, they're more into it than boys are. The blokes I talk to, for them, the first time, when they crack it – well then that's it, really: they cool right off, after that. But girls – with girls, it's the whole opposite thing: they see it as the beginning of, oh – Christ knows what. Who knows what gets into their heads? Romeo and Juliet, or something – or else all the crappy Barbara Cartlands they've ever read, and loads of those really slushy films that they all seem to go for. Girls, they really are strange, you know – because they just don't see things in a normal way, I don't know why. Anyway – she asked me if I wanted her to stay the night, because she'd just have to ring her flatmates and let them know . . . and I didn't say yes, and I didn't say no. She drifted off eventually, as I'd kind of hoped she would – not touching me nearly so much but still really pouty and saying that she wanted to go anyway because if I put on *Beatles for Sale* just one more time, then she'd just have to kill herself.

Well it was good she was gone, anyway – because I needed the time before I went to bed to be on my own and just go over carefully in my head all the final details of tomorrow. I mean – I'd already gone over it, oh Jesus, how many times? I could picture the whole scene, how it was going to be, as if it was in a film that I'd seen a hundred times before, and knew straight off by heart . . . but there still was room to go over the detail, because if something really matters, then there always is.

Because all this with Sammy – it just had to be right, dead right. And once he was impressed – as soon as I could see in his eyes that he recognised very clearly that his old friend Georgie was no longer a moaning, grumpy and scrounging bum . . . when I could see that he was really impressed with me . . . well then I'd find it just so easy to shoot over to Dorothy's and see to the business with all the confidence I needed. Well I felt it already – confident, I mean – but just watching Sammy's eyes really opening up wide . . . well that, that would really do it for me. First thing I had to see to in the morning though was getting my hair done. Well obviously – because once you sleep on it, it's just no use any more. My hair, it's actually pretty good at the moment because I've let it get a bit longer and I've got short square sideburns which are a bit thinner than I'd like them to be, but I haven't been growing them for long. It's quite Beatley, but not honestly in a Paul sort of a way – which is what I really want, but who doesn't? Because it's a funny kind of texture, my hair – it's got a natural wave which just won't go away, and even in the slightest bit of drizzle it goes all frizzy. So I've booked myself into somewhere just around the corner from Smythson that I spotted one lunchtime recently when I was getting my prawn sandwich, smoky bacon crisps and Individual Fruit Pie, which is what I always get, in this place called Da Silva where I go every day. Leonard is the name of this hairdresser, and it seemed to be full of really trendy people – men and women, all dressed in top groovy gear, and it says in the window that the person who runs it, Leonard I suppose, used to work at Vidal Sassoon, so it ought to be okay. It's a bit of a bloody nuisance having to go into town and then come all the way back to Hampstead, but that's just the way it's got to be, because I wouldn't trust any of the local barbers – not since the last time when that Cypriot bastard gave me a crooked fringe, the bloody cock-eyed Cypriot bastard. And Sammy's flat – it's funny this, but Sammy's flat, it turns out that it's really near to where I'm living: I'm in Belsize, and he's just up the road in Hampstead in a really quiet and leafy street (I checked it out one evening to make sure I wasn't going to go to the wrong place). But still I've decided that I'll be rolling up there in a proper black taxi. Obviously what would have been really great is if I could have arrived in a brand-new Triumph Spitfire – or a Sunbeam Alpine, say . . . or even, ho ho ho, an E-Type Jag. But no, I'm nowhere close to getting a car of my own yet, I do know that – haven't even taken any lessons because there's not a lot of point at the moment . . . but it will come. I'll have it – I'll have it all, and it won't take me long either.

So okay – the hairdresser and the taxi, that's going to cost a few bob, but all that, it's actually okay. Because believe it or not, I've still got a little bit of cash in that battered brown briefcase: everything I have I owe to being drunk and then rolled over by a whore and a pimp in the pouring rain at King's Cross Station. Odd, that. The money, yes – well okay, I spent a lot of it securing the flat and kitting it out a bit . . . a fair deal on clothes and records . . . but there was also Sammy's fifty and I'm earning quite a lot now, so there's still a bit left. And that fifty, Sammy's fifty – I've got it right here in brand-new five-pound notes that I asked for specially at the bank. I've tied them with a bit of ribbon from work around a carton of two hundred Benson & Hedges – still nothing close to the millions of fags that I've cadged from Sammy over the years, but still it's a pretty cool thing to do, I think. He'll be impressed, I just know he will. And that, well . . . that's the whole point of the thing, isn't it?

It's really nice at Leonard: never seen anything like it. All black and pink marble, and then shiny red furniture like in Habitat, or somewhere. Gorgeous dolly birds flitting about the place who look exactly like Mary Quant and they're all wearing tall white boots and miniskirts, and one of them is helping me off with my coat and asking me if I'd like her to bring me a free cappuccino. The guy who's seeing to my hair does seem to know what he's doing – but bloody hell: Rose, just last evening she was asking me if I was queer . . .! Jesus Christ – she wants to come and have a look at this bloke . . .! I'm telling you: unbelievable . . . like a bloody ballerina. Anyway – he's trimmed it a bit over the collar and just above my eyebrows and then he washed it, which felt lovely, and put something on which he said would fluff it up a bit and then I got a bit of a back-comb and a blow-dry and a squirt of some sort of perfume like lavender or something, and now it's all finished it looks absolutely great – as Beatley as I'm ever going to get it, anyway. In the clothes I'm wearing, I'd fit just brilliantly on the set of *Ready, Steady, Go!* I'm pleased with the gear I finally decided on: pale blue shirt with a Long John collar, the black knitted tie (I knew it would be the black knitted tie) and a black-and-white herringbone jacket with buttoned patch pockets, which I've never actually worn before: I've been saving it. Really slim black trousers, Beatle boots obviously . . . and because it was absolutely freezing today, this double-breasted coat with wide sort of rounded lapels in RAF blue that I'd got in the Cecil Gee sale – I don't normally go there, but I saw it in the window, and it was only twelve pounds nineteen-and-eleven, down from nearly forty, so a tremendous bargain, really: they'd only got one left – the one in the window – and it just happened to be my size! All meant, you see – everything's meant.

When I'd first sat down in here, I'd said to the hairdresser – his name's Barry, should be Brenda or something – I'd said to him that what I really wanted was for my hair to look like Paul McCartney's, and he said, 'Yes well I daresay you do – but who doesn't, sweetie? I shall strive, though my genius might just fall short of a miracle.' No honestly – he really did say that: afterwards, I simply had to write it down. And look – I knew this place was going to be expensive, but Jesus . . .! I'm not going to say what it cost me, because I still can't actually quite believe it . . . but this is a one-off red-letter day, so it's all in a good cause, right? But apparently the girl – Barry, he's whispering this to me as I'm just getting ready to leave – the girl, the dolly bird who brought me a free cappuccino, you're meant to stick ten bob in her hand! Ten bob . . .! I don't even like cappuccino – only took it because she seemed so terribly eager: I was only being polite, and all I did was just suck the froth off the top of the cup. So I'm giving her five bob instead – Christ, for that you could get a whole fucking vat of cappuccino at Da Silva . . . but I'd better let it go: can't keep going on about all these things – it's just that sort of a day, isn't it? I got a taxi straight away, no trouble at all – and it's actually taken no time from Bond Street all the way to Hampstead. The West End looked nice – Christmas decorations and everything, but obviously nothing was lit up: it's still only just after nine-thirty in the morning – because I'd made a point of booking the very earliest appointment I could: on Saturdays, they seem to be open not long after dawn. I knew I wouldn't be able to sleep much the night before – and I've been up since God knows what time going through every stitch of clothing I possess before finally deciding on what I was actually going to wear . . . and now . . . well now, all of that's done, I've paid off the cab, and

I'm just about to ring Sammy's doorbell. There's his beautiful red Spitfire, looking as fab as ever – so at least I know he's in, anyway. So okay, then. This is it: the time has come.

'Jesus . . . Jesus Christ . . . I don't believe it . . .!'

'Hello, Sammy. Good to see you again. You all right? Still in your dressing gown – didn't get you up, did I? Sorry – I suppose it is a bit early for a Saturday . . .'

'Hm . . .? No – no no. I was just . . . no no, it's fine. Completely fine. Well *Christ*, Georgie . . .!'

'I know. It's been ages. Can I come in . . .?'

'What . . .?'

'Can I . . . you know: come in? That all right?'

'Yes. Yes of course. Come in. Of course . . .'

'Oh – it's nice here, isn't it? This is what they call the communal hall, right? I know because it's a bit like this at my place. I've moved too, you know. Not in Kilburn any more – Christ no. Not far from here, actually. We're both in NW3 – isn't that funny? Flat. I've got a flat too.'

'Really? Well that's . . . that's great, Georgie. God it's good to see you again. Really is. I'm just on the first floor, so . . .'

'Okay – you lead on. I'll follow. So how have you been then, Sammy? Sorry it's been so long, but . . . well, explain later. How long has it been, actually . . .?'

'Well . . . I don't know. Here we are – just in here. Six months, could be . . .'

'Yep – I think it's about that. Oh yes – very nice. Recognise quite a few things. A lot new, of course. Very nice flat, Sammy. Reminds me a bit of mine, actually. You've maybe got more rooms . . .'

'Sit. Do sit. Do you want, um . . . bit early for a drink . . . I don't know – tea, or something . . .?'

'Don't drink tea, Sammy. Remember?'

'Oh yes. Of course. Well – it's been a while. Coffee, then.'

'Coffee would be nice. Not bloody cappuccino, though . . .'

'What . . .?'

'Nothing. No – nothing. So how's the new job?'

'Not that new any more, really. Great. Yeh great. Advertising. J. Walter Thompson. Heard of them?'

'Yes. No, actually – don't think so. Might have. I'm at Smythson.'

'Oh what – in Bond Street? My dad gets all his stuff from there.'

'I expect he does. Yes, Bond Street – that's them. Look – I printed these cards with my new address on it. Because that's where I am, in the print shop, mainly. Have one. Nice, aren't they?'

'Hm. Very smart. So – very much not at Smith's any more, then.'

'Christ no – dumped them ages ago. You know how awful that was . . .'

'Well that's great. Really great, Georgie. And you're looking . . .'

'Yeh – pretty good, I think. You like them? The clothes? Good, yeah? Just had my hair done, actually. Not quite Beatles – more Herman's Hermits, but it's the nearest I can get. What do you think of *Beatles for Sale*? Fantastic, isn't it? Yeah – absolutely fantastic. Where do you go for your hair now, Sammy? Still Vidal Sassoon with your mother? I go to Leonard. Leonard, he's my hairdresser now. You like it? Not bad, is it? Yes and I'm feeling good too, actually. It's all different now, Sammy. I'm different. Which I never thought I'd say. Better, I hope. Anyway – everything's changed. Well – you can see that for yourself, I hope.'

'I can. I'm very impressed, Georgie. Very pleased. Very pleased.'

'You are? You really are? What you actually are is bloody *amazed* – I'm right, aren't I? You thought I was going right down the drain. Yes you did – oh yes you did! And I don't blame you. So did I.'

'Well . . . last time I saw you, you were a bit . . .'

'Yeh I was. Bloody mess, actually. But no longer . . .! This is the new me! I'm feeling great! Oh look, Sammy – these . . . these are for you.'

'What's all this . . .? Fags . . .? Blimey, Georgie – that's a first! And bloody hell . . . money too? Oh . . . you didn't have to do that, Georgie . . .'

'Oh yes I did. A loan, remember? I said I'd pay it back, didn't I? Didn't I? I know you never expected to see it again – I do know that, Sammy. But, well . . . here it is. First for everything. And don't worry, because I can easily afford it. Promise you.'

'Amazing, Georgie. What can I say . . .?'

'Impressive. Yes? You're impressed?'

'I . . . am. I really am. Terrific – really terrific.'

'Well that's just wonderful. That's all I wanted to hear. Because everything's going to be right now, you see. Proper. All square – the way it's meant to be. And everything already is, actually . . . except . . . well, except for the one big thing. Which I want to talk to you about actually, Sammy . . .'

'I'll just get that coffee. You have it black, right . . .?'

'No – don't worry about that. Don't want it, really. No – just listen to me, Sammy. Well look – you know me, so you probably know exactly what I'm going to say next. It's her, isn't it? Yeh well . . . it always is. I wish to God I'd listened to you, Sammy. You know – about her. Everything you said to me. Well I didn't – and I really messed up everything, I do know that. But I'm going to make it all right. Going round to talk to her in a minute. So sick to death of all the girls I've been seeing lately – oh Christ, I can't tell you. You haven't heard anything, have you? Because I know you do, sometimes. Still with *him*, I suppose. Is she . . .? No – sorry, Sammy. Being stupid. How would you know? Anyway – that's what I'm going to do. Yes. Right, then. Let's have a fag, shall we? One of mine, for once . . .! Fag, Sammy . . .? No . . .? What's wrong? Something wrong . . .?'

'Look, Georgie . . . I have to talk to you.'

'Yeah . . .? Okay, then. Talk. What I'm here for . . .'

'I did try to get in touch with you. Loads of times. Left messages with some Irish person – you know, where you used to be living. You maybe didn't get them, but . . .'

'Yeh – I got them. Some of them, anyway. I just wasn't ready, that's all.'

'Well . . . I do wish you'd phoned me back. I really do. And she . . . she wanted to talk to you too, but . . .'

'Who? Dorothy, you mean? She wanted to ring me? Well that's great . . .!'

'Well . . . it's not that great, Georgie. Not really. You see . . . look – you sure you don't want anything? I can make that coffee if you . . . or there's Scotch over there if you'd like some . . .?'

'Just talk, Sammy. Say what you have to say, Christ's sake . . .'

'Well . . . you have to understand, Georgie . . . she was . . . well she was pretty upset, you know . . .'

'I know – don't you think I don't know that? That's why I want to make it all right again. There's no way that she belongs with *him* . . .! She has to know that.'

'No well she's not . . . she's not with him any more. You see.

Hasn't been for, oh ... months. Not since you last saw her, more or less.'

'Really? That true? Well great. That's great. Well why didn't you tell me before? So where is she, then? You obviously know. So where is she ...?'

'Well ... look, this is really hard for me, Georgie. We didn't know where you were – even if you were still alive. You just fell off the edge of the bloody world – so what were we supposed to think ...? We just didn't know what to think. There was nothing we could *do* ...'

I looked at him. Just looked at him.

'I do hope you *see*, Georgie. There was nothing we could *do* ...'

And that just did it. It was the 'we', of course. I'd had the beginnings of really horrible feelings a little bit before all that ... but when he kept on saying 'we' ... well that just absolutely did it. Several things I could do now. One or two things I could say. What I did was ... turn away from him – couldn't quite stomach it, the way he was just looking at me. He seemed so ... frightened, almost. And then I got up and left. Out of the flat, down the stairs, through the door and into the driveway. Kicked his fucking Spitfire, and headed down the street. People were looking at me because I was crying so hard. And when I got home ... my flat just didn't seem anything any more. Not because it wasn't as good as Sammy's – which it wasn't, obviously: not by a bloody mile – but because it was ... empty. At some point Rose rang and said could she come round and I said no. She said why not and I said because I'm not well. She said is there anything I can do for you darling, and I said no. And then she said are you sure you wouldn't like me to come over and then I can look after you and I said no: what's *wrong* with you, Rose? Why won't you *understand*? No. No no *no*.

Didn't want to think, so drank whisky. Felt so cold. Felt so . . . alone. Because I was now, wasn't I? Completely and utterly alone. My two friends, my two best friends . . . the only two people I've ever really cared about or who ever gave a damn about me . . . well they're gone. Lost them. Lost them both. Because they're together. How did that happen, then? Don't know. Sunday came and went. I played The Beatles and drank a lot of Haig, which I haven't done in a long time. Felt like hell on Monday morning. Just getting ready to go to work when the post came. I sat down and read it, Sammy's letter.

Dear Georgie,

It seems funny to be writing you a letter, because I never have before. But you left so suddenly, and your card didn't have your phone number on it so that's why I'm writing. What happened was, after you went round to see Dorothy and Mike that day, the day you had all that trouble and the last time we met, actually, she came to see me. She was in a bad state, Georgie. She didn't care about Mike, not really. She liked him, that's all. I met him once and he seems a nice bloke. I think she was scared of you. She said she didn't know if she wanted you back or not because it would be the same as it was. I think she did want you back though. We saw each other once or twice, and all we talked about was you. And then we tried to get in touch with you, like I said. I don't really know what happened then. I'm being honest with you, Georgie. But I've always liked Dorothy, you know that. I've always thought she was special. Anyway, she liked me too apparently, and it sort of started like that. I don't know what to say. I don't want to hurt you. I know you're already hurt, but I don't want to hurt you any more. Dorothy says she will write to you, but not yet. Don't hate us, Georgie. We are still your friends and we care about you a lot and I hope that you are still friends with us. You know where to find us, and you'll always be welcome.

Sorry, Georgie, for everything. I didn't know it would turn out like this.

Best wishes, Sammy

I would have set fire to it, but I didn't have a fire. Had matches, obviously – but what I wanted was to screw it up with real contempt and hurl it into a blazing grate . . . yeh but that wasn't going to happen, was it? My flat, there's central heating. Read the letter a few times more and then for some reason slid it back into its envelope and put it in a drawer. I went to work in a sort of daze – wasn't just a hangover, because this, this . . . it was just all over me. I felt I was hovering and blinking as if I was scared and not quite believing it – and I absolutely knew I'd be hurting really badly soon. Got to work not even remembering how. Hadn't even taken my coat off and Rose was there and clinging to me and saying what's wrong, George? Is there something wrong, darling? I was worried about you – do you feel better now? I said I'm fine: there's nothing wrong.

The next few days were as awful as I just knew they would be. Kept going over it all in my mind – drinking Scotch, smoking fags and going over and over it, again and again. If only I hadn't stayed away from Sammy for so terribly long . . . if I hadn't been so ridiculously worried about him being impressed by my flat and my job and my hair and my clothes – when I should have been worried about him stepping in and taking the only bloody thing that I still knew I wanted. And now . . . well now he has it all, hasn't he? Like he always bloody does. Now he's just completely got the lot. Then the thought . . . yes, this thought . . . that when I was round there – God I just cringe when I think back on this – that when I finally had gone round to Sammy's new flat and we were talking . . . well then Dorothy, on that bright and cold Saturday morning, she just had to be in the bedroom right next door in a dressing gown all of her own, and listening to every bloody word – cowering, not daring to show herself . . . and thinking just what, exactly . . .? Oh Christ. I'm right back to not being able to believe it all. But the strangest thing of all, in one way, is that I don't feel . . . vengeful. I don't want to kill them. Once, I would have. Once, I would have been round there – screaming, and waving around a hammer. So what I feel is . . . hurt, hurt for myself . . . but still I don't really want any harm to come to either of them. They're nicer than I am. They always were. I've always liked both of them more than I've ever liked me. So maybe, I don't know . . . maybe it's right that they're now together . . .? Maybe. And maybe it's right that I am the outcast.

I did spend Christmas with Rose and her family in the country – what the hell else was I going to do with myself? It was nice, actually. Apart from . . . well apart from just everything, really . . . but it was nice. Everyone was very kind to me, everyone seemed to be having a really good time – even me, once I'd drunk enough. Must have been eighteen, twenty people – all very upper-class and fabulously dressed: really groovy gear, lots of tartan and ruffles. Huge house – very beautiful, eighteenth-century apparently, and filled with all these lovely things. I envied him, Rose's father. He had a Rolls-Royce. Savile Row suits – and the most amazing purple velvet smoking jacket that he wore on Christmas Day. He smoked

Havana cigars – gave me a few, and I thought they were great. The wine at dinner was amazing – never had anything like it. His garden was like Regent's Park, and seen to by gardeners. I could, I think, have married into all that – Rose was all for it, and I got the feeling that her mother was too. Christ knows why: I mean – just look at me. But what I decided was . . . no, because Rose, well . . . Rose is just Rose, isn't she? She's not Dorothy. Not her fault, but there it is. But I am going to have all that – just seeing it, touching it, smelling it all . . . it made me that much more determined. I am going to get it, but when I do . . . it will be mine. I will have worked for it. I think that's the only way, I really do. Because then . . . no one can take it away from you. I'm going to work and work and work – think of nothing else in the entire world from this moment on, because now . . . well now, if I'm honest, I've got really nothing else to think of. I even wrote it down in my brand-new dark blue leather Smythson diary, on the first of January 1965: 'Resolution: Get Everything'.

And not too long after all that . . . I received a wedding invitation. No really. Dorothy, daughter of blah blah blah, and Samuel, only son of yak yak yak. Well that's very nice: the tin bloody lid. But no not quite: there was more. Because a couple of months on, the next thing I got from Sammy – and it turned out that this would be the last I was ever going to hear of him – was a birthday card. He never forgot my birthday, Sammy: couldn't even tell you when his is, even the season. The card had a picture of The Beatles on the front, the black-and-white Dezo Hoffman shot, and it said in red letters 'Happy Birthday from Us to You'. There was a sheet of paper folded inside it: Sammy's usual very neat handwriting, in fountain pen. He said that they were sorry not to see me at the wedding, but that if ever I did want to change my mind and decide to come and visit them – and he couldn't tell me how welcome I'd be – well then it's maybe better that I know in advance that there was now a little boy on the scene. Both mother and baby doing well. Right. Fine. And then I was reminded of that very first letter from Sammy, when he'd said that Dorothy was going to write to me, but not yet. Well she didn't. Not ever.

CHAPTER EIGHT

A PEACE OF SORTS

'What's going on . . .? What in Christ's name is going *on* here . . .? Have you seen him? Is he in there? How is he? Is this a private ward? Has he got his own room? I can pay for a private room, you know. Who do I speak to? There's never anyone around, in these places . . . Have you been in to see him? What *happened*, Christ's sake . . .?'

'Oh George . . . just sit down, can't you? It's just too . . .! Anna's with him at the moment. He wanted to speak to Anna.'

'Oh right – so he is *talking*, then. Well that's something. Isn't it? But David, though – what did he actually think he was playing at? What's *happened* here . . .? Talk to me, Enid.'

'And Lilian too. She's still in there. Won't leave him. Won't leave him for a moment. She's been wonderfully calm, thank heavens. In a terrible state, of course – you just have to look at her, poor little thing. She told me she wouldn't cry – that she wasn't going to let herself cry yet, because it would only upset him. Amazing, really . . .'

'But you . . . you've seen him, have you? How long have you been here?'

'Well we came as soon as we got the call. I don't quite know how long. Not that long, I suppose. Don't know. Could be hours. But I do think he's going to be . . .'

'What? Going to be what, Enid? Spoken to a doctor, have you?'

'Yes. He said he'd come back, but I haven't seen him since.'

'Yes well that's the bloody NHS for you, isn't it? But look – we don't have to hang about waiting for him. We'll go private. Just got to find someone who knows what he's talking about. Who do I speak to round here . . .? Just nobody about . . .'

'Oh George . . . please do sit down. I can't stand it, you stamping up and down all the time. Please sit down, for the love of God . . .'.

'Well what did he say? This doctor. What did he say?'

'He said that he thought he'd be all right. Oh God, *please* sit down . . .'

'Don't want to sit down. And what the bloody hell is that supposed to mean . . .? He *thought* he'd be all right . . .? Will he or won't he, Christ's sake . . .'

'He said that there shouldn't be any, um . . . now what did he say . . .?'

'Oh God Almighty . . .'

'He said that there won't be any lasting damage. Or shouldn't be – I can't remember what he said. You know – his internal organs. Stomach, and so on. He said they had got to him in time. Well that's Lilian, of course. If it hadn't been for Lilian . . . well. But it's his mental state, isn't it? That's what concerns me. I mean – what can have driven him to *do* such a thing . . .? Do you have any idea, George? Oh heavens, I just can't think of it. Too, too awful. But I mean – whatever it was, well . . . not just going to go away, is it . . .?'

'But Christ Almighty . . .! I mean – what a *bloody* stupid thing to do. Taking pills . . .? What a *bloody* stupid thing to do . . .!'

'Don't . . .'

'What? Don't what, Enid? Come on – say it, God's sake. What is it I'm not meant to do now?'

'Don't . . . tell him that. Don't say it. When you see him, George . . . well don't just barge in and shout into his face that it was a bloody stupid thing to do. All right? Be . . . sensitive. It's a very sensitive time . . .'

'Well I know that. Of course I know that. I do *know* that, Enid . . .! Sort of a person do you think I am? What's that . . .? Enid? What's that in your hand? What are you doing . . .? Oh Jesus, Jesus – what in God's name do you think you're *doing* . . .?'

'It is a miniature. Bell's. They had them in the hotel minibar. I had actually been looking for some sort of a snack. Peanuts, or something. We were going to order food, you see – proper food, room service. Sort of a midnight feast – it was all going to be such great fun. And in the meantime, well . . . I was just looking for . . .'

'Enid. What in Christ's name are you *talking* about . . .? What do you think you're *doing* . . .?'

'Well I'm *telling* you, George, if you'll just let me finish. I was looking for some sort of a snack to fill in the gap, that's all. Peanuts – anything, really. Because Troy, he'd just woken up and I knew he'd want something, thought he'd be bound to. Then I got this terrible call from Lilian, and . . . well anyway. They were just there in the door of the fridge. Goes quite well in this tea. Helps it, you know? Because it's perfectly dreadful.'

'Oh . . . *Jesus*, Enid . . .! I don't . . . I just don't believe it . . .! You're *drinking* again . . .? After all this time, you're *drinking* . . .?'

'Didn't plan to. Wasn't even on my mind – it never is. But like I say, this awful call came through and Anna was busy getting Troy ready, because obviously we had to take him with us, and . . . oh Christ's sake don't *judge* me, George. Not again. Not any more. Look: when you hear that your son, your only son could be *dying* . . . well. I don't know about you, I don't know how it affected you when you heard, but I . . . well I just needed a little help, that's all. It's no more than that. I am *human*, you know. He's sleeping in a cot now, Troy. They set up a little cot for him just next door. He was crying all the way here – I think we must rather have scared him, poor little mite. I was crying too, you see – Anna kept telling me not to, but I just couldn't help it. Awful of me, I know . . .'

'Jesus. Jesus, Enid . . . you're *drinking* again. Oh my *God* . . .'

'Oh don't be so melodramatic, George . . .! I'm not *drinking* again – I've just had a couple of sips, that's all. And by the look of you, well – looks like you've barely stopped. Looks like you've been drinking all day and night. So who are you to talk? Anyway it's David you should be concerned about, not me. But you never are, are you George? Concerned about David. You just never are. And now look what's happened.'

'What? What do you mean? What do you mean, Enid? What do you mean "*now* look what's happened" . . .? Are you blaming me? Is that it? You're blaming me for this, are you?'

'I didn't say that. Did I? I didn't say that, George.'

'Well you pretty much bloody well did, actually . . .!'

'George . . . oh George, please do sit down. I can't stand it any more, all your pacing around . . .'

'Don't bloody *want* to sit down – what's wrong with you? Well – it's obvious, isn't it? What's wrong with you. You're *drinking* again . . .'

Yes she is. Beyond belief. But that's not all that's on my mind. Because now she's blaming me, you see. For exactly whatever it is that has actually happened here, she's putting the blame on me. Yes. And the trouble is . . . I am too. This . . . this almost certainly has got to be my fault. And I'm finding that hard. Very hard. David's lack of character, strength, moral fibre, even simple competence . . . they're what forced his hand, I suppose: he would have seen no other recourse, bloody young fool. But I know him, don't I? I know that's how he is. So how did I imagine he was going to deal with any sort of a crisis? In the way I would? Ha – I hardly think so. Should I have just said yes, then? Bail him out? Maybe. Difficult to say. Oh look . . . oh thank Christ in heaven! It's Anna. Anna has just come out of the room. Well that's just wonderful, because it's Anna I need to talk to now: she's the only one in the world I could talk to about any of this. And other things too – there are other things I've got to talk to her about as well. I feel starved: when I don't speak to Anna, I feel starved.

'Anna, my darling – how are you? I've missed you. Can we talk?'

'Well it's David we're all meant to be concerned about, isn't it? Not me. Hello, Mum – you all right? Yes – you can go in now. Lilian's still there, but do go in.'

'Oh well, David – yes of course. How is he? All right? Not too bad?'

'I think . . . I think he'll be okay. Out of danger, anyway – and that's all thanks to Lilian for getting an ambulance so quickly. If she hadn't been around, oh Lord . . . I just can't think. Few days they think he'll be here, maybe, and after that, well . . . he should be okay again. God, I hope so, anyway. Still in a pretty bad way, though. Shocked more than anything, I think.'

'Yes well. I daresay. So, Anna – can I have a word?'

'Don't you want to see him?'

'What? Oh well yes of course – I'll go in and see him in a moment. If he wants to see me. But could we just go somewhere briefly, do you think? So much to tell you. For just a couple of minutes?'

'Is Mum all right?'

'Well . . . not really, I shouldn't have said. One of the things I want to talk to you about.'

'Why? What's wrong with her?'

'Well look – can we just go somewhere? Yes? And then I can tell you. I thought you maybe knew . . .'

'Knew what? Here's all right, isn't it? Why can't we talk here?'

'Well . . . I suppose so. I just wondered if they had a . . . I don't know – café, or something. Lounge, maybe? Somewhere we can just sit and . . . be on our own, sort of thing.'

'We're on our own here. No one around, is there?'

'No – never is in these bloody places. That's half the trouble. Well all right then – here, if you like.'

'Well sit down, then.'

'Oh Christ – don't you start. Don't want to sit down.'

'Well I do. I'm . . . oh God. I'm actually completely exhausted. Can't really believe all that's been going on . . .'

'No. Nor can I. Listen, Anna – you'll never guess what happened.'

'Oh God. Something else. What's wrong? What's happened now?'

'No no. Nothing wrong – nothing wrong at all. Quite the reverse.'

'Okay – I could do with some good news. Tell me.'

'Well two things, actually. One of them affects you. All I'm going to do is just tell you the basic fact. No more. All right?'

'The basic fact . . .? What on earth are you talking about? I think I'd better go in and see that Mum's all right. She's been crying non-stop since she heard . . .'

'No no – she'll be fine. She's with David, isn't she? She'll be fine. And Lilian's in there too, isn't she? She'll tell us if there's anything wrong.'

'Okay then, Daddy: tell me. You sure you don't want to sit down?'

'I'm fine. Okay then – here it is: this is one of the things. The bastard. I've found him.'

'The . . . *bastard* . . .? What . . .?'

'Him. Your bastard husband. Found him. I know where he is. Okay? Anna . . .? Did you hear me . . .? I said I know where he is. What's wrong with you? Why aren't you saying anything?'

Because . . . I'm thinking. I'm trying . . . I'm trying to decide just what exactly I feel about that. And here is something extraordinary: I already know. I absolutely know what I feel about that. It's maybe not at all like me, everything that's bubbling up inside . . . but do you know what I think? I actually think that I've been through enough.

'What . . . what are you going to do, Daddy? About him.'

'Hm? Oh well – that needn't concern you. Just the basic fact – remember?'

'Well it does, actually. It concerns me very much – but maybe not in the way you mean.'

'Look – I don't see why you should care about what happens to him! Look what he did to you! Look how he treated his wife and son . . .!'

'I am. That's exactly what I'm looking at.'

'Walked out – just walked out on you! What could be worse than that?'

'Well actually, Daddy . . . oh God, I don't know why I'm going to tell you this, because I swore to myself I never would. But I just feel, oh . . . so incredibly tired, I'm not sure I quite know even what I'm doing. But it was worse than that, actually. Quite a lot worse.'

'What? *Worse* . . .? What do you mean *worse* . . .? He didn't . . . *hurt* you, did he? My God – if that bastard ever *hurt* you . . .!'

'No. Well – not in the way you mean. He didn't hit me, or anything. But in other ways . . . yes. Hurt me quite badly. Look, Daddy . . . one day, not now . . . but one day, I'll tell you the whole story. Promise. But listen – will you believe me if I tell you this . . .?'

'Believe you? Of course I'll *believe* you. Believe anything you say – always have.'

'Okay then. Give me the address. Where he is. Is it in this country? Doesn't matter. I promise you I'm not going there. I've no wish to ever set eyes on him again.'

'Oh Anna . . . you have no idea how much it pleases me to hear you say that . . .'

'But I know you. Don't I, Daddy? I have no idea how you found him – there are other people who have been looking for ages . . .'

'Other people? What other people?'

'Just let me finish, okay? Look – I know you didn't find him just for fun, I do know that. I know you've got something in mind. Retribution. It's how you think. But trust me: just tell me exactly where he is, and I will tell the . . . other people.'

'Who in Christ's name are these "other people" . . .?'

'Never mind. Never mind. I told you that one day I'll tell you everything, and I will. But I swear this to you, Daddy:

these other people . . . will not be kind to him. All right? You have to believe that. He will not come out of this well. If . . .'

'If what . . .?'

'Well, I was just going to say . . . if he comes out of it at all.'

'I see. It's like that. So he got himself into serious trouble, did he? With very much the wrong people, I'm guessing. Well I'm not surprised. Shady type – crook. You just had to look at him. I always knew he was no good, that bastard. I knew he was a Grade-A shit the moment I laid eyes on him. Told you, didn't I, Anna? Didn't I tell you? How many times did I tell you?'

'Daddy – not now. Please. Will you do as I ask? Will you trust me?'

'I will. I do. Of course I do.'

'Good. Well then. It's finished. I feel . . . free. Sound so silly . . .'

'I hate to think there was a time when you didn't. But listen, Anna – I trust you, of course I trust you, but I really do have to be sure. This bastard . . . he will get all that's coming to him? He really will?'

'I told you. I have met one of these people . . . they are not . . . nice. But I was fine, so please don't start worrying about that. So – there it is. That's over. You just tell me where he is, and then it will be finished. Okay so listen, Daddy – before I go back in, what's the other thing?'

'I'm sorry . . .?'

'You said you had two things to tell me.'

'Oh yes I see. Well three, I suppose. The not good one is about your mother. I thought you'd know.'

'Look . . . I'm sure she'll come back to you. I'm sure she doesn't *mean* it . . .'

'What . . .? What are you talking about?'

'Ah. Okay. Not that. No – never mind. My head – it's just

spinning with, oh my God . . . everything. Well what, then? Look – I really do think I'd better get back in there – see that everyone's all right. Are you coming in with me, Daddy? I know that David would like to see you.'

'Yes, maybe. Well it's the drinking, isn't it? Your mother. She's been sitting here and quietly swigging bloody *whisky* . . .!'

'Oh God. I . . . I did see her taking them from the fridge. There was just so much else going on, I can't tell you. Troy was screaming his head off – and of course I was just so desperately worried about David . . . I think . . . I think what I've done is just blank it right out of my mind. But maybe . . . maybe just this once it won't harm . . .?'

'Do you remember how she was? Do you remember?'

'I do. I do. Oh God.'

'Well then.'

'So . . . okay, well it's just something else we'll have to deal with, then. That's all. Well look – let's go in now, shall we? And see David.'

'Well . . . there is this other thing I've got to tell you . . .'

'Oh yes – the other thing. Go on, then. And this is good news you said, yes?'

'Yes – oh God yes. So, so good . . .!'

'Heavens, Daddy – I've never seen you like this before! What is it?'

'Well . . . okay then: today . . . or no – I suppose it's yesterday by now, is it? What's the time . . .? Yes, it was yesterday. Yesterday . . .! Oh my God – that's actually quite funny when I tell you what happened . . .! Okay then, Anna – are you ready for this . . .? Yesterday afternoon in Chelsea . . . I met . . . *Paul McCartney* . . .! I know! I know . . .! I can see you don't believe me – but it's true, it's true, it really is true. I . . . *touched* him

His left hand. I actually did *touch* him . . .! Oh my God. Oh my *God* . . .! I think . . . you know I think I actually will, now . . . just sit down for a bit.'

'My goodness, Daddy . . . you really are in a bit of a state, aren't you? You're shaking. Look at you – you're shaking. Can I get you something? Coffee, maybe?'

'No no. I'm fine. But it's ridiculous really, isn't it? I know it is. The state I'm in. I know it's ridiculous. But what can I do? It's just so . . . *important*. Do you see? Well – you do, Anna, I'm sure you do . . . you're the only one who ever would. But yes – I know I am being completely ridiculous, I can quite see that. Look – you go in, you go back in and say to everyone, um . . . that I'll be there, I'll be there in just a minute or two. All right?'

'Okay, Daddy. Okay.'

Yes – I think it is best to leave him for a bit, actually. You know, I'm just thinking . . . in any other context, at any other time, it would be really quite perfectly hilarious, the way he's behaving. I mean – look at it: on the day that his wife has left him – and she does mean it, Mum: I said to him she doesn't, but I know she's made up her mind about this, for whatever reasons she's got . . . and they will have been festering for ages, because that's just the way she is. I don't think I've ever seen it in her before: resolve – or anything like it. The drinking too . . . the way she has just started drinking again, apparently, after all those years of complete sobriety . . . well that's no accident, I'm sure of it. She didn't just knock back a few miniatures because she'd had bad news and they just happened to be there. No – she had decided before that this was what she was going to do, I'm just sure of it, don't know why. To be her own woman again, maybe . . .? Caution to the winds – that sort of thing? Always so difficult to know what she's thinking – she doesn't talk, she never will invite you in. Now what was I . . .? Oh yes – on the very day that his wife of, Jesus, how many years, just suddenly decided to book into a Holiday Inn and never go back home again (without even telling him, clearly – he obviously still hasn't the slightest idea of what's actually going on here) . . . and his son David, meanwhile, was doing his level best to kill himself . . . oh God, poor David . . . it all makes me feel so very desperately sad. Was it about the money? Can it really have been? That money he asked me for? Yes – knowing David, it could easily have been about that . . . because he's not like me: he's not like me at all. His idea of dealing with things is either to panic and quickly try to dump the responsibility on to someone else's shoulders, or else to just run. And in this case . . . having failed to shift the burden, well . . . he attempted to run as far away as he possibly could. And me . . .? Well at pretty much the same time, I was running too. Believe it? Oh yes I was – bundling Troy and anything I could carry into the car and heading off to God alone knows where, because I was panicking too, and quite convinced that I had a pack of killers closing in on me. Jesus, I felt so scared. But thanks to Daddy, I'm not any more. I wasn't imagining it, though – I knew they intended to use the threat of pain or death to me and my child to flush out the one true villain here . . . little understanding that a man who vanishes, a man who abandons his penniless and innocent family has no longer the faintest interest in them. It took my father to find him – no one else could have done it: he has this great and awesome tenacity. And now . . . now I'm going to throw my husband to the wolves – let these horrible people find their diamonds, their money, whatever else it is he took from them . . . and let them tear him apart while they're doing it. Don't care. Simply don't care any more. Just so long as

Troy is safe, that's all I really mind about. So – what's next . . .? Well – won't go back to the flat, of course. Well I can't – it isn't mine, and I still haven't got the rent. I think . . . I think, you know, in the light of, oh . . . just everything, really . . . I think I could move back home. Just for a bit, anyway. Daddy might . . . need that at the moment, when he finds out all that's going on with Mum. Yes . . . and so might I.

Oh yes – my father: that's who I was thinking about, that was the thread. Yes well, on this very day of days, Daddy, quite incredibly, somehow managed to run into one of his boyhood heroes – a Beatle, no less! – and for him, well . . . this really does seem to be the only thing in the world that actually matters. He knows it's ridiculous – he said so, didn't he? A man of sixty-four years old being completely smitten by meeting another man who is, what . . .? Three or four years older, I think. Amazing, isn't it? Ah yes but you have to understand: he's like that, my daddy – not stupid, by no means is he remotely stupid – not obtuse, not insensitive, as Mum and David think he is . . . it's just that he becomes so completely swept up by whatever is concerning him at any one particular moment. And he can never get it, can never really see – that anyone else could ever be as much affected as he is, nor that their elations or problems could ever possibly rival his own – not in scale, complexity . . . or, as he put it himself: *importance*. It's selfishness, yes I suppose it is – there's no getting around that. What it is . . . I think he feels that he's made his way in the world, provided handsomely for all his dependents . . . and now he expects that world and pretty much everyone in it – certainly us, anyway – to revolve around him: what he wants, and what he thinks. I understand. Because I love him. But Mum and David . . . of course I can see that they might not always, what can I say . . .? Appreciate the way he behaves: the things he says, and the things he doesn't.

'Hi. Everything okay . . .? Why's everyone whispering . . .?'

'Oh, Anna. He's asleep. We were just wondering – weren't we, Lilian? Quite what to do. Where's your father?'

'Just gone to the loo – he'll be in in a minute. Well it's good he's asleep, isn't it? Looks so . . . restful. Or rested, do I mean? Don't know. Anyway. Hard to think that any of this has happened now, just looking at him. But sleep is probably the best thing, yes? He must be, oh . . . just completely exhausted after, you know . . . everything they've done to him, poor David. Has the doctor been back? No? Well I expect he will soon. I think they're quite busy tonight, actually. Look, Mum – you haven't had a wink of sleep yourself, have you? Why don't you slip away for a bit, hey? I'll stay with him. Think I've got my second wind, now.'

'What about Troy . . .?'

'He's fine, Mum – just looked in. Sleeping peacefully, and looking completely beautiful. You too, Lilian – you must be dropping. I'll ring you, I promise, if anything, you know . . . happens, or anything. But I'm sure he'll be out for the night, now. Let's just hope he feels better in the morning.'

'I'll . . . stay, if it's all right with you, Anna.'

'Well of course, Lilian. Of course. You do what you want to, obviously.'

Her arm, it's lying across the counterpane, just as it was when I left the room – and even now when she's talking to me, still she goes on staring into David's face, almost beseechingly. When I first got here, poor David was still unconscious – or no, the doctors must have given him something, not quite sure. Anyway, Lilian had been the only other person there: she was clutching his hand so tightly – snatched it away when she saw me, but she really needn't have done that, and I told her so. Her whole face was stiffened with the effort not to cry – it's still like that, as rigid as anything – and her lips quite set . . . but in the depth of her eyes there was and remains this really quite extraordinary welling of devotion. Lilian . . . she has been in love with David for just so terribly long, and everyone seems to see it apart from David himself. Amazing, really . . . but did he never ask himself why this woman would continue to work into the night year in year out for such insultingly low wages in that dreadful little office, always pledging her complete and unconditional belief in the endless succession of David's (I am sorry to say) increasingly pitiful schemes and ideas, each one of which was sure to be, just bound to be – in his mind, and his mind only – the one great breakthrough he had always dreamed of. Her tremendous loyalty, though – this must always have been reserved for David the person, and never whatever idiotic venture was simply the latest in an eternal line – because Lilian, you know, is actually terribly astute: she has a really good head for this sort of thing. She will have put everything into the work, of course, but knowing, I think, that it was all rather in vain. I mean – I don't know her well, or anything – haven't actually met her that often, because . . . well, why would I? But still – often enough, I think, to see that she's certainly got something: there is an air of capability about her. And how many times, I wonder, has her sound business sense prevented him from completely going under? And all the time knowing that every new attempt at yet another brand-new launch was just as pointless as the last. I have sometimes wondered if it actually would not have been better if she had left him – better for David, I mean, if there was no longer anyone there to constantly support every one of his hopeless projects . . .? No, not really – because I think that without Lilian, he might actually have attempted to do away with himself, oh . . . maybe years ago. But he *must* know it, surely – the depth of her love . . .? He gives no sign – but no one, not even David, is that blind, can't be. I think they probably do sleep together, I think that's probably part of the arrangement, if we can call it that – yes but, well . . . it's nothing these days, is it? Par for the course, is what you keep reading. And I can see that it's exactly the sort of lazy convenience that might easily suit David down to the ground – well of course it would suit him, of course it would: he's a man, isn't he? But it won't do for Lilian, no not at all – and nor should it either: she's worth, oh – so much more than that. But I suppose, in common with many women who just seem incapable of admitting even to themselves just how terribly *good* they are, she simply meekly receives and is dumbly grateful for whatever small comforts she can get. Which is wrong, and really very, very sad. Well anyway. Can't go on battling with any of that – I'm utterly exhausted now; I said to Mum that I've got a second wind, but it's nonsense, that: I am utterly and completely exhausted. So . . . what is to happen to David now? When eventually he manages to pull himself out if this latest little nightmare, what on earth is he going to do next? And Lilian – what about her? Don't know. Just can't imagine. Far too tired to even think any more.

'Come on then, Mum. Come and have a cup of tea, yes? Or we can go in and see Troy, if you like. Honestly, you can't do any good just sitting there, can you? And Lilian's staying – aren't you, Lilian? So come on – let's go, shall we? David will be fine. Look at him – he's fast asleep.'

Mmm . . . but I'm not, actually. Asleep. Haven't been for quite some time – though I'm pleased that this appalling exhaustion that has just flooded me is making it appear as if I am. I just couldn't look at them any more – and I had nothing to say, did I? Except 'sorry' . . . and how many times have I said that? Every time I did, Mum, she'd start crying again and saying oh David, oh David – it's not your fault, it's not your fault . . . but it is, of course it is. Who else has brought me to this? I've thought of doing it before, of course – oh God, loads of times I've thought of it before. Been hoarding these sleeping pills that I get from the doctor – and just having them near me has for a long time now been the nearest I've got to comfort. The thought of my mighty collection of narcotics has lulled me into a contented sleep far more effectively than taking them ever did. I sort of hugged myself with the secret knowledge that they were there, if I needed them: that if everything crashed completely, when the very last resort had finally been reached . . . well then: I had, I think they call it, an exit strategy. And today . . . or yesterday . . . don't know: I'm so lightheaded – floating, and yet I feel like a ton weight: strange. Anyway – whenever it was, I used it. I walked through the door. Yes . . . but not really. Because I was so very careful to leave it ajar. Well of course. Because this, even this is just another blind, another sham – one more criminal piece of theatre that will just for a little longer deflect my responsibilities . . . and to hell with what it inflicts upon anyone else. I wish I wasn't like this, I really do. But I am, and so that's that, really.

I would have set it up rather earlier in the day, but Lilian was out. Knowing her, she was probably at the bank again – hopelessly pleading my ridiculous cause for the very last time: imploring hard and faceless men who would coldly and repeatedly explain that the matter was out of their hands. So I waited.

Waited until she got back to the flat – because naturally it was absolutely imperative that she had to be there throughout: I couldn't have chanced upon her getting back in and . . . discovering me lying on the bedroom floor. She might have been delayed, you see – who knows what might have happened? And if that was the case, well – she might be too late: I could be dead. Her face said everything: the last-ditch mission had been fruitless – as, of course, it had to be. I opened a bottle of champagne. 'What are we celebrating?' she asked me. 'Is there anything to celebrate, David?' And I said no, not really – but let's just enjoy the fizz, shall we? 'It's nice,' she said. 'Is it the Cava we got that time?' No, I said – it's Prosecco, actually: I saw it in Sainsbury's. 'Well,' she said, 'it's very nice, whatever it is.' Isn't she sweet . . .? Isn't she just lovely . . .? I wasn't tasting it. I'd just come back from the bathroom where I'd swallowed nine tablets, and my stomach already was in chaos. I had calculated, going by the dosage prescribed, that nine would be right, that nine was the right number: nine would make me very ill – I'd pass out, obviously, though I'd be sure to be clutching the little orange container tight in my fist so that Lilian would be able to pass it to the ambulance people, and then the hospital on my arrival would be fully aware of exactly what I'd taken.

Awful. Isn't it? That I should think like that. As I began to convulse, my swollen eyes were concentrated upon this appalled amazement, fright and anguish in Lilian's own, before they just shut down completely. It's the last thing I remember, at the flat. Poor Lilian. Oh Christ. What sort of a man am I? To think like this. To calmly execute so terrible a thing. Oh dear God. And he's right, my father. Well of course he's right – he always is: you only have to ask him, and he'll tell you. In fact, you don't even have to ask: he'll tell you anyway. But he's got my number, that's for sure: he can see right through me – I think, in terms of my father, I must be the original open book. He doesn't ever come right out and say I'm worthless, but that is the gist of his every word and gesture. And I am worthless – how can you argue with it? I'm not good at things. I fail to bring anyone happiness, and particularly me. All I am is in the way. Yes – and I'm not even brave enough to remove myself: I just have created another whole area of chaos and pain, leaving the few who care to deal with it. No courage to live like a man . . . and far too chicken even to die. My God, it's just as well I never married, had children. Can you imagine all that I would have brought to that particular party . . .? Anger, disappointment . . . resentment and failure. And . . . if I'd had a son like me, I would despise him most utterly. Mostly for being like me. I would behave towards him exactly the way my father does – which is what I've always wanted, actually: to behave like him. But I can't. I've tried – not for a long while, obviously, but I used to try all the time, when I was younger: to behave like him. But it's just not in me. Anna – she's got it, she can do it . . . yes, and she knows it too. That's why he loves her so much. Why wouldn't he? She's wonderful. That's why he's always urging her to come into the business – I know he wants her to run it eventually, and God, she'd do it bloody well. He's never said that to me – never invited me into the business, and who can blame him? Christ – I've never got a business of my own off the ground, have I? As he never stops telling me, as if I bloody need reminding. So Jesus: put a rich, successful and highly prestigious company into my two hands, and well look – be honest: how long do you think it would take . . .? It would be no time at all before I simply reduced it to smithereens – rags and tatters scattered to the wind: shame and bankruptcy for everyone: lovely. I am so not my father. I suppose why I hate him. Certainly why he hates me. But it's all I ever wanted to be. Life would have been just so completely wonderful: all I had to be was like him.

In the ambulance . . . I was for a moment rather concerned: I truly did believe for a time that I had actually gone too far – that nine had not been the right number after all, that nine had been altogether too many. Barely conscious, of course, but beyond the screaming of the siren, I was aware of very concerted effort going on. A man in yellow was urgently doing things to me, no idea what . . . and I was quite beyond feeling. There was an air of alarm, though . . . and I remember thinking that I felt so weak that it wouldn't really be so very bad a thing . . . just gently and silently, to slip into death. Then I was terrified by the very idea. The ambulance was bucking about wildly – or maybe that was only my stomach. I could just about see that Lilian's hands were wrapped around mine, and I didn't feel a thing. I must then have gone out completely – yes, I must have lost consciousness after that, because the next thing I remember, there was a man in a room. Moustache. I was lying on a table, I think . . . and this man with a moustache in a room was shouting at me. To stay awake, maybe. Don't know. Possibly I just annoyed him. Something was in my throat – it hurt most terribly, and I was so, so thirsty. A clatter of metal things. This fantastically bright light that I closed my eyes to. And then . . . well then I was in this bed: that was the next thing I knew. Glancing idly at the pale mint-green ceiling a mile above my head, very aware of either pain or numbness just about everywhere. My throat was still in a bad way. Bones were aching. I felt pregnant – yes, and also disembowelled. A Venetian blind, creamish, somewhere over there, plastic jug much nearer, a picture on the wall: dawn scene, or maybe sunset . . . and Lilian. Of course, there was Lilian . . . and still she sits beside me. What on earth am I to make of this woman . . .? I have always found it . . . so perplexing. Why does she love me? So fastidious in most things, so very acute and capable and really quite discerning . . . and yet this huge and inexplicable lapse in taste. Why does she love me? Why does she love . . . *me*? And there is more, you know. The love she gives, that palpable glimmer is for her just simply unstoppable – but that is merely the seepage, the trickled overflow from a walled-up vat that she just is incapable of completely damming up. I know though that if ever I gave her the slightest sign – if I brought myself to a little bit reciprocate, or even encourage . . . well then she would give out the greatest sigh of stupendous relief at finally being able to flood us both with the full and tremendous love that she has been dutifully harbouring for all these years. Yes . . . and while seeing all this perfectly clearly, still I could never understand it. But . . . I am going to try, I am now going to try . . . to give her a reason to love me: to make myself even a little bit worthy of receiving it.

Because this entire charade, this appalling attempt at 'suicide' . . . although a thoroughly shameful thing, of course it is, still it was always intended to be rather more than merely a stunt. An attention-seeker. More than the temporary deferral of all that I have been so paralytically scared to stand up to. And certainly here was nothing so mawkish as 'a cry for help', or whatever they say: I deserve no help . . . and none is forthcoming, that much has recently been made extremely clear. So I am going to give in. Finally. This will not just make my father's day, but everyone else's as well: I am going to give everybody a break, and that includes me: my God, we all deserve it. This way, it will be so much easier: people will put down my change of heart, a new direction, the seeing of wisdom . . . they will put them all down to this watershed moment, this pivot – catharsis, is it, of having come within a hair's-breadth of extinction. A sham again, you see – but it will serve, it will serve very well. I am going to abandon my so-called company, just as all those in the past have so regularly and predictably abandoned me, and never will I even think of starting up another. There will be no more Big Ideas: all that is done. It must die a natural death – it is the kind thing to do. Salvage all I can, of course – there won't be much, but something. Come to some sort of feasible arrangement about the remaining considerable debt. Get a job – that's the next stage. Can I get a job . . .? What can I actually do? What is my proven track record, apart from buggering things up? Lilian says I can: Lilian, she says that any corporation on the planet would be lucky to have me . . . yes, but that's just Lilian, isn't it? When she says things like that, what she means is Oh David, I love you so very desperately and passionately and I yearn for us to be together and I am not allowed to say so, so I am telling you this instead. I understand that – have known it for ages. Lilian could, of course – she could get a very good job indeed . . . and maybe, initially, that's what we might have to settle for. I say 'we' because, well . . . I am, I am going to be with her properly now. Lilian, let's face it . . . she's the best thing in my life. She's more than that . . . she's . . . all I've got. And I know, I am cruelly aware that I can't offer her much, but she's more than welcome to all there is. Because up till now, well . . . I've never given her anything, have I? Even just earlier, I didn't even let her enjoy that Prosecco, did I? And she said it was nice. Didn't she? She probably dropped her glass on the floor when she saw me writhing, and then had to dash to dial 999. Nine being . . . the right number. This silence all around me . . . is lovely. Now that Mum isn't crying any more . . . poor old Mum, I wish she could have had a far better son than me: she did so deserve it: all she ever did was stand up for me, and I'm not really sure she should even have bothered. And I continue to very deeply appreciate this silence. I feel . . . I feel, actually, what I haven't felt in a very long time – seems like for ever: that it is really very good . . . to be alive. And so now . . . in this room, all that I have in here is peace, and Lilian – I can feel her now, holding my hand so terribly tightly. My closed eyes are hot, and the beginnings of tears are oozing through them.

'So, Lilian . . . how's the patient? Same? I brought you some coffee – expect you could do with it. Not sure how you take it, though – white all right?'

'Oh thank you, Anna – white's fine, thanks so much. Yes – he's still asleep. Hasn't moved. Hasn't made a single sound. I hope that's a good thing . . .'

'I'm sure it is. Doctor not been back, then?'

'Haven't seen him.'

'No well – okay. I expect he will be soon – lots of people to see to, I suppose. So, Mum – what do you want to do? It looks like he's going to be out of it till the morning, now. No point in staying, is there really? Sorry, Daddy – I thought he might be awake by this time . . .'

'No no. No harm done. He . . . looks all right, doesn't he? Not too bad. All things considered. Bit pale, maybe. Never would know anything had happened really, would you? Not to look at him. Well . . . I agree with you, Anna: no point hanging about, is there? You'll tell him, won't you? What I said earlier. You'll tell him when he wakes up, yes? Or maybe just say it to Lilian – hello Lilian, by the way. Hell of a time, ay? Well you've done awfully well, I must say. Very well done indeed. I was just saying downstairs – wasn't I, Anna? You mustn't feel too badly, you know – you mustn't blame yourself, or anything – because I really don't think that David can actually have meant to, well . . . you know: do away with himself. Just a bit depressed, that's all. Cry for help – isn't that what they call it? Oh yes and talking of that – Anna, she'll let you know all about it, won't you Anna? And then you can pass it on to David, all right? And if they try to bung him on a public ward, you'll have to put your foot down. Don't let them dictate to you, all right? I don't suppose for a minute that David's got BUPA or anything, but it doesn't matter – just tell them we'll go private. Get them to send me all the bumf, and I'll see to it. Jolly good. Right – I'll be off, then.'

'Daddy . . .! I just can't believe you said that . . .! Of course she won't be "blaming herself" . . .! Why on earth would she do *that* . . .? Don't take any notice, Lilian. Of course it's absolutely nothing to do with you, all of this – quite the reverse. We do all know that, and I'm sure that you do too. Heavens, if it hadn't been for you . . . well. Honestly, Daddy – what a thing to say . . .!'

'Oh . . . so sorry. I didn't mean, um . . .'

'No well, okay. So anyway, Daddy – either way I'll see he gets the message. I'm sure it'll make him feel, oh – just so much better. It's good news, Lilian – I'll tell you in a minute. So, Mum – what do you think?'

'I think I'll go back to the hotel. Might as well – paid for it, haven't I? Are you coming, Anna?'

'Uh-oh . . . what's that I hear . . .? Anyone else hear that? Yes – I thought it was about time. It's Troy – do you hear him? Well now you can – you can hear him now. But he's been awfully good, hasn't he? Sleeping all this time. Well yes okay then, Mum. I'll fetch Troy, and we'll all drive back there, shall we? As you say – might as well. And I don't know about any of you, but I could actually do with something to eat now. I know I've just had a couple of biscuits, but I'm suddenly absolutely starving. And Lilian . . .? You, um . . .?'

'Yes yes. I'll stay. I'll phone you in the morning, shall I?'

'Oh please. And Daddy? What about you? You be all right?'

'Well of course I'll be all right. Going home, aren't I? And that's where you should all be too. All this bloody "hotel" nonsense . . . I just can't understand it.'

No, Daddy: I think you made that very abundantly clear when we were all downstairs and talking just now, in that really very depressing cafeteria. I'd just suddenly thought that it would be a good thing, getting him and Mum together – grabbing the opportunity, really – and with me as a sort of a, I don't know . . . referee, or something. But I'm not sure it really did go that well. It seemed, I think . . . well, it was rather as if we were all of us talking about completely different things. And thinking about it now, of course . . . it was actually maybe the very worst time and the very worst place for the three of us to be talking at all . . . but look: this is how the day has panned out, isn't it? No one could have seen just any of this coming. David's trying to, Jesus – kill himself. I was running away from danger, Mum was running away from, oh . . . just everything, I'm getting the feeling . . . and Dad – well Dad, he was meeting a Beatle. And now here we are, sitting around a primrose-yellow Formica table in a starkly lit subterranean coffee place, very late at night, and in a hospital. It's nearly empty. The very bored girl behind the counter is stacking wrapped-up sugar cubes until they tumble over, and then immediately starting up again.

There's a policeman a few tables away, very much enjoying being cheeky to a terribly pretty young nurse, who is picking the blueberries out of a muffin, and rather seems to be loving the attention. The policeman, he breaks off occasionally from the rolling of his eyes and his muttered innuendos to shout across at a purple-faced drunk in the corner to keep the noise down. 'Don't make me come over there' is what he keeps on saying.

'Where have you been, Enid? I don't mean when you were here – but where were you before that? Where have you been all day? This coffee, you know – it's absolutely disgusting. How can they get away with calling this muck "coffee"? Hey? And why can't they serve it in proper cups . . .?'

'Oh, *George* . . .'

'It's not an unreasonable question. Is it, Anna? It's not an unreasonable question.'

'Well I don't *know*, George, why they can't serve it in proper cups . . .'

'No! Not that! Not *that* question – I mean the question about where the bloody hell have you *been*? And Anna, she said something about . . . what did you say, Anna? On the phone. Something about being booked into a *hotel* . . .? Is that right? Did I hear that right? I did? Well Jesus – what in Christ's name do you think you're doing in some bloody *hotel*, for God's sake . . .? Should be at home, where you belong. Can't understand what's got into you.'

'I think, Daddy, she just maybe felt she needed a break, that's all . . .'

'Break? Break from what? She does absolutely bugger all from morning till night.'

'Well . . . maybe a break from that, then.'

'Not a break . . .'

'What did you say, Enid? Not a break? Well what, then? Oh God *speak*, can't you? Why does every single syllable have to be ground out of you . . .'

'Oh Daddy – for God's sake . . .'

'No no, Anna – it's quite all right. I'm perfectly capable of handling this. Okay then, George. You want me to speak, well then I will. Yes: it maybe is about time. No – that's not right. It's overdue, of course it is. It's so long overdue, I just can't believe it. I should have spoken up – I should have done it, oh . . . just years ago. Years. Yes and that's my fault – oh yes, I know it's my fault. Staying silent for all this time. Don't know why I did – you just sort of get into the habit of it. Just sitting there and smiling. Nodding away. Well here it is, George: my leaving today – yesterday, whenever it was – it wasn't a break in the sense you meant it. But it was a break. A real break – a break in the proper meaning of the word. A . . . severance. Do you see? I have left you, George. Permanently. I am gone. All that we had . . . if it ever amounted to anything at all . . . well that, all that . . . it's now over. Is that plain enough for you, George? Have enough syllables been ground out of me yet? Or would you like me to tell you more? Exactly *why*, maybe . . .? I don't at all mind – know it by heart. But I warn you now: you won't like it, George. It will bruise your ego massively. I used to think it was an impregnable thing, that ridiculous ego of yours, but of course it isn't. It's actually extremely fragile. Because you're a man, aren't you? Yes – and so it's as flimsy as paper.'

Daddy . . . oh my God: he was simply thunderstricken. And Jesus – why wouldn't he be? I have never before in my life heard Mum come out with just anything at all like that – it was simply unreal! His eyes were bulbous . . . he was gripping the edge of the table, and he just went on staring at her – actually making me feel quite frightened. I thought I had to say something, because Daddy, he still seemed to be just utterly speechless – but I didn't know what. And then I did:

'What have you got there, Mum? I thought you'd used all those . . .'

'I thought so too, but I've found another one in my handbag. Not Bell's, this one – Glen . . . what does it say? Fiddich. Glenfiddich. I think that's rather better quality, don't you? Doesn't at all matter, of course – it's only booze. Isn't it? Helps everything along. Because your father's quite right, you know – this coffee, it's completely unspeakable.'

The policeman was calling over to the drunk again: 'Hoi! You! Keep it down. Don't make me come over there . . .'

'Well there you are. Doesn't know what she's saying. It's the drink talking, isn't it? Christ Almighty . . . I never thought I'd hear myself saying that again . . .! I honestly did believe that you were over it, Enid. I thought all this was done with. What can I say? I just don't know what to say. Jesus – you're an even bigger fool than I took you for . . .'

'Daddy . . . please . . .'

'Well it's true. She was clean. She was off it. She was *fine.* You remember, Anna – what it was like. How she was. So what do you want, Enid? To leave me, is that it? That what you're saying? To leave your home . . .? The house you've been living in for how many bloody years . . .? And then what? End up like that raving bloody derelict in the corner? Swigging Christ-knows-what in the park and then being carried in here every night and falling over in the bloody café . . .? Lying in a puddle of booze? Being shouted at by a . . . policeman? Yes? Is that the plan? Well that's very good. Very nice. Very nice indeed.'

I have no plan. I haven't been listening at all attentively to all of George's customary bombast, because I know every word by heart. But . . . I have no plan, I do know that. Plans are for young people – or at least people with choice and opportunity, those who are assured of some sort of a future. I have none of these. There will have been a time when I did, though I was hardly aware. My choice . . . my one and only choice was George. That's why I pursued him so brazenly. Extraordinary to think of it. Because the here and now, the present . . . it has become a chill and alien place that will never persuade me. I feel as if I have been just in the dark – so dreamlessly asleep for a very long time (longer, seemingly, than I have even been alive) and only just recently have I very gradually become aroused. It was not a refreshing sleep. I do not feel revivified. I awoke with the most terrible hangover . . . which I know, I suppose, is quite funny. Had to escape it. The furthest I could think was just to leave: I wasn't *going* anywhere . . . I was simply getting away. Got myself only as far as the Brent Cross Holiday Inn . . . and now all this has happened. I was just so delighted when Anna and Troy came over to see me. I really did think – it really did look as if all of us were set to enjoy, oh . . . such a very jolly time, for just one evening, at least. But even that was not to be. God would appear to have decided that I hardly deserve it – and I know Him, God, for we commune. We go way back. He is both equable and consistent: He robbeth with one hand, and taketh away with the other.

And then when I heard what David had done . . .! The tremble and passion of Lilian's voice – it infected me horribly. Whenever your child is hurt or in danger, you feel it quite viscerally, I think. If you are a parent, you just do. Any mother, anyway. But if that child has become so very wretched – hating to such a degree the life you have given him as to so desperately wish it away . . . well that is the sort of anguish from which it is not right that you should ever recover. I suppose . . . I used always to complacently believe that I had been what they call a 'good mother', without ever actively seeking to define the term. But apparently not. Oh well – it doesn't matter. Bad wife . . . bad mother . . . whatever it is, whoever I am now . . . soon it will all be over: a peace of sorts. It is better, really it is much, much better that I am so terribly ill, and not just sick at heart. When the prognosis came – wholly anticipated by me, never thinking that between the chances of good or bad news it could ever be the former – I was utterly relieved, and even quietly gratified. There are, he said to me – this bogusly upbeat specialist to whom I had been ultimately referred – certain treatments. I told him that I was sure there were, because there always are, for whatever it is that ails you. Treatments, of course, being easily distinguishable from cures. Some, he said, are less invasive than others: prospects of efficacy and remission, well these too vary. I rushed to assure him that neither of us need dread to be embroiled in discussion nor selection, because whatever angry violence it is that seems so suddenly eager to eat me up from within, will be permitted to continue its aggressive course. I had come here, I explained, for simple confirmation, with no thought at all of evasion. Goodness, you just should have seen his face: it was as if he had been rescued – practically panting with relief – and so I was pleased at least to have alleviated the lowering monotony of his daily round. And then I thought, well all right then . . . what life I have left, I would rather like to keep to myself. Do what I like, and when I choose – alone, or otherwise, according to my mood. Strange, but also extraordinarily uplifting to be thinking like that – I never have before. It actually brings me close to exhilaration. The pleasure I have taken in drinking again is immeasurable – for I have been doing that, of course, for quite some time now: more or less since I started feeling not quite right. No one noticed because no one was watching. It makes me happy, if happy is quite what I mean. It's not happy – happy isn't at all the word, but I'm going to use it anyway, because well . . . why shouldn't I? So it makes me as happy, anyway, as anything ever did. With drinking – it is instinctive to me, this – the trick is not ever to quite stop: to maintain the highly sensitive equilibrium – never to spin away wildly, nor irredeemably implode. And it's positively bad for me, which is a sort of delight in itself – because now, well . . . what isn't? The doctor assured me that it would significantly hasten the process, while admitting that this mysterious 'process' already seemed to be in something of a tearing hurry. So at least things are clear. I have no plan.

'Mum . . . you okay . . .?'

'Oh yes. I was thinking, that's all. How has she managed it, I've just been wondering. Lilian, I mean. It's really quite a mystery.'

'What – sticking with David, do you mean?'

'No, George – that's not what I mean at all. It is very easy, actually, to "stick" with David, as you put it. He's a good boy . . . he's a lovely boy, as you'd know if you ever had bothered to get to know him. No – I've just been amazed by how she never seems to need to go to the loo. She's been sitting there eternally. Hasn't once left that room, even for a minute.'

'She does . . . care for him very much.'

'Oh she *does*, Anna – she really does. I hope he comes to see it. He's going to need her. Well – he does already, of course.'

'So why did he *do* this, then? Do you *know*, Enid?'

'I don't. I simply don't. Just can't imagine. Too awful.'

'Well, Daddy . . . you do know he did have problems . . .'

'That's just money. Money's nothing.'

'Wait a minute, George – just wait one minute. Are you saying, Anna, that David might have done this terrible thing because he, what . . . was in *debt*, or something . . .? Is *that* all . . .? Oh *surely* not . . . he couldn't be so *foolish* . . .!'

'Don't you believe it. He's not like Anna, you know.'

'Well did he come to you, George? Did he ask for your help? Why didn't you . . . *offer* it . . .? Why did he have to *come* to you at all . . .?'

'He might have mentioned something about, I don't know . . . owing the bank a few quid, I don't know . . .'

'"A few quid" . . .?'

'Well – quite a lot, actually. But Christ – nothing to *kill* yourself over . . .! I didn't know what to do. It's not easy, you know. You understand, don't you, Anna? I mean – I've bailed him out before. How many times have I bailed him out before? Didn't ever do a blind bit of good. Just went on gallivanting after just another, yet one bloody more of his crackpot schemes. You have to remember, Enid – he's not a *baby* any more. What should I have done? What do you think I should have said, then?'

'You should have said yes, George. *Yes*.'

'Well . . . okay then. I will. If you like, if that's what you want. You can tell him, Anna, will you? When he wakes up, tell him I'll sub him. Pay off the bank. And anything else. Do whatever he wants. All right? Everybody happy?'

So that's where we more or less left it. Mum said we ought to be getting back to see how David is, and I'd been thinking the same thing. I was pleased with Daddy, though – quite proud of him. He was finally going to help David – and yes I know he had been pretty much backed into a corner, but still.

And by finding that bloody 'husband' of mine, oh goodness – he'd helped me, Jesus, more than he would ever know: saved my life. I'm going to ring and tell them tonight: decided that already. Tell them where he is, the bastard – and then they can do what they like with him, and leave me and Troy alone: oh God, what heaven. So . . . we've left the hospital now. Daddy had another last attempt to get Mum, as he put it, to just stop being so bloody stupid and come home with him, for Christ's sake . . . and she actually laughed when he said it. So now I'm driving the three of us back to the Holiday Inn: Troy, he's so full of beans after all that sleeping . . . I don't think I'll ever get him back down now. It's so very late . . . the streets are practically empty. David was still asleep, when we left him. I think he'll be okay, though – hope so, anyway. And Lilian . . . still she was just sitting in the chair, and looking at him in that way she does. No idea if she ever did go and use the loo. I wonder what will happen now? Between them. Well – their affair, I suppose. I'm hungry now – really hungry. I wonder if the hotel's still doing hot stuff . . .? Wouldn't mind a burger, or something. And I think I'm tired, not really sure any more. I must be. I certainly ought to be, anyway . . . because all round, it really has been, as Daddy would love to call it, a bit of a hard day's night.

* * *

You just never know what's going to happen next. Cliché, oh yes, I am well aware – and a godsend too, I am increasingly convinced of that. Because I'm finding more and more as I get older that the motivation even to get out of bed in the morning . . . it's steadily diminishing, one just has to be honest about it. Do I hurl off the bedclothes, my eyes alight with delight at the breaking of a brand-new dawn? Am I the walking embodiment of a sparkling and muscular youth for whom the early morning knows no greater joy than Corn Flakes, berries, smoothies and yogurt – hysterically consumed from blue-and-white striped crockery in a sunlit yellow gingham kitchen? Mm . . . I rather think not. But to actually know for sure and in advance all that was truly going to happen that day, oh my Lord . . . that would be the tin lid, the absolute finish: you'd just pull the blankets back up over your head, and stay there for ever. Might even regress to habitual thumb-sucking, for comfort. As it is, there remains the solace of a solid routine – *Times* crossword, good strong coffee, evacuation of the bowels on a good day . . . with just maybe still the very faintest lingering glimmer of anticipation – most of it habit, hope and a stubbornly inbuilt optimism rather than any sort of genuine expectation. But still one feels that some small smidgen of encouragement could possibly be in the offing . . . something nice might arrive in the post, say – although I hardly receive any actual post, these days. Bills, of course. The very occasional Premium Bond win of twenty-five quid: God knows how many thousands of these bonds I've still got stashed away somewhere, and yet I never win more than the bloody twenty-five quid. Used to be a fifty-quid minimum, so I scooped a couple of them: now, the minimum, it's down to twenty-five quid, so that's what I get. Two people score a million every week, is what they tell you – yeh well, but not me matey: me, I get twenty-five quid. And then there are all the plastic-wrapped catalogues full of step-in baths and collapsible walking sticks with rubber ferrules and booster cushions and back scratchers and grab handles, whatever grab handles are. It's the internet, isn't it? Some robot god, he knows all about you: every click on Google or Amazon has been scrupulously logged over years by the android equivalent of Saint Peter. And so when you hit a certain age, I suppose, your 'personal' details, ho bloody ho, are released to any set-up willing to pay good money for them, whereupon this unstoppable inundation of 'old man' merchandising begins. Easi-stretch shoes and trouser-band expanders. Nose-hair clippers. Tablets to restore your 'potency', Christ help me – and further tablets of a different shape and colour to encourage your prostate into, if not submission, then at least a pending clemency. Dear God: as if it wasn't bad enough, the ageing process, without this eternal tolling of the bell. But . . . it is better than the alternative, I suppose, as has so often been said. Which of course I have been thinking quite a lot about, since . . . well: since it happened. Was it quick? Was it sudden? Don't know. It was more that it didn't really take too long.

I hadn't thought she really did mean it, Enid. About leaving me, I mean. Thought it was just a mood – while privately conceding, of course, that she had never before actually seemed to have them, moods. At first – despite all of Anna's good counsel – I had found myself in hectoring mode, as how many times before? God's *sake*, I was raving at her – be *sensible*, can't you? What's *wrong* with you, woman? I mean, apart from anything else – don't you think you are a little *old* for all this nonsense? And another thing – where are you going to go? Thought about that? Just going to go and sit on a bench somewhere, are you? Regent's Park. Feeding the ducks – that it? Or maybe you're expecting me to, I don't know – buy you a house, or something. Is that it? Is that the plan, Enid? Well . . . I'm not saying I can't afford to – you know I can afford to, Enid, but what a stupid thing that would be! I mean – you've got a house, haven't you? Our house – the house we live in. It's enormous. Big enough for six. So why do you want to *leave* it, hey? I mean – is there something you don't like about it? Because you've never said so. We can get the decorators in, if you like. Or no – what do they call them? Interior designers, yes that's it. Do you want that, Enid? A whole new look, maybe. Yes? Nice idea? New furniture. Different colours. Yes? Yes, Enid . . .? Well no, apparently: I was, she told me, missing the point. As usual.

'Well what is the point then, Enid? You tell me what the point is.'

'Oh, *George* . . .'

'No no – that's no good. That's no good at all. You do this – you always do this. Whenever I put something to you directly, you just do that sighing thing – it drives me mental. Look: you're telling me I've got it wrong – that I don't understand. I'm missing the, bloody hell – *point*. Well okay, then – I'm asking you, aren't I? To explain it to me. And all you say to me is "Oh *George* . . ." In that pitying voice – like you always do. Well it's not good enough. Is it, Enid? It's just not good enough – not good enough at all. So just *tell* me, for Christ's sake. Just tell me what you *mean* . . .'

'Well I will, then. Might I have another drink?'

We were in a bar, sort of a glorified pub somewhere quite local, because she wouldn't come home. Even just to talk, she wouldn't come home.

'Another one? Jesus Christ. That's be three. I'm still on my first, here . . .'

'May I please have another drink, George? Or shall I get my own? I really don't mind.'

'Okay – yes fine. I'll get it in a minute. You can last out for a minute, can you Enid? Christ Almighty – I never thought I'd see this again. You – back on the booze.'

'So you keep on saying.'

'Well, tell me, then. Go on. Just tell me. And then I'll get you your drink.'

'It's really very simple. There's no mystery about it. There's no great . . . *scheme*, George. I have no plan. All I want . . . all it is, is that I simply want to be elsewhere. I do not hate our house, don't want anything done to it, of course I don't – I actually rather love it, and exactly the way it is. So many memories – and I'll be needing those, I do know that. It's not even you, George – although I'll hardly miss being around you all the time: you're not the best of company, are you? No no – don't you start interrupting me now: you wanted me to speak, and so I'm telling you. I just want to be . . . I *need* to be, really . . . somewhere else. Not quite sure where yet – but it doesn't really matter where, you see: just not here. That's all. And no, I don't want you to buy me a house – or anything else, actually. That's for certain. Don't want anything further from you, George. You've been extremely generous to me in the past, which I'm very grateful for – I hope you do know that. I have plenty of money – easily enough to do anything I want to, as you're aware. Because all that cash that you've been banking for me over all the years, well . . . it's just been lying there – haven't touched it, not for ages. Can't remember the last time I bought any clothes . . . and apart from the hairdresser and a little bit of make-up, well . . . I never really spent anything, did I? So . . . I want to go away. I just simply want to go somewhere – to see what happens, really. It might sound selfish – well it will sound selfish, because that's exactly what it is: it's thoroughly selfish, of course it is, no disguising it. But is that really so terribly bad? After all this time, all these years, to want something that is just for me? I don't see it as a sin. It's not a *crime*, George. It just excludes you, that's all. That's what you can't stand. And it's funny, really – because you don't actually want to be with me, do you, George? I mean – you want to be attended to, you can't bear the thought of being inconvenienced in any little way . . . but anyone could do that for you, couldn't they, George? Anna, for instance: I'm sure she'd love to. So it's not me you want, is it? You have to be honest. All these things you are offering me to stay . . . and yet you don't actually want me to be there. That is rather funny. Don't you think?'

I said nothing to that. She'd hit a nerve. Because everything she'd just said there, it was exactly true. I'd thought it myself, and I couldn't explain it.

'I might, I don't know . . . go on a cruise, or something. Never done that. We talked about it once – do you remember, George? Years ago, now. Children were still at school, I think. Mediterranean, it could have been. I think that's what we'd been discussing. But we never did go through with it, can't imagine why. Probably something came up at your work – because it often did, didn't it? Lots of absolutely necessary overnight stays. Lots and lots of them. So yes – that might be nice, a cruise. I've heard they can be awfully good fun. Yes – I might quite seriously think about that. So there. Have I said enough, George? May I please be allowed to have my drink now?'

So I got her a Scotch – and another of whatever I'd been drinking, can't even remember: didn't want it anyway. And while I was idling at the bar waiting for change, I was . . . what was I doing, actually? Turning things over in my mind, I suppose you could call it: tiptoeing through such unfamiliar territory. And what I thought was, well . . . it's right, what she's saying. Isn't it? You can't really fault it. Ah yes, but here's the nub: it's not what I want. At least I think it's not what I want – not too sure: it might be exactly what I want, I just can't think any more. But whichever way you look at it . . . it's different – that's what you can't get round. Her not being at home, it would make a difference to my routine. I'm not saying I would be desolate – because there are many times, I'm sure, when I wouldn't even notice. Her not being there, I mean. But change . . . I'm not really very keen on alterations of any sort, really, no matter what form they might take. Not that I actually thought she'd be gone for long. I mean – I knew she'd be back, of course she'd be back. Once she'd got all of this childish nonsense out of her system, once she'd sampled the reality, well . . . she'd see it for the lunacy it is, and quickly scuttle back to me. Well okay – but that still left the interim to be dealt with, didn't it? And I'm not quite sure how I'll be able to cope with that . . . so I thought I've just got to talk to Anna about this. Anna, she'll be able to, I don't know . . . sort it out. Or at least make it all appear *reasonable*: explain it to me – which is more than Enid seems capable of. So I did that the very next day – would have done it sooner, but in those days Anna still hadn't come back to the house to live. She's been here quite a while now, good few weeks, and I love that, of course I do. She and Troy have the whole of the top floor, as well as the run of the place – but there are these two garages at the end of the garden, just been sitting there for ever, and I had this idea to get rid of them and build a rather nice little sort of two-storey coach house, for want of a better term. So that she can be completely self-contained, but also close at hand: best of both worlds, I'd say. I'm waiting for planning permission – architect says he's spoken to the council, and it shouldn't be a problem. So what with having Anna upstairs, and her now being a big part of the business, well – I see her every day. She took to it immediately – I always knew she would: how many times did I tell her? The job, it was made for her. These days, I just have to pop in from time to time, show my face, sort of thing. She handles everything, really – and then at home in the evening, we talk about it all over dinner . . . which is something I've never been able to do before, because in all the years I was building up and singlehandedly running the company, Enid, she just didn't want to know a thing about it. 'Your department' is all she said. 'I take care of the house, you attend to the business: that's the arrangement, isn't it?' Which was fair enough, I suppose – it was the arrangement – but still it did irk me from time to time. She's rather a good cook, Anna, which is something I never knew: not too surprising – she's very adept at most things. All this, though – all this happened a fair time later: I'm talking now about the morning after I'd had that drink with Enid in the wine bar.

'So the latest thing, Anna, is that she's talking about a *cruise* . . .!'

'I know. She told me.'

'The most ridiculous idea. I mean – all on her own? Where's the fun in that?'

'Well you're meant to meet new people, aren't you? On a cruise.'

Here was a new thought. How do I feel about that one, then? Enid – meeting new people. On a cruise. Well I just can't say. I just can't conceive of it. As far as I know, the only person Enid has ever known is me. And of course one has to remember this: by definition, I have never seen her when she is on her own. So how might she behave? When she is on her own. Meeting new people . . . on a cruise. Simply can't imagine it. And here's another thing – can't really be ducked, can it? I mean to say . . . might some man, I don't know . . . find her *attractive*, or something? Some damned gigolo. Well – she's quite personable, it's fair to say. For her age. Keeps herself tidy. Christ – I don't know. I really can't project: she's just Enid. That's all.

'David thinks it's a wonderful idea.'

'David? What does he know about anything?'

'He's doing very well, Daddy. Since you ask. Completely recovered.'

'Is he? Oh good. Living on Lilian's earnings, I understand.'

'Only for now. He's doing several interviews a week.'

'Yes well, good luck with that. It didn't take her long to get sorted though, did it? Lilian. She got a damn good job more or less the following day, is the way I understand it. She's a very sound woman.'

'She adores him.'

'Yes. Extraordinary. But listen, Anna – to get back to your mother. I mean – this cruise nonsense, yes? You think she'll go through with it?'

'She *has* gone through with it, Daddy. It's all booked. She got a cancellation.'

'What? But that's impossible – she only said it yesterday. I was sitting in front of her when the bloody idea just drifted into her head . . .'

'Well there you are. New-look Mum.'

'Well . . . where's she going, then? Mediterranean, is it?'

'Everywhere.'

'What do you mean, "everywhere" . . .?'

'World cruise, Daddy. Sounds like everywhere to me. She's off in a few days.'

Yes – and when Mum told me that, I don't think I'd ever

seen her looking so . . . well, I was going to say 'happy', but it's not that, exactly. More . . . serene. Anxiety, her horribly trusty companion, it appeared to have left her. She really did seem to have latched on to a peace, of sorts. She spent the few days before she was due to leave frantically buying clothes – and she hadn't done that in ages: didn't even know what shops to go to. Tell me, Anna, she kept on saying – what on earth are women expected to *wear* on these cruises? And so I helped her get together a decent assortment of everyday deck clothes (because she had absolutely nothing like that) and a few rather glitzy things for the evenings. You should have seen her face – just the look and feel of them you know, I really do think she found it rather exciting. Poor old Mum – she'd never done anything like this before: quite a new awakening. And remember, I told her, they have loads of on-board shops as well, and you'll be stopping off at all these amazing places, so you'll never be short of things: gosh I envy you – and I really do hope you have the most wonderful time, Mum – and don't worry about Daddy, will you? I'll see he's all right. Yes, she said – I'm sure you will. I never really know why she has to say things like that, or even quite what she's getting at. Well . . . I suppose I do, really.

So . . . that's Mum. David . . . well David has done surprisingly well, really. Didn't go to pieces – mainly thanks to Lilian, of course. Paying off all his debts, with a little help from Daddy. Well – quite a lot of help, actually. He says he's going to pay him back, but . . . well, I don't think Daddy's holding his breath. Got rid of that poky little office – and he and Lilian, they're looking for a nicer flat, which shouldn't be remotely difficult. Do you know, I think they might even end up getting married – if David could ever screw himself up to the commitment. It's all Lilian has ever wanted, I'm completely sure of that: maybe she should just get down on one knee – propose, and be done with it: she takes charge of everything else, so why not?

Okay then – so that just leaves me and Troy: what about us? Well, it was quite a question, and I thought about it a lot . . . all the time more or less knowing what I was going to decide. But God – at the beginning, it just felt so absolutely wonderful to be free from the threat of *danger*. The thought that at any moment something could have happened to Troy . . . oh God, it got so I couldn't even sleep at night. So . . . with the information that Daddy had given me, I rang the number. It was the same man – Stanley, the same man who had come round to the flat – and he answered instantly. He said, I'm very glad to hear that, missy: there is people what will be very pleased to know the whereabouts of this gentleman. And I tell you something else, my girl – you only just done it in time. Jesus . . . I didn't at all know what he meant by that, but when I put the phone down I was shivering all over. So that was the end of my brush with the underworld. I still think it's my fault, though – for marrying the bastard in the first place. I was stupid in those days – I so much wanted to be seen to be my own woman, and Daddy's disapproval, of course, that went a very long way. And then I so did love to show him all the beautiful and expensive things my handsome husband had bought for me, while never asking a single question about where any of it might have come from. He took it all with him, of course, the jewellery. That went. Even stole from me my solitaire engagement ring – which I never actually wore because it was just so showy. Left me with the wedding ring on my finger – which not long ago I actually threw away. I was in the park with Troy, and I just flung it as far as I could. And now . . . he could be dead. Max, my husband. Sounds so strange – even saying that. Probably is. If he didn't actually have the diamonds, the money, whatever it was he was supposed to have run away with . . . well then he'll be dead. And maybe even if he did have it. Yes, that's likely – either way, it's very likely. Well – I still don't care. It's Troy and me, now: that is my only concern.

At first we were just staying with Daddy because I had nowhere else I could go. And what with Mum away, it seemed a fairly obvious thing to do. He gave us the whole of the top floor, which is huge – and I said well that's very kind of you, Daddy, but you do know that this arrangement, it's only just for now, yes? Just for the time being – yes? Of course, Anna, he said – of course. I don't think he believed it. Not sure I did either. And then I started going in to work with him once or twice, after I'd dropped off Troy at the nursery. His suggestion: keep me company, he said. It's funny, my relationship in the past with the family business – I've always loved it, but never wanted to get too close. And now I was wondering why: it's absolutely amazing, and the quality of the product – oh, it thrills me. Daddy, he's really done so very brilliantly. He made me the proposition around the time he got the idea to build a house at the end of the garden. Our own little house, just for us . . .! This appealed to me enormously – apart yet together, if you know what I mean. I think that also he was thinking he actually wanted to preserve the main house exactly as it was for when his wife recovered from her fleeting madness and came rushing back to him, in a flurry of apology. He really did believe, I think, that this was going to happen. I knew she would never do that, not now – and I also knew that I was never going to tell him so. Soon – because it really did happen astonishingly quickly – I found myself pretty much running the business: it came to me so easily, and I was loving every single moment. Daddy, he had eased very well into the role of a sort of consultant, I suppose – quite literally the father figure. Yes . . . so that's the way things were. And then . . . well then we got the, oh . . . just unbelievable news.

I've thought about it so much since – about the actual moment when I heard. And still I try to remember quite how it had hit me – what my very first reaction had been. Disbelief, I think – that's the usual thing, isn't it? When you are told a terrible fact, something which you absolutely do not want to know . . . well then you are going to say, 'What . . .? *No* . . .! I don't believe it . . .!' So yes, that's the sort of thing I think I must have been going through initially. And then what I felt was, well . . . really rather injured, I am slightly ashamed to admit: because she had not told me, you see. Confided in me. Even so much as hinted at it. Because once the news of the death of my mother had fully and finally penetrated . . . well then I had assumed, I suppose, that poor dear Mum, she had been the . . . what do they call it? In these circumstances. The unwitting victim, that's it – the unwitting victim of some or other awful accident, or even an unspeakable crime. But as I read further into the actually quite cursory email that had pinged up so wholly innocently from the shipping company, I got the feeling that whoever had composed it was assuming that I would of course be dismayed, but hardly surprised by all that he was telling me. Because the cancer, apparently, had been everywhere. She was riddled – virtually every vital organ. It certainly explained why she had taken up drinking again, which at the time had totally amazed me. She did always enjoy it, of course, even while it was doing her and her family such terrible harm . . . but now, I suppose she must have been thinking, what further harm could it possibly do? I wondered then if this terrible illness had actually been the true reason she had gone away in the first place, and so very suddenly – to spare her having to say it, and us to hear. But I don't think so: I think she went because she wanted to go – just like she said. She wanted to be elsewhere – and I suppose had simply hoped against hope that even with a terminal disease in so very advanced a state, still she might just make it to the end of a three-and-a-half-month cruise. But . . . she didn't. It was sudden, they said – and then what they always say: very quick, no pain. She died in Rio.

Daddy had been with me at home when I heard – Troy was asleep in his bed and I had been idly wondering what I should prepare myself for dinner, because Daddy was due to spend the evening with one of his friends, Georgie I think he said, from this assortment of gentlemen's clubs he's taken to going to lately, not quite sure what any of them is called. He had actually just gone out to the hall cupboard to fetch his coat and hat, so I had to quite quickly decide what to do. The state I was in – which I hadn't yet come close to defining – was not, I thought, compatible with sympathetic expression of any sort at all . . . so I simply touched his shoulder, asked him to sit down, and silently passed over to him the tablet. He looked up at me with enquiry in his eyes – and I must have appeared, I don't know . . . I can't actually imagine how I must have appeared, slightly wild, I suppose . . . but immediately he became quite utterly solemn. My heart, it suffered a convulsion as I watched him now concentrate on the words. It was only then that I was aware of the first hot tears rolling away from my screwed-up eyes, and down my cheeks – which felt just crimson, and so terribly swollen: I did not even know who I was crying for. I continued to study the almost abstract immobility of the top of my Daddy's head – still only a very little pinkness glinting among all that thick grey hair – and I was trying so hard to remain quite perfectly still, and to make no noise. It seemed as if I had been standing there for ever – but however long it was, there had certainly been more than enough time for him to have read this terrible message – yes, and several times over. So then I just whispered to him . . .

'Oh . . . *Daddy* . . .!'

And still he did not move. He just continued to sit there, staring at the screen. Then he quickly stood up, the sudden bark of the chair on the floor quite startling me – and that just fleeting sight of his milky eyes before he turned them away from me . . . oh, it hurt me so dreadfully. He snapped on a smile that had nothing at all to do with amusement, nodded once in a rather distracted sort of a way, and then he quite abruptly walked back out into the hall.

'Where are you . . .? What are you doing, Daddy . . .?'

'Out. Going out. You knew I was going out. I told you.'

'Yes – yes I know, but . . .!'

'I shouldn't be back too late. No. I shouldn't be back too late. Goodbye, Anna. Goodnight.'

And, my dear, dear child . . . I know you want more from me, I am so very vitally aware that now, and maybe more than ever, you very much need what a father must be – but all that you are quite desperate to be given . . . well, I just haven't got it, you see. It's not in me. At this very moment when I see with pain that you are shocked and yearning . . . I have to implore you, Anna, to try to find the kindness to forgive me . . . because this time, well – I just don't have anything for you: it simply isn't there.

In the taxi, I am trying to think straight. I do not want this upset. I do not welcome another alteration. I thought I knew how I would be feeling this evening – I've been rehearsing exactly how I needed to feel – yes but now . . . well now I am feeling quite different, so that's going to need a bit of work. But still I'm going to go through with it all: everything is going to happen just the way Georgie and I have planned it – yes, and it's going to be wonderful, absolutely fantastic, and not before time. There are things . . . important things to be considered, of course – but not now. I shall designate a time for it – sit down properly and work it all out: but it just can't be now, that's all. If I start thinking about it all, then the here and now might just begin to unravel – and that's no good, that's no good at all. But leaving Anna like that . . . oh Christ: unforgivable. What is she supposed to think? What is she supposed to *do* . . .? In that email, that email she showed me . . . after the, oh God . . . information . . . there were questions: how would we care to proceed, that sort of thing. Formalities. Protocol. Logistics. And Anna is stranded . . . left to respond, muddle along. She is abandoned. Already she has phoned me twice, but I've turned the thing off now. I will deal with it eventually, of course I will, and probably very soon indeed – it's just that I can't handle anything at all at this very moment. And the coming diversion – something so totally new – it might be exactly what I'm needing. I mean – it has been, it has been that for just bloody ages . . . but now, maybe, even more than ever. Yes? Do I think that? Yes – I think I do. It will help me be better. Because, Jesus – haven't I talked about it enough? Talked about it eternally. Me and Georgie, during all those chats over lunches and evenings – because we're really very chummy now, keep on finding more and more in common – we always did seem to revert to this one great and glimmering dream of mine.

'But what I keep telling you, George, is that it doesn't have to remain a dream . . .! I do it all the time. This wine isn't at all bad, is it?'

'I know you do, Georgie. I know that. Yes – it's rather good, bit young maybe. No I know you do, I know. I just feel so . . .'

'Nervous. Yes. You've told me. But honestly – how many times do I have to say it? There's really no need. Honestly – it's a truly comfortable experience. You do trust me, don't you? You do believe me?'

'Of course I do. I do, Georgie, yes. It's just that . . .'

'Look: how about this. How about we go together?'

'Together . . .?'

'Yup. Oh look – I don't mean *together* together. Just on the same evening, sort of thing. Share a cab. There's this house in Belgravia – of the ones I know, I think that's definitely the place that would suit you best. You remember I've mentioned it? Deeply luxurious – very plush indeed. It's everything you love. Plenty of choice – oh God yes, every type imaginable. And top-class, George – make no mistake about that. We are talking *Playboy* centrefolds come to life. And then afterwards we can shoot over to the Chelsea Arts, spot of dinner . . . and then you can thank me profoundly for all I have done for you! Champagne into the night. How's that sound?'

'It sounds . . . well, it actually sounds rather marvellous . . .'

'Right then. That's settled, George. That's what we're going to do.'

Yes. And tonight's the night we're going to do it. Meeting for a quick one first – in the good old Chelsea Arts, actually: it's where we mostly seem to end up. I've met such a lot of interesting people there now – the sort of people I've never before encountered, and honestly, I really do enjoy it all: I absolutely amaze myself, how much I have taken to all of this. The few people I've ever known in my life, well – they were just so boring! I maybe didn't think that at the time, but you've only got to mingle with the art crowd for even a little while to see how much they just seem to get hold of life around the neck and simply wring out from it every single minute of fun. When they've got money, they blow it . . . and when they haven't, everyone rallies round. Never known anything like it. And these people I now drink and chat with, it's all down to Georgie, of course. He'll say to me: oh look, there's so-and-so, you absolutely have to meet so-and-so, they're wonderful and you'll just love them. And look over there – there's a woman who used to model for Lucien Freud, simply got to meet her (that just happened last week, that one – and she was fascinating, bit drunk, can't remember her name). I hardly have to say, though, that none of these encounters comes even anywhere close to that very first day in here when I actually met Paul . . .! Oh my God – it still makes me shiver, just the thought of it. Sometimes I just stare at the corner of the bar where he'd been standing – where he reached out his hand to me, and I touched it . . .! Well – that was a one-off: never seen him since, obviously. They say he doesn't come in as much as he used to – but still, I'm always looking out for him. And people are getting to know me a bit too – recognising me, you know? One woman the other day, she actually thought I was a member . . .! Me – a member of the Chelsea Arts Club . . .! I rather enjoyed that, actually: didn't set her right. Georgie is always saying how amazed he is that among all these people we meet every day, we still have never run into his mother and this coterie of all her arty cronies he's always going on about: it's a shame you haven't met her yet, he keeps on telling me, because I just know that you'd absolutely adore her – but then he says that about everyone. According to him, she's in here all the time, is what he keeps on saying, but it's really rather odd because she doesn't at all seem to be – or not when we're here, anyway. My God, though – the bottles of wine we've got through in this place . . .! Georgie, he's at the moment getting the cast together for some new musical – or maybe it's a revival, bit hazy about the details – and he's pretty busy, he says, raising the rest of the money – but still he always seems to have time for a boozy lunch, or a jolly night out. And me, well . . . now I've got Anna more or less running the whole show, I've got all the time in the world: I can do whatever I want, whenever I like. Which is exactly what is about to occur right this very minute. Because I think that in the light of all this, just anyone would have to understand why – despite what's happened – I just have to go through with everything that we've planned for this evening. Yes?

The house . . . it's pretty much everything Georgie had said it would be. A smart but discreet entrance at the very rear of a charming and cobbled little mews that must, I suppose, back on to the gardens of one of the terribly grand Belgravia terraces. You could have walked right past this place and not even noticed the door. Far larger entrance hall than I'd been expecting – and immediately I feel enveloped by a very warming sense of traditional luxury. The black-and-white chequerboard floor, glassy marble, has just given way to the deepest pinkish mushroom carpet which seems to be more or less obliterated by all these red and black Turkish rugs: I have a few like that myself, one or two – and my shoes are just whispering as I make my way across them. The air is heavily scented, though not so as to make you retch – it is really very heady, but in a perfectly delightful way: might be candles, though I can't actually see any . . . so probably just a particularly fine perfume. Georgie, as usual, is being greeted as the long-lost friend by an extremely elegant lady of a certain age: my age, probably. The coat and hat I came in with . . . they're gone, didn't notice that happening . . . and now I seem to be drinking good champagne from what I think might well be a Baccarat flute. Georgie and I are alone in the drawing room now – he is grinning madly and urging me to relax, relax, just relax . . . but I already feel that, I am quite utterly relaxed. And this décor, you know . . . it reminds me of somewhere. Deep panelling and heavy cornice, clusters of individually lit gilt-framed oils and lithographs, heavily fringed sofas, an ottoman or so, pleated cream and burgundy lampshades on brass columns and blue and yellow ginger jars. And it is slightly too warm . . . though undeniably the big log fire sparking briefly beneath a rather fine mantel – Greek key design, probably Regency – it's still very welcome indeed. Annabel's – that's where it's reminding me of. That wonderful subterranean oasis in Berkeley Square where I have been as a guest, though very seldom – and which is more or less just around the corner, now I come to think of it. The clientele, I suppose, might easily overlap – quite possibly they have some sort of a mutual arrangement, who's to say?

So this is all seeming . . . very easy, very natural . . . and yet still, these might be the very strangest moments I have ever spent. There is a palpable air of anticipation – the warm sweet air is thick with it – and this is not just due to the light of eagerness, white and alive in each of Georgie's gleaming eyes: I myself, I feel I might be glowing. And now . . . a woman is coming into the room – that aloof and animal lope of the carelessly gorgeous that we know so well from the catwalk, though here there is no hint of scowling. Another is behind her, and then yet more. They are lined up before the sofa I am sitting on – could be half a dozen – and I gaze up at them in awe. This cumulative wall of sheer and scented femininity is quite perfectly overwhelming. Each one of them is, oh . . . just breathtakingly beautiful, no other word for it, yes but in so many different ways. Their clothes are subtle, and very expensive – evening gowns mostly, in silk and pastels. They seem to be unaware of Georgie and myself – just laughing between themselves at maybe the same old joke, and tossing the gloss of their hair. Make-up, skin – whether deeply tanned or peachily white – all quite flawless. The wink of earrings, the sheen on their mouths . . . the very liquid shine on their fingernails, that's quite dazzling in itself. I have seen this scene in films – and while I never dreamed that I might ever one day be a part of the thing, still I always knew that it wasn't a fiction.

Georgie, I am aware of him asking me what I think. I simply shake my head in wonder – for really, there are no words. He urges me now to take first pick – I glance at him enquiringly, and he is nodding his insistence. Well . . . there is a petite and wonderfully curvaceous Latin-looking woman – long black and wavy hair, equally black and challenging eyes. Rather like that actress – what is she called? She has deftly fielded my dogged stare and she holds it tight in the grip of her gaze, as her lips are softly parting. Penelope Cruz – I think that's the actress I mean. There is a statuesque and even quite sculptural negress – I know they don't say that any more, but I actually think that it is rather a noble word, negress, and here is a truly noble-looking woman who is absolutely deserving of it. I've never had one of those actually, a black woman – I can only think because I never really was moved to, couldn't say why: maybe some inexplicable feeling of unworthiness . . . or even just possibly the fear of contrast. Oh and look at her: the sweetest little girl with ginger curly hair and freckles, heavens she looks so terribly young – oh God, she's just so *sweet*. But in truth, there is no real indecision at all about who I am going to choose: I will choose that slim and leggy girl at the very end of the line – the one with long and straight Swedish blonde hair and a heavy fringe that just is spiking her blackened eyelashes. She is wearing pale pink lipstick on her fat and cushioned mouth. She is the only one wearing a very short dress and long white boots: she is a true dolly bird kept utterly pristine from the distant mists of the Sixties . . . and now she is going to be mine.

I will not point – I think that might seem rude. So I am standing up now, carefully placing my champagne flute on a side table that is crammed with crystal and porcelain boxes . . . I walk across the room, and now I am by her side. She smiles as I touch her hand, and then she is guiding me away. I feel quite drunk on bliss. The room she takes me to, she says it's on the second floor, but I hardly can remember the stairs. I find I am unable to take in too much of the decoration, save to see that it is tasteful, soft-lit and profoundly comfortable . . . I can't really concentrate on any more than that, you see, because my eyes now, they are filling with tears. She asks me if I am all right, and I tell her that I am. Her voice is reassuringly upper-class – it pleases me immeasurably. She says her name is Caroline, and asks me what I would like her to do, and I am just idly shaking my head – this way and that, from side to side. She says, would you like me to take my clothes off, and I think I must have said yes to that, because this is now what she appears to be doing: the rustle of silk, as she is eyeing me. I can hear myself telling her to leave the boots, to please not take off the boots . . . I can just about hear it, yes, but my voice, it seems so faint and distant. My God . . . naked, she is, oh . . . heartbreakingly beautiful: my heart is broken, and stopped. She lies across a big brass bed, and I humbly sit beside her, my fingers trailing amid the heavy pale silk of her hair. I tell her I can't do anything . . . just can't do . . . anything. And she says she will help me, and then she asks me my name. I tell her it's George, George is my name, and that I can't, just can't . . . *do* anything. She asks me if I am all right, and I tell her that I am not. And then I say I'm married – have been for ages, for ever and ever. She asks me if that is a good thing or not a good thing. I say I don't know. And then I say well, I am more than married actually . . . I am over all that: I am widowed, now. I am . . . a widower. She is kissing my cheek so very wonderfully softly and saying that she's sorry to hear that and when did it happen? And I am saying to her . . . today, it happened today. As a matter of fact. And now . . . Caroline, she doesn't seem to be saying to me anything at all. The truth is, I can barely see her, my eyes are so much clogged and thick with stinging tears. Yes, I say eventually . . . because I am thinking that the very least I owe this young and beautiful naked woman is an explanation of some sort. Yes, I say: you see, my wife . . . once, she was a pretty young waitress in a Soho restaurant who had stolen my girlfriend's umbrella, long story, won't bore you. And after that, I wrote to her, you see. Do you know what I wrote to her? Well, no of course you don't – how could you? Well, then I shall tell you, shall I? This is what I wrote to her: 'I will love you unto the door of death, and then eternally beyond.' Yes. That's what I wrote. Then she became ill, yes, but she didn't actually tell me about that . . . didn't see fit to mention it, you see. And now . . . well now she is dead. In Rio.

A FURTHER MEMOIR. YOU MIGHT CALL IT THAT. REALLY JUST A JUMBLE OF RANDOM AND TATTERED, MORE OR LESS IDLE THOUGH HIGHLY CONSEQUENTIAL LITTLE SCRAPS OF RECOLLECTION FROM THE PERFECTLY ASTONISHING AND SURPRISINGLY RECENT PAST. NOW I'M A LITTLE OLDER.

It's been quite a time, there's no denying it. And in one huge way in particular – which still I can hardly believe: just too amazing, and really rather wonderful. More than that, actually – little short of miraculous. I never did really expect surprises in my life – good or bad ones, even when I was young. They came, of course, and on every single occasion I was duly surprised: the nature of it, of course. As you get older though, you not only get out of the way of anticipating anything remotely new, but you actively discourage even the scent or danger of it. Well I do, anyway. But sometimes change can be a good thing. Sometimes change can transform your entire existence, and so much for the better. Good Lord – if I have learned anything at all over the past few months, then it surely must be that. I suppose I had simply assumed that I would continue to potter along, much as I always have, until I and everything else just staggered to an eventual close. But oh dear me no – not how it's been: no, not at all.

Anna – she was one of the first surprises, I suppose, and oh – such a very welcome one. For how long had I just yearned for her to return to me, never really imagining that it was possible – and just take a look at us now! It almost seems as if we've never been apart. She's completely reconfigured the top floor of the house – you just wouldn't recognise it. Precious little more than storage before, and now it's all so bright and cleverly arranged: did it on a shoestring too – mainly just paint and planks, so far as I can see – so she's really quite the little homemaker, on top of all her other extraordinary talents. Won't be living up there for long though, because those builders are progressing so terribly well that it now looks not impossible that she and Troy could be in their new little house by Christmas. Already she's sorted out all the carpets and fabrics and so on – fittings and appliances. She has some rather radical ideas for the internal layout, and I just say to her you go right ahead, my dear: anything you want. Even little Troy seems to be very excited about the project – loves trotting down to the site, anyway, and wearing his special little yellow hard hat with his name across the front in big black letters: his mother magicked it up from somewhere on the Net: you can just get anything, these days. I have got to know the little lad rather better than I did . . . well, let's be honest here – I hardly knew him at all, did I? So far as I was concerned, he was either present or absent, noisy or quiet. But it's different when you're more or less living together, isn't it? He's just become such a part of things, if you know what I mean. Taken to calling me Grandpa – not sure he called me anything before: we were barely ever in the same room long enough. I play him all my Beatles records – the early stuff anyway, it's what I like best now . . . when they were sparkling, still young and fresh, and so was I. And Troy, he really does seem to love them – well, what child in his right mind wouldn't? Dancing around the room, going 'yeah yeah yeah': it's lovely to look at.

Sometimes I'm just watching him larking about, not a care in the world, and I can't help wondering just what sort of world it is that he's going to be growing up in. Bears no relation to anything I know . . . but then all that, everything that was taken for granted when I was young . . . well that, it's been steadily disappearing for decades: practically nothing of it left, now. Basic English and simple mathematics – that was the core at school. Feet and inches. Ounces and pounds. Pints and gallons. Fahrenheit, for God's sake. Communicating by letter – with stamps on the envelopes, yes and you had to lick them too. Ancient history. Which is why people of my age have to keep on learning new bloody ways of doing the same bloody things, and they're never as good, are they? Never as good as the old ways. Sod the public, that's the attitude now. And little Troy, well . . . he's headed for some sort of dysfunctional and frankly terrifying 'utopia', and he won't even have a clue what's different. Ah well. I even go so far as to play with him a bit sometimes, which is something I never thought I'd be saying. Only with actual toys though – cars and Lego and that lovely little Brio push train that I'm rather fond of – because I can't have anything to do with all the electronic stuff. Brain-rot, so far as I can see. Anna says it's perfectly all right in moderation, and I suppose that's true of everything, really. Anyway, I'm sure she knows what she's talking about – leave it all to her, of course I do.

She's been perfectly marvellous in other ways too – well naturally. She's so very happy again – not a care in the world: lifts my heart, just to see it. The business, oh my Lord . . . she's not only taking care of it now – complete managerial control – but she's actually come up with a succession of the most extraordinary and novel ideas for not just its expansion, but also all sorts of ways of tapping into a younger and more fashionable market, with brand-new ranges and colours and finishes that she patiently tells me are 'funky', God save us, and – crucially – retail for rather less than all the mainstream standards. The profit margin remains very healthy, however, and the whole of the work force is fantastically enthusiastic: they have backed her utterly – all of them seem to be totally revitalised by every single one of her innovations. And she has completely redesigned and overhauled the website – she despaired of the way it used to be – said that it was just 'so twentieth-century' . . . which still actually sounds pretty modern to me, but never mind. I'm told that all her efforts resulted in an almost immediate surge in traffic, hits, footfall, whatever they bloody call it, and – this is the point – a considerable boost in sales, and also profile. Well none of that would ever have happened if I'd still been in control, goes without saying. I gave her a raise. Do you know what she said? She said to me oh *no*, Daddy – I couldn't possibly take any more money! You're already giving me far too much as it is – and you're building me a *house*, for heaven's sake! And honestly, Daddy, Troy and me, we've got absolutely everything we want. I gave it to her anyway, the raise – but all that, all her protestation, it did so remind me of Enid. All that she had said to me, so very soon before she passed away.

And that very passing away . . . well that was another thing, yet one more, that Anna was left to cope with, actually. The entire process of, Jesus – just getting her back to us from bloody South America . . .! Well, I took one look at all the forms, all the formalities, this extraordinary succession of hoops and jumps, and I just straight away knew that I couldn't be doing with it. It wasn't, I now see quite clearly, actually all that complicated or even time-consuming . . . it was just, well . . . the nature of it I couldn't, um, handle – the nature of it, yes. The funeral was . . . a brief affair. I was, I am afraid, irresistibly reminded of Eleanor Rigby: apart from family, nobody came. And talking of surprises . . . this whole thing with Enid, well – this had been another one, of course: quite the bombshell. Didn't see that one coming, not in a million years. Because Enid, she never really seemed to be particularly healthy or unhealthy, really. She just sort of jogged along, in the way that she did. And apart from the alcoholism, I'm not really sure that she was ever what you might call properly ill, or anything. Was never one for colds, and so on. Never had any operations – never been in hospital. Couldn't tell you if she took pills – you know, courses of treatment: I never enquired. Obviously consulted someone about the fucking thing that killed her, but of course she never let on. To me, she always seemed okay. Well there you are: you never know what's going on inside you, do you? Until you do. If I ever thought about all this sort of thing, I suppose I always assumed that I would be the first to go – simply because men, they usually are. I wish . . . I wish I hadn't chastised her about the drinking. Wish I hadn't . . . bullied her quite so much. Jesus – I would happily have poured the stuff down her throat if I'd thought it might help her – if I thought it might somehow be easing her passage. But I wasn't to know, was I? How could I possibly have known? Because she never talked, did she? Enid, she never bloody talked about anything. Well – no good going on about it: that's that, isn't it?

And before that, David. Yes, all that palaver with David in the hospital that time, his damned overdose and everyone frightened half out of their wits, and particularly his mother – well that had been yet another one, of course: another great bolt right out of the blue. But David, he was most terribly affected by the death of his mother. Which was rather a surprise in itself. A bond then, clearly – and one I knew nothing about. Anna and Lilian were either side of him at the graveside, practically holding him up between them. Kept on saying he wished he could have been better – as well he might. Dreadful day – pouring down: and there was David, crying in the rain. Wasn't even wearing a black tie – said he couldn't find one. Typical. Seems to have pulled himself together a bit now, though – Christ knows there was scope. Got a job, the Lord be praised – in a bloody *bank*, of all things: can't think how that happened. When I heard, it was all I could do not to laugh out loud. Lilian is working for one of these giant pharmaceutical companies, Glaxo Something Something, whatever it's called: unplumbed depths in that girl, I'm telling you. But my God, though – if only they'd done all this a whole lot sooner like I was always saying to the boy – how many times did I say it to him? – well Christ, who knows where the two of them might be today? Well there – never bloody listened, did he? Tried to top himself instead, damned little fool. She asked us round, Lilian, to see the new flat: very nice, actually – Maida Vale sort of direction. Anna said we ought to bring something – sort of a housewarming present, is what she was saying: cushions would be nice – and I said if you say so. And after a tolerable lunch I said to the two of them: so – getting married, are you? And Anna was hissing at me oh *goodness*, Daddy – what a thing to *ask* them . . .! And I said why? What's wrong? Living together, aren't they? Obviously fond of one another. Perfectly reasonable question. Anyway – neither of them answered it, so Christ knows.

So this . . . all this – it would be enough, wouldn't it? For any man, I should have said. And for someone of my age, well – in the light of recent circumstances, what more could I decently be expecting? Nothing – nothing at all. So yes, I suppose I would have been perfectly contented – more than that, actually: really pretty pleased with the way everything had shaped up. But oh my Christ . . .! Now that the *other* thing has happened, well . . . all of that, everything I had before, it would now just seem to be rather empty, really. Well no – I don't truly mean that. It's not to diminish Anna and Troy and this new domestic situation – all that, it's just wonderful, as I've said. So what I really mean, I suppose, is that . . . I, me – I, George the man, deep inside, would still fundamentally be unfulfilled. Now, though, I am, well . . . replete. Yes I am, and in a way that is utterly different from anything I have ever come close to experiencing, or even would have thought to aspire to. Because I never could have suspected its nature, not even the feasibility of so singular an emotion. The jolt of a stimulus has aroused me from the coma. Recovery, salvation – all of it is mine: I now have the meaningful heartbeat. All to do with Georgie again – yes, but in a way we both never could have imagined . . . and when I think back to it now, that perfectly extraordinary evening in the Chelsea Arts Club, well Jesus: I'm still not sure which of us was the more amazed.

I wasn't even meant to be there – still felt a little bit groggy from the night before, if I'm being honest: I'd been home with Anna – she'd done a lovely piece of sirloin with a Béarnaise, just the way I like it, and I'd opened this rather wonderful Haut-Batailley 2000, really very luscious, and then like the bloody fool I am, I went and opened another, didn't I? Which I more or less had to myself. Greed, you see – what's to be done about it? And I just can't take it, you know – the volume, like I used to: I know this from experience, but it doesn't stop me, does it? Christ, what an idiot I am. But Jesus – in the old days, a couple of bottles of claret . . . no more than an aperitif. Now though, Christ – I really do notice it: don't sleep at all well, and then the next morning, woof – throat and stomach, pretty killing. Now Georgie and I, we're in the habit of going out together really rather a lot, evenings mostly. Which suits me very well, of course – he's such a good fellow – though I do sometimes wonder, with all his dozens of arty and theatrical friends, why he even bothers to find time for me at all, but he does seem genuinely to enjoy my company, some reason or another . . . so there we are. We never did mention the Belgravia fiasco – and certainly I would never contemplate such a thing ever again – because even if it hadn't fallen on that particular, um . . . what shall I call it? that . . . day of days . . . still there was something deeply chilling about the entire experience: can't really explain – it should attract me, all that, it should really very much appeal to me, as Georgie had divined . . . and in theory it does, I do like the idea . . . but in practice . . . well no: it's just not for me. So normally, Georgie and I, we go to the Chelsea Arts, and then there are one or two restaurants I favour, so that I can reciprocate – Wiltons, I've rather taken to lately. But when Georgie rang on this particular evening, I said to him – look, old chap, if you don't mind I think I'll sit it out this time: bit tired, early night maybe. Well he just wasn't having it: you *must* come, George – I'm celebrating having raised the last great chunk of finance for the play . . .! I've already booked a cab to pick you up, and also there's someone who's going to be there tonight who you've just absolutely *got* to meet. Oh Jesus, Georgie, I said to him – not another one! You're always saying that, aren't you? I can't think there's anyone in that club who I *haven't* met now, because of you! So look – maybe tomorrow, okay? No no – he went on and on and on, as only Georgie can: he heard me sighing, which he knows to be the first indication of weakness, and eventually I caved in, of course I did, just as he knew I'd be bound to. Had a bath. Washed my hair. Made me feel a little bit fresher. The cab arrived on time, and half-an-hour later I was sipping pink fizz in the bar of the Chelsea Arts – shying away from the protruding elbow of a very intent snooker player with white floppy hair, because the place was completely jammed that night, and the only spare chairs were right up close to the table. Georgie breezed in at that point, about bloody time, and immediately was shouting over the din, 'Well right, okay, come on then George, we're going to the loggia.' 'The *what* . . .?' 'Loggia, George – you know the loggia . . .!' Well I didn't, actually – do now. Turns out that it's a little sort of glass conservatory tacked on to the deeply beautiful and atmospheric dining room, which is where we usually eat in the evening: never noticed a loggia before, though. 'Why, Georgie? Why are we going there?' 'Well,' he said, 'just look at this place: far too crowded, isn't it? Black Hole of Calcutta – we'll have a bit of space in there.' So I chucked up my eyes to heaven, knocked back the last of the fizz and followed him out to this bloody loggia he kept banging on about.

Well when we got there, it was just as rammed as the bar had been. The usual loud and jolly crowd, all apparently about to have dinner. Far too many people really for the three long tables wedged in rather too close to one another, and covered in bottles, glasses, bread and menus. The customary whooping went up as soon as Georgie showed his face – he bowed elaborately and waved to everybody in the way that the Queen does, as is his rather endearing habit. Even I managed to garner the odd one or two nods and hellos myself, which is always pretty pleasing. Men and women, young and old, just as always in this tremendous place – that's one of the greatest things about it – and I easily recognised quite a number of them. Georgie stooped to gently touch the shoulder of the lady who sat closest to where we were standing – just about the only person, actually, who hadn't turned around to greet us. And then she did.

'Ah,' she said. 'It is you. I'm glad. Georgie – he's told me everything about you. Haven't you, Georgie, my dear? He's quite an admirer. You're terribly good friends, I gather. Isn't that right, Georgie?'

'It is indeed. And I'm just so pleased that after all this time I've finally got the two of you in the same room! George – eventually and at last – I would like you to meet my mother . . .! So she is not, in fact, as you might have begun to think, no more than a figment of my delirious imagination – but a true and living person, as well as an artist extraordinaire. So: you finally meet . . .! I'm delighted – and I'm sure you'll get on brilliantly.'

And . . . I was just looking at her. Gaping, I suppose. Then I'm reaching out and clutching at the back of the chair. Couldn't speak. Couldn't say a single word. And then . . . I managed just the one . . .

'Dorothy . . .'

She smiled, and patted my hand.

'Hello, George. How have you been keeping . . .?'

I simply shook my head. My eyes, they felt half closed, as I continued just to gaze at her. Georgie, I knew, was watching the two of us.

'Hang on . . . is there something I'm missing here, Mum . . .? Do you two . . . know one another? You've met before, is that it?'

'Oh yes, Georgie, my sweet. We're old friends. Aren't we, George?'

And this time I was nodding.

'We are. Oh yes. We are. But . . . *Dorothy* . . . I just can't . . .'

I felt so absolutely dizzied and weak – hardly knew what I was saying. And then . . . just at that moment, she did something simply so perfectly extraordinary – something that I know I shall never forget for as long as I live. She . . . looked right at me with eyes I remembered, inclined her head towards my hand, and gently kissed a finger.

'No, well,' she said. 'There we are.'

* * *

What am I to say . . .? What am I to say . . .? We met again the very next day. My insistence. Because it was clear we'd never be able to talk at the Chelsea Arts. This loggia thing, it was a birthday do for one of the other women, apparently, so Georgie and I sloped back in to the bar, which was even more crammed than it had been before, and I took one look around me and I said listen, Georgie, if you really don't mind I'm going to call it a night. Feel a bit off, touch of a headache. Didn't have a headache, felt fine – well, physically fine anyway, and never mind that I was trembling from head to foot like someone in the grip of a plague. It was . . . strange. So strange. Because this wasn't just Georgie my chum any more, is what I think I was meaning . . . because now, suddenly, I could only see him, Georgie, as her . . . son . . .! Her son! And that meant, then, that my old friend Sammy had to be his . . .! Christ Almighty – can you *believe* this . . .? But I just couldn't now have Georgie starting up with all the endless questions – you know the sort of thing, you know exactly what he would have started doing. Well *Jesus*, he'd be going – fancy you knowing Mum . . .! I had no idea – she never let on. How amazing! So tell me – how do you come to know her? When did you meet? How long ago was this? All of that. Because, I don't know . . . I just didn't want to do it all, actually couldn't have faced just any of that – because I felt it was somehow, well . . . private, if you like. Between the two of us. It was ours. Yes – that's what I felt. And I urgently needed to be in a taxi and then my bedroom with all the lights off so that I could . . . think. I was . . . shocked. Oh yes I was – absolutely shaken, I can tell you. This . . . all this . . . it was, oh – just so perfectly extraordinary. One minute I'm out for a drink with Georgie, and the next minute . . . well. The moment I set eyes on her, I had turned to liquid. I more had *sensed* her, I think, rather than recognised her in the normal sort of a way. She looks . . . well she looks the same, kind of, and yet she is also somehow like another person altogether. I knew her straight away, though – maybe . . . could this be it? Maybe . . . because of all the people in the past, she's the only one I've ever actually thought about. The only one I've actually remembered. So . . . a fair amount to deal with. I had to sort it all out in my mind. Get things straight. I had to know exactly what I was going to say to her when next we met. Which would be the very next day – had to be. Couldn't hang about. So at least I'd had the brain to get her to give me a phone number, at least I did that . . . and so early the following morning I rang it and asked her to lunch – just like that, straight out with it – and do you know what she said to me? She said ooh no, George – you don't want to take me out to lunch, not really: why ever would you want to do that? And I said what do you mean? I've just asked you, haven't I? Why would I ask you if I didn't want to take you out to lunch? I want to see you – I want to talk to you, of course I do. And she said oh George – you're still so very sure of everything you *want*, aren't you? And I said no – well, yes . . . but it's not like how you mean. I'm not like that any more – I'm not like how you remember, if you do actually remember me at all . . . because Christ, it's been so terribly long . . .! Hasn't it? Such a long, long time. But what I mean to say is – I'm not *ordering* you. Do you see? That's not me, not any more. Christ – I had to learn *something* over all these years, didn't I? So please do – let me take you to lunch. Please say yes. We can go anywhere you like – just name it. And she said well, so long as it isn't a picnic. And I, bloody fool that I am, I was going, 'Picnic . . .? Picnic . . .? Well of course it won't be a picnic – bloody freezing outside, why in God's name would it be a *picnic* . . .?' And it was only when she started laughing – and I remembered it, that laugh: just listening to it, I saw before me that young and pretty girl from simply an eternity ago. So yes – while she was still just laughing away at me, it was only then that I twigged to it. The picnic. That picnic, which now I was dredging back up from the bogs of a long-gone age. Of course – that awful picnic. The very day I lost her.

If I didn't mind, she said, she wasn't actually that keen on the idea of going to a restaurant: she doesn't really like them. She doesn't normally go out that much at all, she said, but when she did, it tended always to be the good old Chelsea Arts, but we couldn't go there because there are always just so many friends and so on, she told me, that we won't get a moment's peace. So why don't you, she said, come round to my studio. Would that be all right? Would you like to? Or would it be an absolute pain? I said . . . yes: yes it would, that would be completely all right – I'd like to very much, and there will be no pain involved, I assure you. These days, of course, I know that studio inside out, we're very well acquainted – but still,

I'll never forget that day when I went round there for the very first time. It's only a couple of streets away from the Club, actually – no wonder she's such a regular. An actual artist's studio flat, very large and airy, with quite the most colossal windows at the top of a charming and rather classy redbrick and stucco Arts & Crafts building in a quiet and leafy road: completely idyllic, actually – and Lord, it really does suit her so well. The walls are covered with what are maybe Chinese or Indian fabrics, possibly both – intensely colourful silks and swags. Her own paintings, of course – terribly attractive, what they call vibrant, I think. Echoes of Matisse and others of the Fauves, as well as quite a few abstracts. Her photographs, by contrast, are very sombre black-and-whites – portraits mainly, loads of Georgie, though also a fair bit of landscape. Lots of deeply upholstered sofas, banquettes, ottomans and stools, all of them littered with cushions, elaborately tasselled bolsters and throws – and then there's the piano, of course: a baby grand in rosewood, surmounted by the largest metronome I have ever seen. I like to fool with it when she's playing, and even when she's not: the thunk of the beat I find very pleasing, very calming: there it is. But that very first time when I was on my way round there, well . . . I hadn't slept a bloody wink the night before, just tossing about and thinking thinking thinking, going over all these old and stupid memories . . . and I just didn't know what I ought to bring as a sort of a present, hadn't the vaguest idea – nearly bought a ridiculously decorated cake, but I stopped myself just in time. So I arrived in the end with a bottle of Bollinger, thought that might do the trick. When she saw it, she said oh – are we going to launch a ship? I laughed. So it was a pretty good beginning.

'I've just made some coffee. Do you still like it? Coffee?'

'I . . . do, yes. Thank you. That would be . . .'

'And I think there might be some sausage rolls. There's this terribly wonderful butcher we've got just around the corner. He makes them himself. They're awfully good. Do sit, won't you.'

I sat, and then I just had to remember, didn't I, the last time I had been sitting in a room with her. The flat, near Baker Street. With that person, that man . . . somebody, can't remember. Circus Road, it was – never forget that. It was . . . it was a very bad day. I sipped the coffee, left most of it to get cold. Nothing wrong with it – rather good, actually . . . I just wasn't able to concentrate on it, that's all. Didn't seem relevant. Politely declined a sausage roll.

'Why are you . . . staring at me, George? Rather disconcerting.'

'Am I? I'm so sorry. I wasn't aware.'

'Probably you are horribly amazed – and who could blame you? You are thinking how can it possibly be that a Swinging Sixties young bird in a miniskirt is transformed into a fat old bag in a smock . . .'

'No! No – not at all thinking that. I think you look . . . lovely, actually.'

'Oh please, George. Honestly.'

'I do. I really mean it. It's me – it's me who looks a wreck. Look at me . . .! Jesus – it's awful, isn't it? The passing of time.'

'Not really. I don't see it like that at all. Now is now. Here for the taking. That can never be a bad thing, can it? What has been has been. Right then, George – probably quite enough chit-chat, you are probably thinking. When are we to begin?'

'Sorry . . .? Begin? Begin what, exactly?'

'Oh – you know: all the questions. All the memories. All the raking up. The whole damn thing. I do fear it's going to be most awfully exhausting . . .'

'Well – we don't have to do all that, if you don't want to. There's not much really I want you to tell me – not much I want to say. Not really. We can leave it all, if you like. Just enjoy the moment – like you said. Fine by me.'

'Yes . . . except that if you're being really honest, George, there is one thing you would really like to hear about, isn't there? Sammy. Our mutual friend. Yes?'

'Well . . . Sammy. Yes. I suppose so. I would, yes – that is if you want to, um . . . I mean, I don't want to be, er . . .'

'No. Quite all right. Old wounds. Quite healed. Long time ago now. All right then – let's talk briefly about dear Sammy then, shall we? And then we can put it all away again. Back in its drawer. Nice and tidy.'

What is he doing here? Sitting in my studio. What is he doing here? Why did I actually ask him? He is just someone I knew quite briefly, and a very long time ago, when still I was only a little girl. Except . . . he was never just that, of course he wasn't. Oh God, it all would have been so terribly easy, wouldn't it? If that's all he ever was. If only he knew – because he never did at the time, so I'm quite sure he doesn't now. Why should he? I doubt if he's given me a second thought from the last day we met until yesterday . . . when we met again. I was actually amazed that he even recognised me – but he did, and straight away. But look at him. He is an old man. Sitting there, not drinking my coffee. The love of my life. Impossible to believe it's the same person – not that he's actually changed that much, except in the ways we all do. Still handsome. Bit of a paunch – and look at those little dark brown blotches all over the backs of his hands. Still the long, slim and pale fingers, though. Kept his hair – and now, instead of that rich and glossy auburn, it's the colour of the cigarette ash he used to spill all over everything. One habit he would appear to have given up, then – because back in those days, well . . . by this time he would already have smoked about four. He was so filled with energy, my nineteen-sixties George. Filled with anger too – to this day he is still by far the most selfish person I have ever encountered. And cocky – I think that's the word for him. I maybe thought it was normal, did I? In boys? To just take what they wanted, and to blazes with everything else? The only other person he truly cared for . . . was Sammy, who wasn't like that at all. I actually think George loved him. I don't think that he loved me. I was always taking second place to Sammy . . . because I was just a girl. So why did I love George? Oh and I did, my God – I just so totally adored that boy. I have never loved anyone else – I so have tried to, but I've never come close. Would have done anything for him. And I went on loving him too – for years and years, convinced that one day we would meet again, meet again in mutual rapture, and everything would be wonderful. Yes but not *now* – not so ridiculously late as this . . .! Because I'm old too now – though perfectly happy to be so. I do not need any more – I feel I am lacking nothing. Since Sammy died, I have been perfectly content with all that I have. My dear Georgie, my dearest boy – and all my friends at the Chelsea Arts. My work seems to be passably popular – it usually sells, though not for terribly much. But Sammy, he left me plenty – I certainly don't do it for the money. Art, it is very important to me – the act of creation. Yes – so I am fine. Completely fine. The last thing I require is a complication.

Sammy, though . . . oh, he was just so kind, that man. Always older than his years – terribly mature and caring, the complete and utter opposite of George: I was surprised, actually, when I found out that George had married and had children – I just didn't think he was the type. But the differences between the two of them, I don't know . . . maybe that's why they always got on so well. But when I was in trouble – when I was just a lost and hopeless teenage girl who was amazed, confused, very frightened and so totally out of her depth . . . he cared for me, Sammy. He took me in, He said he had always loved me, and I think that was probably true. I tried my hardest to love him back, but it never really worked. It was George – it was always George for me. Oh I was most dreadfully fond of Sammy, of course I was – who couldn't be? I told him, though, that we didn't have to get married, that he didn't actually have to do that, but he was completely insistent. I was deeply relieved, of course, because in those days, well . . . people talk about the Sixties now as a time of loose morals and enlightened attitudes and anything goes, but it didn't actually feel that way at the time – not to me, anyway. And not to my mother either. Oh my God – you should just have heard her . . .! She died not too long afterwards, and I was surprised by how much I missed her, without actually understanding quite what I imagined I was missing. Heaven knows what George was thinking: when he received the wedding invitation that I had implored Sammy not to send him, and then later, when he heard about the baby. He maybe imagined I had done it all out of spite, or something – to rob him of both of us – but it was never that, it was never anything like that . . . it just happened: if George was astounded, then so was I. Sammy's parents, Chris and Elsa, such nice people, I got to know them so very well over the years – dead now too, of course – they were both so terribly supportive right from the word go, and not all people in their position would have reacted like that: they were extraordinarily good to me.

So I was blessed, really. Wasn't I? Happy enough, married to Sammy. Contented, you know? I would have liked more children, of course, but Sammy, well . . . he had problems in those areas: it made him feel awful, but I kept on telling him that it didn't matter, didn't matter a bit. And for years – yes, *years*, I know it's unbelievable – all through the birth of my son, who I had decided just had to be called George, there were no two ways about it (it was Sammy who took to calling him Georgie) . . . through all of that and the beginnings of my becoming an artist, through all the business of making a beautiful home for my family . . . all I ever thought of was George: he was at the centre of everything. On so many occasions during the course of a normal day I found that I was constantly asking myself: what would George think? What would he have to say about this thing or that . . .? This wallpaper – would George like it? A new LP – George wouldn't care for it, would he? He'd just say that it wasn't a patch on The Beatles. I kept all this from everyone, of course, and particularly Sammy. So it just went on, churning around inside me: my own and very personal turmoil. And still I used to so terribly often just gaze at the one single photograph I ever had of him – the one I took that sunlit afternoon on Hampstead Heath with my old Box Brownie on the dreadful day of the picnic. He must have shifted at the very last moment, because it's all rather blurred – still, though, it captures him perfectly: his sweet allure, and a tinge of cruelty. The colour has faded, over the years.

George, yes . . . who now is sitting in my studio. It is so very odd. No – odd is hardly the word. And what do I feel? How do I feel now? So hard to say – don't even know what I'm thinking. Do I actually know this person? Could we really be said to know one another any more? All so very perplexing, really, because it's as if I am with someone new – and yet just a minute ago, I caught a sideways flash of his eyes, and oh . . . it was just so absolutely him again. When dear Georgie first started talking about this person he'd run into somewhere or other – Savile Club, was it? Not a place I particularly favour, although I can see its appeal to others. Might have been the Savile – anyway, doesn't matter. But when he first started saying the odd thing about him, I was suddenly all ears – something had caught my attention, but I didn't know what . . . rather eerie, that. And then when he told me this person's name, well . . . no doubt about it. I Googled him – how I found out about his marriage. There isn't much more, but clearly his company is enormously successful. I don't know what I imagined George would one day become, but it wasn't that. Possibly one of those people in vulgar blazers that they used to have in the Stock Exchange, waving around bits of paper and screaming at one another: something like that. Maybe a wide boy in the City, driving a Porsche and living in a penthouse loft next to the Thames. And when I learned that he and Georgie had so taken to going to the Chelsea Arts, I concentrated hard on not ever being there at quite the same time. I don't really know why though, because I had to assume that we'd be bound to meet eventually – but just not *yet*, that's all. Is the way I was thinking. Well – it's happened. Here he is – he is here. I thought it would be better on home ground, though I'm not now sure if I was right. And, of course, the only thing he really wants to hear about . . . is Sammy. Well. Little changes.

'Well, George . . . what can I tell you about him? He died too young. Heart attack – right out of the blue. Georgie, of course, was devastated. Well we both were, we both were. I'm sorry . . . I know you were very good friends. And I also feel sorry that, um . . . well that Sammy and I, er . . .'

'No no. Don't be. Absolutely *killed* me at the time, of course – can't deny it. But then I came to think, well . . . she's far better off with him. Good man. He'll take care of her. I was never good to you . . . I'm so very sorry about that. I was young, I know – but still, that's no excuse. So with Sammy, yes . . . you'd be better, I could see that. Better than me – he was better than me. I'm . . . very sad . . . that he's gone.'

'Yes. Of course. But I don't think, you know, that it was a question of . . . it was really more the fact that he was there, you see. Oh of course we both were very passionately in love. I completely adored him. Sammy, well – he was the love of my life.'

I am so completely amazed that I have said that. And George is too – he looks quite shocked. I think we both do.

'Well anyway. There it is. Long time ago, Dorothy. Another world. How long is it, actually?'

'Ooh, let me see . . . forty, more than forty years, must be. Forty-five, it is.'

'No . . .! *Can't* be! *Thirty*, maybe – never forty-five . . .!'

'Well work it out, George. Nineteen sixty-four, wasn't it?'

'We can work it out. Yes – sixty-four. *Hard Day's Night*. Christ . . . you're right! Jesus. Where did all that time go, then? Forty-five bloody years – Christ Almighty. I still think of it all, you know. That time. It was wonderful. Or maybe, I don't know . . . maybe it wasn't wonderful at all. Anyway – still very much a part of me. I have thought of you, you know. I've thought about you a lot. It's never gone away. But that's the thing about the Sixties, isn't it? They just don't go away.

All the fashions are back – furniture anyway, not so much the clothes. My God – the clothes! I loved it all, didn't I? Do you remember, Dorothy? Always banging on about Carnaby Street, all of that. E-Type Jaguars, Julie Christie – *Ready, Steady, Go!*, remember that? Dear dear dear. And who would have thought then that the bloody Rolling Stones would still be touring . . .? And *Sir* Mick Jagger – who ever would have believed it? We thought . . . or I thought, anyway . . . that it was all just for then, that moment, that utterly magical moment. My own thing – just for me. And look at it now. Beatles, well – they never went away, of course.'

'You still love them then, do you?'

'Christ yes, Play them all the time. You still listen to all the old songs, do you?'

'A bit. More into classical now. Opera. Verdi. Love Corelli. Bach, of course. Mozart . . . all of that.'

'So . . . not The Dave Clark Five, then . . .?'

'Ha . . .! No. Not them. Fancy you remembering that. But tell me about you, George. You just turn up out of the blue after a thousand years and I don't know the first thing about you. What have you been doing with yourself?'

'Not a thousand years – only forty-five: we've established that. Me . . .? Oh well – not too much to tell. Went into printing. Got married. She died.'

'Oh. I'm sorry. It's a terrible time. I remember . . . well, I remember what I went through when dear Sammy passed on. Oh but it was very quick. He didn't suffer, Doctors did everything they could, but . . .'

'Oh dear. I really do feel so sorry . . . that he's gone. Always so full of life. I suppose we say that, don't we? About people who are dead. And your mother, I presume . . .? Yes – my parents are gone too. Even my brother Tom – did I ever mention him, Tom? No? Well he's dead. And my wife, well . . . my wife – quite recent, actually.'

'You must miss her.'

'Yes, I must. I must.'

'And . . . you had children?'

'Oh yes. Two of those. My daughter, Anna – she's running my company now, and absolutely marvellously. She's a brilliant girl – you must meet her. I've been saying that to Georgie – think they'd get on like a house on fire. Got a little boy of her own, but she's, um . . . divorced. Georgie . . . he isn't a father, is he?'

'No, alas. Susan, she died so terribly young. Too cruel.'

'I know. He told me. Awful. He's the most wonderful man, I think – well, I don't have to tell you how wonderful he is, do I? You must be very proud, Dorothy – very proud indeed. And he's doing so well, isn't he? I don't know why he wants to hang around with an old codger like me, but I'm very pleased that he does. We can talk about anything under the sun, you know – yabber on for hours. And his taste in wine is very sound, I have to say. And Sammy . . . well Sammy, he must have loved him very much.'

'Oh he did, he did, of course he did. And particularly as he was the only child. I didn't want any more – I was decided on that. But I'm so glad you feel all that, George. He's very fond of you. He tells me all the time.'

'Why didn't you want any more, Dorothy? Sorry – none of my business. It's just that I can quite see you as Mother Bountiful, surrounded by her, um . . . brood.'

'I just thought that one would do, that's all. Oh – enough of all this. Can I get you some more coffee, George? That's gone cold. Maybe something else? Wine, or something?'

'No no – I'm completely fine, thank you. Quite happy just sitting here. And I do like it that he's called Georgie. I like that very much.'

'Family name. Name of Sammy's father, actually.'

'Really? Well. More and more coincidences . . .'

'And . . . your other child?'

'Hm? Oh yes – David. He does an assortment of things. Banking, at the moment.'

'Oh I see – so he's most awfully rich then, is he?'

'No I, um . . . wouldn't go that far. So listen, Dorothy – what do you think of all this?'

'What do I . . .? I'm sorry, George, I . . .'

'No well what I mean is – us, just sitting here, in your studio . . . and talking. I mean – I know it's odd, I know it seems really strange after all this time. Ridiculous in one way, I suppose. But I, well – I'm very much enjoying it, you see, and I just sort of wondered whether you might be, I don't know . . . feeling the same. Sorry if I'm being too blunt, but I always feel now – because I'm getting older, I suppose – that there's no real point in hanging about, if you know what I mean. Just come right out with it.'

'Yes well – I do recall that you were always rather good at that . . .'

'Yes. Sorry. But look, Dorothy . . . do you think you could bear the thought of coming out to dinner with me, say? Oh no – you don't like restaurants, do you? Why don't you like restaurants, Dorothy?'

'Oh – I don't know. I always feel rather on show. Not comfortable, you know? I much prefer the Club. Or here. Quite like to cook.'

'Well – where else would you like to go, then?'

'Look, George – what are you doing, exactly? You're not asking me out on a *date*, are you? How terribly funny . . .!'

'Well . . . I suppose I am, in a way. Don't think it's that funny. Is it funny? Maybe it is.'

'Listen, George . . . let's . . . why don't we leave it for a little while. Shall we? See how we feel. Let's both think about things, yes?'

Yes, George . . . please let's do that. Because I think at the moment that you yearn to fall in love with me, and very possibly for the very first time. You maybe have convinced yourself that you are already there. And me – you want me to be in love too, and just the way I used to be. You are craving devotion . . . though I can see very clearly that you also need to give in return, in the sort of way that you never ever did before. And . . . I just don't know if any of this can happen.

'Well . . . all right. If you say so, Dorothy. We can think about things, if you like. If that's what you want. I suppose. I mean – I don't have to think about it, I know what I want. But it's up to you, of course. Of course it is. So . . . anyway . . . let's talk about something else, then. Are all these pictures yours, Dorothy? Remarkable. I do think they're awfully good. I like them, I really do. Love the colours. And you play the piano too. Overwhelming. I never knew you were an artist.'

'No. I didn't either. One of the things I grew into. But when you knew me, George . . . well: I was nothing, was I? Just a little girl, really. Finding her way. And not awfully well.'

'Well I didn't think you were nothing. I maybe behaved that way – it kills me to think of it now. But I never thought that. I never did. Oh *please* let's see each other again, Dorothy. It would be, I don't know . . . meeting again like this, out of the blue, after all these bloody years . . . it would be such a *waste* if we didn't see each other again. Don't you think? Because for me, being here with you like this . . . it really means so much to me. Can't really properly explain . . .'

'Well look, George – we can always meet in the Chelsea Arts, if you'd like.'

'I do like – I love the place, actually. Oh my God – you'll never guess who I met there . . .! The very day I first met Georgie, actually – amazing, really.'

'Tell me.'

'Only . . . are you ready for this? Only . . . Paul *McCartney* . . .!'

'Oh yes. Paul. Of course – you're such a fan, aren't you? Yes, we're really quite used to him in there.'

'Oh. So you mean you've met him too then, have you?'

'Wait here, George. There's something . . . let me try to find it. There's something I'd like you to have.'

And now, weeks later . . . oh, I remember this so indelibly well – because she was gone from the room for quite a while, so I was left to just potter around for a bit. I was gripped by this perfectly extraordinary sense of quite unaccustomed exhilaration – I was so very elated as I was just wandering about the studio, and it felt as if my feet, I don't know . . . as if they were barely even touching the ground. My emotions, in truth, were in something of a riot, and I was finding it impossible to focus on any one thing. Peering closely at her acrylics, stroking an unfinished clay maquette, picking up a snow globe and giving it a shake, activating and much enjoying the heavy thunk of the metronome. Yes, and the thing she gave me – already it is one of my very most treasured possessions: a glossy photo of Paul, taken a few years ago, I'd say – and he had written boldly across it in black felt pen 'For Dorothy and Sammy. All the best – Paul x'. She was holding it before me, and then she carefully placed it on the palm of my hand. My stomach convulsed. The tears were streaming from my eyes, I could hardly believe it: hadn't cried like that since I was a child. She held me, Dorothy. Hush, she was saying, and telling me not to be silly. She stooped to kiss my fingers. And then she whispered, 'It's for you.'

* * *

And now I am back here again. I really know it rather well, the studio. Been round here so many times, I feel perfectly at home. Love all the brightness, the richness, all the colours. And did I ever mention the books . . .? They are absolutely everywhere – art books, largely, very lavish, but also lots of novels by people I've frankly never heard of. Never gone in for any of that myself – the colours, I'm talking about now – but I rather wish I had. Lifts the spirit. Once Anna and Troy are settled in their new little house, which won't be at all long now – two or three months, I should say – well then I think I might get the old place completely done up. Let Dorothy design it, come up with all the ideas – I'm sure she'd be wonderful at it. She's been over a few times for dinner with Anna and me. Georgie too, of course. We all seem to get on so terribly well – like we've known one another for ever: just as if it is meant, almost. Anna, when I told her the whole extraordinary story – how I completely by fluke had run into Georgie (who she likes very much, that's quite plain to see – whenever they're together, there's a sort of palpable fizz in the air: I love it – I'm all for it) . . . yes, so when I told her about all of that, and then who Georgie quite miraculously turned out to be . . . all about Dorothy, the far-off distant days, all the rest of it . . . well, she was really quite fantastically encouraging. Simply happy for me, is what she said. Well I mean I wouldn't have expected anything else of her, but still I do know that a lot of children in her position would not at all have reacted like that. It all being so soon, you know, after Enid's passing, and all that. David is typically down on it, of course – yes but frankly, who cares? Not that Dorothy and I could yet be called, what do they say . . .? An 'item', yes. We're not quite that yet, but I have every hope we will be. Better late than never, ay? And all the signs are there – she does seem to like my company: maybe I even add a little something to her life . . .? I'd certainly like to think so. She has altered mine, oh – immeasurably. There doesn't seem to be anyone else around – not a man, I mean, or no one she's told me about, anyway. We're not in what I suppose I would term a sexual situation, no not really. I mean – we've kissed, and so on. That's always nice. Cuddle up on the sofa, listening to music. I like her taste in classical – never really had much time for it before. I have on one or two occasions attempted to be a little braver in my advances, but I sense she is not at all ready for that. Which is actually fine with me – I just so much revel in the intimacy. I am hardly crazed by lust. She looks very good, I have to say – her face is almost completely unlined, and her lovely legs are just as I remember them, but . . . well: not like the old days, is it? What is?

We talk about everything under the sun. All sorts of things – quite amazing, really. Everything from reminiscing about the Sixties to, I don't know . . . her dodgy knee, say, which she's getting seen to next week at the Wellington. I don't go into all that, though . . . feel quite squeamish about talking about ailments or illnesses of any sort whatsoever. You keep on reading and hearing about bloody cancer and dementia and strokes and, Christ – all the other fucking things that can go wrong with you, if you've had the temerity and sticking power to get this far in your life. Not fair, is it? We survivors, all we people who have got to where we are in pretty reasonable nick, we should be awarded prizes. Bonuses. Life should get better and better. Instead, all there seem to be are forfeits. Handicaps. Until the final whistle blows, and it's game over, matey. Why having someone else in your life to care for is so absolutely vital, of course. And we've got a lot of time to enjoy ourselves in the meanwhile. I hope. Not the way I used to think, this. Dear God, when I was a kid, I really did loathe old people – middle-aged people, anyone really who wasn't a kid like me. Thought they were vile, and took up space. Thought they should be shot. Probably thought that shooting was too good for them. Well . . . I don't at all see it that way now. Being old . . . it's really quite nice. And Anna is right: sixty-four, it's not old, is it? No it isn't – not really. So . . . Dorothy and I, we have woven our own cocoon, in many ways. We don't at all care for the modern world – what it's become. We're completely agreed about that. Dorothy, she doesn't even have a mobile phone, refuses to have anything to do with them – and I only use mine for the odd email, and so on. But more generally speaking, well . . . the trouble is, all around us, everywhere you look . . . it's not really England any more, is it? Not the England we remember, anyway. But because we've both got a bit of money, we can bypass all the nastiness extraordinarily easily. You just make your own little world, don't you? Don't have to go anywhere horrible, don't have to use public transport – don't have to encounter anyone vile. Just cherry-pick the cream: very nice.

She's painting my portrait. Before she does that, she always plays the piano – and she's very good too: very sure, with quite the lightest touch. She likes to play Mozart, mainly – all by ear – but sometimes she'll do something like 'And I Love Her' or 'Here, There and Everywhere', one of the golden Beatles oldies . . . just to please me. To please please me, is what she says: so sweet, so terribly sweet. She kisses my forehead, when she says it. And then after the piano, she'll pick up the brush and set to with the portrait. Can't really say how it's coming along, because she won't let me see it. In the very early stages, I did manage a very swift peek when she was seeing to something in the kitchen. My face is green, I couldn't say why. I don't really understand why modern artists always seem compelled to do this sort of thing, but I daresay they have their reasons. Not my field, is it? I wouldn't know.

And now . . . it's evening. We've just enjoyed an exceptionally fine fish pie that she made for us completely from scratch, and I supplied some rather good Meursault, and also a half-bottle of Yquem with the Stilton. Why not? I love to overindulge her – me as well, of course – and I also love her just slightly bossy display of disapproval, whenever I do it. She's over on the sofa there, and looking very lovely in one of those silk sort of kimono affairs that she favours: pink and turquoise, this one. And clacking away with her knitting – another thing she does. A cardigan for me, apparently – though I'm not too sure about the yellow. Haven't said anything, of course. And I'm just deep in an armchair, and fooling about with the metronome – which I always tend to have close by me, now. It doesn't annoy her. She finds it as calming as I do.

'Do you fancy, I don't know . . . going somewhere tomorrow, maybe?'

'Don't mind. Where, George?'

'Well – don't know, really. Tate, maybe. That sound good? You'd like that, wouldn't you?'

'If you would. Which one? Which Tate are you talking about?'

'Oh Christ – the proper one, obviously. The one that has the actual *pictures* – not that other thing where they dumped all the rubbish.'

'It's not all rubbish, George. Some of it is actually very good.'

'Well all right – we'll go there then, if you'd like to.'

'No no – Tate Britain. That would suit us best, I think.'

'Oh good – because there's this rather nice restaurant there. I know – I know you don't like restaurants, Dorothy, but this place you can think of as an extension of the gallery. Covered in Rex Whistler murals. Ever been? Ever seen them?'

'Well – Tate I know, obviously. Not sure about those murals, though . . .'

'Well you'll very much appreciate them, I promise you. Very grand – very romantic, actually. They also have clarets at unbelievably low prices. Not like it used to be, of course. Christ, I remember the days when you could pick up '61s for an absolute song. '64s as well. Not like that any more, obviously, but it's still pretty good.'

Thunk, thunk, thunk goes the metronome: so tremendously pleasing.

'All right then, George. That's what we'll do.'

'Maybe ask Anna along. What do you think? And Georgie, of course.'

'Maybe. If they're free. If they want to.'

'They get on awfully well, don't they? I love to see them together – don't you? Wouldn't it . . . have you ever thought of this, Dorothy? Wouldn't it just be completely wonderful if they . . . you know. I mean – both of them could do a whole lot worse. They're both quite marvellous people. I think that would be just the most fantastic thing ever. Don't you? I mean

– you must have thought of it. What . . . is it? What's wrong . . .? Why are you looking at me like that? What have I said that's wrong . . .?'

'I don't think so – no, George. It hadn't even crossed my mind. No, George. Not a good idea.'

'But why? I think it's a *terrific* idea . . .'

'George. Look at me. Just trust me, all right? It is not a good idea. All right? That won't happen.'

And so I'm looking at Dorothy now, just as she has told me to. She appears to be very agitated. Well. At first I say nothing: I am taken aback. And now my eyes are open wide, as I continue just to gaze at the metronome. And the beat goes on.

END